Outstanding praise for Antoinette Stockenberg and her novels

"Stockenberg is a fresh, exciting voice. Her writing is delicious!"

—Jayne Ann Krentz

Sand Castles

"Well-drawn, sympathetic characters, exceptional writing, and an intriguing premise that puts a new spin on a classic plot combine to produce a riveting story of selfishness, betrayal, and love."

—*Library Journal*

"Moral dilemmas abound in this intriguing and complex tale."

—*Booklist*

"Twists, good dialogue, and a question to answer at the end . . . an excellent read!"

—*Old Book Barn Gazette*

"A beautifully moving story that touches the deepest recesses of the human heart."

—*Romance Writers Club*

More . . .

Tidewater

"Antoinette Stockenberg is pure magic."

—Susan Elizabeth Phillips

"A spellbinding thriller that is both intense and riveting."

—*Romantic Times*

"*Tidewater* is a fast-paced, intriguing, seaside suspense novel of betrayal, deception, family and love. Stockenberg writes strong emotions, relationships and sharp dialogue."

— *WCRG Romance Review*

"A compulsively readable suspense story."

—*The Romance Reader*

"Sparks your imagination and keeps your interest . . . a very good book!"

—*Old Book Barn Gazette*

"[A] fabulous ability to steam up a small-town environment."

—*Painted Rock Reviews*

"Stockenberg [is destined to become] a major voice in women's fiction."

—*Publishers Weekly*

Safe Harbor

"A complex, fast-moving plot—peopled with winning secondary characters—as well as a humorous and tender love story."

—*Publishers Weekly*

"*Safe Harbor* adds another notch in the growing collection of compelling dramas that Ms. Stockenberg just keeps producing. This author really knows how to tell a story!"

—*Romantic Times*

"This book is fresh and exciting . . . Ms. Stockenberg's stories only get better and better."

—*The Belles & Beaux of Romance*

"*Safe Harbor* is a most entertaining contemporary romance. It has great characters, a satisfying love story, and just enough suspense to keep the story moving . . . [Stockenberg] is very, very good."

—*Romance Reader Reviews*

Keepsake

"Ms. Stockenberg does a stellar job breathing life into this absorbing story that probes deep into the painful heart of a small community. *Keepsake* is a keeper!"

—*Romantic Times*

"Laced with natural, engaging dialogue, and intense narrative, Ms. Stockenberg has rendered a briskly paced, exhilarating story that's impossible to put down. She writes with such depth of perception, I was totally involved in the characters' lives. Don't miss this book . . . it's her best one yet."

—*Old Book Barn Gazette*

"Antoinette Stockenberg is writing some of the smartest, sassiest, and sexiest contemporaries around. This book will keep you reading well into the night. Very entertaining."

—Amazon.com

"Gloriously alive with fresh writing and an intriguing story . . . a standing ovation for Antoinette Stockenberg."

—*Under the Covers Book Reviews*

A Charmed Place

"Award-winning author Antoinette Stockenberg takes a dramatic turn in her new mainstream release. Passion, love, hatred and deceit all collide with unexpected force in the powerful and expressive *A Charmed Place*."

—*Romantic Times*

"Ms. Stockenberg writes with the wisdom and grace of the ageless to create a beautiful story in this intricately woven suspense. I love everything she creates."

—*Bell, Book, and Candle*

"Well-written . . . Every sentence builds the tension as the protagonists try to find their way back to each other and Maddie tries to protect her daughter. Ms. Stockenberg's passion for writing pulses through this superb story."

—*Rendezvous*

"Ms. Stockenberg has a very witty writing style and wonderfully drawn characters."

—*Old Book Barn Gazette*

Dream a Little Dream

"A delightful blend of goosebumps, passion, and treachery that combine to make this novel a truly exhilarating read. Ms. Stockenberg delivers once again!"

—*Romantic Times*

"*Dream a Little Dream* is a wonderful modern fairy tale—complete with meddlesome ghosts, an enchanted castle, and a knight in shining armor. *Dream a Little Dream* casts a powerful romantic spell. If you like modern fairy tales, you'll love *Dream a Little Dream*. Run, don't walk, to your local bookstore to purchase a copy of this magical romance."

—Kristin Hannah

"This humorous, well-crafted and inventive novel is certain to establish Stockenberg as a major voice in women's fiction."

—*Publishers Weekly*

"Well-developed, likeable protagonists; appealing relatives; an intriguing villain; and a ghostly pair of ancient lovers propel the plot of this . . . well-written story with a definite Gothic touch."

—*Library Journal*

Beyond Midnight

"Stockenberg's special talent is blending the realistic details of contemporary women's fiction with the spooky elements of paranormal romance. So believable are her characters, so well-drawn her setting, so subtle her introduction of the paranormal twist, that you buy into the experience completely . . . *Beyond Midnight* has a terrific plot, a wicked villain and a sexy hero. But the novel ventures beyond sheer entertainment and it is easy to see why Stockenberg's work has won such acclaim."

—*Milwaukee Journal-Sentinel*

"Full of charm and wit, Stockenberg's latest paranormal romance is truly enthralling."

—*Publishers Weekly*

"Antoinette Stockenberg creates another winner with this fast-paced and lively contemporary romance . . . a definite award-winner . . . contemporary romance at its best!"

—*Affaire de Coeur*

"A gripping and chilling page-turner . . . outstanding reading!"

—*Romantic Times*

St. Martin's Paperbacks Titles by Antoinette Stockenberg

Sand Castles

Tidewater

Safe Harbor

Keepsake

A Charmed Place

Dream a Little Dream

Beyond Midnight

A Month at the Shore

Antoinette Stockenberg

St. Martin's Paperbacks

A MONTH AT THE SHORE

ISBN: 0-312-98155-4

Printed in the United States of America

St. Martin's Paperbacks edition / August 2003

St. Martin's Paperbacks are published by St. Martin's Press, 175 Fifth Avenue, New York, NY 10010.

10 9 8 7 6 5 4 3 2 1

For Doris

Prologue

The day after eighth-grade graduation was the best and worst of Kendall's life.

He was minding his own business, which happened to be tracking down a snowy owl that had been sighted in a woods just outside of town, when he heard boys' voices farther up the trail.

He was sorry to hear them. He didn't want to be caught with a pair of expensive binoculars around his neck and looking for birds, so he got back on his bike with every intention of leaving the way he had come: quietly. As he pedaled off, the voices got more shrill—whoops and yelps, the sounds of small-town kids on the warpath. He would be fair game for them, he knew from experience, so he picked up his pace.

And then he heard the scream. It was a girl's cry, frightened and angry at the same time, and it sent chills up his back and arms. He slammed on the brakes so violently that his bike skidded on the soft path and went out from under him, falling on top of him and scraping across his pale, thin legs.

He righted the bike, but his hands and legs were shaking as he mounted it again and set off in the direction of the scream. Part of him was hoping and praying that it was all just fooling around; but part of him knew better.

He found them in a clearing next to the trail where he knew kids liked to hang out drinking and smoking—and, he had always assumed, having sex. Four boys had a girl cornered.

She was standing in front of the campfire rocks. Ken couldn't see her very well because she was shielded by the four boys. They were practically shoulder to shoulder, but one pair of shoulders stood higher and broader than the rest: they belonged to Will Burton, the doctor's son, a bully who had squeezed more than one allowance out of Ken on a Friday afternoon. Will's younger, red-haired brother Dagger was there, too, and two other kids whom Ken didn't recognize.

"Hey!" he yelled at their backs, almost before he could think about it.

They all turned around at the same time, surprised and therefore pissed. But Ken wasn't looking at them, he was looking at her. He was stunned to realize that she had breasts; how had he never noticed that? She was clutching her torn shirt to herself, but he could see her dark pink nipple. Instantly he looked away. When he looked back again immediately, he saw that her face was all flushed and her cheeks were wet, and he felt desperately ashamed.

"Leave her alone," he said in a voice filled with fury.

Will Burton just laughed. "Ooh, I'm scared. What're you gonna do? Run and tell your daddy?"

The other boys snickered and approached him as he stood astride his bike.

He could have taken off. He didn't, because he wanted her to make a break for it. But she stayed right where she was! He couldn't believe it. She wasn't moving. It was like she was hypnotized or paralyzed or something. She was looking straight at him and nobody else. He was ashamed in advance for what he knew was going to happen to him.

He became aware of the crack of branches underfoot as

one of the boys he didn't know took up a position behind him. Instinctively he glanced over his shoulder at him. At the same instant, Dagger Burton grabbed his binoculars out of his bike basket.

Dagger turned away and aimed the binoculars straight at her breasts while Ken and the others remained in their standoff. Everything seemed to go on hold while Dagger did his thing.

"Shit, I can't see anything," Dagger said after fiddling with the adjustments. "Everything's blurry. I must be too close."

Stupidly, Dagger began backing away from her in an attempt to get in better focus.

So that left three.

"Leave her alone," Ken said, controlling the quaver that hovered at the back of his voice. "Get out now, and I won't tell anyone."

Will Burton was only a year older than Ken but just then seemed twice his size, minimum. He snorted and said, "Who's gonna make me? You—Skinnykenny? What a dork."

Ken tried to make his voice sound strong. "Leave her *alone*." But his voice broke and the last word came out like a hiccup, and everyone laughed, except her, of course.

He didn't dare look at her; he was so totally mortified. For her, for him, for both of them. He was rich and she was poor, but at that moment both of them were equals.

Hulking Will Burton waited until the snickers died down, and then in a voice that was way calmer and deeper than Ken's, he said: "Dork."

It was true. Ken was a dork; he knew he was a dork. But there was something about being called one in front of *her* that made something inside of him snap. He threw down his bike and went wading into Will Burton: head down, arms flailing, landing punches half in the air. But he made contact, too—for the stolen allowances, for the snickers, and mostly for that exposed nipple, which he knew was now burned into his memory for life. He hated them all, hated them for their contempt for anyone who wasn't as cool as they were.

They punched him and kicked him and he tasted his own blood, but still he kept flailing. His eyes were shut, so he couldn't tell if she was taking off or not. Before he could get the chance to look, he felt a hard whack on the back of his head—he was pretty sure, from his brand-new binoculars.

Chapter 1

"Here he comes at last."

Against a blood-red sun sliding into a dark blue sea, a beat-up Subaru without a muffler wheezed its way toward the two sisters standing on the knoll.

Laura Shore was dismayed by the bedraggled sight: it was so typically Shore.

"Well, he missed Dad's funeral," she said, sighing. "Why should I be surprised that he's missed the memorial?"

"You're not being fair," her sister protested in their brother's defense. "Six months ago, Snack was in jail for stealing a car."

"Yeah. Obviously not the one he's driving," Laura said dryly. "Will you look at that wreck? I'll bet he went out of his way to drive right down Main in it, tooting to everyone in sight."

Corinne grinned and said, "That's our Snack."

It had always amazed Laura that her sister was so willing to accept their brother's outlandish, provocative behavior. But then, Corinne had managed to live at home with their father until the day that he died. She'd been tempered in a very hot fire.

"What do you want to bet he stopped at Foxwoods?" Laura said.

"*Today?* Snack wouldn't do that."

"Wouldn't hit the slots? Since when?"

"Not today," Corinne insisted.

It might have been the ocean damp, it might have been their father's grave: suddenly Corinne shivered in her thin cotton sweater and had to hug herself. "I'll bet he had car trouble. It's a miracle that he made it all the way here from Tijuana in that thing."

"Tijuana. God." Laura turned her back on the noisy, smoking car in time to see the last sliver of orange dip below the horizon, leaving behind a rich tapestry of gold, blue, and lavender sky. It was a spectacular Cape Cod sunset, and despite her resentment at being summoned back home by her younger sister, Laura felt the pull of the moment.

"Why," she asked with grudging wonder, "would Snack move to Tijuana when he could have stayed here?"

Corinne shrugged. "Why did you go off to live in Oregon? To make a mark, I suppose."

"I could just as well have made my mark in Chepaquit," Laura said quickly, rounding on her younger sister. "That is *not* why I left. I left to get as far away from Dad as I could."

"And from everyone else around here, Laura. Admit it."

"If you mean, from some of the people in this stifling, small-minded town—then, yes, I suppose so."

"Mm-hmm. You and Snack. You're more alike than you know."

It was a startling comparison, and Laura didn't like it at all. Corinne was a shy, sweet, totally naïve homebody who'd virtually never ventured off the Cape. How could she possibly have any insight into people?

Laura had to ask. "Corinne—just what, exactly, did you mean by that?"

Corinne shrugged. "You know. Big chip on the shoulder? You and Snack just deal with it in opposite ways, that's all." Her gaze was locked on the Subaru now, and she was waving her arm in broad arcs.

"I do *not* have a chip on my—"

Snack beeped loudly half a dozen times in return, making Laura wince. "The man is driving in a graveyard," she snapped, "not in a St. Patrick's Day parade."

"Laura, stop. You haven't seen one another since Mom's funeral. Bend a little, won't you? It's been so long since we've all been together."

"Three years isn't so long. Anyway, Snack could have come to visit this past Christmas, when you did."

"How? He had to be in court."

Laura smiled grimly. "Case closed. So to speak."

But she was still smarting from her sister's observation. Laura and Snack, two sides of the same warped coin? It wasn't possible. Corinne didn't know what she was talking about. She hadn't taken a psychology course in her life—hadn't had the chance to go to college, period—whereas Laura had worked and scrimped and saved and earned not only a degree in computer science, but a minor in psychology as well.

And never once, during all of the psych courses she'd taken at Oregon State, had it occurred to her that she and Snack shared the same motivation for their respective behavior. The same genes, yes. Apparently. But not the same motivation.

Please. The very thought was laughable.

Snack stopped at the end of the winding lane, got out of the car, and began climbing the rest of the way with long-legged strides. A cigarette dangled from his lips; he pitched it over a headstone and smiled at his sisters sheepishly.

"Brakes went kaput," he explained when he got near. "Just over the line in Jersey. I had to tip a mechanic thirty extra bucks, all I had, to work late. So I'm starving, incidentally. And I blew it anyway—didn't I, big sister?" he added with an edgy and yet good-natured smile at Laura. "I know, I know: thirty-one, and what a mess. Go on. Say it. I'm waiting."

Same old Snack.

Laura said nothing.

He laughed and took in the sweep of Nantucket Sound that lay before them and, with a wink at Corinne, said, "Great view. Dad picked a good spot. Morning sun, sheltered from the wind—not bad. Not bad at all. Ever notice that about graveyards in these old towns? They're always on primo real estate. Yep. Every single one I've ever—"

Suddenly Corinne threw her arms around Snack and began to cry. Taken aback, Snack murmured comforting words without making whole sentences out of them, patting her back as he spoke. Over her shoulder he cocked his head at his older sister, a half-smile of query on his lips: were *they* friends, or were they not?

Laura brushed a few grains of sand from the silk skirt of her dark gray ensemble and then let her glance drift from it to her brother's greasy jeans and denim jacket. "I see you dressed for the occasion?"

A corner of Snack's thin, finely drawn lips lifted a little higher, and he shrugged. "Dad wouldn't have recognized me any way else."

Laura made a dismissive sound and said, "The fog will be rolling in soon. We'd better get back to the house. Come on, Rinnie. Snack can follow us in his car."

Corinne withdrew from her brother's embrace and wiped her eyes with outstretched fingers. "No, wait. Snack needs to say . . . hello, and I guess goodbye. We'll wait for you by your car," she said to him in gentle command.

She linked her arm through Laura's and led her away, giving their younger brother a quiet moment in which to pay his respects, whatever they happened to be.

Corinne walked down the grassy knoll without looking back, but Laura had no such compunctions. She glanced over her shoulder to see Snack standing at the foot of their father's grave, its new headstone obscured under bunches of flowers from the family nursery. Snack's head was bowed, his thumbs hooked in the pockets of his jeans.

Despite her desire not to care, Laura found herself wondering what was going through Snack's head. Was he really reflecting, or was he just faking it? Was he feeling what she had felt earlier in that same spot—confusion, and a horrible, wrenching emptiness? Or was he simply wondering what Corinne, a wonderful cook, had whipped up for them for supper?

With Snack, it was always hard to tell.

After a moment, he bobbed his head and then turned and hurried to catch up with his siblings. Even in the fading light, Laura could see that his thin, boyish face was pale. His voice was subdued as he said, "I could damn well use a drink about now."

"What else is new?" Laura murmured from the other side of Corinne.

Her brother snapped, "Not your attitude, that's for sure."

"There's nothing wrong with my—"

"Stop! Both of you—stop. Think where you are."

Embarrassed by the reprimand, Laura said stiffly, "She's right, Snack. Truce." She held out her hand and shook her brother's firmly when he accepted her offer.

Corinne, presiding over the handshake, sounded relieved. "Good. This has to be a team effort if my plan's going to be a success."

"Success? I'm not used to the sound of that word," Snack quipped.

"What're you talking about?" Laura asked. "What plan?"

Corinne pulled out a rubber band from the pocket of her skirt and began binding her long, sun-streaked hair in a ponytail. With a sweet and gentle smile, she said, "I'm going to make you both an offer you can't refuse."

Snack was all ears. "Oh? Whaddya got?"

"Follow me. You'll see."

Corinne climbed into the nursery's pickup truck, a blue Chevy that was older than Snack's Subaru but not quite as rusted, and Laura climbed in beside her.

"What're you up to, Corinne?" she demanded to know. "Whatever it is, it had better be quick. I leave tomorrow."

Corinne merely smiled. "You'll see."

They were about to pull out when they were halted by the sound of Snack yelling after them to hold it.

Laura groaned. "Now what?"

They climbed back out of the truck. Snack was standing beside the Subaru. "It won't start," he announced in that half-smug, half-defiant voice that they knew so well. "If I had to guess, I'd say it's the solenoid, but who knows? I think the old girl took a look around and thought, 'What the hell, this is as good a place as any to die.' "

"Do you want us to tow you?" Corinne asked.

"No," Laura said quickly. "We'll leave it here. A tow truck can come for it in the morning. It's not exactly blocking traffic."

Them towing Snack. It was all Laura needed: a decrepit truck towing a decrepit car through the middle of town on a Saturday night. She could hear the old snickers so clearly. Oh, how she hated being back!

Snack took his duffelbag out of the Subaru's trunk and tossed it in the back of the pickup, and then he squeezed into the front seat next to Laura. It was predictably tight, and Snack was ripe from his long drive.

"Just like old times, huh?" he said, tugging at Laura's blunt-cut hair. "Remember how Dad used to throw us all in the back of the truck for cranberry harvest?"

The word "cranberry" sent Laura hurtling back in time. For a year or two at the end, when money was especially hard to come by, their father had dragged them off to the cranberry bogs like migrant workers, and that's exactly what they had looked like as they rode in the back of the truck in plain view of everyone in Chepaquit. Oliver Shore was the sole surviving heir to a fourth-generation nursery, and yet he ran it so badly that he'd had to farm out his own children.

Driving out to the bogs hadn't been too unbearable, because few people were up and around at that early hour; but coming back, they had felt painfully on display. They were teenagers, after all; the experience was excruciating. Laura used to pull her baseball cap as far down over her eyes as she could, not because she thought she was disguising herself, but because at least then she couldn't see who was laughing at her.

Often they'd miss school; she hated that even more. Snack, of course, was happy to skip, and even Corinne was relieved—she'd always been shy—but Laura had wanted desperately to make something of herself, and the cranberry bogs were not the place to do that.

"I do remember Octobers here," Laura said quietly. "All too well."

She much preferred her Octobers in Portland, where her garden was a feature on the annual fall tour in her neighborhood, and where afterward she held an open house for the other entrants, treating them to various coffees as well as desserts, none of them baked by her.

"Hey, isn't that the old Sumner place?" Snack said, peering through the deepening dusk. "Holy shit, I hardly recognize it. Who lives there now? The fricking governor?"

"Oh, some trust-fund baby bought it," Corinne explained. "He's playing at being a gentleman farmer. He has sheep."

Whereas the Sumners had pigs. Even so, the Sumner girls had never occupied the lowest rung of the social ladder. That position had been reserved exclusively for the Shore kids.

Laura scarcely glanced at the shingled, gabled farmhouse, now trimmed in pristine white and surrounded by a fenced-in, gently rolling field. She didn't need a walk-through to know that the kitchen was filled with Sub-Zero appliances and that the new wing held a master bedroom with a walk-in closet the size of an Olympic pool. The same kind of gentrification was going on back in Portland. Bigger, better, more: it was the mantra of the new millenium.

"I wonder what became of the Sumner girls," Laura said, only vaguely curious. She was far more curious about what had become of Sylvia, the bright, shining star who had suddenly appeared in their evening sky, and then not long afterward had orbited out of all of their lives. Sylvia, who had been everything that Laura was not: sexy, confident, beautiful, and most of all, free as a butterfly to go wherever she wanted and do whatever she wanted.

"Jean Sumner got married and lives in Indiana; I think she's pretty happy there," Corinne said in a home-town, gossipy way. "Jan, I'm not sure about. I think she's moved to Maine."

Snack said, "So who's still around? Besides you, I mean."

"Lots of people," Corinne argued, sounding defensive. "Two of the Bosenfield kids still live nearby, and so does Nonni Pritchard. And Kendall Barclay, naturally, because of his bank. Will has a practice in Chatham. And, let me see, who else? Oh—Leon Borkowski!"

"Porky Borky?" said Snack fondly. "*He's* still around?"

"He lives with his mother over the liquor store."

"Gee-eez."

Every name felt like a pinprick to Laura, and two of them were red-hot needles. Which was why coming back to Chepaquit was always a hundred times more painful than leaving it had been.

She remembered vividly the day she moved out. By then the dazzling Sylvia had been gone for nearly a year. Laura had had all that time to reflect on what exciting and dramatic lives people like Sylvia led, and to contrast it with how empty and limited her own life was.

By six P.M. on her eighteenth birthday, Laura was packed and ready to run. After a final, bitter fight with her father, she hadn't even stayed for cake, breaking her mother's heart. It was her single regret.

That, and leaving Corinne. Corinne had been too loyal to their parents and to the family business to leave. Well, that phase of her life was behind her now. As soon as she sold the nursery, Corinne would be free to follow her heart's desire. She had paid her dues, with interest. As sole heir, she was going to enjoy her well-deserved reward. No one was more pleased about that than Laura.

She glanced at her sister and let her gaze settle into a thoughtful study of her profile. Corinne might be thirty-two, but hard work and the sun had taken their toll: even in the near-dark, Laura could see thin lines branching from the corners of her sister's green eyes, and a deepening of the line that ran from her nose to the full, well-shaped mouth that presided over a strong, resolute chin.

Was she alluring? It was hard to say. She was Corinne. Laura knew her too well and loved her too much to know how someone seeing her for the first time would respond.

She was Corinne: sweet and loyal and loving and therefore, in Laura's eyes, achingly desirable. For Laura, it was as simple as that. Why couldn't some man, somewhere, see what she saw?

Because men were jerks. Men were all the same. Jerks.

"What? Why are you staring at me?" Corinne asked, cocking her head before turning her attention back to the road.

"I like what the sun has done to your hair," Laura improvised. "Women pay big bucks for that highlighted effect."

"You can't even see my hair in this light," said Corinne, grinning.

"I see fine."

"You do not."

"Yes I do. And I'd forgotten how perfect your teeth are. Whereas I had to suffer through braces at thirty. What a birthday present to myself."

"Okay, enough girl talk," said Snack, cutting in. "Rinnie! What's that offer that we won't be able to refuse, hmm?"

Corinne said smugly, "Right in front of your nose, Snack."

The road had dipped and risen and taken its familiar bend, and now they were at the turnoff to the nursery. Even in the romance of dusk, the place looked as sad and forlorn as ever—a run-down collection of shops, sheds, greenhouses, and outbuildings, all of them presided over by a large farmhouse built on the highest point of the property. Nothing had been fixed or painted in decades, and—for a nursery—very little seemed to be either green or growing.

True, several tables sat haphazardly in front of the shop, but the few pots on top of them held nothing in bloom. It was early in the season for flowers . . . but still. A solid display of spring perennials and bulbs would have gone a long way to attracting customers and distracting them from the woebegone state of the rest of the site. As it stood, no one but a longtime resident in the area would even know the place *was* a nursery: the carved and painted sign that once crowned an arch near the entrance was faded and unreadable, even in daylight.

SHORE GARDENS. A wonderful name for what was once (Laura had seen the photos) a delightfully charming and well-stocked garden center.

No more.

"Will ya look at that?" Snack said in a voice of wonder. "I used to think that it was the peeling paint that held the buildings together. But the paint's all gone and they're still standing. I guess it's by habit."

"Smartass," Corinne said, but with surprising good humor. Clearly she had something to say, and nothing was going to wreck her mood. "Everyone out," she commanded.

Snack and Laura climbed down from the truck like high-school kids on a prison tour: whatever was ahead, they didn't look all that excited to learn about it.

Positioning Snack and Laura next to her on the wrap-around porch of the house, Corinne threw her arms wide and said, "Okay. What do you see out there?"

Not the ocean, that was for sure. The porch faced away from it.

"I see ruins," Snack said candidly.

Laura didn't have the heart to agree out loud.

"Squint a little," Corinne ordered them. "You'll see a thriving business with not only annuals and perennials and shrubs and trees, but garden furniture and water fountains and bird feeders and decorative pottery and . . . squint! You'll *see*."

"Corinne. I have a one-thirty flight out of Logan tomorrow. Cut to the chase or I'm going to miss the damn plane," Laura said, more leery than ever. "Just tell us what you have in mind."

"Just this: I want you to spend a month at the Shore."

Chapter 2

"One month. That's all I ask. I know it's a huge, huge favor. I know I'm asking you to hand over a chunk of your lives to me. But . . . one month. That's all. I've never asked either of you for a favor before," Corinne added in an earnest, heartrending voice.

It was late, two in the morning. Snack and Laura were drooping over the kitchen table: Snack, because he was in his cups; Laura, because she'd spent the previous night crossing the country by plane. Only Corinne, who should have been sleepiest, was still wide awake—feverishly so.

Laura yawned and leaned her head back, trying to rub the cotton out of her eyes. It hurt to open them, hurt to think, hurt to argue. She longed for bed, the same bed that she'd been so glad to abandon fifteen years earlier. If only Corinne would stop holding them hostage!

She gazed wearily at her younger sister. "Rinnie, *why* are you so adamant about this? The nursery hasn't made any money for years. In fact, do you ever remember a good year? I don't. Shore Gardens is a lost cause, believe me."

Her eyelids eased the rest of the way shut as she repeated her litany. "Too many bad decisions . . . too little maintenance . . . the overhead, the taxes. If Dad couldn't make it work with three generations of experience behind him," she added, opening her eyes with an effort, "what makes you think *you* can?"

Incredibly, Corinne was still more than willing to explain.

"Because I know what was missing!" she said with numbing enthusiasm. She slapped the table. "*You.*" She slapped the table again. "*Snack.*"

"We never wanted to stay in the business. Ever," Laura said tiredly. "Everyone knew that—Dad, most of all."

"I know, I know; I was there for all the battles, and I have copies of all three wills: the old one, the new one, and the one Dad was willing to sign if only you'd come back."

Snack let out a harsh laugh and said, "I used my three versions to stoke a fire in a cabin I was living in. What'd you do with your set when you got 'em, Laur?"

"Filed them," Laura said briefly.

Corinne sighed and went on. "But after you both took off, I wasn't enough to hold up our end. The first four generations had a lot more family around to work the business. Our generation just had me."

"Hey . . . don't go laying some guilt trip on me," Snack mumbled. "I paid the price." He folded his arms over the table and began a slow slide forward on it. "And it was a small price at that, to get out from under the old man's beatings."

"All I'm saying is that I didn't have the right stuff on my own, Snack. I'm good at some things, not at others."

Laura said grimly, "Or so you were told by Dad. Repeatedly, I'm sure."

"But it's the truth," said Corinne, ignoring the sarcasm. "For example, the water lines are a disaster because Dad didn't winterize anything a couple of years ago, and some of them burst. I don't know anything about plumbing, so now I'm hauling hoses everywhere. Watering takes forever. There's no pressure. The hoses leak." She said sheepishly,

"That's just one thing off the top of my head. There's so much more."

"Like, who *cares?*" Snack said in a sleepy moan.

"But do you have any idea how many plants we've lost? We could have carpeted the highway from here to Provincetown! Plus, we don't have a catalog, we don't have a computer, we don't do mail order, we're not high-end enough for the big spenders, we're not cheap enough for the Wal-Mart crowd . . ."

Snack was letting his head come slowly down.

"Don't go to sleep on me, Snack!"

"I'm just resting," he muttered to his forearms.

Laura's heart went out to her sister, but Corinne was tilting at windmills. For all of the reasons that she had just listed, the nursery was failing. Had failed. Laura had been shocked by the evidence that she saw all around her when she arrived that morning.

It was over. Everything was over. Corinne should just sell the property and use the money to start up a nice business in a related field. A florist shop, maybe.

Outside, the wind was picking up, adding its dispirited moan to the grumbling responses that they'd been giving to Corinne's dogged pleas for their help.

Laura looped her forefingers through her straight brown hair, tucking it behind her ears. "Rinnie . . . honey . . . can't you hear it?" she asked with a sad smile and a nod at the open window. "That's the fat lady singing."

"No! I am not done here yet! I have plans, lots of them! I've thought about this for months, for years, but I never had the courage to stand up to Dad. You know how he is—was," Corinne said, her voice catching in her throat.

"Yes. We do. That's why we left," Laura said softly. "Snack got sick of the strap, and I got sick of the tirades. Neither of us had your strength, Rin."

She leaned over to rub her sister's back, spinning slow circles of comfort between her shoulder blades. When Corinne was six and Laura was eight, it used to do the trick. But that was then.

"Laura, we can *do* this," her sister said, shrugging off the show of sympathy. "You have an artist's eye; look how you fixed up that wreck of a house that you bought in Portland. For gosh sakes, when you were done, it was featured in *Renovation Magazine*! And so was the garden you created—from nothing, I might add. Think of the marketing angle for us; you're famous now!"

"That's so ridiculous," Laura said, embarrassed. "One little article—"

"In a national magazine! It just flew off the shelves around here. And I forgot to tell you, but there was a copy in Dr. Burton's office, and someone tore out the pages for a souvenir. That's how impressed they were."

A wave of irritation washed over Laura. "I cannot believe you persist in going to that quack," she snapped.

"But . . . we've always gone to Dr. Burton," Corinne said, taken aback.

True enough. Which was why, when she was thirteen, Laura made a vow never to get sick enough to need medical attention. She'd kept that vow. The next time she saw a physician was when she was eighteen, living on the West Coast, and in dire need of her first supply of birth-control pills.

Corinne said, "Anyway, you're changing the subject. This isn't about my doctor, Laura, it's about my doctor's magazine. *You were in it.*"

"Yeah, yeah, I'm a real celebrity," Laura said tiredly.

"*Plus,* you know all about computers. You can streamline our accounting system and get us computerized at last."

"But that's not what I do!" Laura said, exasperated. She had tried so many times to explain her career. She tried again. "I'm a systems programmer. I don't decide what a system is going to do, I just decide how it's going to do it," she said.

"But it's all still computers, isn't it?" Corinne asked naïvely.

Sighing, Laura said, "My clients are *big* companies, with very special needs. I generally work as part of a team of ten to twenty people. My expertise is in the communications part: how to make two computers in the same system talk to one another. I implement the program, make sure it runs successfully, and leave."

She got the usual blank look from Corinne.

"*I don't do flowers*. Okay?"

"Gawd. How can you stand that job?" Snack asked, opening one eye. "I'd sooner cut my throat."

"It's challenging, satisfying work—and it happens to pay well," Laura shot back. "It's clean. It's prestigious. And I get to pick and choose my contracts."

"Had your fill of down and dirty, have you?" Snack asked, yawning. He nestled his cheek on his arm, ready for bed.

"Yes, as a matter of fact," Laura said. "If I'm feeling nostalgic for backbreaking labor, I go out in my garden and weed."

Ignoring the crack, Corinne turned to her brother, reaching across the table to cup her hands over his. Snack didn't bother to raise his head, but she pleaded her case anyway.

"And *you've* worked at every odd job there is. You know how to do everything, Snack! You can spruce up the store, and then the greenhouses, and maybe build us a checkout shed for the spring rush. As for this house, it just needs a coat of paint for now, that's all. Not even! Just paint the front, and maybe the west side—just the parts that show from the nursery!"

Snack's answer was a sleepy moan. "Is *that* all?"

"Okay, skip the greenhouses, then," Corinne said, rolling with it. "That's not as urgent, now that the cold weather's over. They're too far gone, anyway. Maybe—maybe just knock down the one by the road! Bulldoze it, that's what you can do! And relocate that giant compost pile that's next to it. It's so in the wrong place."

Snack's head came up. "Bulldoze the greenhouse! Move the compost! What the hell are you talking about?"

Corinne backed off, drawing her pale brows together in a fit of second-guessing. "All right, maybe not; it was just a thought. I have other ideas, lots of them! Please. Snack, please," she begged. "Give me a month of your time to turn this place around. To turn our reputation around. Let's make the name Shore something to be proud of again. That's all I ask."

Snack dragged himself to his feet. "You're nuts," he said wearily. "I'm going to bed."

A look of dismay passed over Corinne's face. "No!" she said, grabbing his forearm. "You can't go to bed. We made a pact: no one sleeps until this is resolved, one way or the other."

"Watch me," he said, sloughing off her grip.

"Oh, Snack. Why did you have to drink all that beer?" Corinne said, more sad than angry. "Why do you always do that?"

An ironic grin, highlighted by a chipped front tooth, came and went on his lean, stubbled face. "Rinnie, dear sister. I do what I want. If I want to get fall-down drunk, that's my perrog . . . prerga . . . prerogative."

Laura decided that she'd better step in. She was all too aware of her brother's moods, which could turn on a dime from bemused to resentful. Although Snack seemed okay about being cut from their father's will, it was obvious that somewhere deep down inside, resentment still bubbled in him.

Laura sat back in her chair and said, "Snack, Rinnie already admits that she's crazy. The question is, just how crazy are *we*? Let's assume for the sake of argument that I'd be willing to throw a month of my life into this broken-down wreck of a business. Would you?" she asked him with a carefully offhand air.

Her brother's laugh was soft and incredulous. "What, kill myself for a lost cause like this? Do what you like, Laur . . . but count me out."

It was his attitude to life: *count me out*. Without knowing why, Laura decided to call him on it.

"Snack, let me put it another way, because Corinne is far too polite to bring it up: it's Corinne—not me, not you—who stayed behind and made life a little more bearable for Mom. She did it for over a decade. She's asking us for a month."

"Rinnie didn't have to stay," Snack said sullenly. "No one was holding a gun to her head."

"But she did stay, didn't she? And we owe her, don't we?" Laura suggested quietly.

"I'm not saying I'm not grateful. I'm just saying—" He frowned again and rubbed the back of his neck, a gesture of frustration that he had inherited from his father. "What happens if we do manage to turn the business around? *I'm* not staying on, and neither are you. Once Rinnie has to pay for help to replace us, that's it: back down the toilet goes Shore Gardens."

"That's Rinnie's problem, isn't it? We're just agreeing to grant her the favor she's asked, that's all. One month."

"Dammit, Laura! Where're you coming from, all of a sudden?"

All evening long, it had been the two of them against Corinne. But sweet Corrine had stood up to their pounding, and an admiring Laura had just decided to switch sides. Snack had every right to feel double-crossed.

Laura pulled at one of the thin gold loops hooked through her earlobes. She said to her brother, "A month, Snack. How about it?"

His face flushed. He threw a longing glance at the worn-down stairs that led to his old room and his lumpy bed. He was tired and crabby and ready to pass out; Laura recognized the signs from their youth.

"Oh, all right," he snapped. "One fricking month. That's *it*."

Corinne leapt from her chair and threw her arms around her brother in an enthusiastic hug. He grimaced and caught her wrists from behind his neck, breaking the circle of her embrace. "Now can I go to fricking sleep?"

"Yes, yes, anything, yes," said his overjoyed sister. She watched him go, virtually hopping up and down in place, and then she called out after him, "Snack!"

He turned around, sagging visibly. "Now what?"

"Win *or* lose, I'm making you and Laura co-owners."

"Of—?"

"Everything. The business, the buildings, the land. Everything; just the way it should be. If I can't turn the business around and I'm forced to sell, then you get a third, and so does Laura."

"What! *Corinne!*" cried Laura, stunned by what she was hearing.

Bleary-eyed, Snack asked, "You serious?"

"Yessir!"

"Well . . ." He looked uncharacteristically at a loss. "Whatever," he muttered awkwardly, and he turned and began ascending the stairs. "G'night."

Chapter 3

As soon as Snack was out of earshot, Laura said to Corinne, "Are you crazy? Why did you say something like that?"

"Because it's true. I'd always planned on reinstating the two of you. It's only fair."

"Not me. Uh-uh, Rin. Count me out. I don't want any part of this. Do not write me back into *anything*. I refuse to accept. Helping you out for a month is one thing, but I've made my own way, and it would feel like—I don't know—wrong. That's all. Wrong. You're the one who stayed."

"Don't be silly. This will work, trust me. I've thought about it for a long time," Corinne said. She began gathering the empty beer cans for rinsing and recycling.

"Thought about it? You haven't thought about it at all!" Laura said, tagging after her. "For one thing, if you tell Snack he's going to get a third of Shore Gardens whether it succeeds or not, do you really think he's going to try to make it work? Get real, will you? You'll be lucky if he doesn't hold an open house for interested developers every Sunday from one to three."

Laughing, Corinne said, "Bring me those dirty plates, would you? This *will* work," she repeated, turning a little sideways so that Laura could stack the dishes in the basin.

"Snack will rise to the occasion. You'll see."

"Corinne. You are so naïve." Feeling churlish for slamming her brother, Laura dropped the subject altogether for the moment. She had other concerns. "One month," she warned. "I can't do more. You have to realize that this is going to be very hard on—"

My career. God, it sounded so mean-spirited, given Corinne's almost saintly generosity. Laura settled for saying, "I can do a month. I had planned to take a couple of weeks off anyway. The only thing is," she muttered as an afterthought, "I thought I was taking them off in Hawaii."

"With Max. I know," Corinne said, looking up from her soapsuds with a tragically sympathetic look.

"Oh, Corinne . . . stop," Laura said, flushing with annoyance. "I will board that plane tomorrow if you're going to be wringing your hands over Max and me every time I turn around. It's over, and obviously it was no great loss."

"I know. It's just that you sounded so . . . happy."

"Well, I was wrong. I just *thought* I was happy."

"Love is blind," Corinne agreed.

"Love is stupid! It has nothing to do with anything. The only thing that matters in life is what you make of yourself, not what someone else makes of you. And on that note, let's get back to your dream. You missed two payments, no more than that, right?" she asked her sister.

"Yes," Corinne said firmly. "I paid this month right on time. So I don't understand why I got a threatening notice yesterday."

"Don't worry; we'll take care of it. I'll write a check for the missing payments tomorrow."

"I'm so embarrassed about this, Laur. But you know you'll get the money back, don't you?"

"Never mind; it's not today's problem." Laura was back in business mode now, and on firmer terrain. Facts and figures, that's what she could count on. Everything else was just fluff. "When did Dad take out this loan from—who's the outfit? Great River?"

"Great River Finance." Corinne shrugged her strong shoulders and said as she dried her hands on a ratty old dishtowel, "I haven't looked at the books close enough to figure that out, yet. They're all just mishmash to me, anyway, especially the way Dad kept them."

"Yeah. I remember. Everything in shoeboxes."

"All I know is that there's a book of payment coupons from Great River Finance for this year. I'm not that worried, though, because Ken Barclay did say something about how if I found myself over my head, I shouldn't panic."

"Kendall Barclay! When did you talk to *him* about this?"

"Originally? A few months ago. I ran into him when I was in the drugstore, getting something for an awful cold I had. I was depressed and really out of it, and, frankly, I didn't register half of what he said."

Kendall Barclay.

Laura could picture the name so clearly, written in her flowery handwriting on an envelope of thick pink paper, the very best she could find in the Chepaquit Pharmacy.

> *Dear Kendall, Thank you, thank you, thank you,* it began. *You're my knight in shining armor. You saved me, and I'll never forget you for that.*

She had rewritten the note at least three times, phrasing her gratitude more effusively each time. Kendall Barclay had been too skinny to look like a knight, and he'd ridden into the woods on a bike and not on a horse—but no one could deny the courage that he'd shown.

To that day, Laura could not believe that she had once been dumb enough to believe that the son of Dr. Burton could have had a crush on someone like her. But that's what she had believed. When Will Burton asked her to go with him for a walk in the woods, she had pictured nothing more daring than a romantic kiss and an embrace.

How naïve. How dumb. How arrogant.

After the doctor's son and his buddies had assaulted her and beat up Kendall and then had fled like the bullying cowards they were, Laura had dropped to her knees beside her fallen hero: blood was trickling from his mouth, and one of his eyes was bruised and swelling. Tearing off a scrap of her already torn blouse, she had wiped away the blood from his chin.

"Are you all right, Kendall?" she'd asked stupidly.

How could he possibly have been all right?

But he had answered with a dazed, "Y-yuh, I'm all right."

And she had taken him at his word.

"Don't look at me," he had mumbled, averting his face. "Go home. Go *home,*" he had repeated more fiercely. "They won't come back now."

He was the pampered son of a town scion; the other kids knew that, and the other kids despised him for it. He was picked on almost as much as the dirt-poor Shore kids, but for the opposite reason: because he was so rich.

Laura, probably more than anyone else, had understood the humiliation Kendall was feeling as he lay on the ground. She had wanted to respect his wishes, whatever they happened to be, so she'd stood up abruptly and run through the woods and made her way home. She'd been able to sneak past her father and change her shirt before he came in for supper and yelled at her for being late.

And the very next day, she had biked to the Chepaquit Pharmacy and had bought the heavy pink stationery.

And very shortly after that, Kendall Barclay had basically spit in her face.

Kendall Barclay.

It must have been twenty years since she'd seen him.

She murmured to Corinne, "So tell me what he said in the drugstore that you do remember."

"Well . . . he apologized for not being able to come to the funeral, I remember that. Wasn't that nice of him? Bankers don't have to do that. And he said we could talk anytime. That I should just phone and ask for him personally, and we would set up a time."

"A time to do what?"

"I guess, to talk about if I need a loan? I'm not really sure. But he knows what's in our account—nothing—so maybe he thought I'd be looking for another loan soon. Needless to say, I've been so busy that I never did get around to arranging an appointment. But when I ran into him in town at Sam's Market last week, he was just the same."

"I don't understand."

"Neither do I. But then he called yesterday and left a message on the machine! He asked if there was *anything* he could do. He sounded very kind, very concerned. I haven't had a chance to call him back yet."

"He's got an agenda," Laura said firmly. "It's obvious."

Corinne blinked. "I thought he was trying to be nice."

"You would. Don't you see what his game is? As you say, he knows you're broke. Now that Dad's gone, he sees his chance. He'll give you a loan, wait for you to default on it, and then put this place up for auction. Guess who'll buy it back? His bank. Well, don't lose a second's worth of sleep over him, Rinnie. I'll take care of Kendall Barclay."

"I haven't lost any sleep over him," Corinne said as she gathered table crumbs into the palm of her hand. "Why do you dislike him so much?" she added. "You've been this way about him ever since I can remember."

"He's a jerk. A rich, privileged, arrogant, money-sucking jerk."

"Laura. Just because his family was rich and ours wasn't, that doesn't make him arrogant. Or money-sucking. Or a jerk. He couldn't help who his parents were."

"But he could help who *he* was. What kind of person *he* was."

"When did you even see him last? High school?"

"I . . . don't remember," Laura said, sliding the chairs back under the table.

"Well, he turned out very nice."

"There you go again! Don't you get it? You may as well stick his business card in the box with the ones from those developers who keep coming around here. Because that's what he's after, you dope: your land."

"Why would he want our land? He has his own land."

"Why does *anyone* want land, especially with sweeping views? Because they're not making any more of it. Don't you remember the time that Dad told us Kendall seemed to be hinting that he'd like to buy us out? You own a nice little piece of the Cape, Rinnie. You're just minutes from Chatham, but with a heck of a lot less danger of being washed into the ocean. Do the math. Kendall Barclay wants your land. Period."

Corinne tossed the paper-towel napkins into the rusted, grimy garbage can that was snugged up against the gold-tone stove. "*I* thought he was just trying to be nice."

Tired as she was, Laura felt too uneasy and too melancholy to sleep. Disregarding the cold spring fog that had rolled in so predictably after the warm day, she propped her bedroom window open with a stick and pulled a chair up close so that she could better hear the plaintive moan of the whistle buoy offshore. She leaned her forearms on the sill and allowed herself to drift.

Laura had grown up to the sound of that buoy. She was able to picture the big red mark lifting and falling as it rolled on the ocean swell; it was part of the panoramic seascape that was visible from the hilltop nursery. When she was a teenager, it had seemed to her that the buoy's breath-over-a-bottletop moan perfectly expressed how she felt about life in the village of Chepaquit.

Bleak.

It was impossible for Laura to call up wonderful childhood memories, as others did, of carefree days on the shore. There weren't any. The nursery was a full-time chore, day in and day out. There were always plants to water, seedlings to transplant, stock to move, orders to fill, plants to water and water and water.

Even in the dead of winter, even in the dog days of summer, the work was never done. Laura had no friends in school because she'd never had the time to participate in any activities. She and her brother and sister were always getting special dispensations, and the other kids naturally looked on them as the hardship case they were.

Of course, it hadn't helped matters that their uncle Norbert had been sent to jail for killing his wife. Uncle? All she knew of him was that he was a man with a violent temper who'd strangled his wife one day after an argument over a burned supper: a dumb, stupid, overcooked roast. Even though the murder had happened before their time, they had all grown up with the horrible stigma. How could they not? Shore Gardens had been co-owned by two Shore brothers, Oliver and Norbert.

Take away the murderer, and then there was one.

Take away Oliver, and now there was none.

The old generations had all passed on, leaving Laura, Snack, and Corinne to find their way as best they could.

Sitting at the window, looking out at gray nothing and shivering from the penetrating chill, Laura couldn't shake her sense of foreboding. Something about Chepaquit wasn't right. It was as though the village had been cast under an evil spell. People ran off, people died young, people were sent away.

In Laura's mind, the one chance to have the spell broken was lost when Sylvia left. Sylvia—bright, beautiful, independent Sylvia, who had breezed into town, made everyone love her, and then had breezed right out again, breaking Laura's heart. Until the day that Sylvia quit her job at the nursery, Laura had truly begun to have hope. She used to think, *If Sylvia likes Chepaquit, then so can I.*

If Sylvia can impress people, then so can I.

If Sylvia can make work seem like fun, then so can I.

If Sylvia fears no one, then . . . why should I?

It was the single, most exciting time of Laura's life, filled with potential. At last she'd had a role model to show her the possibilities.

But then one day Sylvia left as suddenly as she'd appeared, without a goodbye, without a word to Laura or to anyone else . . . and the spell resumed. It truly was like a fairy tale. Life in the village became more oppressive than ever. The ones who stayed, died. First Laura's mother, and now her father. Neither had made it to sixty-five. Was that so much to expect?

I miss you, Mom, came her sudden, fervent thought. She brushed away a sting of tears. *Today, right now, more than ever.*

So, yes, Laura would grant Corinne her month. But Laura would not be able to lift the spell. Only Sylvia could do that. After the month, when they inevitably admitted to defeat, Corinne would have to sell the acreage—to Kendall Barclay and his crowd, in all likelihood—and Laura would whisk her sister off to wonderful Portland, with its impressive blend of high tech and high mountains. Portland, where the growing season lasted year round. Portland, where she and Corinne could grow old together instead of alone.

The wind eddied and lifted the buoy's moan closer to Laura's open window. It was a ghostly dirge, come again to haunt her: *No-o-oh,* it moaned, followed by mournful silence. Again: *No-o-oh,* and mournful silence. And again.

She was sorry, sorry, sorry to be back. They said you couldn't go home again—but that was such a lie.

She sighed and caught a whiff of cigarette: Snack must be awake too, in his room. She wondered what thoughts he was having that were powerful enough to keep him from sleep.

Chapter 4

Laura had forgotten what "up with the chickens" really meant. Over the years she had evolved into a night person; five A.M. was nearer to her bedtime nowadays than it was to her breakfast.

She dressed quickly in the May morning chill and made her way to the kitchen, where the aroma of strong coffee—even of sizzling bacon—wasn't enough to convince her that life was worth living.

"Here's the number one reason why your plan is doomed, Rinnie: the hours," she mumbled as she filled a mug for herself.

Her appallingly cheerful sister laughed and said, "I know. They suck. But you'll fall back into it; it's like riding a bike." She eyed Laura's workclothes and said, "Is that what you're wearing? Skin-tight jeans and a white linen shirt?"

"They're all I have," Laura said, yawning. "When I packed my carry-on, I wasn't exactly planning to dig ditches."

"You look great, by the way," Corinne said, a little glumly. "I'd give anything to fit into those jeans. What are they, size eight?"

Laura laughed. "Get real. Size ten. A very generous ten."

"I keep forgetting what an hourglass figure you have," her sister said, sighing. "And you've lost weight besides?"

"Yeah. After Max dumped me, I—yeah. I lost some weight," Laura admitted. "That's when I bought these jeans—which was a total waste of money," she added wryly, "because as soon as I get done moping over Max, I plan to put those pounds right back on. And that's a promise."

Instantly Corinne was all sympathy. "Is it definitely over, then? There's *no* hope?" she asked as she laid out oversized plates for the oversized breakfast to come.

"Hope? How can there be hope?" Laura had wanted to get in and out of Chepaquit without going into details of the breakup, but now that she was committed to staying a month . . .

Better to get it over with.

"The fact is, I told Max about Uncle Norbert."

"Oh, no. You didn't," Corinne groaned. "You didn't go into any details, did you?"

Laura shrugged. "Max asked how he got caught. I told him that after Uncle Norbert strangled Aunt Mary, he left her body in bed and went off on a camping trip, trying to make it look as if someone broke in and killed her—even though he and Aunt Mary lived in a mobile home a few feet from our house. Even though he hadn't said boo about any trip to Mom and Dad before he took off. Even though he was arrested still wearing the shirt missing the button that Aunt Mary pulled off in the struggle."

Snorting, she said, "I think it was all just a little too gothic for Max."

"But it happened before we were even born!"

"Did that ever matter to any of our classmates? No. They just assumed that we shared our uncle's gene for stupidity. Max did too, I guess."

"Oh, come on. You're a systems programmer. How can

you be stupid? It's not even possible," Corinne said, bowled over by Laura's admission.

"Obviously I must have the gene," Laura said, suddenly bitter. "Otherwise, why would I have tried to be honest with Max before we got married? How stupid was *that*?"

The irony of it was that she had become a systems programmer precisely to show the world how smart she could be, and that's how she had met Max.

And that's how she had ended up suffering new humiliation: because Max had told everyone on the project the whole lurid, stupid story of Uncle Norbert. Thank God it had happened near the end of a job that Laura was able to finish and leave. Thank God at least for that.

Corinne had that teary look in her eyes; she was a bottomless well of sympathy, overflowing at the least provocation.

Laura put her hands up, palms forward, in a gesture of rejection. "Nope. No tears. I'll get through it fine; I'm just about there, in fact," she said defiantly. "Max was a jerk. I'm lucky to be out of it."

"He *is* a jerk; you *are* lucky," Corinne agreed. "So! Where were we? Oh. Clothes. I'll lend you workclothes of mine to wear. We know *they* won't be tight," she said with a wry grin.

Corinne Shore was five feet ten and heavily built. Neither of the sisters had ever been exactly slim, but there was something super-solid about Corinne. On the nursery grounds, she carried her size with an easy grace suitable to hauling big root balls around. When she was in her natural element, her smile was quick, her carriage straight, and her stride, long and sure. She was Wonder Woman.

But once she left her four-acre world, her confidence collapsed. Her shoulders drooped, her head hung forward. She became overly intrigued by her shoes. Often she mumbled. And she was forever clearing her throat.

It had always been obvious to Laura that when her sister

was out in public, she became ashamed of her size and tried her best to shrink in place. Her classmates had picked up on Corinne's hunched-over manner; they used to tease her mercilessly about it.

But right now Corinne was on her home turf, surrounded by people she loved and cooking a meal for them. She was beaming.

"I know I shouldn't be so happy just months after the . . . the funeral," she confessed as she turned the bacon. "And a huge part of me isn't. It's just that—"

"It's all right, Rin," said Laura, stroking her sister's cheek as she passed. "We're all weird mixes of relief and sadness right now."

Only the proportions differed. Laura changed the subject. "Is our brother—ha-ha—up?"

Corinne rolled her blue eyes. "I knocked. Gently. I didn't want to make him grumpy his first day on the job."

"Oh, good. Then I'll be able to."

Still sipping her coffee, Laura ascended the stairs past the landing window, almost opaque now with dust and dirt, and treaded down a runner worn through in places to the floorboards. The condition of the house was utterly dismaying to her, although it had been going downhill for her whole life. Now that she thought about it, the house hadn't been painted her whole life.

The shabby interior had been cleaner when her mother was alive, of course; meek, submissive Alice had always carried all of her energy and dreams in a plastic bucket with a soapy sponge.

Laura wondered what had become of the money she used to send her mother for buying something nice for the house—a carpet, new drapes, a television set. Anything to make her life brighter, a little more cheerful. A little more bearable.

Sunk into the damn business, obviously. A bottomless hole if ever there was one.

After her mother died, Laura continued to send money, but to Corinne—who undoubtedly handed it right over to their father, just as their mother had done. But Oliver Shore had been gone for half a year, and there was nothing new in the house that Laura could see. Where had the money gone?

Into the bottomless hole, of course.

She paused at the door of Snack's room, knocked robustly, and stepped inside. Her brother was sleeping on his stomach in a tangle of sheet, his tattooed arm dangling over the side of the single bed, his toes looped over the edge of the mattress.

She clutched his ankle and shook it, but not too hard. "Hey. Time to go to school."

He didn't answer. His breathing was deep, just shy of a snore. She shook a little harder. "Hey. Up."

After a pause, she heard a muffled, "Go to hell."

"You haven't noticed? We're already there." She waved her mug of coffee under his nose and said, "There's more where this came from."

"Go to hell."

She straightened up and regarded her brother, behaving so much like the baby of the family that he was. "Oh, for Pete's sake, Snack. One *month*. You've just finished doing more time than that!"

It was a sharp little poke, but Laura was determined that, co-owner or not, Snack was going to give the job his all.

He rolled sleepily onto his back. He opened one eye and regarded his sister.

"I did not steal the car. I took it for a ride. Haven't you ever wanted to take a Corvette for a ride?"

"Wouldn't it have been easier to walk into a showroom and *ask*?"

He gave her a wry look from under half-lowered lids. "Well, unlike you, big sister, I haven't acquired that aura of success that would make a salesman take me seriously."

"Good point," she said briskly, annoyed by that taunting gaze. "So I'll give you a couple of tips. A haircut would help. So would a shirt that actually had sleeves. Tank tops won't cut it in the real world." She regarded the skull and crossbones tattooed on his pale arm with obvious distaste.

Snack registered the look and returned it with a disingenuous one. "What? You don't appreciate fine art? Here, watch the eye sockets move when I flex my biceps." He curled his lanky arm across his chest like a sleepy bodybuilder.

Laura said, "Very nice."

"It has a—how would you say?—kinetic quality, don't you think?" he asked.

" 'Kinetic'? Have you been playing with alphabet blocks again?"

"Ooh . . . mean," he said with cheerful relish.

"Thank you. I try."

Impulsively, he grinned and said, "Just like old times, hey?"

That was the hell of Snack Shore: he was smart, articulate, self-taught—and still enjoyed nothing better than acting like an aborigine being dragged kicking and screaming out of the forest. He used to do it out of self-defense, because most of Chepaquit treated not just him, but all of them, like inbred bumpkins. They were kin of stupid Uncle Norbert, after all.

But Snack wasn't a kid anymore, and his act was getting stale. Laura said wearily, "Just get dressed and come downstairs, would you?"

"I will do that. Now leave, I pray you, and let me conduct my *toilette* in peace."

Snack's *toilette* must have been pretty basic. Still in his tank top, he showed up at the table unshaven, unkempt, and uncombed. Laura caught a whiff of heavily applied deodorant: camouflage, barely.

"No shower?" she inquired sweetly.

"Why bother?" he said, tugging Corinne's ponytail in greeting as he passed. He pulled out a chair. "I'll just sweat, anyway. I can catch a shower later."

"Three eggs or four, Snack?"

"Four, please. I'm not called Snack for nothing. Any coffee left?"

"I'm way ahead of you," said Corinne, setting a mug in front of him. "Black and strong and French with a touch of chicory, just the way you like it."

"Your servant, mademoiselle," he said, dropping a kiss on the inside of her wrist.

Corinne giggled and whacked him lightly across the shoulder. "I've missed you, dope," she confessed, and she began expertly cracking eggs into an ancient cast-iron pan.

He was the Snack of old: charming, amusing; bilingual. He'd spent an entire summer on the canals of France as the improbable result of a cultural exchange program—a flukey, once-in-a-lifetime opportunity that their timid mother had insisted he seize. Laura and Corinne had been forced to fill in for him at the nursery for the entire summer. Amazingly to her, Laura resented it still; *her* command of conversational French had come from a Berlitz tape.

He took a pack of unfiltered cigarettes from his T-shirt pocket and began knocking one loose. So French. So irritating.

"Do you *have* to smoke at the table?" she asked.

He took out a Bic and lit up. "Mm-hmm. Why do you ask?"

"I'm allergic."

"Since when?"

"Since I waitressed at a bar for six years while I put myself through school."

Snack rolled his eyes. "Open a window."

"Play nice, you two," Corinne interrupted with a nervous smile. "Or it's going to be a long month. Snack, please put that out."

Snack took a long drag, held it, and blew the smoke toward the ceiling fixture overhead. And then he stubbed the cigarette into the lid of the open jelly jar. He cocked one eyebrow at Laura. "Happy?"

"I've been happier," Laura said, waving away the smoke.

"You wouldn't know happy if you tripped and fell into a vat of it."

Bristling, Laura said, "It might interest you to know that I'm the picture of contentment back in Portland."

"You're wrong. It doesn't interest me at all."

"Stop! Stop it, both of you!"

Corinne was standing behind their mother's chair at one end of the table, balancing a plate of food in each hand. "Laura, you *know* Snack likes to tease. Why are you letting him get to you? Really, I'm just so surprised at you."

She slapped one plate down in front of Laura, a much fuller one in front of her brother, then said, "Have I forgotten—? Oh, right: ketchup for the hash browns." She took a bottle out from the fridge and handed it to her brother, then turned her attention back to Laura. "You okay?"

"I'm fine."

"Well . . . good," Corinne said hesitantly. She fetched her own plate of overfried eggs and made a production of buttering her English muffin to cover the awkwardness of the moment.

Meanwhile, Laura was left to wonder why on earth she was so determined to bite off her brother's head. True, she'd been under a ridiculous amount of pressure in her job, and the assignment she'd just completed had been a brutal, nonstop grind. And, true, the downtime she had booked for Max and her in Hawaii had just been preempted by, oh, Max breaking off their engagement. And replaced by a month of slave labor.

In—as Snack would say—fricking Chepaquit.

"I'm sorry," she said stiffly. "When I'm here, I guess I revert. Anyway, let's talk about something more productive, like today's work list."

Because for God's sake—she was the most well-adjusted of the bunch!

Snack, who had been watching her in uncharacteristic silence, turned from her to Corinne. "Where's the Deere, by the way? Please don't tell me Dad sold it."

"No, no, it's in the garage. Something's wrong with it, though; it overheats. In fact, that's where Dad was, about to check it out, when he . . . um . . ."

Tears began to roll down her cheeks, and she began biting her lip, trying to stop them. It sent Laura into a panic: the one thing she was not prepared to deal with was an uncontrolled outflow of emotion.

She put down her fork. "Honey, don't," she said softly, reaching over to stroke her sister's hair. "This will sound heartless, but—we don't have the *time*. If we start traveling down the road you're going, we'll all become paralyzed with emotion, all kinds of emotion. If that's what you want, then . . . fine. We can sit around and try to come to terms with what Dad's death means to each of us. It won't be pretty. But if you're serious about turning this place around, and if sales this spring are really off to such a miserable start—"

"Then we have to get going," Corinne said through her sniffles. "I know." She blew her nose in her napkin and threw her powerful shoulders back. "Everyone, eat. You'll need your strength."

Chapter 5

Laura's borrowed pants kept sliding down, and she considered going back to the house to change. But she was spending most of her time in the main greenhouse on her knees, groping under long tables for forgotten pots of perennials. Corinne's roomy, thick Levi's were a lot more suited to the task than her own clingy designer jeans.

Baggy Levi's it would have to be. She snugged the makeshift rope belt a little more tightly around her waist and got back to work.

The work list had chores enough for a year and a month, but its top two priorities were obvious: in order to try to survive, they had to have something to sell, and in order to have something to sell, they had to have a tractor to schlep it around in.

So Snack was in the garage, tinkering with the overheating John Deere, and Corinne was in the greenhouse down by the shop, primping the annuals for the fast-approaching Founders Week sale.

As for Laura, she had spent the morning crawling around in the oldest, most decrepit of the greenhouses, sorting out the perennials, most of which were dead. With so many glass panes broken or missing, all it had taken was one vicious cold spell to blast and then wither the more tender plants.

"Of course, it would *help* if some of these things had labels," she muttered, pulling out pot after pot from under the bottom shelf of one of the nicked and worn tables.

She studied several one-gallon pots that held—what? Who knew? The delicate, pale green shoots sprouting in them were undoubtedly weeds that had taken seed there. She poked through the pots gingerly, looking for established roots or rhizomes of some sort, but she came up empty. Into the wheelbarrow they went, headed with the others for the compost pile.

Cross off three more sales of something or other.

She felt as if she were working in a parallel universe. Back in Portland, she liked nothing more than to escape for a couple of hours in her garden, a vibrant, thriving world of color and fragrance. A single dandelion had her pouncing. But this! The sense of neglect and decay was not only wide but deep. Laura could smell it, she could practically feel it in her bones as she crawled around on the dirt floor of the greenhouse, searching for living things.

Could she have made the difference?

It was a question she'd asked herself a dozen times since her arrival on the Cape the day before. Assuming that she had remained in Chepàquit and had thrown herself into Shore Gardens the way she'd immersed herself in her career as a software consultant—would the nursery now be as successful as her garden?

Truthfully, she couldn't see how. Oliver Shore had been stubborn and tyrannical in the extreme, clinging to the old ways of doing business, ignoring the evidence all around him that some of those ways were obsolete. He had listened to no one's advice; in fact, he'd taken every suggestion as a personal affront. In his mind, "change" was a dirty word, and he'd been willing and able to wash out the mouth of anyone who dared use it in a sentence.

Basically, Laura had had the choice of staying and having her tongue taste like Lava soap for the rest of her days, or of following her own star. She had no regrets.

Almost no regrets, anyway. She had removed herself from a life of which her mother and her sister were a well-loved part, and nothing would give her those missing years back. That realization would hurt forever.

But as for leaving the rest of Chepaquit behind? No. No regrets at all.

She plunged through some sticky cobwebs and pulled out half a dozen more pots from their hiding places.

Labels! Hooray! And growth!

"Ah, nuts." The plants were penstemon, short-lived and a tender variety in any case. And forget about the cupid's dart. Goners for sure. The growth was simply more weeds.

Discouraged, she sat back on her calves and calculated the absurd amount of time she was taking to salvage maybe twenty percent of the greenhouse's contents. Cost-effective, it wasn't.

She was about to crawl on when she caught a glimpse of a small, glimmering object lying in the dirt behind where the pots had been, a bracelet of some sort. She reached far under and pulled it out: it was a plain Timex wristwatch with an expandable and now rusted band. One of the band's pins had pulled out of the watch.

She shook it for no real reason . . . maybe to see if it would work. *Takes a lickin' and keeps on tickin'*, isn't that how the ads used to go? But the second hand wasn't interested in waking up from what had to have been a pretty long nap, judging from the rust.

Hers? Her sister's? They'd both owned Timexes in their days. It didn't look familiar, although it was definitely the kind of rugged watch, a man's watch, that either one of them would wear at work. It wasn't her mother's: Alice Shore had never cared to keep track of how fast her life was ticking out from under her.

Laura knocked the timepiece against her thigh to free it of dirt and then tucked it in her pocket to show to Snack and Corinne. Getting to her feet a little stiffly, she stretched her now-aching back. With an effort, she began pushing the laden wheelbarrow through the greenhouse, emerging outside at a compost pile that was filled with years of the nursery's failures and becoming more mountainous with every trip. By the time she finished emptying all of the pots onto the side of the dirt mountain, it was noon.

Thank God.

In bright sunshine, she retraced the worn, familiar path from greenhouse to the main house. The pleasant warmth of the morning was less pleasant now, with a salty, sticky edge to it that was nothing like Portland's somehow more bearable dampness.

Gonna be a hot one, she found herself thinking.

Too hot, surely, for the neighbor she saw approaching the house carrying a large casserole in her hands and walking with halting steps.

"Miss Widdich, let me," said Laura, rushing to help.

"It's just that my cane is in the car," said the gray-haired spinster, turning carefully and nodding toward the big black Ford that she'd parked in front of the house. "So I'm a little unsteady on my pins."

"Please—wait right there and I'll get you your cane and then carry that inside for you."

"*I* can carry it; but, yes, if you would just fetch my stick," she said politely.

The arthritic woman, whose unfortunate last name sounded so much like "witch"—and who was regarded by the town kids accordingly—had been one of the few to attend the funeral of Oliver Shore. She came, not because of Oliver (who more or less agreed with the kids and had always considered Miss Widdich a little "off"), but because she had formed a quiet but enduring friendship with Corinne.

It was a natural fit: Miss Widdich was an herbalist, and Laura's sister sold herbs. The affection between the two was so obvious that Laura had felt a little wistful when she witnessed it at the wake. In Laura's line of work, she had little contact with anyone over her own age.

Laura managed to coax the casserole out of Miss Widdich's grip, after all, and the two women walked into the house together, exchanging chat about the weather.

"I had hoped to do something about that fog yesterday," Miss Widdich announced. "It can be so gloomy, and I didn't want you children to feel any sadder than you did."

Do something? As in, control the weather?

"Well, that's awfully nice of you, Miss Widdich," Laura said vaguely. "But at least we all have one another."

"For now," said the elderly woman, her smile wistfully sweet.

An unexpected chill passed over Laura, as it often did when she was in the other woman's presence. She chalked it up to childhood memories and concentrated instead on the woman's kindness. Setting the glass dish on the kitchen counter, she said, "Still warm, and it smells wonderful. Thank you so much; we'll have it for lunch. What's in it?"

"Cheese; noodles," said Miss Widdich. "A little of this, a dab of that."

What, like eye of newt and heart of toad?

"Yum, a secret recipe," Laura said, quailing inwardly. "I can hardly wait to dig in. Speaking of which, I really ought to wash my hands; look at them!"

She walked over to the sink, mostly to avoid having to make eye contact, and began a hearty scrubdown.

Although herbs were not her field of expertise, Laura knew enough about them to understand that they could be powerful influences, on personalities as well as in stews. Many herbs were drugs, pure and simple. It was an unnerving and entirely unwished-for thought.

And a silly one. At her father's wake, Laura had overheard Miss Widdich and Corinne making small talk about tarragon, of all things. Surely their shared interest in herbs was no more than culinary.

And yet, Corinne seemed *so* fond, *so* attached to Miss Widdich . . .

But surely not because of drugs. More likely, Corinne had simply transferred her longing for their mother to Miss Widdich after their mother's death. After all, it couldn't have been easy, living in a house with only Oliver Shore for company. A surrogate mother might have filled a real need in Laura's shy and lonely sister.

"Corinne should be back here any minute, if you'd like to wait for her," Laura ventured as she dried her hands.

"But . . . don't you hear her?" Miss Widdich cocked her head and fixed her penetrating blue eyes on Laura; the expression in them was intense. "She's talking with someone—somewhere in the house."

"I don't hear a thing," said Laura, shaking her head.

"Of course you do, dear. She's talking to a man."

To humor her visitor, Laura walked out of the kitchen and into the adjacent sitting room of the high-ceilinged, rambling Victorian house and made a pretense of straining to listen in the direction in which Miss Widdich was jabbing her bamboo cane.

And darned if she didn't pick up faint echoes of her sister talking.

Seeing Laura's face, Miss Widdich smiled. "Corinne has a very pretty voice," she explained. "I'm very attuned to it."

"I *guess,*" said Laura, blinking. Miss Widdich might not have the best knees in town, but her hearing was downright preternatural.

Laura invited her to have a seat while she found out how long Corinne would be, but Miss Widdich waved Laura's invitation away with a flutter of a gnarled hand. "This is a bad time, bad time," she said darkly, and off she toddled, as fast as her knees would let her, leaving Laura mystified.

Curious about the voices, Laura tracked them down and was surprised to find that they weren't coming from the house at all but from the back porch, a small, utilitarian affair with a wasted view of the Atlantic.

Built off a summer kitchen that was no longer used, the back porch was merely a place to slough off muddy shoes or hang a wet oil slicker. It was the porch on the front of the house—overlooking the nursery and facing away from the sea—that was large enough to hold their assortment of half-broken beach chairs and the punched-in wicker loveseat.

Boy, someone had had their priorities *so* reversed, Laura thought, not for the first time. From the inside of the screen door, she caught her breath all over again at the grand expanse of bright blue ocean. It was the one thing her charmer cottage in Portland lacked, that view of the sea.

Unwilling to disrupt the conversation between Corinne and her visitor, who together were now strolling away from the house, Laura opened the screen door quietly and let it close gently behind her. She wanted to eavesdrop: it wasn't every day that they had a visitor who came in a suit.

He was no one she knew. Someone from the funeral home, maybe, asking if they were satisfied with the new headstone? It couldn't be the director. This man was much younger, with thicker hair, broader shoulders, and a more relaxed style, despite his spiffy threads. He was standing with his hands in his pockets, apparently willing to let Corinne do the talking.

He was nodding, as though he'd heard it all before. They definitely knew one another. Laura couldn't imagine who the guy was; Corinne had never spoken to her about anybody who could have afforded a suit like that.

Corinne pointed to her right and he followed her direction, partly revealing himself in profile to Laura. She realized that he did look familiar, after all, and yet she wasn't able to place him. Her sense was that he was—and yet was anything but—a local.

Before Laura could analyze the vaguely negative reaction she was having to him, he turned and gave her a sharp look, as though she'd beaned him on the back of the head with a spitball. Embarrassed to be caught staring, she shifted her gaze to Corinne, who was still blithely chattering away.

"Sorry to interrupt," Laura said, yanking her sister out of her monologue. "Rinnie, Miss Widdich just stopped by to see you. She was behaving a little oddly, and—"

She saw the visitor barely suppress a smile; obviously he, too, was familiar with the odd Miss Widdich. Who the hell *was* he? She marched up to him and, over Corinne's belated effort, began to introduce herself. "I'm Corinne's sister—"

"Laura. Of course. I'd know you anywhere," he said, his smile broadening.

When she looked blank, the visitor added quickly, "Ken. Ken Barclay? We went to the same grade school?"

Laura was speechless. She blinked and stared and finally said, *"Kendall?"*

"One and the same. How are you?"

Skinny, geeky, brainy, rich, and haughty *Kendall*?

"You're him?"

He laughed and said, "Last time I looked at my driver's license, anyway."

She wanted to see that license. The man standing in front of her was six-foot-something, solidly built, and knock-down, drag-out sexy. Not to mention devoid of braces and a bumpy forehead. Those fierce blue eyes: something about them looked vaguely the same, but even there . . .

Kendall Barclay.

The effect he had on her was dizzying, almost violent. Laura's cheeks went hot with the recollection of their fateful encounter. Suddenly she was thirteen and ill-dressed, with dirt under her fingernails and surrounded by a group of cruel, taunting boys grabbing and pawing and tearing her shirt.

No wonder he'd been able to recognize her so easily. Damn it, she still looked the same!

Her cheeks fired up even hotter with embarrassment when he extended his hand and she was forced to extend her own, with its bloody, bruised knuckles and dirty fingernails. She kept the handshake firm, though, as she explained, "I'm working the greenhouse detail today."

"So I see. Nice to have you back. Corinne tells me that you're working like gangbusters on the West Coast as a computer consultant?"

It was that question mark, coupled with a furtive glance at her clown-sized pants and her belt of rope, that instantly got under Laura's skin. It was so obvious that he found the idea of her success a hard one to swallow.

"Well, you know what they say about the self-employed," she said, recovering enough to give him a very dry smile. She gestured with both hands toward her pants. "Every day is casual Friday."

He followed her gesture, looking blank for a second. "Oh. You mean—" He dipped his head in a nod at her getup. "I never even noticed."

"Well, thank you for *that*."

Even worse. To someone like Kendall Barclay, she would always be one of the Shore urchins, beneath notice. It didn't help that his neck was turning red. Clearly he felt that she was putting him on the spot, taking everything to a personal level.

Which she was. For God's sake, she hadn't actually talked to him in, what, twenty years? Surely she could handle a chance encounter better than this!

But she couldn't. All she could see was a blurry circle

of boys around her, taking turns grabbing at her breasts and at her crotch.

"Laura? What, um, was it that you were saying about Miss Widdich?" Corinne's voice was faint with fear, as if she were watching her sister standing in a pit with a cobra and poking it with a stick. *You are messing with the man who holds the key to our survival.*

Maybe yes, maybe no. In an almost wrenching act of self-control, Laura swept away the memory of the circle of cruel boys and said to Corinne, "I think Miss Widdich would like to talk to you whenever you have time, Rinnie."

And then, still feeling fierce about the cruel note she'd got from Kendall all those years ago, she said in a fiercely pleasant voice, "Miss Widdich brought us a huge casserole for lunch. Cheese and noodles. You're welcome to join us in our peasant fare."

He backpedaled from the invitation as fast as politeness allowed. Shooting an arm through the sleeve of his jacket, he glanced at his watch. "Ah-h, thanks very much, but I have another appointment. I'm running a little late as it is, so I'd better get going."

With a friendly smile to Corinne, he said, "I'll see you on Wednesday, then."

When he shifted his attention back to Laura, his manner changed. He cleared his throat. Compressed his lips in a tight smile. Gazed doggedly at her chin. "Well. Good seeing you again after all—"

He had to clear his throat again. "These years."

It was obvious to Laura: he remembered. He remembered, and he was embarrassed about it. He *should* be, damn it. If she had not been a Shore, would he have been so arrogant and unfeeling in his note back to her?

You shouldn't be writing to me.

Don't do it again.

And don't ever try to see me.

Laura was a big girl now, but those scribbled words still cut like razorblades across the thin surface of her self-esteem.

"Good to see you, too—after all these years. But I'm sure I'll be seeing you again," she said coolly.

Not only that, but she was already planning what she'd be wearing when she did.

As he walked back to his car, Ken pulled irritatedly at his tie: he felt too buttoned up by half. The way his blood was pumping, he was ready to burst a blood vessel.

And it wasn't because of the heat of the day. Seeing Laura so unexpectedly had set his pulse roaring along, trying to keep up with his libido. Even now, he was at a loss why: she had just done everything but cross her forearms at him.

Maybe he shouldn't have been surprised. Maybe he should have been willing to let old ghosts lie. But he wasn't. Damn it, he was not willing. One look into her gray eyes—as dark and as threatening as a squall in July—and he was ready to take her on. There were issues here, issues between them that were unresolved.

One way or another, he planned to resolve them.

Chapter 6

In the kitchen, Laura found Snack standing over Miss Widdich's casserole with a soup spoon, helping himself.

"Who was that in the Porsche?" he asked through a mouthful of food. "He just about ran me down."

"Mr. Kendall Barclay, our friendly local banker," said Laura dryly.

"Here because?"

"He wants Corinne to show up on Wednesday at the bank to make her case."

"For?"

"Being allowed to continue losing money hand over fist."

"Ah. Damn, this stuff is good," he said, shoveling away. "So. Little Kenny holds our fate by the purse strings. No surprise there, I guess. The man owns the only bank in town."

"Excuse me, but he inherited that bank; it's not as if he earned that bank," Laura said, sniffing. "And, incidentally, little Kenny is not so little anymore," she had to admit. "He's all grown-up and looking . . . not that bad."

She was still in a state of disbelief at just how not-that-bad he looked. Or, for that matter, at how bad *she* looked.

Ah, screw it, she thought. She was in Chepaquit. Things always went bad in Chepaquit.

She got a spoon out of the drawer and dipped it alongside Snack's dug-out trench. He smacked the back of her hand lightly with his spoon and said, "Hey. Stay on your side."

"Sez you."

It was like old times. Laura and Corinne had always had to fight for their fair share of the casserole; Snack's boundless appetite, coupled with his baby-of-the-family status, guaranteed that he got dibs on any available seconds.

Laura butted him in the hip good-naturedly and said, "We'd better save some for Corinne. I'm sure Miss Widdich made it for her, not us."

"Whoa! This is *Witchy's* food?" Snack asked, bug-eyed.

"You bet."

Snack suddenly choked and gagged melodramatically, dropping his spoon to the floor and clutching his throat. He let his tongue hang out and his eyes roll back as he staggered around the kitchen, gasping for air, all to Laura's amusement.

Corinne walked in and took in the scene. "Now what?" she asked, grinning in response to her sister's laughter. "Has Snack bit off more than he can chew again?"

Her brother pointed to the casserole and gasped, "Bell . . . belladonna. I'd . . . know it . . . anywhere." And then he did a complete circle, stiffened, and fell to the worn linoleum floor.

Laura applauded his inspired performance, but by then the grin had faded from Corinne's face. "Miss Widdich made that for us?" she asked, putting two and two together. In a stern tone, she said, "Get up, Snack. That is not funny."

Snack continued to lie dead.

"At least get your poisons straight. Monkshood might have you flat on the floor, or oleander, maybe. Or dogbutton. Belladonna would take longer, you fool."

Snack opened his eyes and looked at Laura. "Since when is she an expert?"

"She works in a nursery," Laura said quickly.

"So did I. So did you. Knowing the names is one thing; knowing the symptoms, that sounds like 'Double, double toil and trouble' stuff to *me*."

Corinne's face went beet-red. "Don't be such a jerk! Get off the floor and either eat or go to work. You can relieve me down at the shop; the new girl doesn't have a clue how to handle a register."

It was such an uncharacteristic, Laura-like response to Snack's behavior that he was actually chastened. "Hey, Rin," he said softly, looking up at her, "I was only kidding. Remember? I'm the one who likes to tease? Sorry."

"Well . . . some things just aren't funny," she said, barely mollified.

It occurred to Laura that this was the first real instance of their working together without their father giving the orders. They were like orphaned wolf pups, playful and snarling by turns, clearly not ready to work seamlessly toward a common goal.

But they had to try. "How're you coming on the tractor?" she asked Snack as he got to his feet.

"No sweat. I've changed the oil and the filter, and next thing, I'll go into town for a new thermostat. We'll be up and running this afternoon."

Corinne said, "Oh, you're going to town? Would you mind doing a delivery for us? I just took an order. Mrs. Atkins is out of the hospital and—"

"Mrs. Atkins!" Snack said. "She's still alive?"

"Ninety-seven years old and going strong—more or less," said Corinne. "She still asks about you and wants to know when you're going to settle down and get a steady job mowing lawns."

"Well, there won't be a tip in this one for me, that's for damn sure," Snack said with a snort. "What happened to Billy? Last time we talked, he was still doing deliveries for you."

Corinne shook her head. "I had to let him go. I just couldn't afford to pay him, even by the job."

"Geez. After all these years."

Sighing, Corinne shook her head and added, "I really feel bad about that. Who else is going to give him work? A lot of people are uncomfortable around him. Because he's so big," she added softly. Her cheeks colored, and Laura knew why.

So did Snack. He said quickly, "Yeah, well, the best thing about Billy is he didn't give a damn if you tipped him or not. Say thank you, and his face would light right up. I can picture that broad, dopey grin right now. Poor dumb bastard. So how is he? Has he found anyone to feed him besides his mother?"

"I don't think he's seeing anyone, if that's what you mean. But who knows? Billy's not much for small talk."

Again it felt as if they were talking about Corinne instead of Billy. Snack shrugged and went over to the fridge, holding open the door while he searched inside. "We're out of beer already? I'll pick some up on my rounds. You running a tab somewhere, Rin?"

"Not anymore. I'll give you my Visa, but . . ."

"Yeah, yeah, I know," he said, obviously embarrassed. "Don't go crazy with it."

Laura interjected herself between Snack and Corinne's credit card. "This trip's on me," she said. "I'll get my purse."

She took the stairs two at a time so that she could get back down to the kitchen before Corinne could reach her plastic. The purse was on a chair in her bedroom; Laura fumbled with it in her hurry, dropping it to the floor. The wallet fell open; she must have forgotten to snap the closure tab shut. She reached inside for a bunch of twenties—and realized that she had barely a hundred dollars left.

No, that couldn't be right. She had only taken cash enough for a weekend, but . . . that *couldn't* be right. Besides a slew of credit cards, she had closer to two hundred dollars in cash in her wallet, she felt absolutely sure. Reasonably sure.

Snack? Was it possible? The unsnapped tab . . . and the wallet hadn't been tucked in the deepest part of the bag where she liked to keep it.

And Snack had a history of "borrowing" from her before, when they were growing up, although she'd rarely been able to prove it.

She had money. Snack didn't. That would be rationale enough for him.

Hell. Now what? Confront him during their first day on the mission? What would be the point? He'd just deny it again. And Corinne would be devastated: the whole insane scheme of hers would blow up, practically immediately, in her face. They would all go their separate ways again, and who knew what would bring them back together?

No, the money was gone, and that was that. For the rest of the month, Laura would hide whatever she took out of an ATM, and Snack could just—

Hell. She grabbed the last of the cash and ran down the stairs with it, determined, if only for Corinne's sake, not to destroy whatever tenuous relationship she had with their brother. It would take more than sixty or eighty dollars to do that.

At the foot of the stairs Snack was waiting, a look of impatience on his face. "We're burnin' daylight, big sister," he said, plucking the bills from her hand.

Without another word—certainly without any appearance of guilt—he was gone. If he was a liar and a thief, he was a damn good one.

With a sigh of disappointment, Laura made herself turn back to the business at hand. She caught up with Corinne on the back porch, where she was lacing up her heavy work boots.

"Rin, come down with me to the greenhouse a minute,"

Laura said, slipping into her own more fashionable leather clogs, already ruined. "We need to talk."

"Sure. You're going with me on Wednesday to see Ken Barclay, right? Because I'll get absolutely tongue-tied when we start talking business and money."

Laura said grimly, "Wild horses couldn't keep me. But I really don't think you have to worry about being tongue-tied. You looked perfectly fluent when I came on you two together just now."

She gave Corinne a sideways glance and added, "Is there something going on here that I should know about?"

"Oh, please. You're asking me if I have a thing for Kendall *Barclay*?" Corinne said without looking up from her laces. "What would someone like him possibly see in me?"

"Putting aside that impressive display of self-confidence," Laura said dryly, "that's not exactly a 'no.' "

"No." She looked up at Laura. "No, no, no." Smiling, she added, "No."

It was the answer that Laura wanted to hear. She couldn't bear to see Corinne setting her sights for him and then getting crushed the way she herself had been.

"It's just that you seemed so animated when you were talking to him," Laura couldn't resist adding, she wasn't sure why.

"Of course I was animated. I was talking about my plans for the nursery." Corinne threw out her arms, the mortgaged mistress of all they viewed. "When else have you ever seen me excited?"

"Mm. I suppose that brings me to my next question," Laura said, falling in alongside her sister as they headed for the greenhouse. "Are you seeing anyone? I realize that I'd know if it were serious, but—anyone at all?"

Corinne shook her head. "How could I? When would I? *Where* would I? This is it for me. Shore Gardens."

Laura glanced at her sister's face with its sun-darkened

skin scattered over with freckles, and she saw purpose and contentment there. Maybe Corinne was one of those self-sufficient women who didn't need someone else to round her out.

Maybe none of them did. After all, here they were, all in their thirties, and none of them was married or engaged or even seeing anyone. Or even looking.

"Shore Gardens, hey? You think it's better than sex?" Laura asked, only half joking.

Corinne said with a surprisingly evil smile, "I guess you'll find out."

Laura laughed, but she couldn't shake the feeling that she and her siblings were fated to singlehood. She vividly remembered one day at quitting time, watching Sylvia brush her long black hair before heading off on a date. Laura had asked her whether she ever planned to get married.

Sylvia seemed to know where the question was going, because she had smiled and said cryptically, "If you're afraid of being lonely, don't ever get married."

It was years before Laura understood what she meant, and now that she and Max were no longer a couple, the words seemed downright comforting.

A fresh breeze whipped Laura's blunt-cut hair across her face. For the hundredth time, she readjusted her barrettes to hold back the sides; but it was as pointless as trying to hold back the tides.

"Buy a hat," Corinne suggested. "It'll keep your hair in place. You'll need a hat to go sailing, anyway."

"Oh? On whose boat?"

"I don't know," Corinne confessed. "But you're on the Cape. It's what people do. The water's still cold, but the weather's been great. You should have some fun while you're here."

"On whose boat?"

"Details!" Corinne said, laughing.

They were at the greenhouse. Laura said, "We'd better start to go over the books tonight after work. So I have at least *some* idea of what's going on here before we show up in Kendall Barclay's office."

Corinne sighed and said, "After work? Yeah, right. We're not kids anymore, Laur. You work outside all day, you will be wiped. I usually am, which is why I haven't done a thing about the quarterly taxes," she confessed. "I assume the IRS will tell me what it wants me to do. We haven't made any money, anyway," she added with a downcast shrug.

"Not today's problem," Laura assured her. "The greenhouse and the compost pile are today's problem. You're right; they're both in terrible locations. I'm with you on this one. We should bulldoze the one and relocate the other."

"Yes, but Snack—"

"Snack doesn't want any more work on his list, that's all," Laura said, dismissing her brother's objections.

The sisters stepped inside the greenhouse. It was an absolutely glorious day in May, a warm and sunny knock on summer's door, but the temperature inside was no different than the temperature outside—not much justification for keeping a greenhouse. To repair all of the broken and missing leaded-glass panes was unfeasible; only a millionaire restoration hobbyist would have the money and the zeal to do that.

"Almost everything in here is dead," Laura told her. "I suppose that once I clear it all out, we can fill it for the season with herbs, bulbs, maybe the tropical vines and standards that you ordered. But down the road, this greenhouse will have to go."

Corinne nodded eagerly. Laura was dismayed to see how her sister hung on the words "down the road." They implied that there was a road to go down besides bankruptcy or selling out to a developer.

Laura gave herself a mental kick in the head. A one-month commitment was one thing; spinning future fantasies for her sister to grab hold of, that was something else altogether.

They had emerged from the greenhouse and were standing by the mountain of half-decayed compost. It hadn't been turned over in a long time, that was obvious: the south side of it was covered with a carpet of grass and weeds.

Laura said, "Once Snack gets the tractor running, I can relocate this pile myself."

"No, you have too much to do already," Corinne argued. "I'll do it."

"No you won't. You have the shop to see to, and the annuals. God, you must have a thousand geraniums over there."

"Yeah, I went a little crazy on the cuttings, and they're the one thing people always have money for. I've got even more impatiens than geraniums ready to bring out. There's a great new introduction; have you seen it? Kind of a fuchsia with a peachy pink heart—?"

"Mmm," Laura said vaguely, but her mind was on getting the job done, not on savoring its passing pleasures. "Moving this pile is simple grunt work," she said. "I wish we could pay someone—say, a field hand from the cranberry bogs. Do you know anyone?"

"I can't think of anyone," Corinne said, trying hard.

"Corinne . . . I'm not asking you for a name to round out a formal dinner party," Laura said, disheartened that her sister was obviously still reluctant to leave the reservation. "Just someone who's willing to move a pile of dirt for a few bucks."

The wince on Corinne's face vanished, replaced by a relieved grin. "Here's Gabe," she cried, waving. "We'll ask him!"

A year older than Laura and two older than Corinne, Gabe Wellerton was one of a very small number whom

Corinne considered friends. He'd worked on and off for the nursery through high school, and Laura herself had had a passing crush on him. Even now, she felt a warm rush of pleasure, mostly nostalgic, for the way he had stirred her adolescent yearnings. He was the first one to do it, and that would always make Gabe Wellerton special.

She studied him as he approached, impressed all over again by his broad shoulders and beefy arms. He'd been a star fullback on the high school football team and had been recruited to play for the Florida Seminoles, which didn't surprise anyone in Chepaquit: he was their golden son, a boy with infinite potential. He wasn't just all muscle, he had brains as well: he wanted to go into law. Everyone was so proud.

And then, a month before graduation, his parents were killed instantly in a head-on crash with a drunk driver.

In a state of shock, Gabe came back to Chepaquit to clear up their estate, and somehow he never left, never got his degree. He bought a small, local fence-making company which he still owned. Eventually he ran for town council, winning easily; he'd recently been elected to serve a third term. There was no doubt in anyone's mind that he was going to be Chepaquit's next mayor. People wanted him to run eventually for U.S. Congress, where he'd be able to realize his full potential after all.

Nonetheless, despite his political involvement, Gabe still lived alone, almost as quietly as Corinne. People who knew of his plight were convinced that he'd never be completely over the tragedy.

Laura was one of them. "Hey, Gabe, it's been a while," she said in a sympathetic tone that she instinctively used with him.

His smile, above his square-cut chin, was simultaneously familiar and reserved, sincere and somehow just a little bit sad.

"You're right; long time, no see, kiddo," he said, and

then added, "I've been out of town on council business—scouting a possible sister city for Chepaquit in Ireland—and I just got in a little while ago."

He said to Corinne, "Thanks for feeding the mutt, Rin, and for letting him in and out. It had to be a pain, running back and forth across the road all day. Too bad Baskerville's so neurotic about kennels."

"You've spoiled him, that's why," Corinne said, swatting Gabe playfully across the arm. "Trust me, he was absolutely pining for you."

Smiling, Gabe said, "Baloney. He was pining for *you*. I saw the hambone out in the run."

Color flared prettily in Corinne's face as she said, "Well, it was either feed the bone to him or make pea soup. I hate pea soup."

"Sure, sure," Gabe said, laughing. "Anyway, here's a little something from my trip. I know it doesn't say anything about Ireland, but somehow it reminded me of you."

He handed her a mini-shopping bag and Corinne pulled out a T-shirt in a pretty heather-rose color, hand-painted with a bundle of posies and discreet lettering beneath that said, "All natural."

"I *love* it!" she said with a gasp of delight.

"Well, good. I was hoping you would." He turned back to Laura and said hesitantly, "I wasn't sure I'd have the chance to see you this trip."

Had Corinne tipped him off to her cockamamie scheme to kidnap her siblings for a month? Laura couldn't tell, and she couldn't really ask.

She changed the subject and said, "We're just standing around trying to figure out who we can con into moving the compost pile farther back from the road. It's taking up prime display space—and it's not exactly high on charm," she added wryly. "Do you know of anyone who'd be willing to do the job for a few bucks?"

Gabe surveyed the dirt mountain that loomed before

them and nodded. "How about if I offer to move it for you, no charge? I could do it at the end of the week."

"No, we couldn't ask you to do that," Corinne said immediately. But the pleased look on her face stayed right where it was.

"It's not a problem, Rin," said Gabe. "Come on, let me do this. I owe you. I know how to operate the equipment—are you forgetting that I used to drive that same John Deere way back when? I'm done with my crew by four; that'll leave me plenty of daylight to tackle this. It might take me a couple of evenings, though."

"Deal!" said Laura before her sister could offer any more tedious objections to the offer.

It was clear, at least to Laura, that the plan had advantages for Gabe as well: he couldn't be too wild about looking out his front windows every day and seeing a pile of dirt. "And when you're done, come to the house for supper," she said to him impulsively. "We'll celebrate the removal of this blight from the landscape."

"Thanks for the invite," he said, looking away. "I'd like that."

How shy he was, she thought, bemused. He didn't used to be that way.

Oh. She glanced from Gabe to Corinne and back to Gabe again. Was it possible?

Well, well. She was going to have to watch and find out.

Gabe sounded reluctant as he said, "I guess I'd better get myself over to Bayview Estates to check on my crew."

"You're the ones doing the fences for that?" Laura asked, impressed. "That's a really upscale project; we drove past it on our way in yesterday."

"Yeah. The developer's thrown a lot of work to the locals, a nice boost for Chepaquit. Every job helps when you've got a payroll to meet and families to feed."

That's what a businessman and politician would say,

Laura realized; but it was also what someone who cared about people would say.

She glanced again at her sister, who was carefully folding her all-natural T-shirt to fit back in its bag.

"I love this," she said with touching sincerity. "I really, really do."

Chapter 7

By the end of the backbreaking day, Laura had cleared out the greenhouse, salvaging less than three dozen perennials for possible sale. Every bone in her body ached: working in a nursery took ten times the effort as playing in a garden.

Snack had disappeared in town for longer than he should have. When he came back from his errands, there was beer on his breath and a swagger in his walk that Laura hated to see. But he went back into the barn, and he replaced the thermostat, and he still had five cans of the six-pack under his arm when he returned to the house to join his sisters for supper.

The three of them, tired wolf pups by then, polished off Miss Widdich's casserole, newt eyes and all, and then they lined up to take turns showering under the rickety arrangement of pipes in the clawfoot tub. It wasn't until Laura began emptying the pockets of her dirt-covered Levi's that she remembered the watch that she'd found.

She stepped out of her room into the hall and said, "Hey! Guys! Take a look at this."

Corinne had just finished showering. Wrapped in a robe and with her hair bound in a towel, she emerged from the bathroom all shiny and sweet-smelling. At the same time, Snack, stripped to the waist and not at all sweet-smelling, came out from his room.

Laura held up the rusty watch by the pinless end of its expandable band. "Look what I found in the greenh—Oh, my God, will you look at this? It works! It must be a self-winding watch and I got it going again. Too cool. Anyone need a watch?" she said, dangling it in front of them both.

"Let me see," said Corinne, taking it from her. "It's not an old one of mine; I've always used the strap style. How about that? A mystery. I wonder whose it is? If we at least knew how long ago—"

Snack cut in to say, "It must have been a customer's. Toss it."

Laura took it back from her sister and scrutinized it. She was fascinated by the fact that the spunky little watch still worked. "I hate to do that. It's waited all these years for someone to discover it and let it be a watch again."

"Oh, yeah. Like a watch has karma," said Snack irritably. "It's a piece of junk. We're not exactly shy on junk. *Toss* it."

Reluctantly, Laura said, "I guess you're right. Oh, well."

The little group dispersed to their rooms, and Laura dropped the watch into one of the wastebaskets, then had second thoughts about the thing. It seemed symbolic of their own struggle against all odds. She retrieved it and dumped it in a small notions drawer before going out, at last, to have her turn at the shower.

Corinne was right. After a day of working outside, a person's brain felt as alert as a bowl of pudding.

The shower had helped restore Laura a little, but it was still all she could do to hold a pen in her hand and a yellow pad on her lap while hovering in a near coma over a desk strewn with paperwork that made no sense.

"Dad never talked about the loan?" she asked her equally tired sister.

"No. He never talked about money, period," Corinne

said, stifling a yawn. "The different versions of the will, that was as financial as he ever got with me."

"I do not understand this. I don't see how missing two payments can justify this nasty notice. We have to find the original document; that will explain everything. It must be around here somewhere."

She closed the drawers that held the financial records and slid open the drawer on the other side of the desk, poking through the files there.

They were exasperatingly random and unrelated: sales brochures on rose trellises and insecticides; L.L. Bean catalogues mixed in with colored blank sheets; mailing labels thrown in with flyers from a local furniture store. At the back, though, was a file she easily could have missed. It was labeled in faint pencil, "Great River Finance Co."

Laura plucked it from its innocent neighbors the way she would a thistle from a bed of zinnias.

She flipped through the file quickly, and then, with a sinking heart, scanned the document that lay at the bottom.

"Oh, my God," she whispered.

"What? What is it?" Corinne asked, trying to read over her shoulder. "You're scaring me, Laur."

Which was the last thing that Laura wanted to do. She tried to seem calm. "Well, if I'm reading this right, Dad took out the equity loan with Great River Finance almost five years ago."

And then, slipping into fury despite herself, she said, "It seems the good folks at Great River now feel they're entitled to call in the loan. They want full payment by next Wednesday."

"That's . . . eight days away!"

"Yes, it is. I guess we'd better move up the date of our big sale," she added in a dismal attempt to seem light.

"How much? Laura, how much do we have to come up with?"

"Well . . . a decent amount, I'm afraid," she said, her

voice breaking a little. "Seventy-five thousand dollars, give or take."

Tan as she was, Corinne went pale at the number. She sank into the oak chair next to Laura's worn-out swivel one and whispered, "You can't be serious. Not that much. Not that soon. That can't be true. It *can't*."

"Maybe I'm wrong. Give me their letter again."

Corinne handed it over with a trembling hand, and Laura compared loan numbers and reread all the fine print. She shook her head. "Nope. This is the loan, all right, and that's the deal."

"Oh, my God. We have less than a thousand in cash. That's it."

"I can't believe Dad would have done something this stupid," Laura said, seething. "Why wouldn't he just have gone to Chepaquit Savings?"

Her head shot up. "Hold it. Where's the bank file?"

Corinne pulled a worn folder marked "Chepaquit S." and handed it over. Leafing through the mountain of monthly statements, Laura found what she knew would be there: an application for a line of credit, which was denied, and one for an equity loan—also denied.

"That son of a bitch!"

"Who? Dad?"

"*No,* not Dad," Laura said irritably. "Tell me again, Rin," she said in a soft and dangerous voice. "What, exactly, did Kendall Barclay say to you when he came by earlier today?"

"Something about a payment that was due. Well, there's always a payment that's due for *something*. I didn't think anything about it. But if he was talking about this monster payment, this balloon payment or whatever it is—how would he even know about that?"

"Excellent question," Laura said, not too weary to pace the room. The bare floorboards squeaked underfoot as she worked through possible scenarios. "Barclay could be in league with this Great River outfit," she muttered. "It could be some kind of a scam."

"*What?* You're being paranoid, Laur. Not to mention, I'm sure that would be illegal," her sister argued.

Laura stopped long enough to say, "All right, maybe he has nothing to do with Great River. But somehow, he knows about this loan being called in. I was right. He wants to be sure you go to *him* to bail you out, and not someone else. That way, he gets to be the one to foreclose on you."

"Is that even possible?" asked Corinne, looking bewildered.

"Of course it is! What he's doing is fishing for foreclosure rights. Incredible. It's incredible!"

She began pacing again.

Corinne hugged herself and began rocking gently in her chair. "All I wanted was to grow my flowers and be left in peace. This is so humiliating," she whispered.

"No it's not," said Laura, rounding on her. "Don't you dare be humiliated! This is Dad's doing, not yours!"

"But I'm the one who missed those two payments."

"Yes. All right. And we'll get advice about that."

"Why don't we ask Kendall Barclay? He should know."

Laura threw up her hands and said, "Corinne! For God's sake, haven't you heard anything I've said about him?"

Corinne shook her head. "No, I haven't, I haven't," she admitted, in tears now. "All I know is that we don't have the money."

"We'll get the damn money," Laura said darkly. "One way or another."

With the tractor back in commission, Snack became free for commandeering. Laura snapped him up for some carpentry work: she needed a pyramid of shelves for the store, where she planned to display an enticing arrangement of whatever happened to be in bloom around the nursery.

She planned to launch the display with red Siberian iris and blue forget-me-nots and miniature roses of pink and white, and a sampling of whatever impatiens were farthest along, and some Asiatic lilies that she'd noticed were beginning to open—all with little signs of where in the nursery to go for more.

"I'll put the flowering lemon tree in the middle, so that its fragrance drifts over the customers as they head for the register," she told her brother.

"When exactly do you want these shelves?" Snack said with a typically wry look. "Yesterday, or the day before?"

Happily oblivious to his whining by now, Laura added, "And after that, can you make me a small display for the end of the counter? I'll put some scented geraniums there with a 'Pinch Me' sign tucked in each pot. Customers may not take home the hundred-dollar lemon tree, but they'll certainly pick up a four-dollar lemon-scented geranium."

Snack wasn't interested in the psychology of marketing. "What about these walls? I thought you wanted 'em whitewashed," he said, more and more sulky as the morning went on.

"Yes, do that first so that I can put the seed rack against the wall, and rehang the small hand tools. It won't take you long."

"Uh-huh."

"I'll come back and help just as soon as I'm done calling the paper and the printer about the ads for Founders Week. Oh, and Rin and I are going to dash out to T.J. Maxx at lunch, so you're on your own then. Okay, let's get moving," she said, handing him one of the paint rollers she'd picked up in town. "We've got a lot to do before the big sale."

She spun her lanky brother around to face the drab beige wall that she'd cleared. "Walls. Shelves. Little shelves. And then, if you're good and have finished all of your chores," she teased, "I'll give you your *after*-supper list."

He turned slowly back around, his green eyes narrowed under a scowl of genuine wonder. "You're nuttier than Corinne, you know that? Why are we doing this? The wrecking ball's gonna knock down these walls whether they're whitewashed or beige, you *know* that."

It was just as she'd predicted. Corinne's impulsive promise to reinstate them as partners in the family business no matter what happened—that silly, rash promise of hers practically guaranteed that Snack would merely go through the motions until the month was up. He might just as well have been doing time in a Tijuana jail.

What could she do? How could she goad him?

"You're a bum, Snack," she said with a perky, cheerful air. "How do you like that? You are a bum."

His cheeks flushed, but he returned her look with one just as ironic. "This is news?"

Deflated, she sighed and said, "Come on—you're better than that. Somewhere deep down, some part of you is better than that."

"Now *that* would be news," he quipped.

"You can be particularly irritating, you know that?" she snapped, all patience gone again. "If you think for one minute that I'm going to let Corinne do something so stupid as to hand over—"

She cut short her diatribe because two women—actual, paying customers—came in pulling one of the nursery's rusted little red wagons, filled with coral-pink geraniums.

"These are twice as big as the ones I've seen in the discount stores for the same price," one of them said happily. "So healthy!"

Laura beamed and said, "Love makes all the difference."

The geraniums were in fact the best buy in the nursery. Laura took her place behind the register—since Melissa was late—and rang up the purchase, talking up the Founders Week sale which was fast approaching.

"We're going to have how-to seminars, and tea and cookies—oh, and a clown to make balloons for the kids," she added out of the blue.

She glanced at her brother, who was spreading a drop-cloth on the floor, and made a mental note to ask him what he knew about balloon-making, and how he felt about wearing a rubber nose.

"And everything will be twenty-five percent off except select trees and perennials. It's a grand reopening for us. We have a huge inventory of stock on order," she boasted as the women carried their trays of geraniums out the door.

Laura hurried back to the office in the house to make her calls, aware that the part about the huge inventory, like the part about the clown, wasn't quite a done deal.

Corinne had told Laura of a small place in rural Rhode Island that sold annuals and perennials at ridiculously low prices. The plan was to drive there, load up—hopefully at a volume discount—and then mark up the amounts when they returned to their much more visible stretch of New England.

The idea wasn't to make a killing, but to present a picture of plenty. If that didn't work, if the customers still didn't come, well, then they were screwed. It wasn't much more complicated than that. Everything was hanging on the Founders Week sale.

Maybe not everything. There was the matter of the money they owed Great River. Laura could easily come up with the cash to pay Corinne's missed installments, but she didn't have seventy-five thousand dollars just lying around in a desk drawer.

Which is where banker Barclay came in. Laura's plan was a simple one: dress for success, pitch him a basic business proposal, and accept the loan he was bound to offer them.

All they had to do after that was to keep up with their monthly payments to Chepaquit Savings. No tricks, no scams, and the only balloons she wanted to see were the ones that Snack was going to be shaping for the children at the Founders Week Sale.

Because Shore Gardens was not going to fail. Period.

"I have no idea when your plan went from being dumb to being brilliant," Laura said, flipping quickly through the dress suits at T.J. Maxx in the outlet mall, "but here I am, determined to make it work."

"Because you like a challenge." Corinne held up a little black number, simplicity itself. "What do you think? Or do you like lapels on your jackets?"

"It lacks something. Besides lapels."

"Sex appeal?"

"There you go."

Corinne hung it back up and they returned to the hunt. The fact was, Laura wasn't sure what image she wanted to project, standing in front of Kendall Barclay.

Sylvia would know what to wear. She'd know exactly how to play Ken Barclay.

The thought came and went. Laura had none of Sylvia's fashion confidence, but she knew what image she did *not* want to project: one of an ill-dressed, ill-bred, ill-mannered Shore.

She laid a power-red suit with a short jacket and a shorter skirt across her basket, then added several more.

In the dressing room, the first one she tried on was the red. She came out and modeled it for her sister, walking on tiptoe to fake high heels.

"You look bossy in it."

"Not boss? Just bossy?"

"Mm-hmm."

That wasn't the look. Laura went back inside the tiny booth and changed into a bright coral silk outfit with a form-fitting jacket, then returned for Corinne's assessment.

"Yikes. All that's missing is a pink flamingo draped around your neck."

Back she went, and emerged quickly, this time in gray.

"You have gray. If you want to wear gray, just wear the gray you have."

All that was left in her meager haul was a pale yellow dress with a short jacket in a tone-on-tone floral, as pretty as could be. Laura had been saving it for last.

Corinne shook her head. "You look pasty in it. Buy it anyway, though. It'll look good on you eventually, after you've worked outside some more and got some color."

Laura scowled and said, "You know, for someone who spends her days in coveralls, you seem pretty damn opinionated."

Her sister laughed breezily—*she* wasn't the one about to go on stage—and said, "What about this? It was hanging on the return rack."

She held up a simple challis dress in pale blue and overlaid in a pattern of equally pale green fronds. A line of covered buttons ran from the scoop neck to a point above the knees, pretty and sexy and modest and sophisticated all at the same time.

Laura felt her heart do the little ka-thump that women's hearts do when they find what they've been looking for all along but just haven't realized it.

Five minutes later, they were headed for the checkout line with the blue dress and the yellow dress and a pair of better jeans for working in, and Laura was embarrassed when she handed over her Visa card because her fingernails still had dirt under them.

They were in such a rush. There was so much to do.

"Plus, we don't dare leave Snack unsupervised," she said, throwing their pickup into gear and tearing out of the lot.

"Snack? Forget Snack! What about the new hire?" said a giggling Corinne, still high from the hunt. "Melissa's on the register all by herself, handling our money as we speak."

"You know, I don't know how that girl manages to make change. I think she counts the studs in her ears."

Laughing, Corinne pointed to the Dunkin' Donuts that anchored one end of the strip mall. "Do we have time to stop for a Coolatta?" asked Corinne. "Please please? I love their strawberry."

"Yes. No. Yes! No. No, really, Rin. Look at that line of cars. And it's not even Memorial Day yet. Where are all these tourists coming from?"

"Don't think of them as tourists," Corinne said. "Think of them as potential customers."

"You wish. I do worry about your customer base," Laura admitted. "Let's face it, the bulk of your business will have to be from locals. And we know what the locals think of us."

"I know what they think of *me*. And I can guess what they think about Snack. But I don't know why they'd have a problem with you, Laur. Don't forget: you're a celebrity."

"Ah, yes," said Laura dryly, driving resolutely past the Coolata store. "But let's get back to you. *You* didn't kill anyone; Uncle Norbert did. *You* didn't blow up bridges all over town by picking fights; Dad did."

"Maybe Dad became defensive because of the way people looked at him after Uncle Norbert."

"Whatever," said Laura, unconvinced. "The fact remains that you are a businesswoman, the same as Kendall Barclay is a businessman. You deserve just as much respect."

"Oh, I don't know about *that*—"

"Listen to me. You have more worth in your little finger than Kendall Barclay and his family put together!"

"Why do you say that?" Corinne asked. She sounded uneasy, as she always did, at that particular tone in her sister's voice. "What do you have against Kendall Barclay?"

"He's an arrogant snob," Laura said flatly. She couldn't help herself.

"He's always been nice to me when I've run into him."

Corinne still had no idea. Humiliated beyond measure by the way she'd been handled by so many at the edge of the woods, Laura had never said a word about it to anyone, not even her sister. And now it was too late. Even Corinne might advise her just to grow up and move on.

What a fool she'd been to keep her silence so sacred, so long.

Corinne said pensively, "Do you honestly think that we can turn the nursery around?"

"Hey. Gardening is the number one hobby in this country. There's no reason why you can't get a bigger piece of that pie."

Corinne smiled and after a moment said seriously, "I haven't really thanked you for coming East, Laur. I know what a sacrifice you're making for me. Canceling your trip to Hawaii . . . delaying your next consulting job . . . putting up with Snack! I'll never forget this."

"It isn't anything. Stop."

Corinne was cradling the T.J. Maxx bag in her arms. She opened the bag and peeked inside, fingering the soft fabric lovingly. "You're going to be such a knockout in this. He'll *have* to lend us the money."

"He'll lend us the money, all right," Laura said as the rolling land of the nursery hove into view. "The trick for us will be to pay it back."

Chapter 8

Laura dumped her T.J. Maxx bag on a kitchen chair and then noticed the clean casserole dish still sitting on the counter.

"Oh, shoot; we forgot to return that thing to Miss Widdich, and she wanted it right back."

Snack, splattered with whitewash, was searching the fridge for something cold, but he was out of beer again. "Where's Corinne?"

"I dropped her off at the shop; she's keeping an eye on Melissa."

"Want me to run that dish over for you?"

If he did that, Laura would lose him for hours: Miss Widdich was neighbor to a bar and grill.

"That's all right, I'll do it," Laura said quickly. "You're a mess, and I still have decent clothes on. How's your beer supply?" she asked as a concession. "Want me to pick something up?"

He flashed her a genuinely friendly grin. "Hey, yeah; thanks, Laur. I'm almost done with the whitewash and about to start on your shelves," he offered, eager to give her something in return.

"Great."

God, I've become an enabler, she thought on her way

out the door, but she shrugged off the guilt. Better to be an enabler than a slave driver with no slave.

She drove in a hurry to Miss Widdich's house, aware that she was wasting precious minutes of another fine day, the kind of day that made people have spendthrift thoughts about their gardens. In fact, she had seen four cars parked in the front lot, a record so far. Presumably some of the locals had heard that the Shore clan had got back together and were curious to see what new mischief they were up to.

Good. Let them talk. As far as Laura was concerned, it was free advertising, as opposed to the full-page ad she was taking in the *Chatham Herald. That* was costing an arm and a leg.

Just past Pete's Bar and Grill was the overgrown and now almost hidden turnoff to Miss Widdich's house, set at the back of a wooded drive. Maya Widdich had always been a reclusive woman, and the house's location was a perfect fit.

Laura had only been there three or four times in her life, all of them deliveries for the nursery. When she was young and impressionable, the winding drive had seemed spooky and fraught with peril, especially during her first delivery one particularly foggy evening, which she later realized was a summer solstice.

It hadn't helped her jitters that the house was a dark Victorian cottage with gingerbread trim and lurid, leaded red glass over and alongside the door, and that the massive door knocker on it was shaped in the head of a gargoyle.

Laura would never forget that night. She was well aware of Miss Widdich's reputation, well aware that there was no moon behind the murk of fog. Unnerved and clutching her box of white roses, she had knocked timidly and waited, half expecting to be grabbed, trussed, and stuffed in an oven.

Miss Widdich had answered the door dressed all in

black. Her dark hair was beginning to go gray at the time, with a startling white slash across the front that added to the overall drama of the woman.

"My goodness, you took your time!" she had said, sharply for her. "I've got half a mind to send you back with those."

"I'm sorry, Miss Widdich; I had to drive special to Chatham for them, and then I had to wait, and I only just got back," Laura had whimpered.

"Why're *you* delivering them? Where's Sylvia?"

"We're really short-handed at the nursery. My . . . my father wanted Sylvia there with him."

"Oh, I'll bet," Miss Widdich had said in a way that had confused Laura and made her even more uncomfortable. She couldn't imagine what difference it made who delivered the roses.

Thankfully, Miss Widdich had removed the lid and inspected the flowers, and instantly her face had softened with pleasure. "Ah, they're fragrant. You were able to find fragrant. Lovely, dear. I'll keep them, with pleasure. And here's something for the extra trouble."

She had given Laura a ten-dollar tip, far and away the biggest that she'd ever received—and Laura had split it the next day with Billy, who almost never got tipped because people knew he was simple and had no real concept of money.

What Laura had never told anyone about that delivery on that particularly eerie night was that besides hearing soft, strange music and seeing the flicker of many candles dancing on the ceiling, she had smelled the distinct odor of marijuana. It was no big deal, considering the times; Snack was always sneaking off with a joint. But it had seemed odd, almost amusing, that someone Miss Widdich's age—she had to be over fifty!—would be listening to sitar music and smoking pot. Unless, of course, she was a witch.

But that was then. Today it was mid-afternoon, and the

sun was shining and a warm breeze blowing, and Laura was old enough not to have goosebumps just because a single woman with a white streak in her hair had liked to indulge in sinful pleasures.

She parked next to Miss Widdich's big black Ford and walked up to the porch of the little cottage, which was newly painted in the same dark gray. The porch was only two steps up and was surrounded by a wall of white azaleas in full bloom; leave it to Miss Widdich to find hybrids that were intensely fragrant. Inhaling deep, Laura lifted the old gargoyle and gave it two loud raps.

When no one answered, she assumed that Miss Widdich was in her herb garden; it was far too fine a day to waste lingering over lunch inside. Leaving the casserole dish on the vintage wicker porch glider, Laura went around to the back to announce herself.

Miss Widdich was indeed in her garden. But Laura was stunned to see that she wasn't simply puttering and fussing the way older gardeners do, but digging a massive hole, obviously for the balled-and-burlapped pear tree that was waiting alongside. Corinne might be strong enough to dig that kind of hole, and so might Laura, on a good day. But for someone to do it who normally hobbled around with a cane . . .

"Miss *Widdich*!"

The woman looked up from her digging, saw her flabbergasted visitor and instantly dropped her spade, which fell into the hole. A look of confusion and pain replaced the fierce concentration that Laura had seen in her face.

"Oh, thank goodness you're here," Miss Widdich said weakly, gesturing toward the back porch. "Can you fetch me my cane? Billy was supposed to dig the planting hole last week, but he hasn't come, and I—well, I was frustrated enough, and foolish enough, to try."

She hobbled over to a nearby stone bench and dropped onto it with a groan. "Stupid me. Stupid, stupid me," she lamented. "It's so aggravating to get old. You're young, I know, but wait. You'll see. Oh! It's terrible."

On and on she went, until Laura had the chance to explain why she had come, and then to make her escape.

She drove back to the nursery in a state of heightened unease. Miss Widdich was certainly feisty enough to take on a project that was more than she could handle—but she seemed to have been handling it just fine. Laura had a vivid image of the arthritic woman pitching a shovelful of dirt to the side and coming right back for the next. There was nothing infirm about her.

What was the point of the deception? Why try to convince everyone that she was so infirm? That's what Laura wanted to know.

The blip of suspicion vanished completely from her radar screen as soon as she saw the cars in the nursery parking lot. Seven! On a Tuesday! Oh happy day!

"It's as if that Dunkin' Donuts crowd hung a left and drove straight here," Laura told her sister during a lull later that afternoon.

Corinne was in remarkably high spirits. "Actually, you're not far off. Word about my geraniums got out to the Chepaquit Garden Club," she explained. "You know how competitive those women are; no one wanted to miss out, especially on the variegated ones."

"*Geraniums*. Who would've thought?"

"Everyone asks me how I got them so big so early," Corinne said proudly.

"And you tell them—?"

"Compost. The geraniums are potted in almost pure compost. They love it."

"Well, we have enough of the stuff. Maybe we ought to bag it and sell it."

"Great idea!" said Corinne, removing a bunch of twenties from the register. "We could call it Cheppy Chips."

"Hey, start talking it up," Laura said, laughing. "We'll get Snack working on them. In his spare time."

Their brother entered the shop just then, bearing painted shelves that he arranged in the exact pyramid shape and dimensions that Laura had requested. He'd even made a special stand to place in the middle opening for the lemon tree.

Laura was delighted, and Snack was clearly pleased with the fact.

"It was fun," he confessed. "I like making stuff, especially making stuff fast." He went out and came back with the lemon tree, its nodding branches covered in tiny white blossoms of powerful fragrance, and set it on its throne. Immediately the area was awash in its perfume.

"Oh, my," said an elderly woman buying packets of seed. "Oh, that smells so good. It's going to be hard to go home to my wick freshener." She drifted over to the lemon tree and scrutinized the price on the plastic tab in the pot. Sighing, she said, "I'll have to think about it."

"This is our last one," Laura coaxed. Also the first, but it was nothing the customer needed to know.

"Oh, well." The woman drifted out with her three-dollar purchase.

"That was Mrs. Schmidt," said Corinne. "Remember her?"

"Do I? She never bought something in a pot if she could find it in a packet. Surely the most tightfisted Yankee in—"

Laura stopped herself short when she saw the woman coming back through the door.

"You know what? I think I'll just take that tree after all," said Mrs. Schmidt, astounding both sisters. "Delivery is free, correct?"

In fact it wasn't, but history was being made, and Laura was not about to quibble. She answered, "For you, absolutely," and Snack actually volunteered to deliver it after work.

In every way, it was proving to be an historic afternoon at Shore Gardens.

The blissful mood lasted right through quitting time. Laura and Corinne replaced the lemon tree with their only other citrus, a lime tree with no flowers but covered with dozens of budding fruits, and by the time they were ready to close up shop, the shop itself had been transformed. Flowers, houseplants, tools, seeds, wreaths, planters, ribbons, garden markers, cachepots, stepping stones, sundials, little frogs and turtles, even a couple of verdigris-finish birdbaths: every available wall, shelf, nook, cranny, and counter was filled. The only thing missing was Sylvia behind a counter, creating her typically whimsical and wonderful floral arrangements in keeping with the season.

"Of course, we've skimmed the best of everything to create this illusion of plenty," said Corinne, counting their money. "In the greenhouses, we've got bupkis."

"We'll get more. Remember Rhode Island." Laura was sitting on the counter's edge, swinging her feet and watching her sister work. "So—how'd we do, coach?"

Corinne looked up and, grinning, waved a fistful of cash at her. "We scored. This keeps up, we're going to have a blowout of a Founders Week sale. Laura, honestly—we can *make* it," she said excitedly.

"You bet your petunias."

Next up: Kendall Barclay.

Chapter 9

"I'm nervous."

"Why? The guy puts his pants on one leg at a time, same as everyone else."

"Oh, Laura. You know what I mean. What if Kendall says no to a loan again? He did once, when Dad asked."

"Then why would he make a point of seeking you out and asking whether you needed help?"

Corinne had no answer to that, so she settled for a pessimistic sigh. She was that kind of woman: one with infinite faith in her own ability to work hard and get the job done, but with little confidence that anyone else would see that strength in her.

They climbed down from the pickup in their Sunday best: Laura was wearing her pretty blue dress with the covered buttons, and Corinne, a simple shift of lavender which flattered the deep tan that came inevitably with the late spring season.

Of the dozen historic buildings that comprised the town center, Chepaquit Savings Bank was the crown jewel: a historic clapboard house, painted barn red and with a gambrel roof, that two centuries earlier had served as a country tavern.

Its cobbled parking lot was now dotted with cherry trees

that were a day or so past their peak bloom, evidenced by the blanket of pink petals that eddied and swirled around the sisters' ankles as they walked up to the paneled front door of the building. It looked like such a friendly bank; it was natural to assume that its officers would be kind.

Laura and Corinne were about to find out. "Here goes nuttin'," Laura said, squeezing down on the heavy brass doorlatch.

Her heart had begun to beat at a different rhythm altogether, and her emotions were a soup mix of fear and fury, regret and longing. When she was thirteen, Kendall Barclay had been her knight, and then he'd pushed her away and had galloped off. Twenty years later, here she was, forced to seek his services again: he was the only knight in town.

Inside, a too-cool woman wearing a forties-look rayon dress, and with a retro hairdo that was parted and kinked and falling over one eye, came out from a small office and asked them if she could be of assistance. She looked like something out of a Hepburn-Tracy film.

"We have an appointment to see Kendall Barclay," said Laura, filling in for her tongue-tied sister.

The assistant's smile was immediate and deferential; apparently not everyone got to see the bank president. She led them through a narrow hall, still floored with wide butterscotch planks and overlaid with a subdued oriental rug, and ushered them through a small anteroom directly into the office of Kendall Barclay himself.

It threw Laura off balance, somehow. She hadn't expected to skip right past the wait-and-be-seated phase.

The bank's president was at a mahogany desk and looking hard at work: the sleeves of his pale blue shirt were rolled up, and his red tie, printed with colorful hot-air balloons, was loosened to allow room for the opened buttons of his shirt.

His smile included them both, but it seemed to Laura that it came back and settled on her, lingering over her dress. She was convinced that he'd been expecting to greet two clodhoppers in overalls and carrying pitchforks.

He came around to the front of his desk to shake their hands. Laura, who had scrubbed her nails during her shower until her skin hurt, was caught and held in his warm, callused grasp. Again she was surprised: he had the grip of a lumberjack.

"Have a seat," he said to her, snatching up the navy blazer that had been thrown across the chair nearest his desk. "The air-conditioning's on the fritz again. Historic building, lousy systems," he explained. "It's like a sauna in here, I know; sorry about that."

Laura was glad to hear that she wasn't the only one feeling the heat.

Nerdy, geeky, skinny Kendall Barclay. What *happened*? From his squared jaw to his broad, easy grin, he was nothing—nothing!—like the kid who'd gone to her school. She had to force herself not to stare at the new and improved version of him, so she glanced around the room as if she were considering making an offer on its contents, leaving her sister to open with whatever small talk she could scrape together.

In a scarily eager voice, Corinne said, "Y'know . . . I remember back when the outside of the bank was mustard-colored! But . . . I like the red much better!"

"Thanks for your vote," Barclay said amiably. "After my father died and I took over his desk, I thought it would be useful to do something dramatic—but not too dramatic—to announce it. A color change was all I dared," he added with a wry smile. "I dropped the idea of building a new facility; Chepaquit would never have stood for it. Hence today's sauna."

"Oh, that's all right; we'd rather sweat buckets and have our old bank," Corinne quipped, and then slapped her hand over her mouth, obviously afraid that she'd already said something wrong.

Still smiling, Barclay said smoothly, "I assume that *you'd* like to keep things just the way they are, as well. Keep the nursery a nursery, in other words."

"Yes! And we're doing that, only better. You should see the main shop now. Laura has a real gift. She just . . . well! If you could just see . . . it's nothing like . . . everywhere you look, it's just so really, really . . . *full*," she said, slowing down but nowhere near a halt. "We've *never* looked like that before. Ever! I don't know why. Maybe because we were there so long and couldn't really step back and see. Because you have to have a fresh eye, and Laura went off—I mean, she didn't *really* run off, that's not what I meant, it's more like she just moved—and when she came back, well, she just had a really, really . . . fresh . . . eye."

She looked ready to burst into tears.

Yikes.

"What I think my sister recognizes is that my brother and I have brought a huge amount of enthusiasm with us to revitalize the nursery," Laura said in a monumental lie. "We have an excellent facility, a perfect location, and we're a brand name in the area." (They were more like a branded name, but never mind.) "All Shore Gardens really needs," she said, "is some simple updating. And then it'll be a landmark facility."

"It's interesting to hear you say that. I've been wondering what would happen now that Mr. Shore has . . . passed on," Barclay said, using the old-fashioned phrase.

It annoyed Laura. Did he think they didn't understand that all living things died? They worked in a nursery, for crying out loud. They could handle the word "die."

Turning to Corinne, he said, "I thought maybe you'd be feeling overwhelmed, having so much responsibility now. I didn't realize that your brother and your sister were both returning to help you run the business."

Back to Laura he came, with brows upraised in mild query.

Ah, shit. Was he just calling her bluff?

"Well, we're here for the foreseeable future, anyway," she said pleasantly. A month was foreseeable enough for her.

She was impatient with their back-and-forthing. If Kendall Barclay was going to kick them out on their butts, she'd rather it were sooner than later. Still in a breezy tone, she said, "We have absolutely no problem generating enough income for the day-to-day running of the business."

The statement made Corinne's eyes pop open, but she was smart enough to keep her mouth shut.

Laura crossed one leg over the other, batted her eyes at the man, and gave him a hint of an ironic smile.

He knew why they were there, obviously, and he was waiting for them to beg. Well, too bad. She'd rather show him her knees than fall on them.

She continued. "There's just one thing that we haven't *quite* got on top of yet."

"The loan from Great River Finance?"

Aha! So he *was* aware of it. She knew it: he was in cahoots with them.

"How did you know about the loan?" Corinne blurted.

Barclay didn't flinch. In fact, his smile seemed completely sympathetic, which Laura also found annoying.

"Can I speak candidly?" he asked.

Corinne nodded almost violently, and he said, "Great River is what's known in the bank business as a predatory lender. We were aware a few years ago that they were going literally from door to door on properties that—I'll be frank—looked as if they could use cash. They offered easy credit but brutal terms.

"Since that time, several properties in the area have defaulted and have had their loans called in. A couple of the owners have come to us to bail them out; but one or two of them just gave up and surrendered their holdings. I wish they hadn't," he added.

I'll bet, thought Laura. "And yet," she said grimly, "you denied my father a loan when he came to you for one."

Barclay leaned back in his chair and locked his blue gaze on hers. "Yes. I did. I had no choice. Your father refused to have his property appraised, a formality that was required for any loan to be approved."

"Why would he refuse something like that?" asked Corinne, dumbfounded.

Barclay shrugged with his eyebrows. "He was offended that I even dared ask, I think. He lit into me and then stormed out of here."

"My father? Not possible," Laura said dryly.

Barclay's tone was just as dry as he said, "My assistant remembers the day not fondly, but well. As do the tellers. And the security guard."

"I'm sorry," said poor Corinne, bowing her head.

He laughed softly and said, "Good Lord, why? You're not the one who threatened to blow up the bank and teach us all a lesson."

Corinne sucked in her breath. "He *didn't.*"

But Laura could easily imagine the scene; she had faced the withering blast of her father's temper too many times to be shocked by it. "I'm surprised you didn't have him thrown in jail," she said evenly.

"Oh, I admit I considered it," Barclay said, leaning back a little farther and tapping his fingers on his grand mahogany desk.

He was watching her now, assessing her as carefully as she was him. Their gazes locked. They were in some kind of contest, but Laura had no idea how the game was played or what the prize for winning was. She tried not to notice his square chin, or the faint shadow of his beard, or the way his dark hair threatened to go unruly if he gave it the chance. She tried to see a heartless snob, but all she could see was a rock-solid and very sexy man.

Over a galloping pulse, she said, "You considered having him arrested—but?"

"He was a Shore," Barclay said simply.

Laura started to say something, then saw her sister's warning look and stopped herself.

Ever so briefly. "Yeah, well, I remember *your* father," she blurted, picturing the aloof banker as he cut various ribbons at various town functions. "*He* would've called in the cops in a heartbeat."

"You may be right. But I'm not my father."

"I can see that. Let me get this straight. You didn't give my father a loan although he was a Shore, but you didn't have him arrested *because* he was a Shore."

"That's right. Make sense?"

"None at all."

"What can I say?" he said with a sigh. "I try."

"I'm sorry," she said in stiff apology. "I suppose I still have issues where my father is concerned."

"Don't we all."

Was he being snotty or simply candid? Laura couldn't tell. She only knew that she hated borrowing money from this man. It made her feel not only beneath him but beholden to him. She hadn't realized how hard it would be to come to him hat in hand. Until now.

She tried to make it seem as if she were doing him a favor by throwing some business his way. "I assume that your rates are competitive?" she asked.

"As low as a point over prime."

Which was a competitive rate indeed. "Well! *You're* not predatory," she acknowledged with a grudging smile.

His look was both amused and suggestive. "Not usually."

You don't have to be; women must hunt you down, she couldn't help thinking—because she was damn sure that they weren't talking about money anymore. She wondered who he was seeing, and then instantly wondered why she was wondering.

Aaagh. This is a business meeting, you twit.

"Well, sir," she said with perky irony, "it's good to know that when we finalize our plans for Shore Gardens, we'll be able to seek the funding locally."

"But . . . isn't that what we're doing?" Corinne asked, bewildered.

Barclay leaned forward on his leather chair and laid his forearms on the desk. They were solid, muscular. Unnerving. Laura found herself pressing into the soft back cushion of her chair, edging away from his strength.

"Look," he said, "what it boils down to is this. I assume—I know—that Great River has called in your loan. I know that your property has plenty of equity. What I don't know is the amount that you need."

A pause. "Seventy-five thousand," Laura said with sullen iciness.

"Not a problem. You have, what, a week or so to produce it for Great River?"

Laura clenched her teeth. "Yes." God, how she hated this. Hated him. It was the haves versus the have-nots, all over again. Her life in Chepaquit, all over again.

"All right. I'll have an appraiser out there this afternoon. See my assistant Nancy about the paperwork. And . . . best of luck to you," he said with a nod that somehow seemed perfunctory.

Had he seen the resentment in her face? Well—good.

"Oh, *thank* you," said Corinne, springing up from her chair. She forgot to slouch, forgot to seem timid or cringing or anything else but happy.

Not Laura. She felt oddly cheated by the entire interview. She had come there expressly to show off her marketing savvy, but he clearly wasn't interested. "But . . . what about a business plan?" she said. "I've brought one wi—"

"Corinne says you're a very smart woman. I trust her judgment," he said, letting his glance slip down before coming back up to meet her gaze. Had he stopped at her breasts? She couldn't tell, and she was embarrassed even to have had the question pop into her head.

She was embarrassed, too, to be endorsed by her kid sister when it was supposed to have been the other way around.

"Thank you, in that case," Laura said, completely upended by the swirl of her emotions. "I'm sure you—your bank—will not regret the decision."

"I rarely regret a decision I make," he said, his smile relaxed. He was enjoying himself now.

"Really!" she answered. "I myself would have had second thoughts about that tie."

With a surprised but good-natured laugh, he said, "It was a gift from my niece. She's seven."

Corinne said quickly, "I love the colors!"

He rose and shook Laura's hand again. No lingering grip this time; she barely allowed him to make contact with her.

He accompanied the two sisters to the door. His assistant appeared from another office as if by telepathy to take them under her wing.

They'd made it through the application interview in under ten minutes. It took longer than that to order a *café brêve* from Starbucks.

Chapter 10

"Two words," Laura droned. "Curb. Appeal."

"I get it, already," Snack moaned as she pushed and prodded him from job to job.

No matter; Laura was relentless. "We could have as much product as Home Depot and Wal-Mart put together," she warned. "If we don't get people to turn into the lot, we don't stand a chance."

"For crissake, Laura—they're turning, they're turning!"

Snack was right. There were almost always a couple of cars parked in front of the main store, which was far more attractive now that they'd put up huge window boxes overflowing with Corinne's famous bright red geraniums. Something about bright red flowers against weathered, silvery shingles simply cried out "Cape Cod" to passing vehicles.

Even the parking lot looked trim and pretty. Snack had filled in and overlaid the potholed area with a truckload of new gravel, and he'd replaced all of the missing stiles of the rustic fence that lined the road. Laura had attacked the fallen roses that lay in a tangle below the fence, trimming away the deadwood and somehow getting the roses to tumble attractively over the stiles again. For her effort, she carried away scratches up and down her arms and legs, but she didn't care. She was on fire with her mission now.

All three of them were on fire. They worked like demons from sunup to sundown and (with the help of the truck's headlights) sometimes beyond. They dug, hammered, painted, fertilized, arranged, primed, deadheaded, sprayed, and watered, watered, watered. Then they showered, collapsed, and the next dawn they started all over again.

A month was a very short time.

Laura and Corinne were trying to decide what to do about the toolshed. It was hardly worth fixing, a ramshackle affair with holes in the roof, and an even worse eyesore than the main greenhouse with its broken and missing panes.

"Do we have time before the grand reopening sale to bulldoze the shed?" asked Corinne. She deferred to Laura for virtually every decision now, a practice from which Laura was soon going to have to wean her.

"I do hate the sight of it," Laura confessed.

"We all do."

Laura knew what her sister was thinking: it was to the toolshed that Snack had been taken for a whipping whenever he'd get into trouble, no matter how harmless.

To the shed for a whipping. How quaint it sounded.

Except that after the last beating, the worst beating, Snack had run away. He hadn't come back after that except in times of illness or of death, and he hadn't even come back for one of those.

Standing with Corinne in front of the shed, Laura could still hear her own hysterical crying as she'd pounded on its door that night, screaming for her father inside to stop. To this day, she had no idea what Snack's offense had been, other than coming home late on that particular night; he never afterward would talk about it.

The memory was still so vivid. She was there again, in her pajamas again, shivering and screaming in the fog under a pale, watery moon. So futile, so pointless. Her father couldn't possibly have heard her; Snack had been howling too loudly for that.

She remembered racing back to the house to call the police, only to realize that their only phone had been torn from the wall. Her mother—well, her mother. What could she have done? Shy, timid, and cowed, Alice Shore had been beaten by her own father; she'd considered it a blessing that her husband mostly spared their two daughters and aimed the roughest punishment at their son.

"We'd have to empty out all of the tools and equipment first," Laura said softly.

"Yeah. And then where would we put everything?"

It would be a time-consuming project. Founders Week was about to kick off, and with it, the future of Shore Gardens.

And they still hadn't done anything about the mountainous compost pile.

"Let's just pretend the shed isn't there for now," Laura said with a shrug, and together they turned their back on it.

Corinne went on her way, and Laura went to work arranging an outdoor display of flowering thymes on a carefully spontaneous pile of flat rocks. At the last minute, she decided to add some creeping rosemary to the display; she was hauling a cartload of it from one of the greenhouses when she saw Kendall Barclay coming her way.

Oh, great. Now what? If he was there to take back his money, he was fresh out of luck. They'd handed it over to Great River Finance.

He smiled and waved. Anyone would have thought they were friends. *She* felt as if they were friends, seeing that smile, seeing that wave. He was wearing the usual—khakis and blazer—but his tie this time was sober and banklike. She hated it.

"I've been wandering around, looking for you," he said as he drew near.

"Looks like you've found me," she answered, instinctively cautious. Her cheeks felt suddenly warm and her hands, as usual, were covered in dirt. She put on her gardener's gloves, not only to hide her chipped and broken nails but because it was something to do.

"So. What can I do you for?" she asked lightly as she began emptying the big-wheeled cart of its pots of rosemary. "You're not here about the loan, I hope?"

"In a way," he said, and immediately her heart plunged. "I wanted to know how it went with Great River," he went on.

"God, you scared me," she confessed with a far too nervous laugh. "I thought you wanted your money back."

Now why did she have to tell him that?

He took a pot of rosemary out of the cart and passed it over to her. In his hand, the plant looked impossibly small, a rip-off at two ninety-nine. "Thanks," she said as she took it from him, "but, really, I've got it under control."

He didn't take offense at the rebuff, but seemed content to watch her work.

She didn't want him watching her. Something about his nearness had set her nerve ends humming, and it was impossible to focus on which rosemaries looked best where. She dumped several pots on the stones and began moving them around haphazardly, like a flim-flam artist working a shell game on a street in New York.

With a glance at him over her shoulder, she said, "I want to thank you again for putting our loan application on the fast track. We were thrilled to be out of the clutches of Great River Finance. Corinne said she felt as if she'd been tied to the railroad tracks, and you came along just in time and saved her."

Chuckling, he said, "Your sister has a vivid imagination."

"Not as vivid as mine—believe me," Laura said, straightening up from her work and looking him in the eye.

It would have been extremely satisfying to say flat out, *I know what you're after, buster: our land. As far as I'm concerned, you're Great River all over again, but in a good-looking suit.*

With a boring tie. "I think I liked the hot-air balloon one better," she said, nodding at his chest before she took up several pots from her cart.

"The hot—? Ah. Hey, that's easy enough." With practiced ease, he undid the knot and stuffed the tie in his pocket. It was probably silk, probably Saks, but what did he care? There were more where that one came from.

She tried to match his offhand manner. "I wonder what you'd do," she said dryly, "if I said I didn't like the cut of your pants."

He blinked. Paused. Smiled. And actually said, "Try me."

Why was she provoking him? It was insane. "Can we talk about something other than your money and your clothes?"

Apparently chastened, he took it down a peg. "You've made amazing progress here. The nursery looks great. Your display is looking nice," he said genially, pointing to her work in progress. "Even I want to buy some, and I don't know what the hell they are."

"Thyme. Rosemary."

"Oh. Herbs. Like parsley, right?" he offered in a display of knowledge.

"Impressive, but I'm afraid you don't get the job," she said. Still, there was a smile in her voice that she was sure he could hear.

He startled her by taking out a handkerchief from his inside pocket and lifting the square to her face. The temptation for her was to step back from his outstretched hand, but the greater temptation was to let him do what he was going to do: wipe her cheek.

"You have a smudge," he said gravely.

"Only one?"

"It's a big one; there isn't room for two," he said, rubbing gently.

Great. A dirty face to go with her dirty hands. She said with a defensive sigh, "You know what? I'm working. Gardening is dirty work—clean work, but dirty, too, if you understand what I mean." She went back to her task, as if she were on the clock.

He shoved the hanky back in his pocket, then said, "You're used to sitting in front of a computer all day; this must be a real shock to your system."

"You forget that I was born and raised here."

He shrugged. "I guess I thought you'd left it all behind."

"I did—for more than one reason," she said pointedly. Before he could ask her to list them all, she added, "But I'm enjoying myself. Really. Everyone's happiest in a garden; it goes without saying."

"Except that this is a nursery. Ratchet any pleasure up high enough, it can turn into pain."

"Very profound," she said, not necessarily in sarcasm.

"Laura."

She turned. He gave her a look that made her frown and then—for whatever reason—blush. There was just something about the look.

But he said innocently enough, "Corinne tells me that in addition to all of your other talents, you have a gift for landscaping. Is that in the works—a career change?"

"Hardly," she said, balking at the suggestion. "I'm not planning to stay here any longer than a month."

His eyebrows shot up. "That's not what your sister says."

Laura sighed and said, "My sister is wrong. She wishes and she hopes, but the reality is that I have a career as a software consultant in Portland, on the other side of the country."

"But can't consultants consult anywhere? Couldn't one consult . . . for example, here?"

"It helps if there are customers available. With all due respect to Chepaquit, there is no 'here' here."

"Mm," he said with a reluctant nod. "Still, it's a nice place to live. Clean air, great light, warm water, inspiring views, and all the sand you could ever want for a backyard sandbox."

Laura smiled politely. "Except for the water temperature, I have all that in Portland, Oregon."

She had emptied the cart of her load of pots and was simply standing there, mystified by his chattiness. "Well, sir, I envy you your banker's hours, but around here, we don't stop until the sun goes down, and usually not then. So thank you again for moving along so smartly on the—"

"Damn it, Laura, look . . . I wanted to ask you . . . to see you . . . to do something with—"

Exasperated, he tried another tack. "Things got complicated once the loan request became a reality. I felt it was best to wait until after the approval process was over. Now it is. And so—"

She couldn't suppress an incredulous snort. "You're asking me . . . *out*? Oh, that wouldn't be the best idea. Really. I've already said that I'll be leaving the Cape soon—"

"Oh, sure, well, naturally. But uh-h . . . " he said, his cheeks reddening. "What I was trying to find out was: would you have time in your schedule to look over my property and give me a few landscaping tips? The front lawn is a dead-grass disaster, and the backyard is basically an all-you-can-eat buffet for deer and rabbits. I need advice, and fast."

"Oh!"

"I'd pay you, of course," he added.

"You'd—oh."

"I don't know how anything ever grew anywhere on the property; my mother must have stood guard with a broom," he said with a pained chuckle. "But she's moved to a condo in Boston, and since I've taken over the family homestead, I haven't been able to convince her to come back once a week and beat up the deer."

His eyebrows went up over a hopeful smile, and then drifted back down again in resignation. He sighed. "No, I can see how flat-out you are here. I understand."

A tour de force of diplomacy, Laura thought. And an expert application of guilt.

It didn't seem possible that she could be mortified in his presence in so many different ways. Surely by now she should have exhausted the possibilities. Confused and thoroughly humbled by her own presumptuousness—she assumed he was going to ask her *out*?—she said, "I could steal an hour or two after work, if you like. Say, tomorrow? No charge," she added breezily.

"Oh, but I would have to insist."

"No, *I* would have to insist," she said, scraping together what crumbs of dignity she could. "I'll be there at six-thirty tomorrow night, if that's all right with you."

"That's perfect. I'll come for you."

"Not necessary, thanks," she said, lifting her cart by its bale. "I'm sure I can find you."

God, what a fool she'd been. Ask her out!

He was about to intercept her, but the sound of Snack's voice raised in anger had them both turning in the direction of the compost pile.

They saw Gabe sitting on the tractor, and Snack looking determined to knock him off.

"Now what?" Laura moaned, and without bothering to excuse herself, she rushed over to defuse the situation. Snack was working hard and staying sober, but he tended to get cranky by afternoon, probably because he was working hard and staying sober.

She got there in time to hear her brother say angrily, "Gabe, I said get off. Get off the goddamn tractor. *Now*."

"What're you, nuts? What's the matter with you?" Gabe looked dumbfounded, but he wasn't moving. "Your sister asked me a week ago to move the compost pile, and I'm moving the compost pile. You have a problem with that, talk to her, not me," he said, pointing over Snack's shoulder at Laura.

He started the tractor up and began dipping the blade into the side of the black hill of decayed, rich soil.

The action infuriated Snack; he grabbed Gabe by his belt and literally yanked him part of the way out of the ancient tractor's iron seat. With a surprised oath, Gabe resisted and managed to keep himself upright, then suddenly reversed himself and jumped down to the ground on his own, ready for battle. Laura rushed at her brother, and from somewhere, Kendall Barclay jumped between Gabe and Snack.

"Gabe, get a grip," Kendall warned, pushing him back. "Christ, man, let it go, let it *go*."

Laura was having more trouble than that in subduing her brother. For the first time in her life, she realized that he was bigger, stronger, and more volatile than a baby brother by rights should be. She wouldn't be able to control him at all, if he weren't willing to be controlled.

This time, he was willing. He whipped his arm out of her clutches, but he settled for nothing more violent than a fierce glare at their neighbor and councilman.

"If anyone's moving that pile, it's going to be me," he growled. "Now get the hell out."

Gabe exchanged looks with Laura and then with Barclay. He hunched his shoulders and threw out his hands, like a merchant who's made his best offer. "Fine with me. I've got other things to do, believe me."

He tucked the side of his shirt back into his jeans and

shook his head at Snack like a disappointed parent. "You don't even bother to vote, do you?" he said in quiet reproach, and then he left with Barclay, who was doing his best to escort him out quietly.

Laura was furious. "Snack, you *idiot*. We could've really used his help. Not to mention, he's on the town council, and who in his right mind wants to piss off a councilman? *Not* to mention, Corinne is going to be crushed when she hears about this. I swear to God, if you've fouled things up between Gabe and her—"

"Fouled what up? There's nothing to foul. What're you talking about?"

"Oh, forget it. Why wouldn't you let him move the compost? What were you thinking?"

He got that evasive look that Laura knew so well and that more properly belonged on the face of a teenager—but Snack was thirty-one years old.

Thirty-one, and what a mess.

"I didn't like the way he just walked in and took over," Snack said at last. "Like he's John Wayne or something, here to save the ranch. If we're going to do this, we're going to do it ourselves."

"Fine. We'll leave the compost pile right where it is. It's been an eyesore for thirty years; it can stay there another thirty, ah *reckon*," she said, mocking his John Wayne comparison.

"I'll move it myself," Snack promised grimly. "I'll start tonight—after you go to bed and leave me the hell alone."

That night, a weary Laura lay on her lumpy single bed.

She'd been there two weeks. It felt like two years. The long hours were getting to them all. Gabe and Snack in a near fistfight? They'd all grown up together, for heaven's sake!

She thought of her sister, bursting into tears after Laura

was forced to explain why Kendall had been seen escorting Gabe off the property.

Rinnie has a thing for Gabe; I'm sure of it now.

And Kendall Barclay—what was *that* all about? Why would a bank president take such a personal interest in them?

Easy. Because the personal interest was in their highly desirable property.

Still . . . Laura had dated her share of men; she knew the signs of one coming on to her. It certainly seemed as if he were coming on to her.

Or not. She'd grossly misread his intentions. All he'd wanted was a little advice. For which he apparently was willing to pay. How kind of him to throw her that bone.

I'll give him an hour, she decided. *Not a minute more.*

But it still seemed . . . somehow it seemed . . . as if he'd been coming on to her. And the amazing thing was, she wanted that to be true. And it wasn't. Which she found as disappointing as it was annoying.

But! The good news was that she must be over Max; why else go second-guessing about whether Kendall Barclay, ooh, ooh, liked her or not? How pathetic. She was thinking like a thirteen-year-old. If it weren't so sad, she'd confess all of it to Corinne.

No, not Corinne. Corinne wouldn't understand. Right now, the person Laura most wanted to confide in was not Corinne, not one of her friends or neighbors back in Portland, but Sylvia Mendan—Sylvia, wise beyond her years, who knew everything there was to know about the male sex. She knew it as a teen; God only knew how much wiser she must be now.

Sylvia. Where was she now? Married? Divorced? Kids? It was impossible to imagine her as being anything but a stunningly beautiful, superbly confident young woman. She would always and forever be eighteen, and Laura would always and forever be a novice at her feet.

• • •

An hour later, Laura was awakened by the sound of low voices from the front porch below.

It was Corinne, having a conversation with Gabe, and they both sounded on completely friendly terms. Half-asleep, Laura let out a huge sigh of relief—and then, intrigued by the thought that the two could be carrying on an intimate conversation so late at night, she did a bad thing and crept over to the open window to eavesdrop.

Silly her; she should have known better. Her sister was much too considerate to speak in anything above a whisper. Still, it was obvious that she sounded very happy, and that was very good.

Gabe Wellerton's voice carried more clearly than Corinne's, and Laura was able to hear enough to know that he was sorry for the ruckus he'd caused earlier.

"Snack and I . . ." Something something, "oil and water . . . Snack's got major, major problems . . . your father . . . good kid . . . working . . . listen to him go . . . ever sleep?"

And in the distance, not far from the shed where he had been beaten by their enraged father one terrifying night, Snack worked the tractor, burrowing, lifting, and filling the rusted dump truck that stood silently by, ready to move the compost someplace more discreet.

Chapter 11

The letters on the white banner were three feet high and painted in different bright colors: FOUNDERS WEEK SALE, May 24–31.

"The finishing touch; it's perfect, Snack," said Laura, genuinely impressed. She'd forgotten how skilled he was with a brush.

But above and beyond the variety of her brother's talents was the unexpected surge in his output. "When did you *sleep*?" she asked.

He shrugged. "Haven't, yet. I'll grab an hour or two after I hang this across the front of the shop, then come back out and start hitting the compost pile again."

He had the slightly crazed look of someone on too much espresso, and yet he seemed intensely focused. Snack was a man with a plan—possibly the first of his life.

She watched him set a rickety twelve-foot ladder against the front of the building and wished they could afford an aluminum one. "How long were you out there last night, anyway?" she asked. "I fell asleep and you were still going."

"I packed it in around two—when Officer McCray came and told me to knock it off. He wasn't just passing by either; someone had called and complained. I wonder who," he said dryly as he nudged the ladder into a better angle.

"Don't go there, Snack," Laura begged. "Don't. The sale starts the day after tomorrow; it would be *nice* if it weren't to the sound of gunshots. Besides, you know it wasn't Gabe. Someone in town must have seen you and decided to pull your chain."

"It worked." Snack suddenly registered that Laura wasn't wearing jeans and a T-shirt. Acknowledging it with a low whistle from his perch on the third rung, he said, "Steppin' out?"

Laura was wearing the pretty yellow dress she'd bought at T.J. Maxx; she now had the tan to set it off. She was wearing makeup that she'd applied as artfully and subtly as she knew how. She was even wearing lacy underthings instead of her cotton work versions, simply to revel in the delicacy of them. And, most luxurious of all, she was wearing thin strappy sandals which—after weeks of wearing heavy work shoes—made her feel sinfully exposed and feminine.

She felt pretty. She felt good.

She felt guilty for leaving Snack and Corinne toiling in the fields when she herself was not.

"I am not 'steppin' out.' I have a chore to do," she said defensively. "Just so you know, it's strictly business."

"Of course. That's what I assumed," Snack said with a deadpan look. "Let me take a flier: business with Kendall Barclay?"

"I'll be back in an hour."

"Uh-huh."

"An hour and a half, tops."

"Uh-huh."

"Cut it out, Snack," she said, annoyed. "It's important to me that I look good for this meeting—for reasons you wouldn't understand."

"Please. I'm a guy; don't insult me."

"I didn't think that was possible."

"Tsk-tsk. That tone definitely doesn't go with that dress."

"This from the resident expert on good taste. Oh, why am I standing here bickering with you?" she said, glancing at her watch. "I'm going to be late!"

"Hey, you can't go now. Someone has to feed the banner up to me while I hang it."

"I'm not that someone," said Laura. She was feeling a surge of tension for no real reason; Triple Oaks was only a five-minute ride from the nursery.

"Hold on, I see Billy. Billy! Over here!" she cried, waving to the heavy-set man just getting out of his car in the stone-topped lot. "We need a favor."

Billy, who was back to making flower deliveries for them after a six-month hiatus, came right over—as always, happy to help. He was tall, six-foot-three or -four, the perfect candidate for the job. Snack explained, slowly and clearly, what they were going to do, and Billy picked up the free end of the banner and clutched it in one of his beefy hands while he waited for Snack to pound in the first nail.

"Thanks, Billy," said Laura. "Please tell Corinne to give you something extra when you go in to be paid for today's delivery."

Billy looked confused by that, so Laura took her wallet out of her bag and began fishing for a couple of dollars.

"You look real pretty today," he said, staring at the hem of her dress. "*Real* pretty."

"Thank you, Billy. This is for you," said Laura, handing him the singles.

He stuffed them into his shirt pocket with his free hand.

"Don't forget to see Corinne and get paid after you're done here," she reminded him.

He gave her a disarmingly confused smile. "But you just paid me," he pointed out.

"No, that was for helping Snack. I mean for the delivery."

"Oh . . . okay," he said, but it was obvious that things weren't okay.

In desperation to get on with her task, Laura said, "Tell you what. I'll pay you for the delivery myself, how's that?" She got her wallet out again. "And Snack will explain to Corinne what I did."

Billy jammed the ten and the five—twice his usual pay—into his shirt pocket without looking at them. He said, "Should I wait to hang the banner before I see Rinnie about getting paid?"

"But I just—! Yes. All right. That would be good. First the banner. Then Corinne. Thanks, Billy."

She glanced up at her brother, who was waiting on the ladder and shaking his head in resignation. "Billy. *Billy.* Will you hand me the goddamn banner?"

Billy whirled toward the ladder, wrapping the banner around his legs like a Roman toga.

"Thanks, Billy," Laura said to the back of his balding head. "See you all later."

She hurried to the pickup, aware that putting Billy back on the payroll was going to eat mightily into their profits, if they didn't lose money outright on his deliveries. It seemed to her that he was slower now, dimmer now, than he used to be when they were all in school together and he worked part-time at the nursery. Or maybe she had just become used to the high-tech overachievers in the rat race back in Portland.

The wonder of it was that Billy was still able to drive. She made a mental note to verify that he actually had a valid license. Their insurance company might frown on a fender bender that involved a subcontractor who did not.

Triple Oaks was named after three huge white oaks that once dominated the front lawn of the Barclay estate. In 1991, Hurricane Bob roared through and took out the eastmost tree. Now there were only two, both on the west side of the entry, and they gave the house an unbalanced, lop-sided look.

Item number one: replace the missing oak.

Laura sat in the pickup, parked at the far end of the drive, and took notes as she took in the view. She saw nothing growing under the two remaining oaks except for the occasional, pitiful blade of grass; the rest was dirt, with scattered remnants of a layer of mulch.

Item number two: ground cover. Pachysandra, if nothing else. Even dull ivy would do.

At the head of the drive stood the house itself, a stately piece of architecture in the Greek Revival style that was painted white, with many windows, a low-pitched roof, and a triangular pediment on the front and side gables. But virtually every one of its extra-long ground-floor windows was completely hidden behind overgrown rhododendrons.

Item number three: whack back the rhodies, and let the sun shine in.

Item number four: replace some of the rhodies altogether with Japanese andromeda for variety and also for fragrance when the windows were open.

But the andromeda would need to be mature from the get-go in order to compete with their muscular cousins. Where could she get her hands on some? Corinne would know. Yes.

Laura sat with her yellow pad, jotting down ideas at a furious pace. The one thing she did not want was to show up on Kendall Barclay's doorstep without a thought in her head. That impression went a little too well with dirty fingernails and a smudgy face.

So engrossed was she in recording her suggestions that when she next looked up, it was to see the lord of the manor himself with a bemused smile on his face as he strolled down the brick drive to her rusted pickup.

Laura tucked her clipboard under her arm and scrambled

down from the truck. She had no intention of accepting any money from Kendall Barclay III, but she had every intention of handing him a list of landscaping ideas that would blow his argyle socks off.

It amazed Ken, simply amazed him, how the mere sight of Laura Shore reduced him to a fourteen-year-old kid again. The raging hormones, the hungry looks, the crushing desire to see her naked—that was him, all right, then and now.

She had avoided him every chance she got back then, and in retrospect, he couldn't blame her. In school he was Skinnykenny Barclay, local rich geek, spurned by every kid in class for trying to be one of them.

Well, he wasn't one of them. Never had been, never would be; he'd had too much money behind him for that. Ken had understood, even if his old-fashioned father had not, that it was false to pretend to be less than you were—as false as pretending to be more than you were. He never should have tried to act as if he were just another middle-class Chepaquit kid; it had only got him more reviled. For better or for worse, Ken was what he was, a privileged townie.

Laura Shore had lived a life devoid of privilege, and yet look at her now: smart, sassy, and sexy as all hell. The soft bounce of her breasts beneath her dress as she walked gave him a sustained rush of pure pleasure. He couldn't think of a single woman he'd ever been with who'd affected him quite so viscerally.

This, despite the fact that she was waving a clipboard in greeting, which reminded him that she was there on business.

Ostensibly. The fact was, he had been on the verge of asking her out when she'd snorted in disbelief. Taken aback, he'd punted and come up with Plan B: an offer to pay her for some landscaping advice. Not too imaginative, but . . . here she was.

"Mr. Barclay, how are you this fine evening?" she asked with light formality.

She was being ironic again. She liked to do that, and he didn't know why. To put more distance between them? It was maddening, when he was trying to put less.

"I'm pretty well, thanks." He gestured around him. "Well, what do you think? Have I overplayed the disaster aspect?"

She sighed and said, "No, I think you got it just about right."

"The shade from the trees is too deep," he said, oddly driven to defend himself. "Nothing will grow."

"Yes it will. We can fix that."

"And on that side, the grass won't grow at all where the tree used to be, even with sun."

"Because you didn't take out the stump completely. We can fix that too."

"And, I don't know—everything doesn't look right. I can't put my finger on it, but it all looks ignored, somehow. I don't like that look."

"Really?" she asked, angling her head at him.

"I take it personally. I don't tend to ignore things."

He didn't have a clue what he meant by that. He was finding that when he was around her, his mind occasionally turned into a potato.

They were walking slowly toward the house, and she was saying something about groundcover, and something else about the overgrowth in front of the windows, and he realized that he would be perfectly content to walk with her across the country and back again.

Actually, that wasn't quite true. He liked the sound of her voice, true enough, but it was the accidental brush of her bare arm against his that had him resolved to find some reason, any reason, for her to hang around. This was new, this instant, electric response; he was curious to see where it went.

"You know what your problem is?" she finally said, snapping his reverie in two.

"No. What?" He wasn't aware that he had a problem, but if anything, *she* was the damn problem.

"It's this: you have a very formal-looking house, but it's in a woodland setting. In my mind, you have two choices: knock off the third story and turn the house into a cute little Cape, or formalize your landscaping a little."

"Hmm. Why do I think the second option would be more doable?"

She laughed—actually laughed!—and said, "You think so? Wait till you see what it costs to dig out a stump."

She was so pretty; her smile lit up her face in a way that made him think of Christmas morning, waterskiing, and a triple-overtime basketball game: you just never wanted to let it go.

"So . . . there's hope?" he asked, bemused. God only knew what he meant by that.

"Sure there's hope. I'm not talking about creating an eighteenth-century maze or anything," she said, still trying to reassure. "Just some selective pruning and planting."

She seemed so cost-conscious; did she honestly think he couldn't afford it?

Apparently so. "Although, I have to warn you," she went on. "Mature andromeda don't come cheap. Not to mention, you'll want a good-sized shade tree to get a jump-start on the two remaining oaks. The sky's the limit, there. You could spend upward of fifty thousand dollars, depending how in love you are with the idea of a tree. I know: it's crazy. But people do it."

He shrugged and said, "All of your suggestions so far make perfect sense. I plan to have Corinne coordinate the effort—unless you change your mind and decide to stay and make landscape design your real job, which you should—so I hope you won't have any objections to writing up your recommendations for her."

When she looked dismayed, he said quickly, "Or, you can just talk your ideas into a recorder. I'll have my assistant transcribe them later."

"Ken, I'd love for you to order everything through the nursery—I'd be ecstatic," she admitted with a sweet, earnest smile. "But I also really believe you'd be better off having a professional landscaper run the show."

As soon as she said it, he realized how not better off he'd be. "Come around to the back," he said, ignoring her confession, "and tell me what you think." He turned to head off in that direction.

For some reason, she dug in her heels and wouldn't move. She was staring at him, looking so baffled, so conflicted. He could not understand what the problem was.

"It's not very far," he said lightly.

She started to say something and then stopped. After compressing her lips in a hapless smile, she said, "Lead on."

Whatever it was, he would deal with it later. For now, he wanted simply to hear her voice and share her dreams for a place he was fond of.

Right. Who was he kidding? He wanted so much more than that. He wanted to slide his hands through her hair, draw her close, breathe her in. He wanted to kiss the freckle on her cheekbone . . . run his tongue across the fullness of her upper lip . . . nip the place where her neck curved into her shoulder. And that was just for starters. It shook him, the degree to which he wanted different things from her.

That undeniable, painful surge of longing—where the hell had it come from?

"—too much?" she was asking him.

"Not at all," he said, so bemused by his fascination with her that he'd missed what she'd said. He was going to have to get a grip on himself, and he didn't exactly know how.

Obviously something about her had seeded itself in his soul. He hadn't had any contact with her since she was—what? Thirteen?

And even then, he, at fourteen, had made a spectacle of himself, getting so soundly whupped. He could only hope that she'd forgotten the incident.

"A deer will eat almost anything if it's hungry enough," she was saying, "so I can't offer you any guarantees—but you should be safe with the Japanese andromeda in front, which aren't very tasty to them. Your rhododendrons seem to be surviving, after all."

"Yeah. It's back here that the deer prefer to camp out. I imagine that they like the view."

They were standing on the patio in the shade of a towering hickory, with a view that slid past the sulking lawn and ravaged garden, under a canopy of tall pines, and out to the water. It was a sublime evening, with a soft breeze and a benign sea . . . perfect, just perfect, for an evening sail.

But all Ken could think about was how much more fun it would be to be rolling around his bed with the woman beside him, having mad, passionate, sweaty sex.

Chapter 12

"It's a wonderful view," she said, envying his deer. "It's more charming, more intimate than our windy, wide-open one."

"Mm."

"It's nice to see so many bird feeders—and even nicer that they actually have seed in them."

"Mm-hmm."

She didn't dare look at him. Her heart was beating too hard, and she was afraid that he'd see it thumping against her rib cage.

What was going *on*? She'd looked up, seen him sauntering down the drive, and that was it. Something got knocked off balance in the gyroscope of her emotions, and she'd been trying ever since to set it right again. Without success.

"Did you say that you'd like a garden back here? Have you figured out what you want?"

"*Oh*, yeah," he said. He shot her a look, then let it drift back out to the barren border where a few six-foot stakes leaned like a row of drunken sentries.

"You planted tomatoes, I take it?"

He nodded. "They lasted a day. Deer couldn't gobble 'em up fast enough. You should have seen me in my underwear, running after them with a rake one morning."

She couldn't help a smile. "Well, at least you tried."

"I'd do anything for a ripe tomato."

She was picturing him in his underwear much more vividly than she was picturing him with the rake, and that easy leap of her imagination made her incredibly uneasy.

"If . . . if it's any comfort," she said, feeling the heat in her cheeks, "you don't really have enough sun here to grow tomatoes. I'd leave that job to the farmers and just buy from a stand."

She found herself sucking a deep lungful of air, for no other reason than to slow down the beat of her heart. "But there are a lot of . . . shrubs and perennials that would still grow here . . . and that the deer would . . . leave alone. Probably."

He turned to face her, and she saw a new interest in his eyes. "Like what?" he said.

Laura, even Laura, knew that the look she saw there had nothing to do with shrubs and perennials.

"Oh . . . like astilbe, for instance. They're colorful . . . feathery . . . reliable . . ."

"I like reliable," he said softly. "Tell me more."

"Well . . . four-o'clocks would work. So would Jacob's ladder."

"Charming," he said, smiling. "Pretty. Tell me more."

Clearly he wasn't talking about flowers.

He drew a tiny gasp of pleasure from her when he reached up to tuck her hair behind one ear.

"Li . . . ly of the valley. And foxglove . . ."

"Foxglove?" he said with languid surprise. "Isn't that poisonous?"

"Very," she said on a sigh as he tucked her hair on the other side.

"I'm not that mad at the deer," he said. "Actually, I owe them. I wouldn't have you, if they hadn't had my garden."

"Goatsbeard," she said, catching her lip between her

teeth. "Ajuga." She was racking her brain now, trying to think of deer-proof plants. It was so much easier than focusing on what was happening. "If you had more sun—"

"Then what?" he said, lowering his head to hers, feathering her lips in a kiss that took the rest of her breath away.

"Verbena," she whispered, closing her eyes. "The fragrance—"

"You smell much better than any verbena ever could," he said, nuzzling his lips below her ear.

Her head was ringing with the nearness of him. "There's always coreopsis; they hate coreopsis . . ."

"I'll never remember the name."

She was still clutching her clipboard. He slid it out of her hand, and she heard him lay it on the wrought-iron table next to them. He threaded his fingers through hers, pinning her gently in place, and slid his lips in a series of kisses along the curve of her neck, bringing her to the edge of a swoon.

She was completely, utterly in shock. "*Bee* balm," she moaned.

"I like the sound of that. Yes," he said, and she could hear the smile, hear the confidence.

She fought back with her arsenal of ideas. "Helio-oh . . . trope, damn it," she whimpered. He was tonguing the hollow at the base of her throat.

"I've been wanting to do that," he said with a sigh of longing that tore through her.

She was standing absolutely still. "Barberry."

"Is it edible?" he asked softly. He came back to her ear, licked the edge.

"Potent . . . potentilla."

"And how. Lots of it."

He released her fingers, then cradled her face in his hands. "Laura," he whispered, "something very obvious is going on here."

She tried to joke. "Besides your disappearing garden?"

He silenced her with a kiss, a question at first, and then, with his tongue, a statement of fact. She answered in kind, tasting him, loving what she tasted, pressing for more. He made a sound in his throat, low, hungry, ready.

With a wrenching effort, she pulled back.

"I'm not like this!"

He laughed, a shaky sound.

She was staring into his blue eyes, trying to understand what she was seeing there—and what she was seeing there was confusion. Of course he was confused. He'd just taken a running leap over the railroad tracks and had landed in the middle of shantytown. It must have come as a surprise.

"Well, we're obviously under a spell," she said in a wobbly voice, and she forced herself to snap her fingers in front of his face and smile. "There. All broken."

He blinked at the jarring gesture and studied her hard, his dark eyebrows pinched down, his lips parted as though he were about to say something cutting and trying not to.

Turning almost primly away from him, she resumed her review of his garden. "Here's . . . an idea: why not lay down a path of bluestone, interplanted with foamflowers and periwinkle and mosses?"

"Laura—" he said, turning her back around to face him.

"Okay," she said sharply, pouring all of her frustration into the word. "Pachysandra. Even you couldn't kill pachysandra."

"Jesus Christ, who cares?"

He took her by her shoulders and kissed her hard and deep, pounding some silence into her. No more play, no more evasions; this was for real. His mouth dragged across hers, nipping, teasing, diving in again and again, leaving her senseless.

She gave as good as she got, returning fire for fire, the drumbeat of her pulse filling her head and blotting out thought. Her hands were as restless as his, pulling, tugging, trying to disrobe. There was a chaise longue on the patio, thickly cushioned and hidden by the encircling stone wall. They half-stumbled onto it, lying close along its narrow length. He kissed her again and again, leaving her senseless. "Here?" she said between ragged kisses, dizzy with the thought of him, crazed with the illogic of him. She opened her eyes to a high canopy of leaves. "Out here?"

"Here, right here, right now, Laura, right now—" The words tumbled from him in a rush, exploded from him, as though they'd been building like seas that became breakers on a rocky shore.

"Ken, Ken . . . why did you . . . why—?"

"No, *not* here, what am I saying, here," he said, suddenly propping himself up over her. His breathing was hot, heavy, coming from the place where passion simmered and then boiled over. "For God's sake, not out here."

He staggered to his feet and pulled her up, urging her along with a string of kisses, then levered down the brass latch of a heavy French door that he shouldered inward. They were in the master bedroom now, a room as serene and well-mannered as they were hot and unrestrained.

The bed was steps away. He pulled her down onto it, and they renewed the insane frenzy of their kisses, relishing, feasting, hungry for more. His hand slid under her dress and up the inside of her thigh in an electrifying trail, halting over the thinnest of lace. He hooked his thumb into the slender elastic of her panties, tugged them down; she helped the process, wild to be rid of the barriers.

She let out a sultry moan when he slipped his hand onto warm, wet flesh. She was lifting herself to him, offering herself to him, and suddenly she was hit with déjà vu: her response was a physical version of her naïve offer of two decades before.

You are my knight.

"Wait . . . wait, Ken," she said, turning aside, breathless from his kisses. "We have to talk."

"Into the night if you like, but later," he said. He tried for a chuckle, managed a groan.

He began to kiss her again, but she turned away again. "No, wait . . . you have to wait. This goes back some," she said unhappily. She did not want to bring it up—she did *not*—but it had to be done.

His hand relaxed and came to rest against her thigh, and she felt the poorer for it. He lifted his head but stayed inches from her mouth, close enough for her to feel the warm flow of his breath as he said, "How far back?"

"I was thirteen," she said softly.

"I was a year older."

"You do remember, then."

"The woods."

She nodded, not quite trusting her voice. She felt absurd, dragging out a twenty-year-old trauma from the closet of her life. Girls nowadays probably went through worse pawing while they waited for the school bus. But she was what she was because of that trauma—and the letters they had exchanged in its aftermath—and it had to be said.

Ken was waiting for her to go on. When she hesitated, he decided to fill the silence himself. "I'm sorry for that," he said. His face was the picture of painful remorse.

"You are?" She was oddly thrilled to hear it.

"Of course I am." He sounded offended that she was surprised. "When I saw them surrounding you, all I could think of—" He stopped himself and said, "You probably won't appreciate the comparison."

"Tell me anyway."

"You looked like a terrified fox, cornered in a hunt."

He had it about right. Laura had no doubt that the group was getting ready to pin her to the ground and take it from there.

"I *was* terrified."

She saw the muscles in his jaw working in anger. "I know it. I wish I could have done something."

"But . . . you did! You came at them swinging and howling. Who knows what would have happened if you hadn't seen us?"

He shrugged off the idea that he'd behaved heroically, and she asked out of curiosity, "Why were you in the woods, anyway? I've always wanted to know."

His groan was almost comical. "Hell. Are you going to make me say it?"

"Yes," she said, smiling now.

"I was bird-watching. There was a report of a snowy owl in the area. Not that I'd know. The assholes took my binoculars after they used them to knock me out before they ran."

With the pain of remembrance, she said, "They did beat you up pretty bad."

"Mere flesh wounds," he said lightly. "I was easy pickings for that bunch. I doubt that I weighed a hundred pounds back then."

"But look at you now."

Again he shrugged off the compliment. "After that debacle, I started lifting weights—well, not real weights. I was forced to improvise. I stole a few ten-pound ballast pigs from the bilge of my dad's boat, and I worked out with them on the sly in my room. My dad wouldn't have approved of bodybuilding," he explained. "Back then it was still considered vulgar."

He said softly, "Why were *you* in the woods, Laura? I've always wondered, as well."

She could understand that. She searched his face, under its tumble of thick hair, and wondered whether she could be candid with him.

"Will Burton," she said. "For whatever reason, he suddenly began paying attention to me. I was so flattered. When he asked me to go with him on a walk in the woods—"

"You actually said yes?" Ken asked.

Mistake. "You think it was a slutty thing to do," she said with an edge in her voice.

"Come on; you were thirteen. But . . . Will Burton! Jesus. Everyone knew he was a bully and a pig."

"I didn't. He was a doctor's son."

"And that impressed you?"

"It did back then."

"I hope you've learned a little since that time," he said, incredulous.

"Obviously," she answered in a strained voice. But she was thinking, *And yet here I am with a banker's son.*

Was she still just a sucker for flattery?

Ken shifted his weight, and with it, the position of his hand. Instantly she felt the loss of its warmth.

"So," he said quietly. "Three cheers, I guess, for the snowy owl."

The hideous episode in the woods was a huge chapter of Laura's life. Ken Barclay had finally filled in some of the missing pages from it.

But not all of them. "I was so grateful to you," she said, studying one of the opened buttons of his shirt. "You'll never know. Or maybe you do. God knows, I poured it all out in that letter to you. I'm surprised that I didn't write it in my own blood. You were such a hero to me. My knight in shining armor, I believe I called you."

She was sure he had picked up on the disappointment, even disillusionment, in her voice, because for a long moment he said nothing.

And then: "What letter?"

Surprised, she looked up into his eyes. She was searching for truth there, and she found it: he certainly didn't remember.

Painful as the effort was, she felt obliged to jog his memory. "*You* know. The letter to which you wrote the three-sentence response?"

He sat up. "What response?"

"You honestly still can't remember?"

She was humiliated by that. She had let his adolescent rejection of her define who she was in life, and he couldn't even remember writing it. Well, why would he? He probably had got tons of letters from girls that he felt he had to answer. It had to have been hard to keep them all straight.

She kept her gaze steady and tried to keep the emotion out of her voice as she said, "The response that went, and I quote: 'You shouldn't be writing to me. Don't do it again. And don't ever try to see me.' "

"You have got to be kidding me. Why would I do that?"

"I don't know. Why did you do that?"

"I *didn't* do that. I never wrote you a letter. I never got a letter to respond to in the first place."

"That you can remember."

"Laura. I'd remember a letter from you. My God. And can you honestly believe that I'd send something so unfeeling? After what I saw in the woods, can you?"

"You were fourteen," she reminded him. "It's a weird age."

"Oh, come on," he said, dismissing her theory.

"I suppose it was coincidence that after that, you suddenly disappeared?" She was more than a little put off by his condescending tone.

He was obviously still trying to puzzle it out. She could see it in the look on his face, far more focused than it was at the bank, when the mere granting of money was involved.

He got up from the bed, too agitated to sit, and began pacing the tonal carpet that covered most of the floor. He said, "Right after the episode in the woods, my parents shipped me, shiner and all, to Switzerland for the summer to stay with my aunt and uncle."

"Just for fighting?" she asked, awed that there were parents around who would resort to such an extreme.

"It had already been arranged," he said, without the

slightest smile at her cluelessness. "Although I did, in fact, catch big-time hell for fighting."

He added, "I got back from Switzerland at summer's end, just in time to be sent off to Winton Academy in the Berkshires." Mid-pace, he stopped to look her in the eye and say, "During all that time, there was no letter."

"There was. I sent it." She sat up with her legs over the side of the bed and smoothed her wrinkled yellow dress, painfully aware that her panties were still looped around one ankle. She reached down to slip them off and then stuffed them in a pocket of her dress. It seemed more discreet than trying to put them on again.

Obviously he saw her do it. How he interpreted the gesture, she had no idea.

"There was no reply from me," he insisted.

"There was. I have it."

That stopped him in his tracks. "You *have* the letter? Where?"

"Not on me, I'm afraid," she said dryly. Or he would by now have found it on his own, given the way things had just gone between them.

"I'd like to see this letter." He rubbed his hand across his jaw, pulling skin on the return stroke. "Damn, but I'd like to see it."

"And so you shall, since it's so important to you." She stood up, feeling emotionally raw after this second dramatic encounter under the trees with Kendall Barclay III.

She glanced around the bedroom with its subtle, neutral tones and thought, *Heck, I'd rather see more color when I open my eyes, anyway.* "Well," she said with a rueful smile, "I think we can assume that my work here is done."

She began to leave the same way she'd entered, but Ken got to the door before she did.

"Laura," he said, blocking her way. "I promise you I'll get to the bottom of this. I'm wondering now whether my dad—damn, it's way too possible. I remember that my father was all over the principal, what was his name?"

"Smith." He'd come and gone in a year.

"Yeah. Smith. At the time, I assumed that my dad did everything he could to make sure Will and the others were punished—humiliating as it was for me to have my father fight my battles. Now I'm wondering whether he wasn't even busier than I was aware. He could easily have intercepted your letter and then answered it—although it burns my gut to think it."

His father had been dead six years. They would never know.

Laura said wearily, "I have to go."

He was inclined not to let her; she could see it in the way he got hold of the door lever before she did.

The surprise was passing now, and in its place a surge of ridiculous self-pity overtook her. The insult of that letter, heaped on top of the injury of the assault, had been the work of an arrogant grown-up, not an arrogant juvenile. She didn't even *know* Kendall Barclay's father; she'd been rejected by him merely on principle.

Ken stroked his fingers across her cheek, as if he'd seen tears there. "I'll get to the bottom. I promise," he repeated. He lowered his head to hers and brushed her lips in a gentle kiss.

After that, he opened the door for her and she made a break for the rusty pickup parked at the end of his drive. Into it she scrambled, but not before catching her new yellow dress on one of the truck's rusted edges, tearing a triangular rip in the skirt.

Perfect.

In a mood as glum and confused as any she'd felt in her life, she took the long way back to Shore Gardens through Chepaquit. She wanted to face Snack and Corinne with something like normalcy, and she needed more than five minutes to pull herself back together.

So she meandered through the quaint village, parking in

front of the ice-cream shop that had gone up in place of the old pharmacy with its granite-countered soda fountain, and on a whim she went inside and ordered a Sprite to go.

Only she didn't go. She sat at one of the tiny Formica-topped bistro tables in a daze, wondering what, exactly, had sparked that wildfire back at Triple Oaks. What had happened there was not only sudden but . . . well, suspect. Obviously she had been acting out some teenage fantasy, seducing the knight who had spurned her.

Except that he hadn't spurned her.

But he *had* been a knight.

But a young one: fourteen.

But he wasn't fourteen anymore. He was a grown-up, filled-out, full-fledged, totally sexy hunk.

Which obviously had been the problem.

Her mind bounced between Ken in the bedroom and Kenny in the woods until she couldn't separate the two events anymore; she was numb from the effort to sort out her emotions. So she decided not to try, but simply to place all of them on a shelf until she was ready to take them down again, and look them over carefully, and decide which ones to keep and which ones to toss. She had got through life using that system; it was the one sure way to reach her goals.

Don't get emotional.

She had eased that rule exactly three times in her life. The first was with Will Burton, and look where it had got her. The second was with Max: she hadn't fared any better. And now, Ken. Did she really need to go out on that ledge again? She already knew the view from there: down, down, down.

Making a success of Shore Gardens was her current goal. There was only one way to achieve it.

Do not get emotional.

Feeling finally calm enough to face Snack and Corinne, Laura drove at last to the nursery. She was greeted by the wildly upbeat sale banner which now hung triumphantly above the long window boxes spilling over with bright red geraniums. The tidy graveled parking area, the stile fence tumbled over with beach roses, the outdoor carts filled with flowering strawberries and loaded with spring-blooming perennials—what a difference two hard weeks and an infusion of cash had made.

The irresistible sight helped steady Laura and set her firmly back on course. She honked a greeting to Snack, who was attacking the compost pile with the tractor, and got a preoccupied wave from him in return. Gabe's big hound Baskerville was running back and forth alongside the mound, urging Snack on with noisy barks. Maybe Gabe was around. Hopefully he and Snack had buried the hatchet.

Laura was impressed: at the rate he was going, Snack was going to have the pile out of there in time for the sale. She felt like giving him a hip, hip, and a big hooray for being as good as his word.

She parked the truck in front of the kitchen, where she caught a glimpse through parted curtains of Corinne as she moved with ease from sink to stove to fridge, preparing supper. Despite her workload, Corinne had been cooking better and better suppers for them; they had become the highlight of the day. Tonight she had promised to make old-fashioned stew with dumplings, just the way their mother had.

Laura's heart lifted a little. She felt good to be in this new and improved version of home. With a lighter step, she went directly into the kitchen, where her sister was laboring over a pastry board.

Corinne looked up at her approach, and the smile on her face disappeared instantly. "Laura! What's wrong? You look like you've seen a ghost!"

Chapter 13

She laid her rolling pin aside, then went up to Laura and pressed the back of a flour-dusted hand to her forehead. "You're not clammy. How's your stomach?"

"My stomach's fine," Laura said, slipping out from under her sister's scrutiny. So much for disguising her distress. "That smells great, by the way. I'm starving."

"Go wash. You probably haven't eaten a thing all day," Corinne grumbled. "This is why I can't trust you to grab lunch on your own. You don't do it. How'd it go with Kendall Barclay?"

"Oh . . . okay. He could use some work—his garden, I mean."

"Don't I know it. The house is gorgeous; the grounds are a mess. Have been, ever since his mother moved out and he moved in. A gardener he ain't."

Corinne began shaping the dough into a long roll for cutting into thin, chewy dumplings. "I don't know why the man doesn't just break down and hire a service. He can afford it. But no; I see him pushing that ridiculous old hand-mower over that pathetic patch of grass, and I say to myself, why? Why does he bother?"

"Maybe he wants people to feel sorry for him."

"Yeah, right. The most eligible bachelor on the Cape, a

man who's rich, smart, and handsome—who's going to feel sorry for him?"

Laura dipped a spoon into the stew and blew on it to cool it down. "Why hasn't he married?" she asked very casually. "No one in Chepaquit's good enough?"

"Funny you should ask," Corinne said, amused by the very question. "A couple of months ago, I was getting my hair cut at Tess's, and his mother's old cook was going on with one of the hairdressers about him. He's dated plenty of women, but the cook says he's very particular—not that you'd know it, looking at his lawn."

"Well, cheer up about that, at least. He plans to order all of his landscaping needs from Shore Gardens, and he wants you to oversee the planting."

That got Corinne's attention. "Really? Oh, don't toy. *Really?*"

When Laura nodded, she said joyously, "This could be it, Laura—the break we've been looking for! Maybe everyone will take their cue from him and come to us instead of taking their business to Chatham. Maybe they'll stop regarding us like a bunch of weirdos and murderers. Maybe we'll finally get some respect!"

"We'll have a better idea the day after tomorrow," Laura said, not as confident as she'd like to be. "A good crowd would go hand in hand with lots of orders."

"I know what we can do. We can serve more serious treats than cookies. Brownies. I'll make up a few batches and cut them small. We'll have them set up at your seminar on how to dry flowers. That should do it. Now go change, and then call Snack; supper's in fifteen minutes."

She looked so pleased with herself, so hopeful. Laura didn't have the heart to tell her that the real reason she suspected they were getting Ken's landscaping order was so he could talk it over with Laura in bed.

Okay, that was unfair. But for whatever reason, Ken had

a yen, and what did he care if he threw a little business their way to indulge it?

Okay, that was also unfair. Although he seemed mystifyingly attracted to her, Laura had seen evidence that he felt an obligation to his family homestead. His desire to have it properly landscaped seemed sincere. Still, the best way to test that sincerity was to stay out of his bed.

Which was an excellent plan all the way around. "Do I have time to change?" she asked Corinne.

"Laura! Have you heard a thing I said?"

"No," she admitted. "Nothing after the word 'brownies.' "

Ken had to cool down before he punched in the number of his mother's Boston condo. Camille Barclay was very protective of her late husband's memory, and she was convinced that Ken had competitive feelings about his father besides.

Well, she was right. Ken did feel as if he had something to prove. He was determined to be his own man and not just his father's son when it came to running the bank. It was the reason he'd painted it red, the reason he'd pushed for a major upgrade of their data management system.

It was even the reason he'd hesitated about moving back to Triple Oaks, once his mother had made the decision to move to Boston. He didn't want to be a carbon copy of the Old Man; it was such a cliché. But then his mother had gone and called his bluff by threatening to sell out to a developer, so here he was, the owner of the house after all.

And mad as hell. It was one thing to be encouraged and guided and even blackmailed, another thing altogether to have mail intercepted, an answer faked, and his life turned around. Goddammit!

His mother sounded delighted, as she always did, to hear from him. He had to give her credit there; Camille Barclay never nagged if, unlike his sister, Ken happened to slip out of touch for a few weeks. In fact, the only guilt he'd had to endure was over his taking his time on the marriage-and-grandchildren front, and Ken knew that he wasn't alone in his generation to do that.

"Darling, you're going to have to make it fast," she said. "I'm on my way out to dinner."

"All right, I'll cut to the chase. Did Dad once intercept a letter to me and then answer it himself?"

The ripple of cultivated laughter was both reassuring and troubling.

"Ken, your father never opened his own mail. Why would he have opened yours?"

"When I was fourteen."

He expected more laughter, but instead he got silence.

And then, finally, an answer: "No. I'm absolutely sure that your father never did any such thing."

Suddenly someone pulled back the blinds in a back room of Ken's mind, and light began flooding in. "Mother. For God's sake. You were the one."

"Oh, Ken, don't start. I've told you: I'm on my way out the door."

"How could you do that? *Why* would you do that?"

"You were just a boy; you don't remember—"

"The hell I don't!"

"It was an awful event; it could have dogged you for the rest of your life. You meant well, of course you did, but you managed to get involved with the worst sort of—really, I *have* to go," she said. He could see her drawing herself up to her full statuesque five feet and nine inches. "We can discuss this at some other time."

"I'll be up there tomorrow night," he said in a steely voice. "Don't make plans."

"I've made plans."

"Then cancel them."

"I will not! I—"

The regal tone collapsed in a puddle of motherly irritation. "Oh, all right," she said. "This is such a non-issue. But if it makes you feel better to throw a tantrum in front of me instead of over the phone, then fine. Be here."

He hung up in a retroactive fury. As an only son, he'd always had to put up with a certain amount of control and manipulation by both his parents. His father had discouraged his original desire to become a naturalist, and his mother had never given up trying to match him to the Right Sort of woman. He understood and accepted that; they were only being parents.

But this was different. This had been behind his back. The fact that he'd been a kid at the time was irrelevant; this was the first instance he'd seen of either of his parents being guilty of deception. Now, suddenly, he was forced to wonder if there had been other times.

Damn it.

The couple of times that he and Laura had crossed paths in town, she had looked away and then run away. He hadn't run after her because he was tongue-tied and shy. He saw her only one other time, although that time, she hadn't seen him. He'd grown taller by then, and he'd put on some muscle. Didn't matter. He was still tongue-tied and shy.

It wasn't until he went to college and lived free of parental and private-school constraints that he'd had a chance to grow and bloom. He went a little wild, his grades sank, he ran a risk of being kicked out as a classic non-performer. But he turned it around in time and graduated with honors and, more importantly, with a minor in ornithology. Laura was long gone by then.

Had he been happy since? He hadn't been *un*happy. But now all bets were off. When he finally went to bed, the same bed that he'd so fleetingly shared with Laura just hours before, he was aware that he was more miserable than he ever had been as a geeky little rich snot in Chepaquit Elementary.

And he didn't like the feeling at all.

• • •

"It's some kind of plot, that's what it is."

"No, it's some kind of blown gasket. I'll go to town, get a new one, replace the lost hydraulic fluid, and we'll be back in business."

Laura, Snack, and Corinne were standing in front of the ancient John Deere tractor, which looked as if someone had come during the night and stabbed it to death: a pool of dark liquid stained the rich earth beneath it.

"But the tractor was working fine last night when you were moving the compost," Laura said, ready to scream. "How could it just go and collapse in the middle of the night?"

"It's old. It's tired. I've been flogging it for days."

Corinne said, "Whether or not you finish moving the compost, we need the tractor. We have to fix it, Snack. We won't be able to move or load any of the bigger shrubs or trees without it," she went on, her voice getting higher and more anxious. "What if you can't get the right gasket?"

"I'll get it, I'll fix it, you'll have it, *okay*?"

"That'd be great, Snack," Laura said in a soothing tone. "Just . . . do what you can."

She was worried about him. He'd been doing the work of two men, and the strain was beginning to show. The compost project was taking far too long for him, and he'd become increasingly snappish; even Corinne's hearty stew the night before hadn't been enough to restore his mood.

It was a stretch to picture him in twenty-four hours wearing a clown's outfit and twisting balloons into cute little animals for kids. A real stretch. Laura gently set her hand-wringing sister back to pricing the truckload of annuals that had just arrived; gave her brother some money for town; and went back to the house and her laptop, where she was preparing a list of gardening dos and don'ts.

After the sale—and assuming Shore Gardens was still

in business—she intended to compose a Tip of the Week ad for the nursery in the *Chatham Herald*. It was a great way to establish brand loyalty with the gardeners in the area, and once she was back in Portland and getting paid again, the cost of carrying the ads would be nothing for her.

She sat back down at her father's desk and continued plugging away. She already had a list of Top Ten Dos for the Garden to pass out; but she wanted to include the Top Ten Don'ts. She composed at a feverish pace and didn't look up until the printer began spewing the pale green printed pages. She pulled one off the top and looked it over.

1. *Don't water your roses at night; you'll encourage blackspot.*
2. *Don't plant your tulip bulbs in holes that are shallow; you won't get a second season of bloom.*
3. *Don't use chemical pesticides if you want earthworms to make your soil rich. And bees to pollinate your flowers. And birds to feed on the seedpods.*
4. *Don't plant sun-loving flowers anywhere where they can't get four to six hours of sun a day; they'll sulk and just won't bloom.*

Don't don't don't.

Don't think about him.

Don't think about yesterday.

Don't think about his touch, his kiss, his vow to get to the bottom of the letter mystery.

Don't.

Laura proofread the rest of her tips and set the stack aside. Next up: tip sheets for her dried-flowers workshop. She was gratified that the class would be full. Twenty-one women—including Miss Widdich!—had paid the ten-dollar fee, which barely covered the cost of the supplies. It was part of doing business, and Laura understood that, but still. It would be awfully nice if they managed to come out of the week with anything close to a profit.

No one ever promised you a rose garden, her mother used to say. It was kind of a family joke. But Laura needed success, money, and, yes, that rose garden, so she had gone off in search of the good life. She had found herself a city, a job; for a while, a man. But now, looking out the window at the bounty of the nursery and beyond it at the sea, she had to wonder whether she'd made the right choices in life, after all.

Don't.

She brushed away her doubts like aphids off a rose and got back to work, and she didn't look up from her laptop until she heard three easy raps on the open door to the den.

He was standing there with his arms crossed and leaning against the doorjamb, big and broad-shouldered and looking about as un-geeky as a man can get. There was something about his smile—something in the anticipation she saw there—that made Laura feel it right down to her toes.

Chapter 14

"Welcome to our humble home," Laura said—and she wasn't just being modest.

"It's a really nice old house. Good bones. I've never been in it before."

"That's true." She left it at that.

"All ready for your big day tomorrow?"

"Is that why you're here? To find out?"

"Nope."

"I didn't think so," she admitted, almost rigid with awareness of him.

He strolled over to where she was sitting. She watched him carefully, as conscious of his thick brown hair as she was of the threadbare brown fabric of her chair.

She said, "Gee, you're not at work."

"Banker's hours, remember?"

"Oh, right. Whereas over here, we're working our buns off." She gave him a too-perky, too-tense smile and said, "Isn't that just the way?"

"Is there anything I can do to help you?" he asked.

Go away. Leave here. Vamoose. Before I forget everything I am and want to be and have to be. Beat it. Scat. Shoo.

With unbending politeness, she declined his offer.

"Thanks very much, but I think I have things under control. I'm certain of it, in fact."

"Well . . . good," he answered, but her tone was clearly throwing him off balance. He seemed unsure, suddenly, of how to proceed. He began fiddling with the pens and pencils that were stuffed in a chipped mug on the desk, rattling them until they all fit more upright.

"I . . . ah . . . wanted you to know that, in the best tradition of Sherlock Holmes, I have figured out who wrote you that letter way back when."

"Really! How did you do that so fast?"

He said wryly, "I picked up the phone. It wasn't my father who wrote it, incidentally."

"Ah. Your mother, then."

" 'Fraid so. It was a surprise to me. It was my father who'd been on top of the situation. I can't remember my mother's reaction at all, other than an understandable sense of distress at seeing her kid with a split lip and a black eye."

"Maybe she was afraid that I had designs on you."

"Obviously she was afraid that you had designs on me," he said with disarming candor, then added, "You didn't, did you? By any chance?"

The hopeful look on his face left Laura absolutely smitten. He was such a charming mix of cockiness and naïveté. She'd never known anyone like him.

"Ken, I was thirteen years old," she said, trying not to smile.

"I know. I know." He frowned and said, "You don't happen to remember anything from the letter *you* wrote, do you? Since you apparently memorized my mother's?"

She could have lied and said no, but there was something satisfying about having the chance to let him know, at last, how grateful she'd felt all those years ago.

"If I told you, your head would swell and you'd become stuck-up," she went as far as saying.

"Me? Ha. I doubt it."

Now it was her turn to sigh. She already knew him well enough to realize that arrogance wasn't part of his makeup. She'd had him pegged so wrong. All those years. So wrong.

She owed him at least one apology. "The first time I saw you in town after I got that letter," she explained, "I saw your face turn all red when you spotted me. I figured that you were embarrassed by having got involved in such a foolish mission. So after that, I avoided you."

"I had that feeling," he murmured. "And, boy, am I ever sorry to know I was right."

He sat back against the edge of her desk and stroked her cheek in a cloud-soft caress. "If you hadn't run . . . if you hadn't misinterpreted my red face . . . would we maybe have gone to a movie together?" he asked, smiling.

"I doubt it," she said, despite that look. Because it was true.

"Might we have . . . fooled around in the library stacks, maybe?"

She laughed and said, "Without being caught by Mrs. Roberts? Not a chance."

He rubbed his chin, then came up with yet another scenario. "If you had taken sailing lessons, we could have raced together—or even against one another. Heck, I'm easy: I would've let you win."

She blinked. Was he really so oblivious to the differences in their lifestyles back then? "I don't recall that my parents ever belonged to the yacht club," she said dryly.

"You didn't have to belong. Anyone local could have signed up for lessons."

"For free?"

"Well—not for *free*."

"Then I wouldn't have signed up. I wouldn't have signed up, anyway, Ken. We were not only dirt poor—literally—but we worked very long hours."

"Ah. Like now."

"Oh, we're not *that* poor, anymore," she quipped.

He laughed and said, "Okay, I can take a hint; I'll get out of your hair. I know everything's riding on this week. I liked your ad in the *Herald*, by the way: 'Visit us again for the first time.' Very nice."

"Thank you, sir," she said, ridiculously pleased that he'd noticed. She stood up to walk him to the door. It was the least she could do, since he'd stopped by specifically to clear up the mystery of the purloined letter.

"How did you know where to find me?" she asked on their way out. She wanted him to say "by telepathy," so that she could take it as some kind of sign.

But he didn't. "I went to the shop, and Corinne gave me precise instructions: down the hall after the kitchen; second left is the office."

"Well . . . thanks for letting me know that you've cracked the case. I hope there wasn't a dust-up over this," she added, but not with much conviction. How *could* his mother have done something like that? It was so deeply offensive to know the truth.

"The dust-up is yet to come," he said, suddenly grim. "I see my mother later."

Laura winced, and he said, "Don't worry. No blood will be shed in the slaying of this illusion."

"I'm glad to hear it. It was a long time ago."

At the front door, he seemed reluctant to go, which pleased Laura much too much.

He said, "You know, the town's really abuzz about you and Snack coming back and pitching in to put the place in order. The Shore kids, together again—everyone's intrigued. I think the citizens of Chepaquit are really rooting for the nursery to stay in business."

"Maybe they'll actually give us some, then. That would be nice."

Part of her hated to see him leave. The other part was holding her breath until he did.

Suddenly she blurted, "Will you be dropping by tomorrow?"

God in heaven! Where had *that* come from?

"Wild horses couldn't keep me. I'd bring you a good-luck plant for your grand reopening, but I guess you've got that base pretty well covered. On the other hand," he said softly, "maybe *this* will get my point across."

He bent his head down and kissed her, a long, lingering kiss that sent a warm, delicious thrill through her. She wanted to pull away, but couldn't make herself do it.

"Point . . . well taken," she whispered against his lips.

He kissed her again, lightly this time. "Good luck. See ya tomorrow."

He turned and took the steps quickly, and Laura had to make herself close the screen door and not look as if she were memorizing the man as he left.

She moved out of view and, leaning against the nearest wall, hugged herself. He had come there just to see her: Kendall Barclay, ex-knight, there to see Laura Shore, ex–wench-in-distress. He had done exactly what he said he'd do: got to the bottom of the false letter. And not only that, but he seemed truly interested in coming back.

The only question was: why?

At dawn the next morning, Corinne did not have to go around banging on bedroom doors; Snack and Laura were up, dressed, and ready to go. The air was so thick with anticipation that it was obvious to all of them when they'd last shared that feeling together.

"Christmas mornings," said Laura. "Remember how we'd sneak down in the dark, and so would Mom, and we'd all have hot chocolate together before Dad got up?"

"Do I," said Snack with an uncharacteristically nostalgic sigh. "I still can't smell hot chocolate without thinking of ribbons and tags."

"Hey, I know! Let's have some, just like the old days," Corinne said in the middle of frying bacon. "I think I have a can of cocoa around somewhere."

Snack laughed and paddled his clown nose with his open hand, dancing nimbly around the kitchen to keep the game going. "What're you, nuts? It's already seventy degrees out; it's Memorial Day, not Christmas Day," he said, keeping his eye on the bouncing nose.

"So what? I won't make it super-hot. It'll be ceremonial."

"I'll make it," Laura said, surprised by her own enthusiasm for the idea. She found that she was aching for that connection to her past, to her mother, to all the good things that were and might have been. She began rummaging through the cupboards for the cocoa.

"Someone said that there was a huge crowd at the opening ceremonies down at the gazebo yesterday," Corinne told her. "Huge."

"Because the weather's been so unbelievably nice."

"But we don't want it to be *too* hot, or no one will come."

"It's never too hot to buy the plants; just too hot to plant the plants."

"I don't know why I'm worrying; the way the morning feels, we'll have a sea breeze for sure. There's no better place to be than Shore Gardens on a hot day; we catch every whiff of air."

"Tell that to people on the Vineyard."

"Oh, *well*—the Vineyard."

"And Nantucket. And Block Island. Not to mention Cutty Hunk. People on the islands all have cooler breezes than ours."

"Oh, what do they know?" Corinne said, dismissing them with a wave of her spatula. "They all live in Boston and New York most of the year, anyway."

"Whereas you, my little townie, get to live here all year long," Laura acknowledged.

At that moment, in that kitchen, with a breeze beginning to lift the new sheer curtains that she had bought on impulse, Laura could easily believe that Corinne Shore was the luckiest girl on earth. "Just make sure you never give up this day job," she said, patting her sister's fanny with a wooden spoon.

Corinne bumped hips with her and smiled. "Not a chance . . . now."

Ten minutes later, they were sitting down to a farmer's breakfast that was designed to carry them through the day: oatmeal, bacon, eggs, biscuits, juice, and fruit, all served in heaping abundance by the maternal one among them.

But it was Laura who carried the cups of hot chocolate to the table, Laura who raised their mother's angel mug in a toast.

"To the Three Musketeers of Shore Gardens," she said, tapping each of the others' mugs in turn.

"One for all," Corinne added, "and all for one."

Snack lifted his clown nose high above his head and squeaked it twice. "Hear, hear."

They sipped in unison. It was a moment as happy, as hopeful, and as selfless as any that Laura had experienced in her life. In a burst of pride and flush with newfound emotion, she said, "I love you guys, you know that?"

Corinne smiled and said simply, "Sure we do."

Snack groaned and rolled his eyes. "You had to go and get mushy."

Grinning, Laura said, "You love us too. Admit it."

"Do not."

"Do too."

"Do not."

"Do too."

He let Laura have the last word, and that made her feel warm and gratified.

After breakfast, the others went out, and Laura cleaned up the dishes humming a tune. On the family front, life was good. Snack had evolved, during the weeks that they had spent together. He was drinking so much less now. His moods still shifted wildly, of course; he'd never tolerated frustration very well, and that was unlikely to change. But he smiled more easily, and the little boy popped out often from behind the brooding gaze.

If he could find a good woman, Snack would be all set.

As for Corinne, it looked as if she may have found her man, and wouldn't you know? It was the boy right next door.

Despite her low expectations about men in general, Laura's fingers were crossed for her sister. It was heartening to see that Gabe had begun hanging around the nursery during the late afternoons, lending a hand, helping Corinne with stock. Laura sometimes heard them laughing together in the greenhouses, the kind of laugh that has a flirty, sexy edge to it. It didn't take a rocket scientist to figure *that* one out.

Laura was also relieved that Gabe and Snack had apparently patched it up, although she had no idea which of the two had made the first move. Knowing men—neither. Probably the two of them had simply decided to behave as if the near-fight had never happened.

She was able so easily to imagine all of them gathered together at their farmhouse on the hill during holidays, laughing, eating, getting along. That was the most important part of her idyll: that they be getting along. If they were able to do that, they'd be the first in a generation. (Their murderous Uncle Norbert most likely hadn't been very good company, and all of them knew personally what his brother had been like.)

It had begun to hit Laura that it was time—past the time, really—for the Shore sisters to marry, to have children, to begin renewing the Chepaquit branch of the clan. Hopefully, Corinne would do just that.

As for Laura . . .

She thought of Max, but not with any sadness, because the idea of having children with him had somehow never been compelling. It was the first time that Laura had admitted it to herself, and she experienced a sudden, sharp feeling of grief: for the children that she never wanted to have with Max.

What was wrong with her? Was she missing a maternal gene or something? All of her adult life, her one desire had been to be financially and emotionally independent. Given her mother's situation, it seemed a logical goal.

But now, suddenly, here she was, obsessing about her biological clock! Of all the irrelevant daydreams!

It was all Ken's fault. He was playing havoc with her emotions; messing with her head. Or her heart. She wasn't sure which.

She tried to tell herself that her attraction to him was nothing more than a dramatic rebound from Max. Or that she was working through a leftover teenage crush. Or even that she was being insecure and vindictive and trying to get back at Ken's mother by seducing her son. She was ready to buy any theory except the scary one: that she might genuinely be falling for the guy.

No way. Clearly the answer had to be a, b, or c.

Methodically, Laura put away the iron frying pan and drained and scrubbed the sink. Today was not about Ken. Today was about Shore Gardens, and pleasing the customers enough to make certain that they'd come back.

Was that so hard?

She could do that.

Chapter 15

Their first customer was an hour early and came with her own carload of plants: Miss Widdich had agreed to sell Shore Gardens eight dozen herbs to bolster their already depleted stock.

Laura was impressed by the robust health of Miss Widdich's plants; their roots were punching their way out of the waterholes in the three-inch pots. Nonetheless, she felt uneasy about buying from the woman; she didn't know why.

Corinne pooh-poohed her reluctance. "It's not as if we need FDA approval of the plants, for Pete's sake. They're *plants*."

Interestingly, Snack had even greater reservations than Laura. "We don't know what kind of hybrids the old lady's created. Just because she says something is tarragon—"

Corinne was getting in a snit by now. "Well, at least we know it's not marijuana," she said as she added the new arrivals to their stock on an outside table. "I saw enough of your plants to be able to tell the difference."

Taken aback, Snack said, "How did you know I used to grow weed?"

"Please. The things towered six feet into the air. You couldn't exactly miss them."

"Those were for private consumption," Snack muttered. "I was never a dealer."

"Neither is Miss Widdich! What is this thing you have against her? You remind me of certain good citizens of Salem."

Laura hardly heard their bickering, tense exchange. She was browsing through the handwritten ID stakes in the pots and becoming even more uneasy.

Sylvia Savory. Silver Sylvia. Sylvia Sage. At least five of the herbs were tagged with the name, obviously bestowed on them by Miss Widdich herself.

"We're a little heavy on Sylvias here," she mentioned to the others. She rattled off some of the labels.

Corinne shrugged and said, "Sylvia is a good horticultural name. Doesn't it mean 'woods'?"

"Most herbs don't grow in the woods. They need sun. Lots of it. It's not the most logical name to use. Here's what I was thinking—does anybody remember Sylvia Mendan? That gorgeous girl who worked here for a couple of months one summer and then suddenly quit and moved on? Remember? Dad was in a black mood for weeks after she left. *Her* name was Sylvia."

Laura was remembering how disappointed Miss Widdich had been that she, and not Sylvia, had been the one to deliver a dozen fragrant white roses on that foggy summer solstice. It had seemed odd at the time; it seemed even odder now.

Corinne said, "But that was a million years ago; Miss Widdich couldn't possibly remember someone who came and went through here so fast. I imagine she's thinking of someone more recent, if she's thinking of a specific person at all."

"Of course she has someone in mind," Laura argued. "Horticulturalists name plants after specific people all the time."

"I don't see what any of this has to do with us—but if you're so curious, then *ask* her."

"I can't. I'm not her friend the way you are. You ask her. But do it in front of me. I want to see her reaction."

"No! It's too personal. If she'd wanted to explain, she would have. You're the one who seems obsessed with Sylvia Mendan, not Miss—"

"Will you two knock it off? Jesus!"

Laura glanced at Snack, who immediately looked at his watch. "Look, am I supposed to bring down the damned prunus or not?" he snapped. "I've got a lot to do before the opening gun—unless you two plan to find someone else to be your fucking clown."

Whoa. Was that why he was being so testy? Because he dreaded putting on the harmlessly silly clown suit?

Somehow . . . Laura didn't think so.

"No, forget about the prunus," Corinne said, easily as edgy as he. "The plums and the cherries are done blooming, anyway. But why don't you bring down a few shrubs? Say, two or three daphnes, and maybe one or two viburnums. We'll put them near the entry so that people will pick up on the fragrance."

Snack turned to go, but Corinne added, "I suppose, bring a couple of the weigelas too. The buds will give us a shot of color, even though the blooms aren't open yet. As for any trees . . . the weeping ones would have the most impact now. Two of those. We'll move the rest of the trees to their new spot tomorrow."

With an impatient sigh, Snack marched off, only to be called back again by Corinne. "Do you really think you'll have the compost area scraped clear to use for a display area by then?"

"I will if I don't have to stand around *here* all day."

"Go, then; go. I know you're almost done," said Corinne.

Snack practically jogged out of the greenhouse in his

dash for the tractor. Corinne looked concerned. "Is that just enthusiasm, do you think?"

"Hard to say. I wish I knew," Laura murmured.

"Oh, there you both are," came a voice behind them. It was Miss Widdich herself, leaning on her cane and struggling with a gallon pot of Saint-John's-Wort, its cream-and-pink marbled leaves spilling luxuriously over the edges. "Would you be able to ring this up for me, even though you're not open yet? I don't have this variegated version, and I must say, it's stunning. This one is all you have?"

Laura recognized that had-to-have gleam in Miss Widdich's eye; collectors were like that, whether it was a Hummel or a hypericum that they were after.

"I'm afraid that's the last one," she said. "But it will fill out so fast; it should get you started, at least. You don't have to pay for it, Miss Widdich," she added. "Consider it a gift for helping us out."

"Thank you. Then I'll be on my way. I want to get this in the ground, and a bit more done, while it's still cool. It's going to be a scorcher—for May, anyway."

"Another record, I'll bet. And still no rain in sight," Corinne fretted. "Oh, *why* didn't I stock more drought-tolerant plants?" Shading her eyes, she scanned the blue, sunny sky in a fruitless search for clouds.

Laura said, "You did fine, Rinnie. We have plenty of low-water plants. People are going to buy the biggest bloomers, anyway—no matter what the season's forecast."

Corinne's confidence seemed to be drooping under the rising sun, and Laura could see why. This was it, their moment of truth: they were betting the ranch on having a great sell-through during Founders Week. Although serious gardeners had been shopping and planting since April, the more fair-weather types, and certainly the summer people, didn't get going until Memorial Day weekend.

"I'll carry this to your car for you," Laura volunteered.

Miss Widdich took her up on her offer. "Thank you,

dear. I think I overdid, the other day in the garden."

Or something. From old lady to Amazon to old lady again in a couple of weeks: the difference in Miss Widdich's condition was more than a strained muscle or two. Either she had been faking being strong, or she was faking being weak. It didn't take a physical therapist to figure out which was more doable.

Miss Widdich sighed heavily. "And to think I once planted a row of eight-foot-high arborvitae for a side hedge. By myself. And now I can't even carry a pot. Never get old, Laura; never get old."

"Oh, I don't know," Laura said as she loaded the plant in the trunk. "It's better than the alternative."

She was being flip, but the remark went over like a lead balloon. Miss Widdich gave her a withering look and said sharply, "What is *that* supposed to mean?"

"It's just an expression, Miss Widdich," Laura said, backing off quickly. "I didn't mean anything by it."

Astonishing, how the woman was able to turn Laura into a teenager quaking in her shoes again.

Laura gave her an intimidated smile and said, "I'll see you this afternoon at the workshop?"

Please let her stay home with her dolls and her pins.

"I'll be there—if I live that long," Miss Widdich said darkly, and she slammed the trunk of her big black Ford.

Jitters, Laura decided. For whatever reason, there was a plague of them going around. She herself felt as though she were backstage on opening night. What if they didn't come? What if they came and didn't like what they saw?

Take us or leave us, folks, she wanted to shout. *Just make up your minds so that Corinne can get on with her life.*

And by the way, that goes for me, too, damn it.

By ten-thirty, the lot was full, the help—Melissa—was overwhelmed, and Laura was in a state of shock. Everyone in Chepaquit seemed to be there, eating cookies, drinking coffee, collecting balloon animals—and buying everything in sight.

Billy was staggering around like a dancing bear, emptying wagons, loading cars, and generally acting as traffic control officer. His gap-toothed welcome was as cheery as any Wal-Mart greeter's as he flagged cars into tighter and tighter parking spots.

Snack, amazingly, seemed to fit right in with the lively carnival atmosphere. Orange and chartreuse suited him well, and so did big giant feet. He squeaked, he honked, he hammed it up. The kids loved him, even though his balloon creations looked more like aliens than dachshunds. During the lulls—there weren't many—he drove the old green Deere, still wearing his big giant feet, back and forth between the far reaches of the nursery and the loading area, bringing back more stuff to sell.

He hadn't quite finished clearing the compost pile, but it hardly mattered: there wasn't time to set up a proper display of trees, anyway. Besides, people seemed to enjoy roaming the different sections of the nursery, probably as much for the view of the sea and the cool breeze as anything else. What was not to like?

As for Corinne, she was everywhere at once, giving advice, ringing up sales, hunting down just the right plant for just the right person. Freckle-faced and flushed with joy, she couldn't look more radiant if she were wearing a wedding dress and leaving a church. It was a thrill for Laura to see.

Gabe was there and lending a hand, which might have had something to do with Corinne's joy. He had walked across the road shortly after they'd opened their doors for business, and almost immediately, Corinne had drafted him as her assistant. Gabe didn't know much about horticulture, but he was willing and able to find more boxes and trays, snug up the pots to eliminate the gaps on the tables, and do whatever it was that a guy Friday was supposed to do and still maintain a councilman's dignity.

It helped that Gabe knew everyone in town; he was able to talk up the nursery and encourage each citizen, by name, to go out and drag back his or her friends. People teased him about running for mayor a year early and handed over their babies for him to kiss. And meanwhile, his big, gentle mutt Baskerville ran around and barked at the birds and slobbered over the kids who took the time to pet him.

Even Miss Widdich had somehow managed to make herself not only pleasant, but useful. She planted herself, cane and all, next to the table that featured her herbs and took it upon herself to advise browsers on the fine art of herbal medicine and cookery. Never mind that all most of them wanted was a simple pot of basil or chives; Miss Widdich was a fount of facts, and she wasn't afraid to spout them. After hearing her, Laura was sorry that she hadn't invited her to conduct a seminar on herbs.

Maybe next year.

Through it all, Laura kept a weather eye out for Kendall Barclay III. She spotted his assistant among the customers, and a teller from the bank was there too. But the president of Chepaquit Savings was a no-show so far. It was disappointing at first, crushing by lunch. She wanted Ken to witness their amazing turnaround! He would be pleased that his bank's money had been so wisely invested.

Besides that, she wanted him to be there because . . . she wanted him to be there. Period. He had said he would come, and he was a man of his word; she believed in him instinctively now. So she searched for him among her customers, and watched for his car, and tried to be as enthusiastic about the glorious day as her sister was, although she wasn't quite able to match her level.

Laura's late lunch was a half-melted PowerBar that she

had been carrying in her pocket, and a handful of her sister's oatmeal cookies, which sounded healthier than they were. The dried-flowers workshop was coming up. If Ken arrived during it, Laura would miss him.

She put her disappointment aside as she set up the materials for her event, because she knew that a woman did not have the right to be crushed simply because the holder of her loan didn't show up.

She was joined by her sister, who came rushing into the greenhouse bearing a tray of brownies. Corinne was out of breath and on the run.

"Believe it or not," she said as she laid out napkins and paper cups next to the coffee urn on a rickety card table, "someone has just applied for a job here. Lucy something. Nice girl. She's worked at nurseries before. Sounds pretty knowledgeable. Not like Melissa. I think Lucy has appeared as a blessing. I told her to get to work and we'd worry about the paperwork later."

"Oh, *Rin*," Laura argued. "Was that really a good idea? What about liability, what about—?"

Corinne waved away her sister's fears. "It's not as if she's going to fall overboard and drown or something. For heaven's sake—this is a nursery. What could possibly happen?"

"She could pull her back; she could fall under the tractor—which is the number one reason of death in this type of workplace, incidentally," Laura pointed out.

"She didn't look like the type to sue." Corinne picked up a brownie and offered it to her sister. "Here. Chocolate. It'll soothe your nerves. You have pre-presentation jitters, that's all. Stop being so negative; you just have to trust."

The last thing that Laura could easily do.

But she took the brownie and hugged her sister. "You're so damn much better than I'll ever be," she said, her voice suddenly husky and emotional.

Startled into laughter, Corinne said, "What was *that* all about?"

"You. You're so full of hope. But you're a *Shore*. Where do you get it from?"

"Come to church with me next time and see," Corinne quipped. "What, would it kill you to break away from here for an hour?"

"It's not church. You were always like that. You were the shyest and yet somehow managed to be the most optimistic."

"Maybe the two things go hand in hand," Corinne said lightly. "It's easy to be hopeful when you don't know what's out there—"

Her face broke into a sudden happy grin. Laura turned and saw Gabe Wellerton entering the greenhouse with a man who she thought looked vaguely familiar.

Gabe met Corinne's grin with one of his own and matched her ebullience. "Ladies, I want you to meet someone who can throw a hell of a lot of business your way: Joe Penchance. He's certainly thrown it my way; as you know, I'm doing all the fences for his Bayview Estates development."

"Ah, that must be where I've seen you," said Laura to their visitor as they all shook hands.

Her response to him was predictably schizophrenic. He was a developer, after all, which automatically made him one of the enemy in her book. But on the other hand, someone like him could make the difference as to whether Shore Gardens would be able to stay afloat or not.

Better to be nice, for now. "I hope you've had a chance to look around the nursery, Mr. Penchance. We have quite a bit of stock, but it's somewhat spread out."

"I've been roaming all over the place," he said with a congenial smile. "It's a big place. Prime acreage."

He was probably pacing it off and figuring out how many houses he could squeeze in.

"If we don't have what you need," Laura said, smiling, "Corinne certainly can order it for you."

Penchance nodded and said, "Trees. Small, decorative trees."

"Not large shade trees?"

He sighed and said, "Generally the homebuyers go for the pretty ones, not the big ones. Maybe they don't have the patience to wait for a tree to mature. It's too bad. I'm with you on planting shade trees if there's room: people ought to plant for the generations ahead of them."

"But the customer is always right," Laura said laconically. "Isn't that what we keep saying, Corinne?"

Poor Corinne. She was like a fieldmouse searching for grains of corn to keep from starving while a hawk sat on a branch overhead, watching and waiting. She nodded nervously but didn't say a word to their hovering visitor.

What an incredible change in her in the space of sixty seconds.

Laura and Penchance exchanged pleasantries about the terrific turnout, and then the developer smiled at them both and said, "Well, I'd better find my little girl and my wife before the clown runs out of balloons—and you run out of geraniums."

"Well! That doesn't sound so terrible," Laura quipped.

They left, and she said in a musing aside to her sister, "Not so terrible at all."

All of the sign-ups, including Miss Widdich, were present by ten minutes before the appointed hour, so Laura used the extra time for the students to introduce themselves.

Totally unnecessary. Everyone seemed to know everyone, and despite the fact that they were all new faces to Laura, most of them knew her. Or at least, of her. She felt surprisingly notorious. After all, she was the niece of a murderer. In a small village like Chepaquit, that counted for something.

Well, let them satisfy their curiosity about her. She was filled with wry resignation. They'd plunked down good money for the right to know whether or not she ran true to seed like her murderous forebears, and she was going to give them a full hour to decide for themselves.

All things considered, Laura was glad she'd taken the time to duck into the house and change from work khakis to a challis jumper that she'd found on one of her dashes into T.J. Maxx. She felt pretty in lavender. And she felt confident that she knew more about flowers and how to dry them than anyone else in her audience. She felt everything . . . but happy.

Where was he? He said he'd be there.

She put the thought of Ken aside as gently as she would a dried pansy, and then she turned her attention to the class.

Chapter 16

A minor plumbing crisis at the bank made him late, so Ken had to decide whether or not to crash Laura's seminar on dried flowers.

Twenty women.

Shriveled plants.

Nope.

He compromised by parking himself, with a cup of coffee, on a broken-down bench just outside the greenhouse where Laura was giving her talk. Sipping the surprisingly good brew, he sat back and listened to the sound of her voice rather than to her actual words. By now he was so besotted that she could have been explaining the easiest way to rob a bank. He wouldn't have been any the wiser.

She was irresistible. Each time he saw her, she struck him as more beautiful. He remembered reading that once a person had been successfully hypnotized, the person hypnotized more and more easily. That was him, all right. Completely under her spell. He wanted her more than any woman he'd ever known.

Too soon, too soon, knucklehead. You've hardly spent any time with her.

However: at least it was spent in bed.

Yeah, but it was spent straightening out a pathetic misunderstanding.

Whatever. At least it was spent in bed.

She let herself be carried away by you. Literally. That doesn't mean she'd let you do it again.

Like hell.

Why? Why her?

Now that was the million-dollar question. The easy answer was that Laura Shore was an attractive, sexy woman—but he'd been with plenty of attractive and sexy women before. What was it about this one that had him sharing a broken-down bench with a dozen potted ferns just to be able to hear the sound of her *voice*?

Well, they shared a history; there was that. A traumatic history. And from a formative, vulnerable time in their lives. Maybe that was it. He had thought about her a lot over the years, wondering how she was doing, how her life was working out. He knew from Corinne that Laura had gone west to find her fortune and that she'd done well . . . but still he wondered.

And now here she was, right back in Chepaquit. And single. And apparently attracted to him. He broke into a private, irrepressible grin. Laura Shore had had such a profound effect on him that he was happy just to be hearing her telling her audience how to do something or other with paper towels.

So it was all the more exasperating when he heard Gabe's big hound just a few feet away, wrecking the show: Baskerville had a bark straight out of hell, and the name to back it up.

Ken let out an irritated sigh. He wasn't able to hear Laura over the dog's din, and presumably neither could anyone in her class. He went around to the other side of the greenhouse to quiet the animal, who was alternately barking and growling as he pawed and dug at the edge of what was left of the compost pile that Snack was in the process of relocating. The dog was downright gleeful with the thrill of some discovery.

"Hey! Bass! C'mere, boy . . . c'mon," Ken said, modulating his voice as he approached the dog. "What d'ya got there, boy, huh? C'mere. Give it here."

Yeah, right; as if. Baskerville had found himself a bone. It was still stuck in the ground, but it wouldn't be there for long. The dog now had it solidly in his jaw as he worried it back and forth, all the while keeping one eye on Ken as he approached, and warning him off with an occasional growl.

At least he wasn't barking anymore. Ken crouched down at a respectful distance for a better look. Damned big bone, he thought. From what? A horse? A cow? It wouldn't be surprising; the land had been farmed long before it became a nursery. He watched, fascinated, as the dog worked at freeing his half-buried treasure, pawing the ground around it. The compost was rich and crumbly and easily worked. In short order, Baskerville had what he was after.

Gripping the bone—which looked like a fragment, at that—the big shaggy dog went loping off, no doubt to bury it someplace else.

Curious now, Ken walked over to the edge of the small mound of earth to check it out. He had a pal in Hyannis, of all places, who was a cowboy wannabe and had outfitted his den with Western paraphernalia. Pete would get a kick out of having a cattle skull perched on his humongous new HDTV.

Ken toed around in Baskerville's spot and soon came up with the rest of the bones, brown and wormy with age. His mood began morphing from curious to chilled, even before he found the shreds of cloth. And when he found the skull, that's when he knew: it wasn't a cow or a horse or a sheep from a New England farm that had been buried here.

It was somebody's deadly secret.

Ken had shown up at last! And none too soon.

Laura was relieved to see him calm Gabe's barking dog.

Friendly or not, the animal had been making a shambles of her class. But it was quiet now. Life could proceed.

"Before we begin to arrange the dried flowers that I've provided for the workshop," she said, "does anyone have any questions?"

A hand shot up. Rosie Nedworth, who used to run Chepaquit Dry Cleaners and who used to be (and probably still was) the town's biggest gossip, said, "What if we're not ready to use the flowers for a while after we press them in the paper towels? I belong to a Christmas crafts club, and we don't start our projects until after everyone's kids and grandkids are back in school."

"No problem," Laura answered. "After they've dried, a good way to store pressed flowers until you're ready to use them is to leave them between the paper towels and then slide the whole shebang—very carefully!—into a plastic sheet protector. You can get them at any office supply store."

"I suppose that would work," Rosie said grudgingly. "But you said we could do these projects practically for free. I don't want to be running to any office supply stores."

"Well, another way would be to use waxed paper instead of the—"

The rest of Laura's sentence was cut short by the eruption of a furious dogfight just outside the greenhouse. Laura ran out ahead of the others in time to see Gabe's big mutt going at it with another, smaller dog that she hadn't seen before. She was shocked; Corinne had told her that Gabe's dog was the most gentle, easygoing animal she knew.

Gentle or not, it was a scary fight. Laura went running for the nearest hose to turn on them, but luckily the owner of the new dog wasn't far from the scene. He came racing up to the brawl screaming, "Dutch, Dutch, cut it out!"

At the same time, Laura saw Gabe appear out of nowhere and fearlessly nab his much larger dog by the collar.

Baskerville, that was its name; she remembered it now.

"You dope!" he admonished the animal. "Wassamatter with you?"

Someone else, a boy of about ten, piped up with the answer. "They were fighting over that bone. I saw it. The big dog had it first," he said, like some witness to a fender bender.

"You don't get enough bones at home?" Gabe said in a scolding and yet tolerant, dogs-will-be-dogs tone. Gingerly, he picked up the big, dirt-covered bone and began heading for a nearby trash barrel.

"Gabe, don't pitch that!" Ken yelled from behind Laura.

Later, Laura was able to pinpoint the exact moment that her newly fixed-up world began falling back apart again.

It was when a confused Gabe yelled back to Ken and said, "Why not?"

And Ken muttered behind her, "They'll need it."

"For what?" she said, turning to Ken.

"Evidence, possibly."

Laura followed his gaze downward and saw a human skull; it made her turn away so violently that Ken had to steady her.

"Oh, God . . . it's a man," she said in a ghastly croak.

"Or a woman."

A woman? Could her Uncle Norbert have killed two of them? That was Laura's instinctive, appalling thought—that if he could kill a wife, he could kill a lover.

It will start all over again.

She hardly had time to speculate any further than that, because Gabe had reached them with Baskerville's bone.

"What's up?" he asked, and then, after he looked down: "Jesus."

Ken said, "Keep it quiet. I'll call Chief Mellon." He got

out his cell phone and punched in a number.

In the meantime, Baskerville was barking and tugging furiously at his collar despite Gabe's commands. Gabe dropped the bone with the others and then kicked some dirt over the skull to hide it.

"I've gotta get this guy home," he told them, and he began hauling Baskerville away from the scene.

Snack had been outside entertaining a group of kids and had seen the ruckus. He came over, took one look at the bones, and let out a single, ghastly, sick sound. Then, without a word to either of them, he turned and headed for the house.

Maybe he wanted to change out of his clown clothes—because, God knew, they suddenly looked out of place. Or maybe he was just going somewhere to be sick: even with his theatrical makeup, Laura could see that he was getting nauseous.

She looked around for Corinne and saw her pulling a loaded wagon for an elderly customer. Corinne would have to be told, obviously—but, in the meantime, there was the seminar.

Falling in behind Rosie Nedworth like chicks behind a hen, the attendees were all headed out of the greenhouse toward Laura and Ken. All except Miss Widdich, who was nowhere to be seen.

Laura intercepted them before they could draw too near.

"What's going on?" demanded Rosie Nedworth. "Why is Kenny Barclay standing guard over a pile of dirt?"

"There's been a . . . complication," Laura managed to say. "I'm sorry, but the class has been canceled. You're free to keep the materials, and we'll either refund your entry fee, or give you a gift certificate for the equivalent amount."

"Why? What's in the dirt?" Rosie wanted to know. She brushed past Laura on her way to Ken, with several of the class in her wake.

"Rosie," Ken warned, "no closer, please. I'm serious."

He was no doubt her banker—maybe everyone's banker—and presumably enjoyed a certain amount of authority in town. Even so, it took a stern, cold look from him to keep them all at bay. Rosie grumbled, the others muttered . . . but they did back down and begin drifting away.

A scene from *It's a Wonderful Life,* it was not.

Laura went up to Ken again. "I have to tell Corinne. She can't not know."

"Go ahead. I'll stay here," Ken told her.

"Thanks." She began heading for the shop, then stopped and turned around. "But I wish you wouldn't treat this like a crime scene," she said, aware that her wish was a plea.

"We don't have much choice," Ken said grimly.

She turned and left him, then, and caught up with her sister.

Taking Corinne aside, Laura tried to bring her up to speed before the police arrived and pandemonium hit. Already, she could see curious customers drifting out of the shop and heading toward the compost pile where Ken had posted himself sentry.

"But why did Ken refer to the bone as evidence?" Corinne wanted to know. "If you call something evidence, it means you think there's been a crime."

She had a blank, faraway look on her face, as if she had retreated to another place and time. She was chewing on the roughened skin of her forefinger, staring ahead, seeing God only knew what.

"Don't you understand?" Laura said, frustrated that her sister was being so obtuse. "There's a *body* buried at the bottom of the compost pile. I saw the skull."

"Yes, no, I understand," said Corinne, speaking low and with her back to the customers. "I do understand. There's a body buried on the property. But . . . why wouldn't there be? The land has been settled for hundreds of years. It's perfectly natural that some farmers would lay their dead here. Or even Native Americans. They were here first."

She was warming to her theory as she spoke. "There could be an entire burial ground underneath the compost, and reaching under the greenhouses too. They're all right next to the road. The land there has probably never been tilled. What could be more predictable than finding bones there? That's where old cemeteries are always located: next to the road."

"Oh, Corinne, for God's sake!"

"Shh!" said Corinne, glancing around them.

"There's still *fabric* with the bones," Laura said in a hiss. "If the body were there from when you say, the natural fibers from any clothes would've long since turned into dust. Indians didn't wear polyester!"

But still Corinne refused to see. She would not look at the compost pile; she wouldn't even look at Laura. She kept her gaze fixed on that place that Laura knew she retreated to whenever she felt the world around her was being overly hostile.

It was all too surreal: the discovery; the sickening timing of it. The three of them were going to have to get through this, somehow. If all they'd done was inadvertently upset some burial ground, Laura would be the first to drop to her knees in gratitude.

But then she remembered the look on Ken's face: it so clearly said otherwise.

With halfhearted reassurances, she left Corinne to deal with the customers while she backtracked to where Ken was standing guard. From somewhere he had found a couple of sawhorses and had placed them a few feet away from the edge of the compost pile, cordoning off the site.

He said, "Chief Mellon had to detour to investigate a break-in, so he'll be running a little late."

Laura wanted to talk about anything besides the bones

at their feet, so she said, "Since when are there break-ins in Chepaquit?"

Ken shrugged and said, "It's the czarina again. She has a summer house on Old Beach Road and she never locks the doors, so the maids—or their boyfriends—steal her jewelry and the silver, and then she insists that the chief and only the chief investigate the burglary." He added lightly, "The season doesn't officially begin until the czarina's had a burglary."

"Is she really a czarina?"

"No . . . but she acts like one." He added with a smile, "Maybe I'm just being sour grapes because she's too cheap to pay for a deposit box."

He was trying to reassure. In his own indirect way, he was succeeding. Without looking at them, Laura nodded her head toward the pile of bones waiting to be officially unearthed. "This *will* become a crime scene, won't it?"

He sighed. "Probably. For a while."

"The entire nursery, you think?"

"Not as much as this immediate area. But, yes, I imagine an investigation will include at least one pass over the property."

"So we can forget about our Founders Week celebration," she said dully. "I'm sorry. I know it makes me sound hideously selfish."

"No. I understand. It's easier to wrap yourself around the notion of profit margins than it is to comprehend something like this."

"Yes. Because bankruptcy is probably the very least of our troubles now."

"Don't jump ahead, Laura," he urged. "Please don't do this to yourself. Just take things one step at a time."

"Ken, how *can* I?" she said, exploding with emotion. Immediately, she reined herself in. There were too many people finding excuses to walk past the compost pile.

She said in a low murmur, "Were you able to tell what kind of clothing it was?"

If she was expecting him to say something along the lines of, say, "a jewel-neck knit top with a Talbot's label," she was disappointed.

He shook his head. "Brown shreds, that's all. Maybe a pattern . . . but that's for forensics to determine, I guess."

She wanted to ask, "Were there teeth?" because even she, a crime dufus, knew that that was one of the easiest ways to identify a body, and she hadn't registered if there were teeth when she first saw the skull. But somehow she couldn't make herself ask, because every question was bringing her nearer the realization that this had been a living human being that Baskerville had run off with part of. A living human being who wore clothing and had teeth and a smile and a heart and a soul.

"If only it could be a suicide," she whispered, more to herself than to Ken. A suicidal person could certainly dig a hole, jump into it, and kill himself or herself.

But a suicide couldn't cover himself or herself with compost after the deed was done. That was a job for a murderer.

"Oh, God. Oh, God," she said, shivering into a near faint. She was losing it, just like her brother, just like her sister. And she was supposed to be the rational one of the three. What a joke.

Quietly, Ken put his arm around her shoulder and squeezed her gently to him. In no hurry to let go, he stroked her arm and said, "I'll keep the curious at bay. You go on with your sale."

"Oh. Of course. The sale," she said, and she let out a dull laugh. "The only thing we could sell right now is a ticket to our latest melodrama."

"Here comes Chief Mellon already," Ken said, looking over Laura's head. "I'm surprised he got here so fast."

"I'm not. A break-in versus a murder; you do the math,

Ken." She slipped out of his grasp as the chief drew near.

It was déjà vu all over again: a Shore kid, waiting for the police to arrive at their house. Only this time it wasn't because of a fight her father had picked with someone in town. God. It didn't seem possible that they were going to be made to account for bones left over from another age; Laura's mind bitterly rejected the prospect.

Their grand reopening, which had promised to be so memorable, was going to fulfill that promise, after all.

But, oh, for all the wrong reasons.

Chapter 17

Police Chief Andrew Mellon, like the Shore kids, was a townie, the son of a cop and a high school teacher. He was regarded as a stern but fair man, and no one was counting on that more than Laura.

She was sitting with Corinne and Snack at the kitchen table after closing up the nursery, waiting to hear what was next on the chief's agenda.

Corinne's earlier optimism that there could be a perfectly innocent explanation for the bones in the compost had long since faded. "Chief Mellon is going to be prejudiced against us," she fretted. "How can he not be? His father was on the force when Uncle Norbert strangled Aunt Janice."

"What are you saying, Corinne? That he's already made up his mind to accuse someone in our family?"

"I'm just saying that he's not likely to believe it was some drifter."

"But that's exactly who it must have been," Laura argued. It was the only theory that she found either plausible or acceptable. "One drifter must have got into a fight with another one, buried the body, and moved on. A nursery compost pile would have been an irresistible place to dump it—no heavy lifting required, shovels readily available.

What would he care if the body were discovered soon afterward? He'd have been long gone by then."

"*Long* gone," muttered Snack, popping the lid of another Coors.

Laura was keeping track. With three beers under his belt, Snack was still capable of being perfectly civil and sincere. Once he reached four or five, though, things tended to get iffier.

"But one of the nursery dogs would've barked."

"We didn't always keep dogs. There were years when we didn't. Like right now. Same with Grams and Gramps, I'm fairly sure."

"Someone would have seen the murderer digging from the house."

"Only from the dining room. We never used the dining room except for special occasions, and that goes back to Grams again. It would've been just dumb luck, but someone could have got away with it without being seen. And if it were foggy, he'd definitely get away without being seen."

"I guess. The thing is," said Corinne, "we don't have drifters coming through Chepaquit."

"Sure we do," Laura argued. "Especially in the summer. Okay, they're not actual hobos jumping on and off trains, but you do see a bunch of kids renting a house, and they know someone who knows someone, and before you know it, you have a house filled with strangers. Ask any landlord around here."

Snack said, almost eagerly, "I've crashed in houses like that. I've spent weeks in digs where all they knew was my nickname."

Unable to resist a gentle poke, Laura said, "What? You mean you don't go by Oliver Norbert?"

"What do *you* think?" said her brother with a wry face. "Man, with a name like that around *here*," he added, "I may as well just check myself into the MCI."

He took a long slug of his number-four Coors and said under his breath, "*Go directly to Jail. Do not pass Go. Do not collect two hundred dollars.*"

There he went, feeling sorry for himself. "Well, if you feel that way," Laura snapped, "then why not just turn yourself in and get it over with?"

"Laura!"

"Oh, please don't 'Laura' me," she said tiredly to her sister. "You know I didn't mean it."

To her brother, she said, "But for God's sake, Snack—do you have to be so defeatist about everything? And *Corinne*—you of all people! Where's your optimism when we need it?"

"Well, I'm just saying—"

She was interrupted by loud knocking on the front door at the other end of the house. All of them jumped, but it was Laura who said, "I'll get it. You two stay put."

She opened the door to see two men, one of them a twenty-something guy dressed in khakis and an olive-green shirt, the other a jeans-clad cameraman. Hell and damnation, more media.

"Hi. Bret Evanston from *News at Ten*," the one said, introducing himself in front of the rolling camera. He stuck a microphone in front of her face and said, "Do you have any idea who's buried there?"

Laura said coolly, "No—as I've already told your competitor, Channel whatever it was. Who, by the way, have come and gone. What took *you* so long?"

Let him run that quote if he liked, damn it. She closed the door on him as he turned to the camera, undoubtedly to say that the family was being uncooperative.

How she hated this. If there was anything worse than being an object of derision, it was being an object of curiosity. Too restless and annoyed to rejoin her gloomy siblings, Laura wandered off into the never-used dining room, which had a direct view of the ongoing investigation. Several state investigators—where had they found them on such short notice?—were still there, digging and sifting like kids at the shore. So to speak.

What would happen to Shore Gardens now? They'd already been told that they couldn't use the dump truck or the John Deere or the compost—obviously—from either the original site or the relocated one. Most of the nursery would be off limits not only to customers but to them as well. They'd be able to reopen the main shop in the next couple of days (that was a courtesy) but what good was an open shop if they couldn't get anything brought down to it?

Not that it mattered. Who was going to buy anything from them now, anyway?

Stop. Just stop. You sound like Snack.

She stared at the bright yellow Do Not Cross tape that seemed to be growing by the mile and thought how completely ironic it was that Snack had managed to move all of the compost except the little pile that mattered most. If she and Corinne had not constantly distracted him from finishing the job he was trying so hard to do, Snack might have managed to move all of it to the back of the nursery without anyone, including Baskerville, ever noticing the bones.

And the sale would go on.

And the Shore name would be restored.

And Corinne would marry Gabe.

And Snack would run the nursery.

And Laura would not be second-guessing the man who had called Chief Mellon on his cell phone just minutes after discovering the bones.

Ken had to call the police, Laura realized. Of course he had to call. But if he had waited until after the sale, would that have been so unforgivable?

She sighed. Definitely, it would have been unforgivable. Probably.

She stared through parted curtains at the somber scene that was playing itself out in their back yard, all according to well-defined procedure. Her sense of paralysis was profound. Laura was a doer, and for the moment—now that they'd given their simple, initial statements to the police—there was nothing to do except wait.

Chief Mellon wasn't as mean as Laura had feared, nor as kind as she had wished. He was depressingly noncommittal. He knocked politely on their screen door and, seeing them inside at the kitchen table, let himself in. He was a big man, six-three or -four, and deeply tanned. He loved to fish, Corinne had already told Laura, and he spent every free hour on the water, often with his young twin daughters.

He said, "We're done photographing the scene, and at this point we've started to recover the skeletal remains, which seem to be fairly undisturbed—except of course for the dog's activity. The long daylight will help speed the process: the men will keep at it until dark and then be back tomorrow at daybreak. At the moment, we are treating this as a death investigation. If the medical examiner can determine the manner and cause of death, that could change."

"To what?" asked Corinne, looking blank.

"To a homicide investigation." He added quietly, "It would be best if you confined your comings and goings to the house for now. We'll move the investigation along as expeditiously as we can; I know you're concerned about being closed down this week, and if we can avoid that, we will."

"Can you tell yet what he—she?—died of?" asked Laura.

The chief shook his head.

"We're assuming, not old age," said Snack, staring at the can of beer he was clutching. He began lifting and dropping it in a rhythmic beat on the enameled metal tabletop, broadcasting his displeasure at being there.

Oh, great. The beer was kicking in. Laura tried to give her brother a warning look, but he refused to acknowledge it. She saw the muscles in his jaw clench and unclench. He was working up a head of steam, all right.

Corinne took a deep, shuddering breath, apparently to build up her courage, and then blurted, "How long have the bones been there? Can you tell? Couldn't they be ancient? Couldn't that be an uncovered Indian burial ground?"

The chief seemed surprised by the question, but he answered it. "Decomposition rates vary. Although we don't know yet whether the site is a primary or secondary scene, the medical examiner tells me the compost pile is an optimum environment for accelerating the process of decay—but, then, you folks are aware of that, I'm sure."

Was that an insinuating tone? Laura tried not to be paranoid about his perfectly reasonable assumption, given that they had been raised in a nursery.

She said, "You mentioned that we'd have our store back in a couple of days. Do you have any idea when we'll have access to the stock in and outside of our greenhouses? The store's not much good without anything to put in it."

Try as she might, she couldn't keep the resentment out of her voice. The chief picked up on it, and he answered her in a tone that was equally cool. "Like I said, we'll move as quick as we can, Miss Shore."

Snack's answer to that was a snort. Corinne's eyes got wide; she looked as if she wanted to knock Snack's and Laura's heads together in an effort to make them behave.

"And in the meanwhile, I understand you two are staying on for a few weeks?" the chief said, his glance sweeping from Laura to Snack. "Is that right?"

"Only if the crick don't rise," Snack muttered ominously.

"Not a *few* weeks, Chief Mellon," Laura corrected. "I have contractual obligations back in Portland before then." She couldn't bear to look at her sister and see the dismay in her face, so she got up and began clearing the table of its tea things.

"Well, the search of the premises shouldn't take that long," he said. "And as for the interviews, I think we'll be able to wrap them up soon."

"Oh, go-o-od," said Snack, exaggerating his joy. He was being his most provocative. The wonder of Snack was that he wasn't still locked up in somebody's jail merely on principle.

"You'll be around," said the chief with an even look. It wasn't a question, or even a confirmation. It was an order.

Snack didn't take orders very well. Laura jumped in before her brother decided to invite the chief outside for a knuckle sandwich. "Your car's parked out front, Chief Mellon," she said. "It would be quicker for you if I take you through the house to the other door."

"That's all right; I know the way through."

And he did too: Corinne had told Laura that he'd been to the house several times over the years, following up on a variety of complaints by people in town—just like his father before him, no doubt.

Laura tagged along behind him anyway, mostly to watch his back.

At the door, she couldn't resist asking point-blank, "*Can* you tell us if it's a man or a woman?"

"That will all come out in due time," he said. "Good night."

Laura responded with a cursory nod; she was distracted by the black Porsche that had passed the shop and was on its way to the house.

Kendall Barclay pulled up in time to have an exchange with the departing chief. Laura watched from the doorway as the two men shrugged and frowned and nodded and did all those things that men seemed to prefer to actual speech.

The chief left, and Ken took the front steps in twos. Despite the gravity of the day and despite her on-and-off dismay that he had been the one who'd made the discovery, suddenly all Laura could think of was the fact that her hair was limp and her lipstick worn off.

"You're back," she said, feeling a surge of unexpected relief.

"Where else would I go?"

"Well . . . you have a bank to run," she said, stepping aside to let him in.

"We're talking about Chepaquit Savings, not Chase Manhattan," he said, smiling. "And besides, I wanted to take the three of you to dinner. My guess is that Corinne's not much in the mood for slaving over a hot stove tonight."

It was such a vote of confidence in them, such a boost to her sagging morale, that Laura had to stop herself from throwing her arms around him in clinging gratitude. She felt like Sally Field on Oscar night.

"Thanks for the offer," she said warmly. "But I doubt that anyone's hungry. It's been a helluva day."

"All the more reason. C'mon, let's go ask 'em."

Without waiting for her to demur, he led the way to the kitchen, looking as at home as if he'd been coming over to play pinochle on Friday nights for years. Snack was at the table—still nursing beer number four, thank God—and Corinne was standing at the opened fridge and staring blankly into it. Neither of them was speaking.

"Hey," Ken said cheerfully. "We're going to town for Chinese. Care to join us?"

Snack pulled back his chin in surprise. "Chepaquit doesn't have a Chinese restaurant."

"It's International Night at Captain Jack's. Yankee Szechuan."

"Uh, I'll pass. Thanks."

"Corinne?"

"Oh. *Tonight?*"

Of all nights. Too shy to be on display in a restaurant in the best of times, Corinne didn't look all that eager to answer casual inquiries just then about the body in her compost pile.

Tonight, in short, was the worst of times.

"That's really nice of you to offer, but . . . you know, I think I'll just heat up a can of soup. But thanks. Really, thanks," she added with a limp smile.

Ken took the dual turndowns in stride. "Okay. But keep your dance cards free for Hungarian Night next week. The goulash is not to be missed," he said amiably. "Meanwhile, we'll bring you guys back some takeout, in case you get a yen later."

He shepherded Laura out of the kitchen and toward the front door. In the parlor, he stroked her cheek lightly and said, "Of course, you understand that this is all by design, to get you alone for a while."

Sizzling under his touch, she murmured, "And here I thought you were just trying to be nice."

"I *am* nice. You're going to find out just how nice."

"Can I comb my hair? Get my bag?"

"You're perfect the way you are."

Her heart was pumping hard, and for so many reasons. *I'm the niece of a killer,* she wanted to whisper in his ear. *Maybe a serial killer. How perfect is that?*

Out the door they went, and into his shiny car. He held the door for her, shut it after her, turned off the blaring radio for her, did all the things that a proper gentleman does on a first date.

Except it wasn't a date, it was a rescue.

Chapter 18

"Basically, you wanted to save us from ourselves, didn't you?" Laura said.

She leaned back on the glove-soft leather headrest, closed her eyes, and tried to blot out the day: the good, the bad . . . the ugly.

No luck. "If you could have seen us huddled around the kitchen table just now," she said, because she had to talk about it, after all. "God, we were pathetic. I think we were expecting them to bring out the rubber hoses and beat a confession out of one of us."

"What is it with you guys?" Ken asked. He sounded genuinely bewildered. "Where's your confidence?"

"Easy for you to say. Tell me this. Has your family ever been hit by a scandal?"

"My mother stole my mail and forged my signature once," he said, smiling.

"I mean, a real scandal."

"You hated me for twenty years. I call that scandalous."

"Ken. I mean where people looked down at you wherever you went, as if you were lower than low."

"Now, see, I don't get that. Why would any of you feel that people were looking down on you?"

"Hello—because they were? My father didn't exactly

cut an admirable figure around town," she said. "And let's not forget: he was the kinder, gentler brother."

Ken acknowledged her claim with a wry smile as he took the turn onto Main, a two-lane road that divided Chepaquit into waterview properties and affordable ones.

Laura said wistfully, "I wish I could be different. I wish I could have the confidence of someone like you—or even like Sylvia. I don't suppose you knew her."

"Name doesn't ring a bell," Ken admitted.

"If you'd ever seen her, you'd remember her. She worked for us for a little while. She wasn't local; she was from up north. But she had this . . . this fearlessness about people that had Corinne and me in awe. She was our hero."

"I think what you did with your own life is pretty heroic. You followed your star—"

"Hardly," Laura said with a snort. "What I did was run away from Chepaquit as fast as I could."

"Well, all I can say is, that Uncle Norbert of yours must have been a piece of work—not only for what he did to his wife, but for what he did to you all," Ken muttered. "What a hell of a legacy he left you."

She twitched one shoulder in the barest of shrugs. "My father contributed his fair share," she insisted, because that was part of the legacy too. "He also had a temper, and he wasn't shy about using it on anyone near."

Her thoughts rocketed back to an innocent afternoon when Sylvia returned from making a delivery. She could see her father so clearly, his face red with anger, his voice raw with fury.

Where were you? I don't want you drivin' off doing deliveries. My daughters can do that. Billy can do that. Not you.

Since when?

Since now.

But you hired me to—

You heard me. You don't leave the premises! You stay right here!

Laughing, Sylvia had said, *You're my boss, not my master.*

And she had flipped him a finger before turning her back on him and going back to work. Laura had watched in astonishment. No one had ever—ever—stood up to her father that way.

Vaguely distressed by the memory, she lapsed into thoughtful silence.

After a moment, she rolled her head toward Ken and said, "How did it go with your mother, by the way? Dare I ask?"

"Ask away; I have nothing to relate, I'm afraid. A close friend of hers was taken seriously ill and ended up at Mass General, which is where my mother spent the evening and much of the night. Needless to say, my tantrum had to be postponed."

"I'm so sorry," she said, smiling, and added, "I think I'd pay good money to watch you throw a tantrum sometime."

"I'd have to practice first," he confessed. "I've never really done one, despite the fact that I was an only child for years before my sister was born. I guess I don't consider myself spoiled, although I haven't exactly been deprived."

"It sounds as if your parents got it about right. I'm jealous," she admitted.

"And meantime, you're telling me that my parents weren't the thing that drove you away?"

"Not really."

"Huh. One less reason to throw that fit, darn it," he said as he squeezed into the last parking space in front of the restaurant.

Captain Jack's was a quintessential small-town New England eatery, a two-story Victorian house with big square windows split in four on both sides of the door. The place was painted a pleasing shade of slate blue and trimmed in ivory. Its handmade hanging sign was the most ostentatious thing about it: "Captain Jack's" was carved deep into the wood and finished in gold leaf over a relief of a fouled anchor.

"Didn't this used to be a hardware store?" Laura asked as they walked up to the double-doored entry.

"Not for at least ten years. You don't come into town on your visits much, do you?"

"Never, if I can help it."

The restaurant was crowded, which wasn't surprising; it was one of the few in town. The old wood floors from the hardware store were still intact but were varnished now instead of scraped bare as Laura remembered them; they glowed like spilled honey in the late sun that poured through the simple lace curtains covering the lower half of the windows. A dozen tables were arranged in cozy proximity. At the back was a small bar and a take-out register. It was all very casual, all very nice.

All very awkward, when conversations stopped after Laura and Ken stepped inside. It was obvious that everyone had heard about the bones in the compost pile.

Laura was prepared for their stares and murmurs; it was just like old times. What she wasn't prepared for was the sight of Will Burton, sitting at a table with three other men.

Will Burton.

Unlike Ken, he had hardly changed over the years. He had the same blond hair, the same hawk nose, the same air of cockiness that Laura had once found intimidating. The red-haired guy with his back to her had to be Dagger, Will's younger brother. The other two men could have been just about anyone; Will had always moved with an entourage.

Suddenly Laura was thrown back into the woods again, clutching her torn clothes, and with tears streaming down her face. Her heart was knocking as hard as it had those decades ago, and her crushing need, now as then, was to turn and run.

But Ken had tightened his grip on her elbow. They weren't going anywhere.

A pert hostess with a dimpled smile approached them. Ken said, "Dinner, for two. And we'll be ordering takeout."

"Certainly, Mr. Barclay; this way," she said, and they followed her toward an empty table tucked under one of the curtained side windows in a corner of the room.

Laura had no idea how to act. She wanted to take her cue from Ken, but he was now behind her. She was on her own.

Don't let Will get to you; the bastard isn't worth it, she warned herself. But her flushing cheeks were betraying her even as she formed the thought.

And then she tripped. Somehow, some way, she had managed to stumble on pure, thin air as she drew abreast of the group.

She recovered, but not before a smiling Will Burton jumped up with infuriating chivalry and said, "Whoa, easy there. Laura Shore . . . is it really you?"

There was a mixture of disbelief and amusement in his deep, grown-up voice—the voice of a radio announcer selling fine used cars.

"Yes, it's really me," she said, for lack of something catchy.

"They said you were back in town. To stay?" he asked.

The slightest smile betrayed the condescension he obviously felt. He made her feel like someone caught sneaking in under the circus tent. She didn't have a ticket. She didn't belong.

How she hated him just then. She wanted so much to be past all that, but . . . how she hated him. She said in as lofty a voice as she could muster, "I haven't made any plans, one way or the other."

"Yeah? That's not what I hear." Will looked deliberately

from her to Ken and back again. He leered and said, "Just call me Cupid, hey? You don't have to thank me."

She felt Ken behind her make a move for him, but she had the advantage of being in front. She brought up her arm and slapped Will. Hard.

"That's for then," she muttered. *God,* it felt good.

Will was too stunned to do anything, but Dagger jumped up from his chair, ready to rumble.

Ken shoved him back down by the shoulder. "Sit. Enjoy your food. All of you," he said with a scarily rigid smile.

Will looked around the room, which had become even more silent, and then said cheerfully, "You always did have a way about you, Laura." In an undertone he added to Ken, "This isn't over."

"Anytime," Ken murmured back.

They continued on their way to their table.

The rattled hostess pulled out Laura's chair for her. Ken took one look at her face and said in a voice clear enough to be heard around the room, "Hey, on second thought, it's a great evening. What do you say we get takeout for us, too, and have a romantic picnic on the beach?"

She could have kissed him on the spot, but she settled for a relieved smile. "I'm up for it."

Ken asked the hostess very nicely for the take-out menus and a bottle of wine. They ordered Szechuan shrimp, Szechuan chicken, Szechuan pork, Szechuan noodles, Szechuan baby back ribs, and enough rice to feed mainland China. While they waited for the food, they clinked their stemware and downed a fair portion of the bottle.

The food arrived in three reinforced shopping bags. Ken hauled two of them, and Laura, biting her lip to suppress her growing merriment, carried the third. By the time they reached the car, she was exploding with the day's pent-up emotion, all of it streaming from her in the form of helpless, inappropriate giggles.

"Did you see all their *faces*?" she asked as she collapsed in the front seat.

"Before you slapped Will, or after?"

"Either! Both! They were apoplectic!"

"Ah, they were all just jealous. I had the best-looking woman in the room on my arm."

"Ken, don't you realize? Your reputation just went up in smoke!" For whatever reason, she found that, too, hysterically funny.

He grinned at her reaction and said, "You mean that because of you, I've finally made the transition from nerd to bad boy? I'm so impressed with myself."

He pulled into a nearby parking lot in front of Chepaquit Dry Cleaners. Seeing the sign drew more nervous giggles as Laura remembered Rosie Nedworth, fists on her hips, demanding to know about the bones.

She said, "Why are we here? To drop off your cleaning?"

"Wine. Next door."

"More wine? I'm not sure I can handle . . ."

"We have food on the back seat. You didn't notice?"

More giggles. "God, right, the food. We have enough to let us hole up for the rest of the year."

"Promise?"

"Sure! Anything. Absolutely! I just had the *best* time in there. I can't believe it," she said, sitting back, exhilarated. "Why do I feel so great? I should feel mortified."

"You needed that, slugger. It was long overdue."

Ken ducked into the package store and came out minutes later with the requisite brown-bagged bottle. Laura felt like a teen on prom night, something she'd never had the chance to experience firsthand.

"I promise not to get you drunk," he said, sliding into his seat and handing her the bottle.

"Too late!" she answered gaily. "Knowing you, this

probably isn't a screw-cap, though," she said, peeking into the bag.

"My Swiss Army knife has a corkscrew. We're good to go."

He drove the few minutes to the nursery and turned in toward the house, then carried two of the shopping bags inside for Snack and Corinne while Laura purposely waited in the car. She knew that she was walking a high wire made from a strand of a spiderweb; that it could break at any moment and send her plunging back to earth. One look at her gloomy brother and worried sister, and down she would plummet. She wanted to hold on to the high.

Ken came out grinning and with a tablecloth over his shoulder, and Laura felt a rush of relief. He wouldn't look like that if there had been trouble in the house.

"Billy dropped by five minutes ago to see you," Ken said. "He told your sister he'd be back tomorrow."

He tossed the cloth on her lap. "From Corinne. She said to tell you that she understands completely."

What was that supposed to mean? Laura hardly had time to wonder, because Ken was wheeling out of the nursery like a Nascar driver, hugging the turns, shifting constantly, accelerating whenever he could.

"You drive fast."

"I drive well. Okay, I admit it: the car is a brand-new toy. I was torn between this and a Volkswagen Bug; the Boxster won out by a hair."

"I actually have a Bug back in Seattle. A yellow one."

"*Do* you?" he said, throwing her an astonished look which was apparently fake. "I'm not going to go making claims about kindred souls or anything—but to me, that is a very big deal," he said gravely.

"You weren't *really* considering the Bug."

"Okay, no," he admitted with an impish smile. "But I did think they were cute when they first came out. That's close enough to karma for me."

She laughed. He made her feel so good. "Where are we going?"

"To one of the best and most private stretches of beach on the Cape."

"That leaves out the town beach, for sure," she said, intrigued by his air of mystery. "And it's not the stretch of beach below Shore Gardens, which we don't own anymore, more's the pity."

"God, yes. What a bummer that your parents sold it off," he said with feeling. He glanced over at her and said, "Sorry. That was the investor in me speaking. Sometimes he breaks out of his cage."

"It wouldn't be so bad if they'd sold it for a fair price," she conceded. "But they got so royally snookered by that developer."

"Yes, they did."

"Oh, well. It happened before I was born. I don't feel the loss that much."

"Good. Here we are," he said, suddenly pulling off the road and into the side of a sandy ditch.

She was uncharacteristically disoriented. The exquisite houses they had passed were newly built, throwing off her sense of geography. "Where are we?"

"Just an old deer path," he said. "You grab the bottle and the tablecloth and the shopping bag."

Bemused, she said, "What're *you* going to carry?"

"You," he said, slamming the door and coming around to her side. "The grass is high," he explained when he opened her door for her. "Ticks."

"Oh. Right." She was still wearing her lavender dress and sandals, and her limbs were exposed.

"Alley-oop," he said, and he lifted her out of her seat as easily as if she were a bag of laundry.

"Holy cats, those years of working out paid off," Laura said, clutching her wine and tablecloth and somewhat stunned to find herself so easily in his arms.

"Shhh. Only whispers from now on. We don't want the neighbors coming at us with shotguns," he said in her ear. "You know how proprietary Massachusetts shorefront folk are about their beaches. They act like they own 'em."

She whispered back, "But they do. Damn it."

"Shhh."

He lowered her enough so that she could grab the handles of the paper shopping bag of food, and then they were on their way. The dune grass wasn't the only threat; prickly beach roses—and, at one point, a short, hidden stretch of barbed wire—made the narrow path almost impassable. Ken had some tricky maneuvering to get around and through the obstacles; together, he and Laura weren't nearly as aerodynamic as a white-tailed deer.

In the fading light, Laura caught glimpses of houses through the thickets of scrub that grew on either side of the roses. She saw weathered shingles to their right, a small patch of white clapboard on their left. They were snaking between two obviously high-end estates.

Ken managed to get them through the path without her getting a scratch, although she couldn't be as sure about him. They emerged onto a narrow strip of pure white beach that seemed to go on forever in either direction.

"Voilà," he said, lowering her to the sand. "You okay?"

"Of course," she whispered. "I rode a magic carpet."

"*Here's* our magic carpet," he said, taking the tablecloth from her.

She asked in a whisper, "Why aren't you whispering?"

"No need, anymore." He took the tablecloth from her and let it float down over the sand, then anchored two of the corners with the wine and the shopping bag.

"No need? Why not?" she asked, watching him pull off his deck shoes to anchor the third corner. He looked awfully at ease, which was more than she was feeling.

He grinned and jerked his head back over his shoulder.

"I know the owner." Peeling off his socks, he stuffed them into his shoes.

Laura tiptoed a little way to the left for a clearer look at the house he was indicating. "That's *your* house!"

"Yup."

"So tell me why we went the thorny way around?"

He shrugged and said, "Besides the obvious excuse to have you in my arms? To pull my neighbor's chain, I guess. He's such an uptight SOB about people using the deer path to 'trespass' on 'his' beach."

"The barbed wire is his work?" she guessed.

"Yeah. Remind me to take a bolt cutters to it, by the way. Tom strings the stuff up; I cut it down. It's a game we play. Neither of us has ever acknowledged knowing a thing about it. We're so immature," he said. "Really; it's embarrassing."

He dropped down to the tablecloth, crossed his legs Indian style, then began lining up a row of white cartons in front of him. "Woo-ee, this smells good."

She was watching him, utterly bemused. "Sneaking onto your own beach to have a picnic of Chinese food. Well . . . it's just a little on the bizarre side, if you ask me."

"Hungry?" he asked, looking up at her.

"Starved."

He said softly, "So take off your sandals and stay a while."

"I think I will," she said, dropping lightly into place on the other side of the line of cartons.

She unbuckled her sandals while he opened each container in turn. There was food enough for them and for SOB neighbor Tom and for any and all trespassers, past, present, and future. And plastic utensils, for which Laura was grateful; she'd never mastered the use of chopsticks.

He said, "I'll open the—ah, *nuts,* I forgot about glasses. Now what? Let's think . . ."

"You could always break into that nice-looking house

over there," she said in a deadpan attempt to be helpful. "I'm willing to bet that the owner's not home."

"Nope, nope. I draw the line at breaking and entering," he said with an equally straight face. "Wait. I know." He got to his feet and went to the edge of the dune grass behind them and came back with a child's sand pail, brightly decorated with starfish and shells.

"I noticed this the other evening when I was sitting on the beach—alone and pensive, I might add," he said as he passed her on his way to the water's edge. "My nieces must have left the pail out on their last visit. I liked seeing it there because it reminded me of their visit, so I left it where it was. Now I'm glad."

He rolled up his pants and waded in a few feet to give the bucket a saltwater rinse. "Hoo! Still cold," he said on his way back out.

"Not compared to Portland," she boasted.

"So why are you there and not here?"

"I told you. To get away."

"Not from your father, anymore." He dropped back down on the tablecloth and shook the pail dry. "Why not come back?"

"I have a job—"

"You can consult anywhere."

"And a house."

"We have houses here."

"I have . . . unfinished business."

"So finish it and move back East. What's so hard about that?"

She laughed softly and said, "You're very persistent."

"Wait till you see how much." He poured wine into the bucket and handed it to her, then touched his bottle to her pail. "A toast: to new beginnings. I know it's a cliché, but humor me."

"Sure. I'll drink to that," she said. She lifted the plastic bucket to her lips and tried to take a sip. Instead, she ended up spilling a wave of Chablis down her dress.

It came as a shock, but a laughable one in which Ken joined in. "Swear to God, I thought I was giving you the daintier vessel. I swear," he said, coming up with a clean, folded handkerchief. He began frantically patting her chin, her dress, the folds in her lap.

"Stop, stop, it's okay," she insisted, laughing. "Here, you take the bucket. It's too lethal for me. We'll try again."

They switched, and she tapped the bottle to his pail.

"New beginnings," she said, and he added to that, "Take two."

She sipped from the bottle as he lifted the sand pail to his mouth—and ended up pouring an even bigger wave over himself.

He swore good-naturedly while she shrieked with laughter. "We're hopeless!" she said.

"Can you just picture us on *Survivor*?" he said, flapping his shirt back and forth against his chest.

"Or in a commercial for Carnival Cruise Lines?"

"We reek."

"We do," she agreed.

"Okay, I give. Let's retreat to the house and clean up. I'm sure the owner, who I understand is a first-class dork, won't mind," he said dryly.

"*I* think the owner is a first-class charmer," she countered. She was still grinning, still happy, still thoroughly diverted from the hideous situation at Shore Gardens. "I pronounce the evening a wild success so far."

"Talk about an easy date," he quipped, tossing the unopened paper cartons back into the shopping bag.

"I suppose your mother warned you about girls like me?" she asked, not without irony.

He looked up from his packing to say, "Oh, darlin'. My mother instinctively knew right where to put you: in a league of your own."

Was it the look in his blue eyes; the tone of his voice?

Who could say? All Laura knew was that suddenly she was having a harder time breathing, because her heart seemed to be stuck in her throat. "What . . . do I do with our bucket of wine?"

"Offer it to the sea," he said easily. "In thanks."

She waded in ankle deep and poured the wine, with some ceremony, into the lazy, sliding sea.

Her prayer was simple: *Please, whatever happens, let it be the right thing, the true thing. No more false steps.*

She returned the pail to where he'd found it in the dune grass.

"Did you make a wish?" he asked.

"Oh, yes."

"Then I hope it comes true."

Chapter 19

They shook out the tablecloth, grabbed their shoes, and walked barefoot up a sandy path toward the house. It was dusk now, that long, languid moment when the day has wound down but the night hasn't yet asserted itself, a moment when anything could happen, or nothing at all.

They entered through the set of French doors that led into the bedroom. "I never lock them," Ken explained, which was par for the course in Chepaquit.

"Us, too," said Laura. "Of course, in fairness, we've never had anything to steal."

He flipped on a light inside, and they wiped the sand from their feet on a rug of silky, shaggy flokati. Laura couldn't help observing that the bed was unmade. Ken saw her looking at it and said, "The housekeeper only comes once a week. You were here on her day, last time."

Embarrassed to have been caught fixating on the state of his linen, Laura said, "At least you're not compulsive about that kind of thing."

"But I am. For example, I hate leaving dishes in the sink," he said, opening a set of doors that led to a softly lit closet and dressing area.

"Me, too!"

"So I leave them stacked alongside on the counter."

She laughed. "You don't have a dishwasher?"

"I'd rather do them by hand. It lets me think. The view over the sink's not so bad: straight out to sea."

She pictured him at the sink, doing dishes alone. Sitting on the beach and watching the sun go down. Alone. Doing all of the things that people do every day, but doing them alone. It didn't seem right. It didn't even seem possible.

"What?" he said, glancing over his shoulder and seeing the look on her face.

"You must know what I'm thinking," she confessed.

"That nothing in here is going to fit you or even be the right gender?"

That you're too good-looking, too successful, too charming—too damn rich—to be wandering around feeling either pensive or alone.

"Why aren't you taken?" she blurted before she could stop herself.

He shrugged and said, "I guess no one's used a big enough club. Why aren't you?"

Laura hadn't expected him to turn the question around on her, and she felt her cheeks flare up as she tripped and stumbled through a noncommittal answer.

Misinterpreting her response, he said, "I'm sorry; that was nosy of me."

"Not at all; I asked first."

She let it go at that. The perfect opportunity to admit to him that she'd just been dumped: blown. It seemed to her that it was something he should know—that he *had* to know—about her.

Ken pulled a clean polo shirt out of a drawer and said, "Is your dress dryable in a machine? Because I can lend you a robe while—"

"No! It's almost dry," she said too vehemently. "The fabric is thin, and it was just alcohol, after all. It evaporates. I'm fine."

"Okay . . . well, I'm soaked," he said, clearly puzzled by the shift in her mood.

He took a step deeper into his dressing room, and the next thing she saw was his gray polo shirt go sailing into the opposite corner. He came out tucking in a dry navy version and smiling sheepishly, as if he'd just stripped for a crowd of screeching females at a bachelorette party.

"I guess we'd better tackle that food," he said. "It's gotta be almost cold by now."

She nodded, still feeling off balance and not certain why.

He picked up the shopping bag and flipped off the lights and stepped aside to let her leave the room first, and then, when she was abreast of him, unexpectedly shot his left arm out ahead of her and blocked her way.

Down went the shopping bag. He eased her into his embrace and gave her a long, hard kiss, catching her completely off guard. She let herself slip into the erotic thrill of it, crushing her lips to his, aware of spreading heat, aware that she was burning all over and willing for more.

And then suddenly he broke the kiss off so abruptly that she caught her breath in a moan of distress. But he remained close, his breath mixing with hers, smiling down at her in the near dark.

Dazed, she said, "What . . . was that all about?"

"Just checkin'," he said softly.

"And what have you found?"

"It's still there."

"Well, thank heaven for that." A second later, she said, "What's still there?"

"That thing they call—"

"Chemistry?"

"Yep," he said, sliding his hands up and down the sides of her body. And then he added, "I hate this dress."

Which surprised her. "I feel really good when I wear this dress."

"Sure you do, because you look really good. I hate this

dress because it's on you and not on the floor," he said softly, and he caught it on each side of her hips and began peeling it up over her torso, reversing the fabric on itself.

"Lift your arms," he said.

Just like that. Her dress was coming off, just like that, and she could feel a cool breeze from somewhere whispering across her back. And she thought, irrelevantly, that waterfront properties were like that: all about cool breezes. And it seemed to her that while she was assessing the temperature outside, the temperature inside of her was heating up, burning up.

He slid the sundress over her head and let it drop in a puddle at their feet, and then he pulled his clean, dry shirt up and off in an easy swoop and dropped it on top of her dress.

She said, a little nervously, "Tsk. More laundry. You were probably Rosie Nedworth's biggest customer."

"How do you think she got to retire early?" he quipped.

He unsnapped the catch in the front of her bra—with startling ease for a one-time nerd—and slid the garment from her shoulders. More cool May air washed over her, followed by the even more startling warmth of his hands cupping her breasts. He stroked her nipples with his thumbs, and she became light-headed from the pleasure of it. She closed her eyes, bit her lower lip.

"Second . . . base," she said in a soft moan.

"One base farther than I ever got with anyone in school," he murmured, and he lowered his mouth to hers for another kiss, hot and warm and tasting of the wine they'd spilled over themselves. Her bare breasts were pressed against his bare chest, her fingers threaded behind his neck, an invitation if ever there was one for him to head on down to third.

He did just that, pulling away the elastic of her underpants and slipping his hand inside, seeking and finding her clitoris and making her jump, then stroking it lightly, then backing off to a broader, more sensual rub with the flat of his hand, then pinpointing her clitoris again, all of it reducing her knees to rubber, her breathing to a series of helpless pants. He was simultaneously holding her up and taking her down, and she was caught in the crossfire, victimized by her own surging desire and her basic inability to move.

He asked, "Am I doing it right?" but she caught the easy confidence in the voice behind the question. He stroked and rubbed and stroked again, and she whimpered, "I'd say . . . oh-h . . . not . . . so . . . bad." And the smile came through as he said, "This is third base, right? I never knew who to ask."

By now her forehead was bent into his chest, her legs parted, her arms limp as she waited for the release from the unbearable tension that was coiling inside her. It didn't seem possible to feel so good and so bad—and so utterly focused—at the same time. The pace of her panting picked up, and he picked up the pace of his strokes, until at last a long, low moan slid out from her on a full-body shudder.

He wrapped his arms around her and held her close—she assumed, as a courtesy, to keep her from collapsing to the floor.

Satisfied. It was a profound sensation, ending a string of frustrations at work, at the nursery, and—she hated to admit it—in bed. *Satisfied.* She'd forgotten how good it felt to be at the end of a job well done.

"Thank you," she whispered, because it was the first thing that came to her mind and because it was true. She was grateful. She wasn't even embarrassed that she was grateful; he was that good.

His laugh was soft, bemused. He tilted her chin up and kissed her. "My pleasure," he said. "Believe me on that," he said, nibbling her lower lip, dragging a trail of soft kisses from there through the curve of her neck.

"So it's . . . your turn now?" she said, arching her neck for him.

"Our turn," he corrected. "Come," he murmured into her heated skin. "What do you say we make love properly now? We won't even have to undo the bed."

She laughed, a little flutter of reviving passion. "As long as you put it *that* way . . ."

"Wait until you see how many ways I can put it."

He took her hand to lead her to his bed, and that's when it began to sink in: they were about to make love. She was going to take him inside of her, to give herself to him. She was going to hold him close against her heart. And when they returned to their separate lives—as they inevitably would—Ken was going to have a claim on that heart.

She saw no other possibility. She wouldn't be going to bed with him merely for release; he had just taken care of that. No, this would not be about having sex. This would be about making love. This would involve her emotions—and those emotions presently were a mess.

"Ken," she said, pulling back gently.

He turned. She could see that he was surprised by the gesture. She felt like a shy schoolgirl hanging back on that dread first day. "I can't do this."

He looked truly blindsided. He cocked his head, as if he hadn't heard her right. "Because . . . ?"

"Because I can't. Not now. I just can't," she confessed miserably.

She knew how it looked. It looked awful. As if she were the worst kind of tease. That didn't stop her from saying again, "I just . . . can't."

He still looked confused, but there was an edge to it now. "Was it something I said?" he asked a little dryly.

"No, no, it's not you at all," she insisted, which was a lie. "It's . . . it's everything. It's the wine, it's the bones, it's Will, it's Snack, Corinne, the nursery, it's . . . oh, God.

Everything." She sighed a deep, shuddering sigh. "Suddenly it's all hitting me at once."

He let out a sound of exasperation, and automatically she winced, expecting an outburst to follow.

He saw her fear and said, "Laura—God. Don't ever react that way to me. Did you think I was going to force you? It's myself I'm mad at. I had my brain on hold. I wasn't thinking; I should've considered what you've been through . . ."

Relieved, she said, "I didn't want you to believe that just because *I* got satisfied—"

"I don't think that," he said quickly. "I ambushed you."

"But I didn't stop you."

"Why would you? How could you?" he said simply. "You needed the release."

"You make it sound so mechanical," she protested.

"In a way, it was," he said, taking her in his arms. "There's nothing wrong with needing to let off steam, even if it's sexual steam." He held her close—but his chest was bare, and so was hers, and it was hard to find real comfort in his embrace. She was far too on guard.

Clearly he felt her tensing up, because he said wryly, "I think probably this isn't such a great idea." He freed her, then scooped up her discarded dress and her bra and handed them to her with a smile that was both resigned and bemused.

She felt terrible. "I'm sorry," she said. "I'm sorry."

"No regrets," he admonished gently. "Never apologize, never explain. Not about something like this."

And meanwhile, she was only wearing underpants. Feeling way too much like a go-go dancer, Laura turned her dress right-side out, stuffed her bra in one of the pockets, and slipped the dress over her head. Armored now in lavender, she felt more able to face the shirtless man in front of her.

She was so grateful to him for not being angry at her

that she blurted, "There's something else you should know."

He leaned back on his Art Deco dresser and crossed his arms over his too-bare, too-broad, too-male chest. Looking calm but warily intrigued, he said, "There's more?"

"It's not really relevant, but . . . you should know that I just broke it off with my fiancé. Or rather, my fiancé just broke it off with me," she felt obliged to admit.

"Jesus Christ!" Ken said, straightening back up again. "You were *engaged*?"

"More or less."

"Until when?"

"The month before last."

He let out a long, slow stream of air, clearly trying to get himself back under control. He looked away and then looked back at her. His eyes seemed somehow darker, the way water looks when a cloud passes between it and the sun. He had to unclench his jaw to say, "I wish you'd told me that before now."

She had to challenge that. "When?"

"I don't know," he admitted, and she heard definite irritation in his voice. "Sometime. Before tonight, anyway."

"I didn't know we'd be ending up here," she said in self-defense.

"*I* did," he shot back.

"Oh." Well, so much for spontaneity. "I had no idea," she said rather primly.

"When I suggested a romantic evening on the beach, bells didn't go off?"

"Back at Captain Jack's? I assumed you were playing to the audience."

"Yeah. You."

"I didn't take you seriously. Why would I?" she said, trying to sound unconcerned as she looked around for her sandals. "I mean, you're who you are and I'm who I am."

"What the hell is that supposed to mean?" he said hotly, turning her around to face him.

Ah, now *this,* she understood. An angry male was familiar territory to her, easier to flee than one who was a charmer.

Don't respond. Don't argue, don't say boo. Just keep your head down and you'll get out without getting hurt. That went double for matters of the heart.

Her answer was to ease out of his grip.

"Laura! Damn it, I asked you a question," he said, clearly getting more and more frustrated.

"You already know the answer," she told him, despite her vow to stay low. "You're the bank president, a member of the ruling class. I'm just a Shore."

You'll love me and leave me and then where will I be?

"Oh, please. You're not serious," he said.

"Never more so."

"Are you just looking for an excuse not to go to bed with me? Christ, Laura, you had plenty of valid reasons, chief among them, a broken engagement; you didn't have to go reaching for something so dumb as class warfare."

"It's the truth!" she snapped.

In fact, he sounded very patrician as he said, "This isn't Victorian England, you know. Wake up and smell the country, will you? We live in a democracy."

"Yeah, sure. Now where did I—? Ah." She found her sandals half buried in the thick, soft shag of the flokati. Scooping them up by their slim straps, she said, "Good night, Mr. Barclay. Don't let the bedbugs bite." And she let herself out onto the terrace, closing the elegant French door carefully behind her.

No more false steps. Wasn't that what she had just got done wishing for?

Good thing she remembered her shoes.

Chapter 20

Laura may have left with her shoes, but she'd forgotten about her car: at the moment, she didn't have one.

Fine. It would be a two-mile trek and in the dark, but she had absolutely no intention of asking Ken for a lift home or even for the use of his phone to call one of the town's two cabs.

It was late. She was exhausted. But she had her pride, damn it. There was absolutely no need for him to assume that Max was part of any list of reasons for her refusal to jump into bed. How anyone could go from being so understanding to being such a total jerk was an infuriating mystery to her.

Suddenly a couple of garden lights went on, casting a soft glow over the brick patio. A doorlatch clicked. Laura whirled around to see Ken fully dressed and slapping his car keys against his thigh.

"Do you want to talk about him?"

"Who?"

"I don't know his name. The guy who broke it off."

"Max? Why would I want to talk about him?"

"Maybe it's something you have to work through," Ken said slowly, as if he were feeling his way. "Now's your chance."

"I don't have to work through Max," she said, exasperated. "I've worked through Max. It's over. Done. Finished." *Aaagh.* She didn't have the energy for this. After a quick and forceful sigh, she said, "It's been a long day." She pointed to his car keys. "Are you offering to drive me home?"

"If that's what you want."

"Thank you," she said, and she sat in one of the teak patio chairs. "I just have to put on my shoes."

He stood and waited while she buckled first one sandal and then the other in self-conscious silence. She felt far more awkward now than she had when she was standing half-naked in front of him.

Of all the ways for the evening to end. She fought back a sudden sting of emotion as she stood up and said briskly, "Okay, I'm all set."

"Watch your step," he warned her quietly as they walked out. "The rest of the way isn't lit."

Now what?

That's what Ken kept asking himself as he drove a silent Laura back to Shore Gardens. How could it have gone so wrong? Granted, he'd had other dates that hadn't ended up as ideally as he would have liked—in bed—but this one had just hit a new low. To have a woman as desirable as Laura Shore in his arms for one intensely erotic moment, and then to have her slip away . . .

He *was* a knucklehead. He hadn't been able to resist her, and he had rushed her, and now here she was: not speaking. Only a knucklehead would have tried to take advantage of her in the state she was in. He was disgusted with himself for having lost control. If he had known that she'd just been ditched by some obvious moron, he wouldn't have touched her with a ten-foot pole. A woman in that position, and with everything else going on in her life besides . . .

Not with a ten-foot pole.

And yet there was something about her—a surprising vulnerability, despite her in-your-ear attitude—that made him want to be near her, and take care of her, and keep all the Will Burtons at bay. There was something about a woman who was determined to fight her own battles that made you want to share the battlefield with her. Laura was that kind of a woman.

The question was, since when had he become that kind of man? He wasn't unhappy or restless with the life he was living. Why the need to go and complicate it with a complicated woman? Hell, the last time that he'd felt such a protective surge about someone was . . . well, with Laura, that day in the woods.

The realization brought him full circle to the payback smack that Laura had given Will Burton in Captain Jack's. Smiling inwardly despite the chill in the car, he glanced at Laura. "Everything okay over there?" he ventured to ask.

"Perfectly fine."

She could have been answering from a neighboring ice floe.

His thoughts went back, inevitably, to their recent confrontation. She claimed that she was over this Max character. Ken wanted to believe her, more than he wanted to admit. But how could she possibly trust her own judgment right now? She had arrived in Chepaquit at a time of financial crisis; had spent punishing hours in an all-or-nothing effort to save the family farm; had seemed to be pulling it off; and had just been upended by the discovery—*his* discovery, no less—of human remains in her compost pile.

Clearly, the best thing he could do was to leave her some breathing room for the moment. The truth was, he could use a little breathing room himself. Things were moving way too fast, and that was all his fault.

His headlamps bounced their beams off yellow tape as

he drove past the site of the search; he was relieved to see that the police hadn't set up lights for an all-nighter. The rest of the nursery was pitch-black, the way it was every night of the year: everyone knew that the Shores had never been ones for wasting electricity.

The house was dark, too, except for two rooms at opposite ends of the second floor.

"Looks like everyone's about to turn in," he said, trying to make ordinary conversation.

Sounding equally offhand, Laura said, "It's been a long—interesting, but long—day for all of us."

He pulled to a stop but left his engine idling, because he didn't want her to feel even remotely obliged to offer him coffee.

Fat chance. She had the door open before he had time to pull the brake.

"Laura—"

"You don't have to say anything, Ken. Tonight never should have happened."

"I know. That's how I feel."

They both said, "I'm sorry," at the same time, and then they both chuckled awkwardly at the same time, and then she closed the door and said good night through the half-opened window.

He said, "See you—"

She was gone before he could say "tomorrow."

Before collapsing for the night, Laura went in to see her sister. Corinne was still awake, sitting on the side of her painted iron bed and twisting her hair into a single long braid. In her plain white nightgown and posed against a backdrop of peeling, faded cabbage-rose wallpaper that had been there for at least half a century, she looked like what she was: a farmer's daughter.

"When did they leave?" asked Laura. No need to explain who "they" were.

"Around dark, just like Chief Mellon promised. I almost couldn't breathe while they were here. I was just so *aware* of them; of what they were doing. They kept filling black plastic bags and then labeling them."

She shook her head slowly, clearly reliving the scene. "Bag after bag after bag . . . It was brutal."

"I know. Hopefully they're done digging."

Unless they planned to go hunting for more bodies, of course.

"Lucy called."

"Who?"

"You know—the girl I hired when I thought we were going to be overwhelmed with customers?"

"Oh, yeah. That Lucy." It seemed like at least a decade ago.

"I had to tell her that we wouldn't be needing her," Corinne said, obviously disappointed. "She was really nice. She said she loved what we'd done with the place, then told me to cheer up and said that she was ready to come to work for us whenever we were ready for her. I felt like she was *my* boss. She was so calm, so reasonable. It really is too bad that we can't hire her."

"Did you ever find out her last name?"

"Oh, gosh. I forgot to ask."

"Oh, well. If she wants us, she'll know where to find us."

"We'll call her Lucy in the Sky," said Corinne, and then added, "Did you have a nice time?"

Laura dropped like a sack into a low-slung, quilted armchair positioned across from the bed. "Yeah. I had a good time," she said with a doleful smile. "Too good. By half. One could say."

"Because when Ken said you were going to have a picnic on the beach, I have to say, I was surprised."

"Oh, the beach was fine, actually fun. It's when we went into his house that things took a turn for the worse. Or the better," she corrected, "depending on how you want to look at it."

"You're not making much sense, you know. What exactly happened?"

"There wasn't penetration, if that's what you're wondering," Laura said glumly. She jammed her fists in her pockets and came up with her bra.

Corinne said with obvious disappointment, "Oh. The cotton one. Too bad you weren't wearing the bitsy thing from Victoria's Secret."

"Who knew?" Laura grimaced and stuffed it back in her pocket.

"So you chickened out. Laura, why?"

"Why do you think *I* was the one who chickened out?"

"He's a man," Corinne answered, surprised by the question.

With a sigh, Laura said, "You're right, I got cold feet. The timing just didn't seem to be optimal."

Her sister said with a knowing nod, "Because of Max, you mean."

"*No,* not because of Max. Why is everyone fixated on Max? Max has nothing—nothing!—to do with my feelings about Ken."

"Okay, okay," Corinne said, backing down. "So what *are* your feelings about Ken?"

"I don't know," Laura admitted, shaking her head. "I don't have a clue. There's chemistry. That's all I know."

But she was thinking, Max would never drink wine from a child's pail the way Ken had. Max didn't even like the beach; he was afraid of getting sand in his laptop. And would Max have carried her in his arms through thorny roses when he could go the easy way around? Not very likely. And forget about wearing a tie with hot-air balloons all over it.

Corinne stood the pillows on edge against the iron posts of her headboard and sat back against them, then pulled her knees up to her chest and wrapped her forearms around her shins, just the way she used to do before bed when they were growing up. She was ready for girl-talk.

"Was there any chemistry between you and Max?" she asked.

"Max again!"

"There wasn't, was there? I knew it," Corinne said without any glee. "I could tell that from your phone calls, but I never wanted to say anything. Don't take this wrong . . . but if Max was so unexciting, why did you get engaged to him in the first place?"

Laura had propped her legs up on the footboard and was studying her feet, which she never really liked. Why on earth did she keep sticking them in sandals for all the world to see? No wonder she'd felt self-conscious back at Ken's patio. It was probably all because of her feet.

"Laura?"

Reluctantly, Laura looked up to see her sister waiting, not too patiently, for an answer.

"You want the truth?" Laura asked.

"What do *you* think?"

"All right. The truth is—I wanted to get married, I *have* to get married," Laura said, still surprised and exasperated by the fact. "My clock is ticking. I can't wait forever for the perfect man. I watch *60 Minutes*. I read *Newsweek*. I know my eggs are doing a nosedive even as we speak."

"You want kids?" Corinne said, astonished. "Since when? I can't remember you ever talking about it."

"Because I've hardly ever thought about it. It always seemed like something that was down the road. Well, guess what? I'm a fair way down that road."

"But what about your career?"

"I can do both. One of the reasons that I became a consultant instead of signing up for some big-benefits job was so that I could work from home. I *can* do both. I *will* do both."

"The question is," said Corinne, posing her chin on her knees, "who you gonna do it with?"

"If that's a pun, I plan to ignore it," Laura said wryly. "Anyway, just because there's chemistry between Ken and me, that doesn't mean he's husband material."

"Oh, come on. Who better?"

"Okay, let me rephrase: that doesn't mean I'm wife material."

"Aha. *Now* we're getting at it," Corinne said, pointing a triumphant finger at her sister. "You don't think you're good enough for him! And you're the one who's supposed to have confidence in yourself. God, you sound like *me*."

"Yeah, but I'm the one with a track record," Laura said. "Let us not forget dear Max."

"But Ken has always known about Uncle Norbert. And that didn't stop him from—"

"Trying to get me into bed. Right. Because, as you said yourself: he *is* a guy. It doesn't mean a thing. Anyway, I doubt that he'll try again. I told him tonight that Max dumped me."

"Really! Before or after the bra?"

"After. The fact had nothing to do with my backing away from the bed, of course, but at this point Ken thinks I'm an emotional wreck in general, and he thinks Max is part of that."

"Are you? Is he?"

"If I am, it's not because of *Max*. Oh, I don't want to talk about it," Laura said miserably. "Let's talk about your love life instead. How were things with Gabe after this afternoon's little horror? Could you tell?"

"He's concerned," Corinne said, biting her lower lip. "And very worried about me, about how this will affect me. And Shore Gardens. My dreams for it."

"I'm glad to hear that he feels that way, though I'm not

surprised. I half expected to see him on the porch with you when we got back. He's been here every night lately."

Their courtship was so old-fashioned and sweet—tailor-made for a woman like Corinne.

"He stopped in, but he couldn't stay—although he did steal a couple of the Szechuan ribs from Snack on his way out," she added, smiling. "There's a council meeting to-night."

"It's so nice that you've grown up as neighbors," Laura mused. "Not like Ken and me. We hardly know anything about one another except that we have chemistry."

"It's better than *not* having chemistry," Corinne pointed out.

Laura asked, almost shyly, "Do you, with Gabe?"

Corinne nodded. "When I see him, my heart goes up, up, and away," she said, fluttering her hand upward. "And when he touches me or kisses me, it's pure heaven."

"You're going to be so happy together," Laura said wist-fully. "You're taking it slow but sure. That's the best way."

She was surprised to see her sister's eyes suddenly glaze over.

"How can we be happy, now that this has happened?" Corinne asked. "Gabe wants to run for Congress down the road, everyone knows that. I might have been able to . . . to fit in that picture if Shore Gardens were a success. People might have forgotten about our unsavory family. Uncle Norbert might never have been an issue. But now, with *another* murder here—"

"You don't know it's a murder," Laura said quickly.

"It almost doesn't matter! Bones are bones! That's all people will remember. You know what happens to politi-cians who are tarred by scandal, even if it's by association. If Gabe were content simply to be the mayor of Chepa-quit—but he has bigger dreams than that; he has plans!"

Sighing, Laura said, "Rin, you worry too much. Stop. We're all going to have to take this one day at a time.

Gabe's a good man; you ought to trust him."

She got her exhausted body out of the comfy, overstuffed chair by pure force of will and went over to hug her sister. "Now hand me one of those pillows. I'm sleeping here tonight."

"Really?" Corinne said, pleased.

They had shared a bedroom nearly all of their childhood, and Laura used to climb down from her upper bunk to comfort Corinne whenever she was scared or nervous—which was often, given their father's temper.

Tonight, judging from their brooding silence as they lay side by side in their parents' old bed, they were both scared. Both nervous. Eventually, when Laura was on the verge of dropping off to sleep, her sister whispered, "Do you think Uncle Norbert did this one too?"

"I sure hope so," Laura murmured, and then she let herself fall the rest of the way into darkness.

Chapter 21

Breakfast was late. There seemed no point to getting up with the chickens anymore.

"For all practical purposes, we're under house arrest," Snack said, fuming. "What're we supposed to do—sit here twiddling our thumbs? I have *work* to get done."

As frustrating and appalling as the situation was, Laura found herself laughing out loud at his lament. Work! Snack! Same sentence!

"Little brother, you're officially all growed up. We are so proud of you," she said, planting a big kiss on his newly stubbled cheek. "And you will look *so* cute when—if—that beard fills out," she teased.

"Quit it," he said, half good-naturedly pushing her away. "We've got to get those trees, and the bigger shrubs, brought closer to the shop; the customers aren't going to hike all the way back to the east end to look them over, even if they were allowed to. Who the hell do these guys think they are, impounding the Deere? I need that tractor. *Now*," he said, standing up. He looked ready to take on the entire Chepaquit police force.

"Oh no you don't," Corinne said, capping his head with one large hand and pushing him back down. "I spent good money for the blueberries in these pancakes, and you're not going anywhere until you've had breakfast. Sit."

The syrup was hot, the bacon sizzling. Snack was persuaded to stay where he was. A minute later, Gabe showed up at the screen door and was waved in. He was dressed in work twills and a dark polo shirt and on his way to work.

"Joe Penchance wants to talk with me about a couple of upgrades," he explained. "As you know, when Joe says 'Jump,' all *I* say is 'How high?' "

He stole a strip of bacon from Corinne's plate and added, "Let's hope he's heard even half the yammering I've done about Shore Gardens. In which case, you'll have all the business you can handle."

"Thanks, Gabe," Laura said warmly. "We appreciate your putting in a good word for us."

"Oh, and I meant to ask you," Gabe said to Snack. "I hear the Deere's off-limits for a couple of days. Could you use my Bobcat loader?"

"All-wheel steer?"

"Sorry," Gabe said meekly. "Skid steer."

"Hey, it's better'n a sharp stick in the eye. Yeah, man. Definitely, I could use it."

"It's back of the house. Keys are in it. Help yourself."

"Cool," Snack said, breaking into one of his cloud-parting, sunshine grins.

It was heartwarming to see that Gabe wasn't abandoning them. Corinne looked ready to burst into tears yet again—now of just plain joy. She was at a loss for words. The shock of the discovery and the fallout from it were clearly affecting her the most deeply—but then, Corinne was the most emotional of them.

However Gabe felt about the current mess, it was apparent to Laura that he knew more about the discovery than they did. She waited until he finished his bacon and his pleasantries, said goodbye, and went outside. Then she caught up with him.

She kept her voice low and her back to the screen door

as she said, "Gabe, you've obviously talked with the police. Do they know yet if it was a man or a woman? They *must* know. That part's not rocket science. Fat skull or delicate one? Big bones or little ones? *I* could probably tell the sex if they gave me the chance."

He looked very uncomfortable. "I'm not really supposed to say."

Laura was not in the mood to take no for an answer. "Come on, Gabe," she coaxed. "It's going to come out very shortly; you know it will."

He glanced in the direction of the greenhouse, where the men had progressed in their investigation. Without looking at Laura, he muttered, "It's not a man."

"Oh, damn."

"Remember: I didn't tell you what it was."

"No, I know. But . . . oh, damn." It didn't bode well for her theory of two drifters who'd got drunk together and into a fatal argument. She said, "Do they know how old she was? How long ago it was? Can they tell any of that yet?"

Gabe shook his head. "That'll take longer. They have their theories, but nothing solid. They did find part of— Well, look, I can't go rattling this stuff off, Laura!" he said, turning to her and clearly angry with himself. "It would compromise the investigation, you know it would."

She felt like saying, *Your Chepaquit chums seem plenty willing to tell* you *all they know,* but she couldn't shut down the only avenue of information that was available to her, so she made herself agree with him. Besides, if she'd stuck around in Chepaquit, who could say? Maybe she'd be one of the in crowd too.

As if.

Deliberately changing the subject, she said on a more pleasant note, "Are you going to any of the Founders Week events? Since the shop is going to be shut down today, I thought I'd drag Corinne to something. The strain of this on her is unbelievable; she deserves a reprieve. Do you have any recommendations?"

Gabe didn't hesitate. "Take Rinnie to the kite-flying contest. It's a lot of fun and the perfect diversion."

He added with a hapless smile, "I'd love to take her myself, but . . . the powerful Mr. Penchance has other plans for me this afternoon."

Gabe didn't have to offer that sweet admission about wanting to take Corinne, but Laura was so glad that he did. She would bring it wrapped up in a bow to her sister, and Corinne could carry it around with her until she saw him again.

"Thanks, Gabe," Laura said softly. "Thanks for everything so far."

"Hey, come on. What're friends for?"

For marriage, she wanted to inform him. *Kids. A big old dopey dog like Baskerville running around with a chew-toy in his mouth, instead of someone's thighbone.*

"Don't give up on her, Gabe," she said impulsively. "It would break her heart."

He gave her a steady look and said, "You didn't have to tell me that."

And on that wounded but reassuring note, he left.

Like many Cape Cod villages whose year-round populations numbered in the low thousands, Chepaquit tried hard to make the most of what it had come summer, when tourists flooded the Cape like a hurricane surge at high tide.

There were difficulties, though. Chepaquit was not as old or refined as Sandwich, not as hip and swinging as Woods Hole, not as charmingly commercial as Chatham. Chepaquit didn't even have a lighthouse to flaunt (Chatham had that). Chepaquit had sand and water, and that was pretty much it—except for the Legend of the Founders, which Chepaquit played up for all its worth during Founders Week.

The story of the town's beginning was packed with drama: in 1836, approaching the height of the whaling era in America, a heavily laden ship bound for Nantucket became disabled in a fierce storm and was driven off course until eventually it sank halfway between Nantucket and the stretch of beach that came to be known as Chepaquit. In the last minutes before losing his ship, the captain and eight of his crew took to one of the longboats, the remainder of the crew to the others.

So fierce was the storm that only the captain's longboat survived, wrecking on a beach near a group of fishermen's shacks. In one of the shacks lived the widow of a fisherman; she had stayed on to be of general service to the others. It was she, a woman of rough-and-tumble descent, who nursed the surviving crew and especially its handsome, rugged, and wealthy captain.

Some say the woman, Eliza by name, cast a spell on the captain. In any case, he fell in love, and when he was recovered, he bought the land on which the fishermen were squatting. Although he was exonerated from blame for the loss of the ship, Captain Barclay wasn't able to get over the loss of lives under his command; he couldn't bear to go to sea again.

Eventually he founded a town on the land he had purchased, and he named it Chepaquit after one of his crew, a Native American who had distinguished himself in an act of heroism aboard ship. Chepaquit and several others of the surprisingly loyal crew settled in the new village with Captain Barclay and Eliza—among them, the ship's steward, James Wellerton.

And now, one and three-quarter centuries later, all that remained of the maritime beginnings of Chepaquit were a few poignant reminders: the handwritten record of Captain Barclay's autobiography in the town's one-room library;

the tiller from the longboat that had smashed up on shore; and some of the descendants of captain and crew, none of whom any longer derived his living from the sea.

"The problem was to make the legend marketable," Corinne explained to her sister, "so five or six years ago, the council came up with 'Chepaquit—Pitcairn of the Cape.' What d'you think?"

Laura stared at the huge white banner, its Pitcairn slogan emblazoned in nautical blue and flanked by stylized ships, that was strung across Main at its intersection with Water Street.

"I think the slogan's a stretch," Laura admitted. "First of all, how many people know that Pitcairn is the island where the crew of the *Bounty* settled after their mutiny? And Bligh's crew headed for Pitcairn on purpose. Captain Barclay didn't have a heck of a lot of choice about where to aim his longboat."

"Well—don't go telling the tourists. The idea is that we're supposed to be a wonderful destination."

"And you are," Laura said, looping her arm through her sister's.

It was another in a string of improbably glorious days, warm and breezy and absolutely tailor-made for flying a kite. There were dozens of them visible from the town center where the sisters were currently taking in the scene.

"It was Gabe who came up with the Pitcairn concept," Corinne explained. "He's so proud of Chepaquit's history."

"And well he should be. He's a Wellerton, after all, descended from one of our founders."

A discouraged sigh escaped Corinne. "He is, isn't he? Oh, God. What was I thinking?"

Laura said, "Now, wait a minute. He's a Wellerton, not a Washington, for heaven's sake. Let's not get *overly* impressed."

"You're not impressed that Kendall Barclay is descended from Captain Barclay himself?"

"No! Well . . . maybe I was once. But I'm willing to bet that Kendall Barclay takes his pants off one leg at a time," she said dryly, "just like everyone else."

Corinne laughed and said, "Isn't the expression supposed to be 'Puts his pants *on* one leg at a time'?"

"Oh, Gawd. You're right," Laura said, embarrassed. "How Freudian of me." She decided that there was absolutely no point in dwelling on either the man or his pants, since she didn't expect to see him again after her panicky meltdown of the previous night.

She and Corinne got in line to buy cherry slushes from an ice-cream truck parked in the blocked-off street. All too aware of their current notoriety, they waited in discreet silence until suddenly Corinne groaned and said, "Oh, shoot; I forgot to take something out of the freezer for Snack."

At the mention of their brother's name, the woman ahead of them turned her head around sharply, took in who was standing there, lifted her chin, and yanked her grandson out of the line.

"We'll get the slush later, Joshua. Let's go look at the quilt exhibit first."

Little Joshua was having none of it. "No! I want my slush first! You said!"

"Don't be naughty. We can come back when the line is smaller, Josh. Come with me; we'll go see the quilts."

"I don't *wanna* see quilts, not now, not ever. I want my slush!"

He began to bawl loudly.

The woman turned to the sisters with a baleful look. "I hope you're happy now," she snapped. "You are *nothing* but trouble, you Shores."

She gave Joshua's arm a yank that might have dismembered a less robust child and marched him, howling, toward the village hall.

"Who was *that*?" Laura asked, abashed.

Corinne's tan did nothing to hide the crimson flush in her cheeks, but this time her high color was from anger. She was as stunned as Laura was.

Under her breath, she said, "You didn't recognize her? That was Patsy O'Hara's mother. Josh is Patsy's kid."

"Mrs. O'Hara? Oh, God, it figures. She *never* let Patsy play with us. I remember one time I sneaked over to Patsy's house and Mrs. O'Hara came home unexpectedly; I hid under the bed for an hour before she left again and I could escape. It was the most humiliating hour of my life."

Once again Laura remembered why she'd left Chepaquit. How did you change people's initial convictions about you? It couldn't be done. There they were, two grown women, dressed very prettily in summer skirts and pastel tops and politely minding their own business, and what did they get? Bushwhacked.

Of course, the latest scandal couldn't be helping their case for acceptance very much. Still, bones or no bones, it was completely unnerving to have Mrs. O'Hara whip her head around like that at the mention of Snack's name. Was it the Shore clan in general that everyone was focused on—or Snack himself? The town had never had much use for him.

Laura could see that Corinne was wondering the same thing. Their spirits dampened, they skipped the cherry ices and headed off for the kite-flying arena. Corinne was always happiest with the wind in her hair, anyway.

There was no line at the popcorn cart, so they bought a bag apiece and munched on the snack as they threaded their way through strolling tourists and townspeople—no huge crowds, despite the fine weather and the Pitcairn comparison. They wandered down a side lane that led to the town beach, a wide strip of pure white sand with a weathered concession shed in the middle and dotted with humble trash barrels painted with childlike renderings of gulls and shells.

The kites, of every conceivable type and color, were swooping, diving, climbing, and skittering across a sky studded with cotton clouds. Bird kites, twist kites, box kites, dragon kites, stunt kites, trick kites, and several plain old everyday diamond kites filled the air with their jubilant solo dances.

Laura was enchanted.

"They didn't have this during Founders Week when *we* were kids," she said.

"How would we know? We would've been working."

"Too true," Laura said, yearning once again for that childhood she'd somehow missed. "Well, we're not working now, so let's make up for a few lost years."

They took off their sandals and trekked leisurely across the warm sand, digging their toes in now and then to watch a particularly perilous maneuver and, at one point, crying out together when one of the kites crash-landed in the parking lot.

"Don't worry, it's cool," the teenage owner assured them as he began reeling in his fierce-looking F-16.

Relieved to see no damage done, they walked on, pausing at the very end of the exhibition to marvel at the twenty-five-foot-long dragon kite that wiggled and wallowed above them. Its great size and bright yellow, green, and red color scheme made it easily the biggest and brightest kite in the sky, humbling the charming Harry Potter diamond kite that snapped and fluttered alongside.

"It's hard to believe that the same wind can keep both those kites aloft," said Corinne, shading her eyes from the afternoon sun.

"I know," Laura said, squinting up at them. "You expect the one to sink like a stone, and the other to blow apart. I don't understand the aerodynamics of kites at all. You know what, we should just ask some—"

One. The one. The one, the only. What was he doing here, of all places, and with a Harry Potter kite, of all things?

Chapter 22

"Hey," Ken said, seeing them at about the same time that Laura saw him. A grin spread across his face, leaving Laura giddy.

When I see him, my heart goes up, up, and away.

Corinne had got it just about right, Laura realized. Her own heart was lifting and soaring alongside that Harry Potter kite. She was astounded by the coincidence of their meeting. Never mind that the beach was filled with locals. This was extraordinary. This was fate.

He was wearing a shirt and tie with his khakis, way overdressed for Oregon, but somehow not that weird for a beach in New England.

"What're you doing here?" she asked, and she was hoping the answer would be, "Waiting for you, of course."

"Banker's hours, remember?" he teased, and then he went on to explain. "I had the kite—my nieces and I made it when they were visiting—and it was just sitting at home. I figured I'd take it down to the beach and give it to the first kid I saw."

He said with a gallant smile, "Corinne? That would be you," and handed her his string-wrapped stick.

"Me?" she squeaked. "Oh, I couldn't, honest, I don't know how . . . I've never flown a kite, ever. Take it back, take it back, *plee-eeze.*" She looked as if he'd just handed her the controls of a jumbo jet.

"You're doing swell. Just pump it two or three times, and you'll be able to keep it right where it is," he said, laughing. "Okay, ma'am, you're on your own. Mind if I steal your sister for a couple of minutes while I take in the rest of the show? I didn't do it when I first got here."

Corinne nodded nervously, her gaze fixed on the kite, and Ken took Laura by the arm and said, "Shall we?"

And when he touches me or kisses me, it's pure heaven.

Corinne had that part right as well. Oh, damn, she had it so completely right.

When they had strolled a little ways away, Laura said to him, "You do realize that my sister will die of embarrassment if Harry Potter crashes and burns, don't you?"

"Harry's fine. Those instructions I gave her basically cancel one another out. It's a perfect day; the kite will fly itself."

"Oh. Well, in that case . . ."

She let herself fall into strolling mode with him, perfectly happy, for once, just to be. Maybe it was her imagination, maybe it was the kites, maybe it was because when you smile, the whole world smiles with you—but everyone they passed on the beach seemed willing to make eye contact with Laura without a hint of suspicion, much less hostility. A couple of women even asked to know when the nursery would be open again for business; they'd heard so much about the jumbo-sized annuals for sale there.

It's Ken, she theorized. *They're trying to score points with him.*

But why would young mothers with children and little old ladies in hairpins want to do that? Wasn't it possible that Chepaquit was simply evolving into a vibrant, small-town alternative to Boston? The town was clearly growing. Laura had seen the new construction, seen the new faces.

What she hadn't seen, until that moment, were the possibilities for a future there.

Frightened by her own optimism, she walked beside Ken in thoughtful silence. He seemed content to do the same. But she was practically throbbing with awareness of him, despite the bright sun and the people all around them. If they'd been alone on the deck of a yacht in the moonlight, she could not have been more aware of him.

And yet Ken seemed truly to have nothing to say. Once or twice he glanced at her, but he seemed content just to walk. It rattled her, and she got a little silly, as she sometimes did when she was flustered.

"Wanna hear a kite joke?" she asked him.

"Sure."

"A man is in his yard," she said, "trying to fly a kite with his son. Every time the kite gets up into the air, it comes crashing down again. This goes on for a while. Finally, his wife sticks her head out the window and yells, 'You need more tail.' The father turns to his kid and says, 'Son, I'll never understand your mom. Just yesterday I told her I needed more tail, and she told me to go fly a kite.' "

Ken burst into a loud laugh. "I'm shocked," he said primly. "Who told it to you? Snack?"

Caught off guard by the question, Laura had to say: "Max."

Ken gave a single upward jerk of his head by way of an acknowledgment. After they walked a few more steps, he said, "I'm pretty sure I hate that guy."

Surprised, she said, "Why? Because he dumped me?"

"Because he knew you well enough to tell you dirty jokes."

She stopped to do a double-take. "You want to tell me dirty jokes?"

"I just want to know you well enough to."

If she expected to find burning desire in the look he was giving her, Laura was disappointed. She saw wariness in those sea-blue eyes, and, worse, distrust. The question was, what was it that he distrusted?

"We really have spent more time in the trenches than we have at the pool, haven't we?" she said. Before he could answer, she added, "And, face it: it doesn't look as if my life will be normal anytime soon."

"Doesn't look like it," he agreed. "What's your point?"

"My point is that unless you have a taste for the bizarre situation, I'm not sure you want to continue this walk with me."

"Well," he drawled. "I guess we're even now."

"Oh? How so?"

"This time you're the one who's ambushed *me*."

The phrase vividly called up a picture of them in the doorway of his bedroom; Laura could practically hear her own moans.

"I didn't intend to ambush you," she said, pressing her lips together. "I just want you to know that there's no obligation to get to know me well enough to tell me dirty jokes."

Without a smile, he said, "How about if I just try to get to know you, period?"

It was an odd proposal, possibly innocent, probably intimate. Laura didn't really know what to make of it, but she knew what her answer had to be. "Yes. Okay. I'd . . . like that."

Suddenly they heard Corinne yelling at them. "Ken! Help! That dog ran off with my sandal! Come and take the kite!"

Laughing, Ken yelled back, "I'll get the shoe." He took off after the golden retriever, who apparently had decided that the sandal could use a good wash. Into the sea went Ken. After a brief showdown with the animal, he was able to return the sodden shoe to its rightful owner.

Laura watched him, delighted by the sight. His khakis were soaked to the knees, his yellow tie was blowing sideways like a kite-tail in the wind. He had a grin on his face that would have melted the most hardened of hearts. For all of his education and breeding, Kendall Barclay was a townie to the core: it was obvious that he was perfectly content being on that particular patch of the planet. The captain's genes ran true.

Corinne herself looked wonderfully carefree and relaxed. She and Ken were in animated conversation, which just went to show that Corinne *could* fly a kite and talk at the same time, despite her fears. As Laura approached them, she could see that Ken was having a lot to do with her sister's mood; there was just something about him that put people at ease. The dog's owner had joined them, and a couple of passers-by. Everyone was having a laugh over the purloined shoe.

This was a whole new Chepaquit—and it was definitely where Laura wanted to be. The realization came like a bolt of lightning and an immediate crack of thunder; she felt it race through her body and leave her in a state of electrified shock and with her ears ringing.

But was it Ken or was it home that was claiming her?

It couldn't be home, not with someone's bones in their compost.

It had to be Ken, she decided, dumbfounded.

"Hey, here's an idea," Corinne suggested. "Since they won't let us work in the nursery, why don't we work on the house? We have a lot of daylight left. We can do . . . windows!"

Snack, alas, did not do windows. But he did do painting, so he dragged out an old gallon of gray paint from the basement and went to work on the floor of the wide front porch, while the women tackled the windows on the side of the house that faced the sea.

Laura suspected that they were all somehow whistling

past the graveyard, but it felt good to be doing something constructive again. The first window she tackled was the filthy one on the second-floor landing. She was sitting on its ledge, cleaning the painted-shut upper pane, when the phone rang. Slithering back out into the hall, she answered before the machine kicked in. It was Ken.

"Hi," she said, unable to keep from smiling. She was picturing him on the beach in his soggy pants, returning Corinne's hijacked shoe.

"I'm at Creasey's Marina," he told her. "They're launching my boat in the next hour: we have to wait for high tide. Come down and help me eat all the fortune cookies in my pocket."

"Is that all you do? Play? Come here and wash windows," she countered, not entirely kidding.

"Ah . . . sorry, sorry, can't," he said. He sounded sincere, as if there were nothing he'd like to do more. "You know the old saying: time and tide wait for no man."

"I know another saying: something, something, men and their toys."

"Hey, unfair. Except for the car, the boat is really my only toy. And it's a hand-me-down boat at that."

"Such things are called 'antiques,'" she said dryly. "In this case, the correct term would be 'antique yacht.' "

He sighed. "It's just a small old boat, Laura. Still carrying that chip on your shoulder? I thought we'd been through all that."

"Are you kidding? I have enough material for years of therapy."

"Baloney. You just want to think you do."

"Excuse me?"

"Come over to the marina," he coaxed. "And I'll elaborate."

"Ken . . . really, I can't. Everyone here is too on edge. We need to hang together now. To do something together.

But . . . open a cookie for me," she said impulsively. "Tell me my fortune."

"Can do," he said, and she heard the rustle of cellophane. "Okay, it says, 'Come down and help me eat all the fortune cookies in my pocket.' "

Her laugh was beguiled as she asked, "What does it really say?"

There was the slightest hesitancy in his voice before he answered, " 'Be careful what you wish for.' "

"Oh, that one. That's so overused," she said, actually resenting the slip of paper. "Open another one."

"Okey-dokey." Again the crackle, again the slight hesitancy before he said, " 'Be careful what you wish for.' "

She humphed and said, "There is *no* quality control in fortune-cookie factories anymore. Do another one."

Sheepishly, he said, "That's all I got. I had three with me. I may have exaggerated my holdings."

"What did yours say?" she asked, almost afraid to ask.

His soft laugh was more bemused than cheerful. "Actually, mine had the complementary sentiment to yours: 'Things are not what they seem.' "

"Good grief," Laura said, more affected than she would have liked to be by the ominous proverbs. "Whoever the fortune-writer was, he could use some prescription medication. What a downhead. Whatever happened to cute little sayings like 'You will gain wealth and live long'?"

"Ah, the guy probably just had a bad day at the office," Ken said, dismissing him. "When will I see you again?"

"We have lots of Windex. When can you be here?"

"An hour, an hour and a half."

"Too late. The sun will be down and the streaks wouldn't show."

"Can I come over anyway?" His voice was a low, irresistible plea. "We could play Scrabble."

"How persistent you are," she said, smiling.

"I'm a good speller, that's all; I like to show off."

She was charmed into capitulation. "All right. You win. Scrabble it is."

"An hour and a half, tops," he promised.

Whatever game they were playing, it wasn't Scrabble. With a smile that wouldn't go away, Laura returned to her Windex and was surprised to see that her sister had abandoned her post. Wandering through the farmhouse, she tracked Corinne to the front porch.

She was standing alongside Snack, facing down the law.

No question, Laura felt as if she were watching a scene out of a Western. There they were: homesteader Corinne, in bib overalls and clutching a window-cleaning rag; prodigal son Snack, looking lean and rough and dangerous with his stubbled chin and a red bandanna tied around his head; and the posse, in the form of two investigators who weren't looking too terribly thrilled with Snack at the moment.

"You got a warrant?" Snack was asking with barely concealed contempt.

Laura couldn't believe he was actually saying that. "Snack, don't," she commanded.

The men, dressed casually but looking official all the same, sounded equally contemptuous. "All we're *saying* is, it's not the best thing to be painting the porch right now, before the death investigation is complete."

"And all *I'm* saying is, if you don't have a homicide investigation, then you don't have cause. Go away and let me paint."

Jumping in to save Snack from being dragged off in handcuffs behind their horses, Laura smiled sweetly and said to them, "My brother is only home for a very limited time, and naturally he wants to get as much accomplished as possible. Since we can't conduct our Founders Week sale as we'd planned, you can see how frustrated we all naturally feel."

"It can't be helped, ma'am."

"Yes. We understand. I'll speak with Chief Mellon about

whether we can paint or not, and in the meantime, we will leave all the bird poop DNA right where it is on the porch so that it's available to you in your ongoing investigation."

She picked up the brush lying across the gallon container, then picked up the paint. "Snack? The sooner they get done, the sooner we can get back to the business of saving the ranch. Shall we leave them to it?"

Put that way, Snack couldn't say no. He turned to go back into the house and then, maybe to have the last word, he turned back around. An expert spitter from way back, he let loose a missile of phlegm that went flying over the banister and within a foot of the investigator who both looked and talked like Joe Friday.

It could have been worse, Laura told herself, sighing. At least Snack was still a good shot. Without daring to look at the investigators' reactions, she followed her brother and sister inside.

Chapter 23

Ken stood on the sidelines at the marina, watching Jay Creasey slide his hydraulic lift under the bow of sweet *Eliza* in preparation for her launch.

He shouldn't be feeling so good, he knew. With Shore Gardens shut down and a forensic exam in the works, there was more than enough gloom to cast a pall over the moment. But the moment was traditionally one of the sweetest of the year, and savoring it was almost automatic.

And besides, there were reasons to feel optimistic about the ongoing investigation. He had learned from Chief Andy Mellon that the woman's bones had been in the compost pile for a long time, perhaps generations. That was the initial word from the ME, and Ken had taken heart from it. He wanted no one—no one—in Laura's own generation to be under a cloud of suspicion.

Still, assuming that it was a murder, which seemed likely, it was disheartening to realize that an obvious suspect was Laura's uncle, and that another might be Laura's father. Ken did not want it to be Laura's anything.

He had never known Norbert Shore, who'd been in prison with cancer by the time Ken became old enough to learn the story of how the man had strangled his wife. But Ken certainly had known Norbert's brother, and as far as he was concerned, Oliver Shore had been nothing less than a foul-tempered menace. No wonder Laura and Snack had run as fast and as far as they could to escape him.

Ken's newly avowed goal was clear: somehow he had to make Chepaquit accept Laura and Snack and Corinne for who they were and not hold the sins of their uncle—or of their father—against them. He was ready and willing to throw his name, his money, and his time into the effort.

If Laura would let him. She had this thing about fighting her own battles, and Ken wasn't altogether sure that she was currently signing up enlistees in her cause.

His revery was broken when Jay Creasey leaned out the window of his cab and yelled, "Hey, Cap! You got all your dock lines set up?"

"Yessir," he told the marina manager. "And fenders at the ready."

"You're gonna need 'em. Wind's pickin' up. Want some help takin' her around?"

"Nah. But if someone's on the dock to take a line, I wouldn't mind."

Creasey nodded. "Last thing you need is a big fat gouge in that paint job," he agreed. "Nice work, by the way."

High praise, coming from Jay Creasey. Ken said to the older man, "Thankee, sir. I try my best."

"You ever quit your day job," Creasey added with a gruff nod, "you come round to the office, and I'll put you right to work."

It would be dream work, as far as Ken was concerned. Messing around in boats all day? Dream work. He grinned and said, "I might take you up on that offer—but only if you let me pay *you*."

Creasey snorted and then began barking instructions to the help, a muscular kid with a ponytail who looked as if he would run screaming from anything so terrifying as a desk.

He'll probably end up skipper of a windjammer in the

Caribbean, whereas I—I'll still be running Chepaquit Savings.

Ken had to smile. It happened every year around launching time: the restless wanderlust, the second-guessing about might-have-beens. So it was coming as a bit of a pleasant shock that this year, he was feeling happy to be sticking around Chepaquit. He envisioned taking Laura sailing, taking Laura dining, taking Laura dancing, taking Laura to bed. Stick a bottle of Windex in his hand, and he could even envision himself . . .

Okay, something was going on here. The day that Ken Barclay could picture himself with a bottle of Windex in his hand was the day that he was in trouble. What the hell *was* going on here? The biggest commitment he'd ever made in his life was to something called *Eliza*. Someone called Laura—that was a whole new level of commitment. Man, a whole new level.

His musings were so intense, so real, that he had to be chided back to the present.

"Yo! Move it!" Creasey roared.

Ken was standing right in the path of the truck that was guiding the *Eliza* down the ways and into the sea.

Embarrassed to be yelled at like some landlubber, he jumped clear and watched with his usual fascination as the small, graceful sloop made her annual slide into the warming waters of Nantucket Sound. The *Eliza* slipped off the padded arms of the hydraulic cradle and dipped and bobbed becomingly; she was afloat again.

Ken climbed aboard the sloop from the wobbly floating dock that was casually moored alongside the deep end of the ways. The little ship yielded gently to the pressure of his boarding and then righted herself, ready to go.

It felt good—it felt great—to be waterborne again after months of being on land. Ken thought of his ancestor Captain Barclay, as he always did, with a mixture of awe and sympathy. To captain a whaling ship successfully around the world with nothing but the stars to steer her by, only to lose her so close to home—that was enough to break any man's spirit. Never mind that at least half a dozen other vessels in New England foundered during the same storm, and with far greater loss of life. By all accounts, Captain Barclay after the storm was not the same man as before it.

What was it like, to have responsibility for a man's life? Ken had never even baby-sat, let alone had complete responsibility for the crew of a square-rigger. The grief had to be crushing.

He tossed Creasey a stern line and his crew a bow line to hold the boat temporarily. Then he flipped the secured fenders over the port side, which he knew would be driven into his slip by the raw southeast wind that had come up and was still rising.

Rain soon, he thought as he scanned the dull gray sky.

He turned the key to the sloop's auxiliary engine. After a slow start, the diesel knocked to life and thumped solidly, a heartbeat in a winged angel. Ken was glad to hear it: no mechanic, he considered it a minor miracle whenever the engine awoke from its winter sleep, stretched, yawned, and began moving again.

"Okay, you can cast off; I'll take her around now," he told Creasey and the yardhand.

The men unfastened the lines, coiled them loosely, and tossed them back on deck as Ken put the sloop smartly in reverse, compensating for the adverse wind. He backed all the way out from between the two rows of slips, turned into the Sound, and then threw the boat into forward gear, heading for the same berth that had been in his family since the marina was built half a century earlier.

It took some smart maneuvering, but Ken knew the boat and he knew the slip. He didn't really need anyone to catch the lines—but he'd got a *damn* good paint job on the hull this year, and he wasn't taking any chances. Hell, everyone knew that bankers were conservative folk.

As he approached, he was surprised to see Billy Benwith weighing down one end of the narrow float as he tried to squeeze his big body out of the way of the two men arriving. Ken acknowledged Billy with a distracted nod and threw the boat into neutral and then reverse and back to neutral again, gauging the wind speed and direction well enough so that the boat made a painless soft landing. The men tied up the *Eliza*, Ken thanked them for working late, and they knocked off for the day.

Not Billy. He carried his bulk forward a little sheepishly and said, "They told me you were launchin' tonight. Is this an okay time?"

"For—?"

"Because I've got something, y'know, to tell you. I was gonna tell Laura, but then I thought, she's such a delicate lady. And this isn't delicate, what I have to say. You been giving me work, just like the Shores. For years and years." He took a deep breath after his long speech and said, "So—can I tell you now?"

"Sure. Now's good," Ken said, baffled by what he was hearing. Billy was known around town as the gentle giant, but just then, he had Ken's hairs standing on end. "C'mon aboard," he said.

Billy grabbed the stanchions on either side of the gate and hauled himself up. The *Eliza* angled sharply to take his weight, then righted herself as well as she could, which wasn't completely: Ken felt the boat take on a slight starboard list as Billy settled opposite him on the cockpit seat.

"What's up?" Ken asked, even though in the back of his mind, he was thinking that he should first take the time to rig a forward spring line. The wind really was picking up.

Billy always looked a little ill at ease when he talked to anyone, but his manner just then went far beyond his usual awkward shyness: the man looked genuinely scared. "It's okay, Billy," Ken found himself saying. "Whatever it is, we can make it right again."

"I don't know," said Billy disconsolately. "I don't know."

"What happened?"

"I'm not sure anything happened. But it could've. Maybe. You know those bones?"

"Oh, yes."

"Well, I think I know how they got there."

God Almighty. "Okay," Ken said, nodding calmly. "Tell me how you think they got there."

Billy seemed eager to spill it all out, frowning as he concentrated on what he had to say. "Well, I was doing deliveries for Shore Gardens," he began. "We were real busy with graduations and weddings and all. And back then, the flower arrangements were usually done in the greenhouse. You remember?"

"Not exactly, but that's all right; go ahead."

"Mr. Shore used to keep Laura and Rinnie working in the store because of handling money and all, which nobody else ever got to do but them. The flower arrangers, they were just people he hired around busy season—usually from Easter to weddings. And also before Christmas, 'course."

"Sure. That makes sense," said Ken, wondering where Billy was taking this. "Spring through June is a busy time, and so is Christmas."

"But Christmas season, that's only a coupla weeks. But it would be too cold to heat the greenhouse in December, so then they used to make do in the shop. But it was really crowded when everyone was jammed in there like that. They had to make do."

"Yes. I understand. So what then? What about the flower arrangers?"

Billy looked a little huddled, rubbing his bare, massive arms briskly in the chill wind. He stared at his reflection in the brass ship's bell that was mounted on the bulkhead as he said, "There was this one girl . . . she was younger than the usual. Prettier. The prettiest of all. Prettier than—promise you won't tell?"

"Promise."

"Prettier even than Laura. You remember?"

"Ah . . . can't say that I do," Ken admitted. He was becoming more baffled by the second. "What was her name?"

"Sylvia. Her name was Sylvia. I don't know her other name." He sighed. His brow twitched in the effort to focus. "No, I don't know it. If I ever knew it."

Sylvia again. Ken said carefully, "Well, this Sylvia—she must have been really good-looking, because she sure seems to have made an impression. When did she work at Shore Gardens?"

"She worked there when I worked there," Billy said, blinking at the question.

"No, I mean, how long ago was that? Do you remember?"

"Yes," Billy said, nodding eagerly. "I had my driver's license. Laura and me both. We practiced in the same car in Driver's Ed. We were in the same grade—well, me because I was held back. And on driving too. I didn't like that part!"

Ken felt obligated to apologize for his lack of knowledge. "I was going to school in western Mass by then," he said, "so I guess I kind of lost touch with everyone."

Billy nodded again and gave Ken a look, as if he were taking it personally. *You went K through 8 with us, and then you ditched us for a fancy high school. What, we weren't good enough for you?*

Or maybe that was just Ken, projecting. He said, "So you were delivering flowers for Shore Gardens, and a very pretty girl named Sylvia was doing the arrangements. Did she work in the greenhouse or in the shop?"

"For sure, the greenhouse! She started work during Founders Week. I said when I got my driver's license, right? *Everyone* knows the driver's test is in May."

Except Ken. "Right, right. Sorry. And then what?"

Suddenly Billy seemed not to want to continue, after all. He said to Ken, "Would it be okay if I rang the bell?"

"Uh . . . sure, go ahead," Ken said, wondering at the wild shift in subject matter.

Billy carefully took hold of the macramé lanyard attached to the clapper of the brass bell and gave it a timid rap against the strike.

"Ooh! It's loud," he said with a startled giggle.

Ken made himself smile. "That's so other boats can hear you in the fog."

"Yeah. It wouldn't help if no one could hear; they wouldn't know where you were," said Billy. "Then what would be the point?"

"Exactly," said Ken, nodding.

"It's Snack," Billy blurted. "Sylvia had a *big* fight with Snack. They were screamin' at each other, just screamin'. I didn't even go into the greenhouse, that's how mad they sounded. They were just screamin' at the top of their lungs."

That's all this was about? Thank God. "Ah, so you heard an argument between Snack and this girl Sylvia. And because of that, you think—?"

"He could've done it. I wish he didn't," Billy said miserably, "but he could've."

Relieved that Billy's big news came down to overhearing an argument between Snack and a girl, Ken was nonetheless thrown into a quandary. The news about the exceptional length of time that the bones had been in the compost pile wasn't common knowledge yet—but on the other hand, Billy could do a lot of damage spreading his story around. Ken understood how small towns worked. The simplest event could be twisted into something unrecognizable within the space of a single conversation over a picket fence.

That was unacceptable. "Billy," he said, "you have absolutely nothing to worry about; I have great news for you. But first: can you keep a secret?"

"I think so," said Billy. He looked as if he'd never been asked to do it before.

"It won't be forever. Just temporarily."

Billy looked excited, relieved, and curious, in that order. "What's the secret?"

"I've already been told that the bones were in the compost pile for much, much longer than when you're talking about," Ken explained. "The bones are not Sylvia's, Billy. You don't have to worry about that. Okay?"

Now came really happy nodding of his big, shaggy head. *"Okay!"* Billy said. He looked ready to hug Ken.

And Ken was just about ready to hug him back. What profound relief to know there wasn't anything to Billy's fears. Ken was jumpier about the investigation than he'd realized.

"Well, I'm glad that's settled," he said, smacking his hands together. "How about a Coke?"

"Yeah, that would—oh. But . . . then what were they doing, dragging it into the compost pile?"

"Who?"

Billy cringed visibly, as if his teacher had asked him to name the capital of Baluchistan.

"If Snack didn't do anything, then I guess I don't know. I always figured it musta been Snack."

"Dragging what?"

"I . . . don't know. Something heavy?"

"When, for God's sake?" Ken snapped.

"That's what I been trying to say: after the fight."

"Right after it?"

"Not *right* after it. Later that day. Maybe about eight o'clock? It was really foggy, and practically dark, I don't care if it was June or not. I was late because I was driving real slow, because I just got my license. I got it the same time as Laura. We were in the same grade, because I was held—"

"Yes, yes. Do you remember what the person looked like that you saw dragging something heavy into the compost pile?"

"Not hardly. It was really, really thick out. I drove the van up to the greenhouse like I always did, so I could just load up the next day and go. So I wasn't *real* close to the compost pile. And then a song came on that I liked a lot—'I Dream of You.' You know it?"

"Yeah, sure," Ken said, lying through gritted teeth. *Don't rush him.*

Billy went on, even more earnestly. "Anyway, I waited until the song was over, and then I guess I fell asleep in the van. Not real asleep, just nap asleep. I almost forgot about that part. Maybe that's why I wasn't so sure of what I saw when I woke up. Maybe I was still dreaming, even. Or maybe just sleepy."

The furrows on the broad expanse of his brow were deep. He was trying so hard to get it right. "But, no, it *wasn't* because I was sleepy; I think it was mostly the fog."

Ken felt as if he were in a free fall into hell. "I can see why you had a hard time," he said reassuringly. "Around here, you can cut a June fog with a knife. But try to remember: was it a big person? Small person? Tall person? Short person? A man? A woman?"

To every question, Billy shook his head. "They were too hunched over. All I know is, they were having a hard time dragging—well, not Sylvia, so I don't know what it was. Maybe a bag of manure or something?"

He sighed heavily and said, "I remember I was thinking of going over to help, but . . ." He dropped his voice to a whisper. "I think maybe I was afraid someone would tell on me."

"Tell what?" Ken asked, surprised.

Up came the massive shoulders in a sorrowful shrug. "I

don't know. But it didn't look right. It made me feel funny to see it. I guess I was afraid."

His pale green eyes looked watery and full of contrition, so much so that Ken began to be suspicious of what it was that Billy was actually sorry for.

Nonetheless, he said to him, "You don't have to be afraid, Billy. You've told me what you saw, so now you don't have to worry. You did the right thing by coming to me and getting it off your chest. All that worrying, and see? It was for nothing. Because it couldn't be Sylvia."

In his mind Ken was thinking, shit, shit, shit. What if there was something to all of this?

Billy smiled sheepishly. "I feel kind of dumb."

"Don't ever feel dumb," Ken said, shaking his head. "You have a much better recall than a lot of other people. Look how long ago that happened, and still you remember it."

"Because I was afraid, that's why," Billy said simply.

"And you didn't have to be."

A hard gust of wind sent the bow rubbing into the dock. Ken stood up and said apologetically, "I've got to tie up the boat a little better; it's supposed to blow like stink tonight."

"I'll go," Billy said, jumping up as if his pants had caught fire.

Ken assured him that there was no hurry, but Billy was convinced that there was. Rather than step carefully down onto the dock, he leaped from the boat, tripping on a stanchion support in the process, and ended up landing on his feet with a heavy thud. Ken was surprised that he didn't break both his ankles; a sailor he was not.

"Mr. Barclay—"

Ken, who had dropped down to the dock behind him and was cleating off the first spring line, said, "We've been all through this, Billy. Call me Ken. I'm your age."

"Okay. Could I ask you a favor?"

"Shoot."

Billy pointed a ham-sized hand at the little brass ship's bell. "Would you count to a hundred, and then ring the bell? It would be fun to hear what it would sound like if I was on one boat, and you were on this boat, and we were in the fog."

"I'll go you one better, Billy. We'll go sailing on the next foggy day, and you can hear for yourself."

"Uh-h-h . . . well, maybe." It sounded like a very iffy maybe. "I don't really like water," Billy admitted with a squeamish look. "I get kinda sick."

Smiling, Ken said, "I understand. All right: I'm countin'. One. Two. Three . . ."

Hurrying off the float and onto the main dock, Billy said over his shoulder, "All the way to a hundred, don't forget."

"Eleven! Twelve! Thirteen!"

Ken watched the bulk that was Billy make his way to the parking lot, where he'd left his old, rusting Hyundai.

Grabbing the lanyard, Ken gave the bell a real whack, something he hadn't done since he was a boy plying the waters with his father in the same chill fog that was now blowing in ahead of the rain. The clear peal of brass on brass was almost shocking in its quaintness, a throwback to an age before air horns and radar and digital readouts.

Not to mention, an age before sophisticated forensic tests like DNA analysis.

As Billy drove off with an answering, happy toot-toot, Ken poured all of his growing and as yet baseless fears into making the *Eliza* doubly secure, adding extra lines and fenders. It was the only thing he could do to control events that were currently out of his hands.

He wanted desperately to believe that Billy had just overheard two teenagers arguing over something as inane as, say, which was the best rock group, and that Billy later had seen someone hauling a bag of something as innocuous as manure and dumping it into the compost pile. What Billy had seen was probably all very ordinary, all very accountable.

Assuming the medical examiner was right.

Chapter 24

The morning after Chief Mellon confided to Ken that the bones were decomposed enough to have been there for generations, the examiner decided to revise his time line downward.

The ME's change of mind had a lot to do with the discovery of a brass belt buckle in the shape of a maple leaf that had survived the belt to which it had once been attached. Inscribed on the leaf were the words "Canada Cup" and the year "1987."

"So now we know," said the chief. "The body was dumped no earlier than 1987."

"Huh." Ken had no comment beyond that one syllable; he was reeling. He'd gone to the chief for further confirmation that the bones couldn't possibly have belonged to the girl named Sylvia that Billy had been so worried about, and instead he had taken a one-two punch to the gut.

Not that Andy Mellon was aware of the impact of his remarks. The men were sitting on the chief's back deck, having a pre-supper beer and watching the chief's twin girls playing badminton with a couple of kids who were there for a sleepover. The smell of wet grass, the squeals and laughter of the children, and the aroma of marinara sauce drifting through the sliding doors of the kitchen behind them almost made Ken wish he'd said yes to the chief's impromptu invitation to stay to dinner. There was something reassuringly stable about the scene, and just then, Ken's footing felt anything but.

Ken was exploiting a friendship, he knew that. Andy Mellon kept a modest cabin cruiser a few slips down from Ken's at Creasey's Marina, and the two were friendly, as all men are who share a common passion. Gabe Wellerton kept a boat there, too, and so did Captain Jack, who once had owned the restaurant he'd named after himself. All of the men had caught dock lines for one another, and at the marina's end-of-summer barbecue, they had grilled burgers and dogs side by side. They weren't exactly family; but having lived in Chepaquit all of their lives, they were the next best thing.

Because of that, Ken could trade on a certain amount of good will, and that's what he was resolved to do. He had to learn as much as he could for Laura's sake. He was in too deep emotionally even to think of watching from the sidelines as the investigation unfolded. It frightened him to think how deep.

The chief came back with another cold one for each of them, and Ken picked up the conversation where they'd left off.

"So . . . they figure the buckle belonged to the woman who was buried there?"

The chief gave him a somewhat condescending look. "It was with the remains."

"Yeah . . . but a *woman* wearing a buckle commemorating a hockey series? Sounds a little butch to me."

"Not if you're Canadian. Not if Gretzky was playing. She was probably a big Gretzky fan. Hell, who wasn't? Come on, man—you don't remember that year? The greatest hockey ever played was played in 1987."

Ken himself was a football fan, but he nodded in arbitrary agreement, then said, "Yeah, but still. There's no chance the bones could be of a small-sized male?"

The chief shook his head. "There are anatomical differences. Besides, this woman was tall, young, and in good health."

"They sound sure."

"They are sure."

Suddenly a remark that Laura had made about Sylvia came skipping to the forefront: *She wasn't local; she was from up north.*

The almost unnecessary question was, how far north?

Ah, hell.

Ken felt like a shit. At best, he was betraying the chief's hospitality. At worst, he was withholding evidence.

That's a crime, you moron. Tell him what Billy said and let the chips fall where they may.

He'd do it—but not until he'd seen Laura. After Billy left him on the previous evening, Ken had begged off going over to the Shore house. He wasn't convinced that he could mask his concern, and he had hoped to buttonhole the chief and pump him for an update. It hadn't happened. Now it had. How the hell was he going to manage to be reassuring to Laura today, now that he knew about the belt buckle?

"So . . . what's next?" Ken asked.

"Now that we have a time line, we'll go through the records of missing persons in the area for the last fifteen years or so."

"Will that kind of information be computerized between states, going so far back?"

"Nah. Some of it will; a lot of it won't. This is bound to take a while."

And all that while, the Shore kids were going to live under a cloud of suspicion. As for Shore Gardens itself . . . it didn't take a rocket scientist, only a banker, to know that its future looked bleak.

They heard a high yelp from Team Badminton: one of the chief's twin daughters went diving for the shuttle and slid onto her fanny, then scrambled back to her feet in a race to make the next shot.

"Hey!" her father called out. "You're getting grass stains all over your shorts, Amy; I hope you know that."

"Yes, Dad," his daughter said without taking her eyes from the shuttle. "I know that." Whack went the birdy.

"And you're wrecking my newly seeded grass; I suppose you know that too."

"Yes, Dad," Amy's sister said. "We know that too." Alice ran back and made a wild swing, slipping on the wet grass and also landing on her shorts, but with a whoop of joy that she'd sent the bird over the net and scored a point.

"Why do I bother?" the chief said, sighing. He leaned back in his new plastic Adirondack chair and put his feet up on the matching resin stool. "Comfortable," he said with approval. "Of course, we could've had real wood if I didn't own a boat, as the wife likes to point out."

Smiling, Ken said, "Your girls love being on the water as much as you do."

"Don't they just? Alice, she's the one. She wants to go into the Coast Guard, and I'll tell you, I'd be proud. Still, it's Amy who's the better fisherman. Nothing fazes her, not blood, not guts. She's the one who cleans the fish with me; Alice won't go near. They're like any twins, I expect—as different from one another as they are the same."

He was beaming. Ken felt a surge of real envy for the life the chief was leading. Suddenly he realized that he would trade everything he had for Andy Mellon's setup, including the plastic Adirondack chairs, if he could be married and sharing a beer and watching his kids play badminton on wet, newly seeded grass.

"So. This is a fine mess, no?" asked the chief, shaking his head. "The uncle, the father. And now this. What a family."

"Hey, come on, Andy," Ken said, demurring. "The kids are a good bunch."

"Oh, yeah, Snack's a real peach." The chief made a wry face. "To employ a cliché: the boy's got a rap sheet a mile long."

"Nothing serious, I imagine," Ken said stolidly. "He's not the type."

"Stole a car, ditched it. DUI. Driving with a suspended license. Breaking and entering—although, to be fair, it was an ex-girlfriend's place and he was allegedly after his clothes."

"Kids will be kids."

"Cut it out, Ken. I know where this is going," the chief added gruffly. "The word's out about you and Laura. Walkin' up and down the beach on kite day didn't exactly go unnoticed."

Oddly enough, Ken was glad to hear it. "I'm not surprised. It's a small town," he said with a shrug.

He went back to watching the kids at their game while Mellon hid behind a long slug of beer, then rested the can on the wide arm of his new resin chair.

"Hey."

Ken turned to see the police chief giving him a steady look. Mellon said quietly, "You sure you don't want to maybe come out of the water for a while? You don't know where this investigation is going; you might end up being caught in an undertow."

It occurred to Ken that Andy Mellon had been waiting for just the right opportunity to warn him away from the Shore family, and now he was taking it. "Too late, Chief. I guess she's got me hook, line, and sinker, to mix your metaphor."

And the funny thing was, Laura hadn't even been trolling.

Mellon nodded and said,. "Well, hey. You're a grown-up." He added with a crafty look, "Does the *mater* know?"

"Cute," Ken snapped. "The short answer is, there's not a hell of a lot for the *mater* to know. I've still got a long row to hoe before Laura will trust me enough to—"

"Get out. Someone like that would jump at the chance."

"She sure as hell hasn't so far."

Ken didn't care for the way the conversation was going, and he used that as his excuse to say his goodbyes without a word about Billy. There was time enough for that. He stood up.

"You've always been an odd piece of work, you know that?" said the chief. "I never could get a handle on you. As a kid you always marched to your own drum. Picked on, bullied, and yet as stoic as hell about it, even though your dad was jumping up and down for us to do something. I'll give you that: you took it like a man. On second thought, I've changed my mind," he said dryly. "I'm thinking you and the Shore girl might just be a match made in heaven."

"From your lips to God's ear," said Ken, rapping his empty beer can against Mellon's thigh. "I'll say goodbye to Beth and get out of your hair."

"Seriously. Think about what I—ow!"

A shuttlecock went whizzing into the side of the chief's neck and he let out an oath. "That's it!" he barked to his kids, and he stuffed the feathered cork into the pocket of his T-shirt. "You're gonna put out someone's eye with this thing; it's lethal. I told you there's no room in the yard. You wanna play something, play bocce or horseshoes when someone's sitting out here."

One of the twins said, "Oh-h-h, come on, Dad. Please? The game's tied at ten to ten. Just let us finish—please?" She gave him a winning smile that would have had Ken tearing out the deck to give them more room to play.

Reluctantly, Mellon tossed the bird back to Amy. Or Alice. "Finish the game and that's it. I mean it." To Ken, he muttered, "No kids—you lucky bastard, you."

Oh, yeah, Ken thought on his way out. *Real* lucky bastard.

• • •

Laura opened her eyes and was depressed to see what a clear, beautiful morning it was. She'd been rooting for another day of wet weather, because at least that way they wouldn't feel bad about the business they were losing to the ever-expanding investigation.

And it was expanding. The sheds were now all officially off limits to them, and the store still hadn't opened, and Laura had no doubt that soon the house was going to be gone over with a fine-tooth comb as well.

The police knew something that they did not. Just before the rains came, she had seen the investigators in a huddle at the site of the new compost pile, where they logically had been concentrating their search. She had gone off on a search of her own for binoculars to spy on them, but she hadn't found any and hadn't wanted to ask Corinne and raise the alarm. They would all find out any new developments soon enough.

And in the meantime, she was having to soldier on without Ken. She had yet to see him since their accidental meeting on the beach: he'd backed out of seeing her twice in a row now—and she was getting a sinking feeling about their barely launched relationship.

She didn't seriously think that he was afraid to be seen with her simply because she was a Shore girl. He'd been just the opposite, in fact: downright flagrant. No, if Kendall Barclay was cooling down, there were other, more plausible reasons to consider.

She didn't believe either of the ones he'd given her for not coming over. On window-washing night, he had called back and said that he had some unexpected work to do. Him? Please. But okay, she gave him the benefit of the doubt.

It was the second night that had left her both tense and depressed. She had seen his Porsche parked in Chief Mellon's drive when she'd detoured past the chief's house on her way to town. She was curious to know whether she could pick up any clues as to how the investigation was going. Seeing Ken's car there—the last place she would have expected to see it—had given her a major jolt.

She couldn't ask Ken what he was doing there without explaining what *she* was doing on that particular back road. It wasn't on the way to anything. Unless she wanted to admit to some ditzy spying, her only options were to wonder and worry.

He had said he would drop by that evening. Laura hated to admit it to herself, but it was her only reason for getting out of bed.

Breakfast was another late affair, and Laura had managed to be late even for that. She dropped into her regular chair and immediately had a warmed plate of waffles with a side of sausage and bacon placed in front of her. "Eight o'clock means eight o'clock, and not seventeen minutes after," her sister said with a sniff.

Laura apologized and then said to Snack, "Can you load the sycamore into the pickup for me? Thank God for Gabe's Bobcat. At least we can deliver the few orders we do have," she said in a desultory voice.

Snack nodded. He was as subdued as she was. Only Corinne was keeping up a brave front as she served one of her typically mammoth farmer's breakfasts.

"Snack? Can you fit a fourth waffle? I have batter."

"Yeah, sure," her brother said, leaning back on the hind legs of his chair to pass her his syrupy plate. To Laura he said, "Can't the sycamore wait? I wanted to get an early start on the rotted floor around the tub. It's gonna drop right through the dining room ceiling if I don't get to it soon."

"I can use Billy for the other end, if he's available," Laura conceded. "But the bathroom floor, that's a big job,

Snack. Is this really the right time to start on it?"

"Why not? There's no place else they'll let me work. If I can't find something to do, there's not much point to sticking around. I may as well take off again."

"Snack! That is *not* funny," said Corinne.

With a melancholy smile, he said, "You're not supposed to laugh, Rin; you're just supposed to pack me a really big lunch."

"Not gonna happen," she told him calmly. "You're staying here. I've got used to having you around."

Laura said nothing, but she couldn't help wondering what was behind Snack's bravado threats to move on. Her brother seemed increasingly antsy—understandable enough, but worrisome to see.

She pushed away her squeamishness about him and said, "So? What about that sycamore?"

"Yeah, I'll load it. But definitely get Billy to unload it. After breakfast, I'm tearing up the bathroom floor. The hell with them."

"Hooray!" cried Corinne. "You'll be another month, at the very least!" With her wooden spoon she conducted an imaginary band while she tum-tum-ta-da-da'd her way through "Hail to the Chief."

She was as up as Laura was down. Way, way up. And Gabe had stayed late. And Laura couldn't remember hearing any good-nights on the porch below her window. Smiling despite her own glum mood, she took a shot. "I see you were with Gabe last night."

Corinne stopped conducting and turned to Laura with a bland look. "Yes, I was with Gabe."

"No, I mean, you were *with* Gabe last night," Laura said, lifting her coffee mug in a knowing salute. At least someone around there was getting some.

Her brother lifted his head. "With Gabe? What's this? Am I going to have to challenge him to a duel?"

Snack's affection for his sister was heartwarming for

Laura to see. "You'll look for any excuse to drag out Dad's shotgun, won't you?" she quipped.

"There will be no duels, and there will be no roundtable discussions about my relationship with Gabe," Corinne announced with surprising gravity. "Now shut up and eat," she said in what had become a familiar refrain. "We still have work to do."

Billy was eager to assist Laura with the deliveries; he showed up at their door less than fifteen minutes after she called him. Laura thought that maybe he was simply happy to make a little money under the table, but he seemed to be more motivated than that: he looked almost possessed by joy, as if he'd lost something and then had found it again.

Laura was glad to see him in a better mood. He'd taken the discovery of the bones very hard and had kept himself scarce since then. "Have you been having a fun time doing Founders Week stuff?" she asked as they headed out for Miss Widdich's place.

Billy nodded his shaggy head. "Yeah, it's pretty nice. Like usual. The juggling contest is my favorite part. The rain stopped just in time for it."

Laura had been so focused on the sale at Shore Gardens that she hadn't realized that there was such an event. "Who won?" she asked politely.

"Beezee. He's a caddy at Thorncrest. That's where he learned to juggle. When he wasn't caddying, I mean. He started out by practicing with golf balls. Now he's awesome."

Apparently Laura had pressed one of Billy's hot buttons: he went on to describe in great detail each of the contestant's acts, everything from juggling balls and clubs to rings and beanbags.

"But Beezee's was the best; he used torches. Those are

always the best. He dropped one, but it was still awesome. It's too bad we have the contest before World Jugglers Day in June. That's when we should really have it. Beezee said that this was good practice, though. To get used to the pressure. Beezee's going to Pennsylvania to compete. He's just awesome."

"Uh-huh," Laura said, pulling into Miss Widdich's secluded drive.

She had been a little surprised when Miss Widdich ordered the sycamore; the lady needed another tree the way Pennsylvania needed more coal. Apparently there was a gap in the natural screen between Miss Widdich and a distant neighbor's new house, and the fast-growing *pseudoplatanus* was the tree that she wanted to plug that hole.

A strange, seclusive woman, Maya Widdich. Laura still couldn't get over what an odd couple she made with Corinne. On the other hand, the last that either Laura or Corinne had seen of Miss Widdich was in the minutes after Baskerville went dashing off with the bone. Some friend.

Backing the truck alongside the house, Laura snugged it as close to the planting site as she could get. She saw that, as agreed beforehand, the immensely wide hole had been dug and the soil amended. By Miss Widdich? All that remained was for Laura and Billy to muscle the tree into the planting hole, fill it, tamp it, and beat it. They had three other deliveries still to make.

They attached the portable ramp to the pickup, and then Billy positioned himself behind the tree dolly. He put the brake on lightly to keep the sycamore and its heavy root ball from roaring down the ramp, and slowly eased the dolly to the ground using his massive size and strength as a counterweight. No one else Laura knew could have done the job, except perhaps her father in his prime.

Getting the root ball positioned properly took even more strength; Laura and Billy pushed, shoved, and pried until she, at least, was exhausted from the effort. Billy was drenched by the time they were done, but he still wore that cheerful, indomitable smile. He probably had strength enough left to plant a whole row of the blessed things. He began to fill in the rest of the planting hole while Laura and Miss Widdich squared up. The job was harder and had taken longer than Laura had thought when she verbally quoted a price; but she had to honor it.

"Could I have a glass of water?" asked Billy when he was done.

He was sweaty, dirty, and not the most appealing guest to invite into a house. Miss Widdich smiled thinly and said, "Wait here."

Laura would have liked to finish the deliveries and get home and into a shower, but she waited, rather awkwardly, with Billy outside while Miss Widdich fetched his drink. Billy hummed a tune as he looked around the lush, thriving garden. Flowering shrubs seemed to be everywhere; the smell of lilacs was pervasive.

Suddenly Billy pointed to a corner of the garden and said, "Oh, look at that. Miss Widdich has a compost pile too. Not a very big one, though, compared to yours," he said, dismissing it.

Laura knew he meant it as a compliment. "Well, we have a much bigger operation at the nursery, Billy. You can see why we'd be able to make a much larger compost pile."

He chewed on his lip for a minute and then said, "I hope you don't feel bad about, y'know, what was in yours."

"I don't feel *good* about it, Billy," she admitted with a weak laugh.

Miss Widdich approached slowly with a very tall glass of water and handed it to Billy, leaning both hands on her cane while she watched him drink. She looked as though she were expecting him to steal the glass when he was done.

He downed the water in one long series of gulps. "Thank

you, that was good," he said, handing it back. He wiped his mouth with the back of his arm, leaving a horizontal streak of dirt across his chin.

And then, out of the blue, he turned to Laura and said, "Can you keep a secret?"

It was an odd request and unlike him. "I guess so," she said, glancing at Miss Widdich. It couldn't be much of a secret, since someone else was there.

Billy took his cue. "Can you?" he asked the older woman.

Miss Widdich seemed equally tentative as she muttered a yes.

"You know when Baskerville found those bones that time? I was really scared," he admitted.

Laura said, "I know, Billy. We all were."

"But not as much as me, I bet. After I got home, when I was in the kitchen, my hands started shaking. Like this," he said, vibrating his fingers in a demonstration.

"That's not unusual, Billy," said Laura. "Sometimes things do hit you later—"

"Because! That's when I remembered about Sylvia, that's why I started shaking!"

Laura and Miss Widdich gasped audibly at the mention of Sylvia's name, but it was Laura who said, "You remember Sylvia? So many years later?"

"Yeah. Who could forget her? Not me."

"What is it that you remembered about her, Billy?"

He hung his head and said, "Well, it was kind of stupid, really. I remembered it all wrong." He looked at them both with sad green eyes and said, "One time she had a big fight?"

When Laura merely stared, he added, "With Snack?" as if he were hoping she remembered.

"Oh," said Laura faintly. "I didn't know."

"And then later I fell asleep in the van, and when I woke up—it's *so* stupid," he muttered, but he finished his confession anyway. "When I woke up, I saw someone in the fog dragging something heavy into the compost pile, and I didn't know what it was, but then when Baskerville found all the bones, I thought for sure it was—"

He giggled self-consciously, inappropriately, and said: "Sylvia."

"Oh, God in heaven."

They were the first words that Miss Widdich had spoken. As for Laura, she was speechless.

"But Mr. Barclay said that the bones were there for way longer, so I was wrong. Don't tell Snack, okay?" he begged them both. "He could get mad if he knew."

He giggled uncomfortably again; clearly he was having second thoughts about letting them in on his secret.

"Billy," Laura said with a fierce scowl, "it's wrong to go around telling people something you know isn't true. I'm really surprised at you. Surprised and ashamed! How would you like it if I went around telling people that I thought you were the one who hit that dog last week and left it wounded on the side of the road?"

Billy's eyes got wide. "I didn't do that!" he said, horrified by the scenario she'd drawn. "I would never do that!"

"I know you didn't do it. And Snack didn't kill Sylvia. -No one killed Sylvia! She quit her job and moved on. She was restless, a wanderer. She had lots of jobs beforeshe came here; she used to brag about how many. Everyone knew that. Really, I'm so disappointed in you, Billy!" she said, hitting him with everything she had. She had to stop him from going around sharing his little so-called secret with anyone who'd listen. And in Chepaquit, that would be virtually everyone.

"But . . . I said I was wrong," he said, crushed by the reprimand.

"Don't say *anything* about it, Billy. To anyone. Come on, let's finish our deliveries."

Laura was almost afraid to look at Miss Widdich, who had stood in rigid silence during the exchange. She was expecting to see shock, but all she saw was a very blank stare.

Chapter 25

The three of them were sitting in the sample twig chairs outside the garden shop, looking as out of place as B-list guests at a Hamptons wedding: Snack, Corinne, and Kendall Barclay himself.

Laura's heart went up and plunged back down and landed on its side. She had no idea what to make of the fact that they were out there and not in the house—until she looked over and saw the official-looking van parked in front of their wide front porch.

The police must have returned with a warrant. If that was true, then the death investigation had become a homicide investigation at last. There was a grim inevitability to it, Laura knew, but it still came as a jolt to her system.

As she pulled alongside Ken's little black Boxster in the customer parking lot, Billy took one gawking look at the assembled group and said, "Gotta go!"

Without waving his usual ebullient greeting to everyone in sight, Billy hurried away to his car—feeling guilty, no doubt, that he'd already spilled his secret.

Laura felt bad for the way she'd scolded him, but not bad enough to regret having tried to put the fear of hell in the man: all they needed was Billy running around telling people that he once believed he'd seen Snack dragging Sylvia's body into the compost pile. Never mind the fact that—according to Billy, who'd heard it from Ken—the bones were there before Sylvia was even born; no one was going to remember *that* part of Billy's chill little tale.

Tense as she was, Laura could see that the three in the twig chairs weren't exactly all sweetness and light either. With his chin on his chest, his hands in his pockets and his legs stretched out, Snack resembled nothing so much as a grounded teenager. Corinne looked mopey too, sitting sideways in her chair with her legs looped over its arm and listlessly snapping off last year's seedpods from a summersweet bush behind her. Ken, ever the gentleman, rose to his feet as Laura approached; but even there, she saw a certain droopy tension in his demeanor.

Feeling like something the cat dragged in herself, Laura collapsed in the chair that he'd vacated and breathed in a noseful of fragrant lilac. It revived her, somehow, as the sight of Ken just then could not. He'd stood her up twice, and he'd kept her in the dark about Billy's so-called secret.

Three strikes. He was out, as far as she was concerned.

He looked edgy and tentative. *Welcome to the club,* she thought. It made her feel as though they were playing on a level field. For once.

She said to him, "When I grow up, I want to be a banker. You never work."

It brought a quick, wry smile. "Laugh all you want. When the bank goes under, so may your loan," he quipped.

Snack let out one of his world-weary snorts.

Laura avoided looking at her brother, and he continued to avoid looking at her.

She nodded tiredly toward the house and said to Corinne, "And to what do we owe the pleasure of those guys poking through our lingerie?"

"I don't know," her sister said, looking all at sea. "They showed up with a consent warrant that they asked me to sign. Then they asked Snack to stop tearing up the bathroom floor. Then they started going through the house. I have no idea what they're looking for."

"*They* have no idea what they're looking for," Snack said. "I ought to know; I followed them from room to room."

"And you, Mr. Barclay?" Laura was angry and hurt and in no mood to be either tactful or adoring; she wanted to know why Billy was in Ken's confidence and she was not. "What're *you* up to? Your new best friend just ran away, in case you didn't notice," she added, unable to hide her irritation from him.

"Ah, hell," Ken said. "So you know."

"I know. Miss Widdich knows. I expect that by dark, all of Chepaquit will know."

"Know what?" asked Corinne. "What're you talking about?"

"Ken, would you like to do the honors?" Laura said, leaning her head back on the chair and nailing him with a perky, insolent smile. It was pointless to try to keep Billy's story from Snack and Corinne; they were bound to hear it sooner or later.

She was gratified to see that Ken looked discomfited. His color was rising, and a frog seemed to have lodged itself nicely in his throat. There was just a hint of the old class geek peeking through that handsome, clean-cut façade—enough to take the edge off her resentment. How could you stay mad at someone who had the decency to feel embarrassed by his actions?

"I didn't handle the thing with Billy as well as I might have," he said, mostly to Snack. "I should have come directly to you and told you what Billy told me. I was hoping to just nip the damn story in the bud, though, and obviously that didn't happen."

He recounted the story, only in more detail, that Billy had told Laura and Miss Widdich.

Corinne was scandalized; Snack, immobilized.

Laura found herself interrupting Ken just to reassure them both. "Fortunately, we now know, thanks to Billy—if no one else—that the bones have been there for a couple of generations. Let's hope people remember that part when Billy goes blabbing his disproved, silly theory."

"Uncle Norbert," Corinne whispered. "It had to be him. *He* was around here forty years ago."

Snack said contemptuously, "Oh, come on, you could just as easily say it was Dad; he had the same vile temper. And anyway, why does it have to be a Shore who did it? There's got to be a murderer or two somewhere in the world who's not a member of our immediate family."

Brave talk. But Laura was watching Ken, and she wasn't liking what she was seeing. He was standing—presiding—in front of the three of them, hands in his back pockets, thumbs hooked outside. He was looking down, listening or thinking intently.

"The reason I told Billy about the age of the skeletized remains," he said to them, "was to reassure him and quiet him down. The thing is—"

He looked up, and the pain in his face was evident for all of them to see. "The thing is, that initial time line has now been revised downward. The ME hadn't taken into account how active a compost pile is as an agent of decomposition. It turns out that he was off by twenty years or more."

"Gee," Snack said contemptuously, "the guy sounds like quite the expert. Next, he'll be telling us the bones were put there last weekend."

"There's corroborating evidence, Snack," Ken said quietly. "The body was put there no earlier than 1987."

"That's when Sylvia worked here!" Corinne blurted.

"I know," Ken said. "Billy worked the dates out for me."

For the first time since he'd returned home, Snack looked cowed. "No one's going to believe a half-wit," he murmured.

"Don't call him a half-wit," Laura said faintly.

"Okay, a three-quarter-wit. Come on, Laur," Snack coaxed with a sickly smile. "Billy is . . . Billy. He's a good guy but he's *Billy,* for crissake. He talks to deer. On occasion, to trees. I'm amazed that he could even come up with such an evil-sounding scenario."

"It's entirely possible that he did actually witness a crime being covered up," said Ken. "Literally."

Snack jumped to his feet; he looked around, ready to run. "This is nuts. This is really nuts! Are you telling me that because Billy has a nightmare and someone else comes up with a date—? Where the hell did they get a year? I suppose the body was buried with a laminated newspaper?"

"Trust me, they have hard proof."

Laura's head was spinning. She had no idea whether she should be thanking Ken or running him over. "You seem to know everything about this case," she hissed. "Why don't you just tell us who did it and spare us the wait?"

"If I knew, I certainly—"

"Here comes *Gabe,*" Corinne said, and for the life of her, Laura could not be sure whether her sister thought it was good news or bad at that particular moment.

They waited in resounding silence as Gabe pulled in beside the pickup truck. Compared to them, he looked reasonably carefree, smiling a greeting that encompassed them all but that dwelled on Corinne. He went one better, coming up to her and slipping his arm lightly around her for a first-time-ever public kiss. Corinne smiled shyly and cast her look downward, the picture of confused desire.

Gabe was dirty and his shoes were covered in caked-on mud. He'd been working the earth, a match for Laura in every way except for the six-pack of Budweiser that was hooked through his fingers.

"I've just knocked off for the day," he explained. "I stopped at Smitty's Package on my way home to a shower—but you guys look like you need a beer even more than I do."

He knows as much as Ken knows, thought Laura. *And he feels bad for Corinne. That's not good.*

Snack held up a hand and Gabe broke out a can from the plastic retainer and tossed it to him; Corinne, Ken, and Laura passed on his offer. Gabe had to have seen the van parked in front of the house but politely wasn't commenting on it.

Corinne felt obliged to tell him about the warrant anyway. She was still talking when they heard a shout from someone standing in front of the run-down toolshed. Almost immediately, two men who were in the house left through a side door to join him. One of them carried a camera.

"They could curb the enthusiasm a little," muttered Snack, holding the can to explode away from him as he popped its tab.

"Does this mean they're done with the house?" Corinne wanted to know. "Can I start supper? I don't want to turn on the oven if they're going to be fingerprinting the stove or something."

Now what? thought Laura. What could they possibly find in an unused toolshed that had been filled with rusty, obsolete farm tools for as long as she could remember?

A bag filled with money, that's what.

The investigators didn't tell them that, of course. They simply walked down to them and held up an old satchel-style, Gucci-looking bag whose fake leather corners were torn brown plastic.

"This belong to anyone?" one of the investigators said, holding up the filthy, dust-covered bag in his gloved hand.

"Not me," Corinne said quickly.

"Nope."

"I've never seen it before," said Laura.

"We'll be taking this," he informed Corinne. "I'll need you to sign for it."

He didn't sound either arrogant or mean, but Laura hated him anyway. She hated all of them and wanted them all to go back to tracking down their serial killer or hit man or whoever it was they were looking for before Baskerville entered the scene with a woof and a bang.

She said dryly, "Can we have our house back now?"

"Anytime you want," one of the men answered, which was no answer at all.

The investigators were walking past Laura when Snack said after them, "I wouldn't go packing my Jockey shorts in that thing; it's bound to be filled with bugs. You'd be better off hopping over to Wal-Mart for a new one."

"Thanks for the tip," one of them said without looking back.

Laura could see by the way he was carrying the satchel that the guy felt sure he was going to have the last laugh. Staring at the bag, she suddenly understood why.

She waited until they were well away, then turned to her brother and said, "What is it with you? Do you have a death wish or something? Do you have any idea what's in that bag?"

"Yeah. Bugs."

"*Money,* you idiot," she said in a hiss. "I saw the tip of a bill sticking out the middle."

Ken said, "Are you sure of that?"

"I know money when I see it!"

"Ken, you're the banker," Snack drawled. "Did you notice any money?"

"I wasn't watching that closely," Ken said quietly.

And Laura knew why: he was watching *them,* watching their reactions to see who was acting guilty and who wasn't. Coming on top of everything else, it absolutely infuriated her.

Meanwhile, Gabe was looking like a Red Sox fan at a cricket match. "I don't get it; I thought they were winding down the search."

So Gabe wasn't in the loop, after all. Laura said bitterly, "Just ask Ken for the latest. He's pretty thick with the chief and his pals. He probably has a copy of the ME's report in his glove compartment right now."

"Okay, Laura," Ken said evenly. "Let's you and I have a quick private chat, shall we?" He took her by the elbow and began to steer her away from the others and toward the aisle of potted roses that were starting to bloom for an audience that was bound to be severely limited.

Laura was angry enough to lift her elbow pointedly out of Ken's grip, but she walked out with him anyway. Whatever he had to say, good, bad, or infuriating, she had an almost desperate need to hear it.

As soon as they were out of earshot, he said bluntly, "You want me to throw myself at your feet and beg for forgiveness because I didn't tell you about Billy. All right. Consider it done."

She said, "Oh, yeah. Just like that. You don't know me very well, mister. I'm a Shore: we're mean and vindictive and we have tempers hot enough to melt paint off a picket fence."

"Bullshit. Corinne, for one, is the gentlest soul I know."

"Oh, her," Laura said dismissively. But meanwhile she felt cut to the quick that he was leaving Laura herself lumped with the rest of the Shores. The realization was a bucket of water on her sizzling temper.

She said in a lower but still lofty voice, "I assume you stayed away the past couple of days so that you wouldn't compromise yourself?"

"Myself? Be serious, Laura. You know me better than that."

She shook her head. "Do I? All I know about you is that you were quick to buy out the mortgage we had with Great

River Finance. Which puts us in your power. As actual facts go, that's pretty much it."

That was so *not* it that she felt her cheeks heat up, as they always did when she deliberately distorted the truth.

"I'll ignore that," he said through clenched teeth. "You're stressed. You're not thinking."

She stopped halfway down the row of roses and turned to face him. A thorny cane that brushed the back of her calf seemed to goad her into continuing the confrontation. "Why didn't you tell me what you knew?" she asked, not backing down an inch into forgiving territory. "What do you *still* know that I don't? Why are they circling around us like buzzards?"

"What do you plan to do with the information?" he asked in turn.

"I won't say a word. Not to anybody." Which was probably just what Billy had got done promising him.

"All right, damn it."

He told her about the maple leaf belt buckle that had been found in the compost pile, and whatever was left of Laura's belligerence dried up like fog under a noonday sun. She was devastated.

"You said that Sylvia was from up north somewhere," he went on. "Did you mean Canada?"

"I . . . don't remember."

"Laura, you do. It's written all over your face."

"She might have been," Laura acknowledged, lifting her chin. "So what?"

Ken glanced around again and dropped his voice even lower. "You have to see that the coincidences are piling up. If it really is Sylvia who was buried in there, what will you gain by denying it? Would you really rather be behind the curve in the investigation?"

"Well, I sure as hell don't plan to fill in any missing blanks for the chief!" she said in a blistering undertone. "Do you think I'm crazy?"

"People will be questioned. You'll be questioned. And you're not going to lie, Laura. You know you're not."

"No? Just watch me."

"You know you're not," he insisted softly.

She looked away. "If that was a vote of confidence in me, I'm not particularly touched by it."

But it *was* a vote of confidence, and she *was* touched by it. He had trusted her enough to tell her what he knew, and he believed in her enough to know that she wasn't capable of lying to the police. That was something. That was big.

He must have seen her anger melting around the edges because he said, "What was Sylvia's last name?"

She waited a long time before answering. There were so many considerations, so many fears that went into that pause.

At last she whispered, "Mendan."

One word. She handed it to him like a gift, a token of her gratitude and faith in him.

"Who *was* this Sylvia?" he said with a certain amount of wonder in his voice. "Should I feel lucky that I wasn't around to fall under her spell?"

"Yes," Laura said, taking his question seriously. "Sylvia was someone you didn't forget, which is why nobody has. She was just incredibly beautiful. Black hair, huge blue eyes, perfect skin, long legs, big breasts, the works. Heads *always* turned when she was around. Man, woman, young, old. None of us could figure out what she was doing working for minimum wage here when she could have been on the cover of *Cosmo*. She knew it too. She was arrogant and not afraid of anyone—including my father," Laura felt obliged to say.

She could picture Sylvia so vividly now—much more clearly than when she had simply read the name on the little stakes in Miss Widdich's potted herbs.

She started up their walk again, compelled by the need

to do something; anything. "Sylvia had a tattoo on her ankle, large for the time," she went on. "A bluebird, of all things. Everyone else was getting butterflies. But Syl was like that; she didn't care what anyone else thought. Definitely, she was a free spirit."

They were beyond the rose aisle now, headed toward a refuge of balled and burlapped trees for sale. With every step that she took away from the others, away from the house, Laura felt better. Ken was perfect in a one-on-one situation like the one they were in just then; she couldn't imagine ever being bored in his company.

But irritated? Yes. He managed to evoke a flash of that when he asked, "What did your brother think about Sylvia?"

"What I just *told* you: that she was gorgeous. Not that a fifteen-year-old would ever admit to it. But he stared. We *all* stared," she insisted, "Corinne more than anyone else, for that matter. She and I were both wildly jealous of Sylvia. Corinne couldn't get over the bluebird tattoo. After she saw it, she asked my mother for permission to get a little bee on her shoulder, and my mother about had a heart attack. I remember that Sylvia thought my mother's reaction was hysterically funny. She couldn't imagine that anyone would care."

Her thoughts went back to Billy's account of what he saw. It didn't seem possible. She said, "I don't see how Billy could remember an argument after so many years. I mean, he's Billy."

"From what he told me, he was as mesmerized by Sylvia as everyone else."

Laura gave Ken a sharp look. "*How* mesmerized?"

"I know what you're thinking. I've been wondering myself whether Billy isn't just projecting a crime he committed onto some fantasy murderer—a kind of twisted version of an imaginary pal."

"Well, couldn't he be doing just that?"

"I'm sure you can find an expert witness somewhere to say so."

"But you don't believe it," she said with a sigh. She was having a hard time believing something like that about Billy herself. And yet, was it any harder than accepting that the killer had been a member of her own family?

"It's such a horror story," she moaned. "This whole thing started as a simple, ordinary dedication of a gravestone. And then I agreed to stay on . . . and worse, I talked Snack into staying on. And this is what the month has brought us to: a murder investigation. Of us, apparently. I can't believe it. And I can't believe that Sylvia Mendan is just . . . bones. Oh, God," she said, sick over the ghastly image. "Not just a headline, anymore. Someone we knew."

She stopped, paralyzed by the thought, and was surprised when Ken took her in his arms. She should have resisted—she still resented his not telling her about Billy—but it felt so right. Just for a moment, it felt so right. She bowed her head in a simple gesture of sorrow. Not for them now, but for poor Sylvia, who'd never had the chance to grow old.

"You'll get through this," Ken whispered, stroking her hair. "Don't worry. One way or another, you'll get through it."

She nodded into his shirt and didn't even try to keep her tears from staining it. Soon other tears were mixing with the ones meant for Sylvia; it had been such a turbulent, grueling, heartbreaking month.

With a wrenching sigh, Laura got herself under control. She said, "How did Chief Mellon react when you told him what Billy said?"

Now it was Ken's turn to look evasive and troubled. "I haven't told Andy yet."

She looked up at that. "You haven't told him? Why *not*?" But of course she knew why not: because of her. "You have to tell him," she conceded glumly. "I know that.

Even Snack won't argue with that. Just . . . get it over with." She eased out of his arms, resentful once more. "Oh, look," she said wearily. "The van's leaving."

"Do you want to go back now?" he asked.

"Yes; I have to clean up." She had a sudden and almost desperate need to be showered and squeaky clean. She'd had her fill of nature and dirt.

She blew her nose on the hem of her T-shirt before Ken had the chance to retrieve his handkerchief for her. He smiled and stuffed it back in his pocket, and they headed back.

But something was off kilter, like a framed picture hanging slightly askew. "If Chief Mellon doesn't yet know Billy's story . . . then why did they get a consent warrant for the house?"

"My question exactly," said Ken. He sounded so grim that Laura's heart took another dive.

"I did think that Andy was behaving a little too much like the sheriff of Mayberry yesterday," Ken went on, "and now I see why. He was setting me up, the wily bastard. He has another piece of evidence besides the buckle. He was assuming that I would come straight to you with that information, and he was waiting to see who would do what as a result."

"But you didn't, so no one did anything."

"And they've decided to take it to the next level anyway. Hell. What do they have?"

"Something that seems to point to us, you mean."

Ken said nothing; Laura took it as a yes. After another moment, she said, "It wasn't Snack."

Again he said nothing.

"Ken—it wasn't my father, it couldn't be my uncle, it wasn't Snack. It *wasn't*!"

His answer to that was a look of horrible, hideous sympathy.

She could feel it building in her, a bitter impulse to

knock down his silence. She wanted him to say blindly, of course you're right, whatever you say, I believe you because you would know.

Any and all of those responses would be acceptable. Instead, he continued to maintain an unnerving quiet. If it wasn't just her luck to fall for a man with such a depressing amount of integrity. Her mood became more and more bleak, and she walked in a silence that became as chill and thick as a Cape Cod fog.

When they got back to the shop, Gabe was gone and so was Snack. Only Corinne was there, and she had news.

"They've taken away all the old office records from just before and just after 1987," she said, agog that it had come to that. "I listened at the top of the cellar stairs; they didn't realize how well their voices traveled up. They took a whole bunch of moldy boxes. I think they're looking for employment information for Sylvia; they must actually think it's her!"

"Lots of luck to 'em, then," Laura said. "We all know that Dad never put seasonal help on the books; he paid them under the table."

It wasn't what Corinne wanted to hear. "Laura! Don't you get it? They really must believe that those were *Sylvia's* remains."

"They don't even know her name yet," Laura said with a sideways glance at Ken.

But it was clear that they were about to.

Hours later and under a black, starless canopy of sky, Laura crept through the nursery to the rose area. She could scarcely see the potted plants, but she was prepared to follow her nose: Summer Wine, that was the hybrid musk she was after. She had noticed it earlier as she drifted in a state of shock and sorrow across the grounds with Ken.

The rose was big and blowsy and bold: a lively coral,

fading to a bright gold center and bursting with red stamens. Summer Wine. Even the name fit. Laura found it easily, even in the dark. She took her secateurs from the patch pocket of her chenille robe and cut off a single opened rose, then inhaled its alluring, heavy scent. Yes. Sylvia would have approved of Summer Wine.

Continuing on her impulsive mission, she made her way to the yellow tape that surrounded the dregs of the original compost pile.

What might she have been?

For a long, sad moment, Laura pondered the multitude of odd twists and quirks of fate that had her standing in her nightgown next to a crime scene in the place she once had no choice but to call home.

"Rest in peace," she whispered into the stillness of the soft May night.

Leaning over the tape, she pitched the rose. It landed on a low mound of loose soil, its frilly, scalloped petals as flirty and feminine as an old-fashioned Gibson girl.

"Amen," she murmured, and then she retraced her steps to her room in the darkened farmhouse and tried again to sleep.

Chapter 26

The Chepaquit Police Station was located back-to-back with the Chepaquit Savings Bank, but Ken saw far more of Andy Mellon when they were on their boats at Creasey's Marina than he did when they were at their desks at their respective jobs. Maybe it was because the bank and the police station fronted on two different streets. Maybe it was simply because, for Ken, business and pleasure didn't mix.

Today he was all business. At eight A.M. he cut across both parking lots and greeted the dispatcher at the police desk with the same friendly smile that he'd given her at Belle's Cafe when they stood in line at seven, waiting to buy the still-warm chocolate-covered doughnuts that (if Belle was to be believed) were famous for miles around.

"Hey, again. Chief Mellon around?" he asked, glancing at the empty cells behind her. Empty. Good. Snack was still at large.

Cindy leaned back in her swivel chair and threw her head back. "Chief?" she called out over her shoulder.

"What *now*?"

She lifted her eyebrows above a smile. "He's in," she said to Ken, and she went back to pecking her keyboard, leaving him to fend for himself.

He walked around the corner to an office that had been

decorated by the art class of Chepaquit High in honor of Chief Mellon's silver jubilee: in front of his desk on the gray-painted floorboards, the students had painted and then varnished a replica of the chief's badge, complete with his badge number.

The chief did not look pleased.

"I wondered how the hell long it was gonna take you," he growled.

"How'd you find out?" Ken asked, dropping into the nearest of three chairs.

"Billy told Helen Jennings who told Agnes Ritter who told our very own Cindy. He's coming over in half an hour to make a statement."

"Then I'd better beat it," said Ken, rising.

The chief waved him back down. "He's down at the Laundromat, watching his clothes dry. One of the loads is a down blanket. You've got time."

Ken nodded. Everyone knew Billy did things according to a schedule. Try to rush or change it, and Billy would be too agitated to be even remotely helpful.

"You're lucky your daddy gave Beth and me a mortgage back when we had zip credit, or so help me, I'd have you up on charges," the chief added. "What the hell's the matter with you, not coming here directly? Are you so besotted by her?"

"Yes. Snack didn't do it, Andy."

"So she tells you. It was a long time ago. Kids do dumb things."

"Have you notified Sylvia's parents?" Ken asked, because he knew how much his own mother would want to know.

"We're trying to locate the next of kin right now—in northern Saskatchewan, no less. Her parents should still be alive."

"Obviously your people will try to get hold of her dental records?"

"Obviously."

If no employment records existed at Shore Gardens, as Laura had claimed, then they must have found something in the satchel—a wallet, an ID—that told them Sylvia had hailed from Saskatchewan.

The phone rang. The chief picked it up, listened, and then said, "Which brought it to? Wait, let me grab a pencil. Nine nine eight zero. Got it. Thanks."

He hung up and Ken began to ask him point-blank what exactly they'd found of Snack's, but the phone rang again.

This time the call was even briefer and the chief was not so calm after he hung up. "Son of a bitch, when it rains it pours," he growled. "Beezee just torched the refreshment stand on the beach, can you believe it? He couldn't have waited until *after* the closing ceremonies?"

He grabbed a key ring from the top drawer and said, "We'll talk about this some more. I'm not done with you yet."

Out he went, leaving Ken a precious few seconds to poke through the crisp new folder that sat front and center on the desk. If he got caught—well, he didn't think about getting caught; he only thought about finding something he could use to get the Shores off the hook.

Right on top: the ME's report, a copy of which Laura was convinced he had in his glove compartment. Ken didn't much care how Sylvia Mendan had been murdered, and unless a bullet, a knife, or a blunt instrument had left a deep impression on the partly decomposed bones, the examiner wouldn't have been able to figure it out anyway.

He passed over the report and fastened his attention on the list of the finds from an examination of the crime site.

Bingo, he thought. An account of the buckle was there, exactly as the chief had described it . . . and also one of a knife. A knife engraved with the initials O.T.S.

Shit! Father, or son?

He scanned the rest of the list quickly. Sneakers, some

fabric, scraps of a bra. What might have been a lipstick case. Assuming that the chief would have the most pertinent stuff at the top, Ken resisted the urge to look further and closed the file, carefully returning it to its original position. He pivoted around and was standing on the chief's jubilee floor badge when Cindy appeared at the door.

"Something I can still do for you?" she asked him pointedly.

Ken himself had approved the loan for *her* mortgage, and he was hoping that he looked like someone severe enough to call it in if she pissed him off.

"Nope," he said. "Had to retie my shoes. New laces. See ya."

He made a hurried exit, and by the time he got home, he had managed to convince himself that losing a knife in a compost pile was practically inevitable if you worked in a nursery.

Laura wasn't all that anxious to have Miss Widdich open her door.

She was thrown back to that foggy, scary time when she had waited on the same porch to deliver a box of white, fragrant roses on the night of the summer solstice. This time the evening was golden, she had no roses, and it wasn't the solstice—but she felt as jumpy as she had been on that long-ago night when she was seventeen.

The door opened a crack. Laura was surprised to see that a chain had been engaged on the other side of it. The room beyond was dark; clearly the blinds were all closed. Miss Widdich's hawkish nose and penetrating eyes filled the gap, and her hair seemed to glow whiter than ever. All that was missing was the flash of lightning and the crackle of thunder.

"Miss Widdich . . . please," Laura begged softly. "Can I

come in for just a few minutes? I desperately need to talk to you."

"About what?" she asked, narrowing the gap another inch.

"About Sylvia. You *know* I'm here about Sylvia."

"I don't know anything—least of all, why you're harassing me."

"But I'm not! I'm just trying to do the right thing for my brother. He's going to be blamed for this, you know he will. You heard Billy."

"How can your brother be blamed? They don't even know who it is," she said, easing the door closed millimeter by millimeter.

"They do know. It's been confirmed. Well, not through DNA yet, obviously. But all signs point to the bones being Sylvia's. There's really not much doubt," Laura added, trying to prod a reaction, any reaction, out of the older woman. Horror, fear, disbelief, she didn't care.

Instead, what she got for her effort was a hissed, "Why don't you just go back to Portland, you evil child!"

And a door shut firmly in her face.

Well, this is rich, she thought, blinking at the gargoyle doorstop. *Ordered out of town by the resident witch.*

She lifted the ring in the gargoyle's nose and rapped sharply. No answer. "Fine!" she said loudly. "If my brother gets tried for this, it'll be on your conscience. Think you can live with that?

"You're the one who's evil," she muttered when no one answered. She turned and stamped down the stairs, determined to return by stealth the next time. With any luck, she'd surprise Miss Widdich in her garden. Even the evil had weak spots.

She got in the pickup and backed out angrily, sending stones kicking into the azalea hedge. What on earth did Corinne see in the woman, anyway? All Laura saw was a selfish, secretive, demanding old maid. And worse.

She arrived home to find her sister ironing a pair of valences for the two kitchen windows. Perky and cheerful, the damned curtains seemed too optimistic by half. And so did Corinne.

"Where did you get lost? I thought you were just going out for bread," Corinne said, smoothing the fabric with long, easy strokes. Clearly, ironing was therapy for her.

"I detoured to Miss Widdich's."

Corinne glanced up. "Why?"

"Too many things about her don't add up, and I wanted to shake her . . . her . . . *arrogance,* damn it. Where does she get off?"

"Oh, not the Sylvia cultivars again," Corinne groaned.

"Not only that. One minute the woman's too crippled to walk without a cane, and the next, she's digging holes like a convict in a chain gang. That limping-along-with-a-cane thing is all an act."

Corinne was more amused than surprised. "Don't be silly," she said. "She finally broke down and got a cortisone shot, that's all, and it's worked wonders for her knee. That's why she's been able to dig again."

"Then why did she fake needing a cane after I saw her digging? I caught her doing it twice. What was the point?"

"I imagine that she was just too embarrassed to admit that she felt better, that's all," Corinne said, laying the crisp, smooth valence over the back of a chair to dry. "Her herbal remedies turned out not to be as good as modern science."

She tore open the cellophane wrapper of her second valence and shook it out. Holding the length of it against herself, she said, "Wouldn't this make a beautiful dress?"

"If you don't mind looking like a bowl of fruit," Laura groused. Truly, her mood was vile. "Corinne, how can you be so serene? Don't you see where this investigation is going? They're going to accuse Snack of murdering Sylvia!"

"No they're not. Snack is innocent, so we have nothing

to worry about." She shook out the valence and laid it on the ironing board, then pumped spray starch onto the first section. The iron let out a satisfying hiss as she slid it over the dampened cloth. "You know how I know that?" she asked.

Laura simply shook her head, unnerved by her sister's serenity.

"Reverend Knowles dropped by while you were gone. I've missed services two weeks in a row now, and he wondered why. Wasn't that nice of him? He didn't have to do that. I told him how afraid we all were, and he said, 'If Snack didn't do it, you have nothing to fear.' Snack didn't, so I don't."

As simple as that. Laura smiled wanly. Was Corinne in total denial?

She was about to suggest it when she heard a truck with a noisy muffler pull up, and she ran to a window to see who it was. If it were anyone who had anything to do with the investigation, Laura had every intention of running him off with the family shotgun. She was so very sick of them all.

She read the lettering on the side of the van: MISTER FIXER, APPLIANCE REPAIR. Suspicious that someone would be gung ho enough to show up on a Sunday, she went back to her sister and said, "Were you expecting someone to come look at the dryer?"

"That must be George. He said he'd try to stop in and get a number for the broken belt, if that's what it is. I hope Snack's right, because it wouldn't be an expensive repair, George said."

"I'm getting paranoid," Laura muttered, and she went back to let the guy in.

George carried a tool bag with him and was as polite to Laura as a country doctor. If the man thought there was a murderer in the house, he certainly wasn't letting on.

Corinne gave him a warm smile and put aside her iron.

"Thanks for stopping by, George. The dryer's in the basement; I'll show you where. I hope you can save it. It really is an old one; we've had it since I was a child, and even then, we bought it used."

"With a dryer, there's not much that can go wrong," George said reassuringly as he followed her downstairs to view the patient. "We'll get it working again, don't you worry."

The phone rang and Laura, alone in the kitchen, answered it.

"Why is it that you never answer your cell?" Ken asked without a hello. "I keep leaving voice mail for you."

He sounded newly tense. She wondered if they were just taking turns being strung out, or if they wore off on one another that way.

"I dropped the phone in the koi pond a few days ago," she said coolly. "It hasn't worked since."

"I need to see you. Where can we meet?"

"Here?" she asked instantly, responding to the urgency in his voice.

"I'd rather not. How about here?"

It crossed her mind to say, "If this is a trick to get me into bed, the mood is *definitely* all wrong."

"How about O'Doule's?" she countered.

"Fine. Five minutes."

Five minutes later, she was sitting at one of the bistro tables that were crammed into the popular hangout. The noise level was deafening: on Sunday night, the bar featured live music.

"I didn't know that," she shouted in apology across the table.

Ken moved his chair so that it was touching hers. He leaned closer to her, his shoulder brushing hers, and spoke loudly into her ear. His message was as electrifying as any whispered words of desire could have been.

He said, "I think I found something today that links Sylvia to Miss Widdich."

Laura started so violently that she whacked her drink, spilling a small puddle. She blotted the rum mix with both their napkins and simply nodded. *Tell me more, more.*

Ken leaned his forearm on the table and swung his other arm around the back of Laura's chair. Anyone looking at them would have seen, at best, a couple on a hot date and at worst, a guy seriously and even obnoxiously on the make. They would not have seen two people desperately trying to move suspicion away from an innocent man.

Over the sexy, pulsing sound of a reggae tune, Ken said in her ear, "When I was in Chief Mellon's office today, he took a phone call. A number got mentioned. I'm a banker; I can smell when a number is an amount and when it isn't. I decided he was alluding to the amount of money they found in that satchel they found in the toolshed: nine thousand, nine hundred and eighty dollars."

Laura nodded, as fiercely attentive as if he were giving her driving directions to heaven.

"On a hunch," Ken continued, "I got to thinking: assuming that the satchel was Sylvia's, where would someone like her get her hands on ten thousand dollars? She could have robbed a bank, but I *am* the bank. She could have robbed a shop in Chatham, but very few shops around here have that kind of cash—then or now. Again, as a money man, I think I might have remembered a robbery. We're not exactly a high-crime district at this end of the Cape.

"I wasn't happy about having this thought, but I wondered whether Sylvia might have been blackmailing someone she'd had a quick fling with: the mayor, the police chief. The president of the local bank," he added wryly. "She was young, beautiful, and presumably out for something, or she wouldn't have been in a backwater burg like ours. With all due respect, the wages you paid her wouldn't have been an irresistible incentive to stay."

Laura closed her mind to the music and the raucous conversations all around them, memorizing every word of what Ken was saying. He was building a case, and it wasn't against Snack.

"Armed with that idea," Ken said, "I spent today going through the deposit and withdrawal records at Chepaquit Savings—not so easy, since, in my infinite wisdom, I moved the bank over to a new database system recently. And guess who took out precisely ten thousand dollars on June twentieth of 1987?"

"She *didn't*!"

"Oh, she did. As for the twenty bucks that were short—maybe Sylvia dipped into the satchel for cigarette money afterward; maybe someone just miscounted. But both totals are close enough to be related. The amount, the timing—"

"The reason? What was the *reason*?" Laura said, bumping his ear in her desire for him to give her the answer to that too.

"That," he said, tucking away the lock of her hair that was tickling his cheek, "is what we're going to find out."

He paid for their drinks and they went in his car, leaving her pickup in O'Doule's lot. Like everything else in Chepaquit, the ride to Miss Widdich's was mere minutes away. It was nearly dark, and the ride down the secluded drive to her house left Laura prickly all over with apprehension; she was grateful that this time, she was with Ken.

He parked back a few yards from the front of the porch. "Maybe you'd better wait in the car," he suggested. "If we both confront her, she may spook."

"She *is* the spook," Laura quipped, but it felt wrong to sound like a smart-ass just then. "Okay," she said more humbly. "I'll sit tight."

She watched as Ken got out and went up to her old pal the gargoyle. He lifted its heavy ring and dropped it down three separate times, hard, each time setting her knees twitching. Laura was just able to make out the door opening a crack; again she saw no light issuing from the room behind. Slowly sliding lower in her seat, she strained without success to hear what they were saying through her rolled-down window. Was Miss Widdich aware that Laura was in the car? She simply couldn't tell.

Suddenly, amazingly, the door opened wide and Ken was admitted inside. A light went on after the door was nearly shut behind them. Laura was wild with curiosity, but she made herself stay in the car. Ken had already managed to get a hell of a lot farther than she had, and she didn't dare blow it; the stakes were simply too high.

So she sat where she was, and she tried to spin different scenarios in which someone like Miss Widdich would give someone like Sylvia ten thousand dollars, and how that could result in Sylvia's death.

Chapter 27

Ken was looking at a woman who had been crying. Her eyes were puffy and red, and her white hair had broken free in places from the bun that usually held it together on the back of her head. The tears had obviously gone on for a while: a mound of crumpled wet tissues covered most of the square oak table next to the sofa, and the Kleenex box was on the floor, empty. On a low wooden table in front of the sofa, a plate held the remains of curled orange peels, a half-full glass of milk, another plate with some saltine crackers on it, and a bottle of gin without a glass to pour it into.

Miss Widdich had clearly been having a very bad day.

She seated herself on the moss-colored sofa and then commanded Ken to sit down. Her voice was thick, maybe with drink, probably with emotion.

Ken chose a straight-backed wooden chair, the least comfortable one in the near-dark room; he did not want to get overly cozy with the woman. Nonetheless, she looked so ill-used that it was easy for him to sound sympathetic. In a way, he was.

After he explained his discovery, he added softly, "They'll be able to put two and two together pretty quickly, Miss Widdich. It's just a matter of time until they figure out the connection between you and Sylvia. I've only been following the money trail. I don't know what else the authorities have discovered, but you can bet that if they have your money, they have a lot else besides."

He felt safe in adding, "Sylvia was Canadian; they know that much. And more."

Maya Widdich's face looked as thoroughly crumpled as one of her used-up tissues. From grief or from fear? Ken couldn't tell. She was simply too inscrutable for that.

"Sylvia didn't have a gun sticking in your back when you withdrew the money on June twentieth, 1987, or we would have had a record of it on tape," he said in a wry tone. "Clearly you were not robbed by her."

Miss Widdich nodded in wordless agreement, and he said more gently, "So the other, more reasonable assumption is that Sylvia was blackmailing you because she was your illegitimate daughter."

She bowed her head on the word "daughter," and Ken felt a thrill of electricity fly from her to him that was downright hair-raising. He'd always made light of the local rumors that Maya Widdich was a practicing witch. The name, the hair, the black clothing; her seclusion and her quaint obsession with herbs—it was all a bit too over the top for him. He had a sense that women of Wicca were somehow more everyday about it. He pictured them in sweats and sneakers and buying day-old bread at the supermarket, just like everyone else.

Now, suddenly, he wasn't so sure. The hairs that had decided to stand up on the back of his neck were slow to ease down.

"Do you want to tell me about it?"

Without looking up, she shook her head, but he pressed on anyway. "We both know that 1987 wasn't 1957. Surely no one would have held it against you that you'd had to give up a baby for adoption, once they'd found out." He wanted to add, "*Especially* you," but he settled for saying,

"It's hard for me to understand why you gave in to Sylvia's blackmail threat. I'm puzzled by that."

"It wasn't about simple blackmail," she muttered.

"What was it, then?" he asked softly.

Maybe it was his sympathetic tone, maybe it was his candor that broke down her reserve, but she said in an unexpected growl, "It was the *way* that I gave her up!"

Something in her voice had Ken imagining the infamous scene in *Rosemary's Baby*. Goosebumps rolled over him in waves as he said, "How do you mean?"

Again she shook her head. He waited. She hugged herself as if she were cold. There was a fringed wine-colored throw on the back of a nearby armchair that Ken considered fetching for her, but something made him hold back. If she were shaky enough and miserable enough, she might just tell the truth.

Suddenly her head came up sharply and she fixed Ken with as penetrating a look as he'd ever had in his life. It shot into him like an arrow and lodged squarely in his throat. He was dizzy from the force of it, angry from the power of it, and something else: aware. Instinctively and against all rational thought, he understood that this was a woman who had dabbled in black art. Maybe she was now reformed, maybe she'd put away her psychic gifts—but she had strengths, still, to be reckoned with.

Without preamble, she began her tale.

"My grandmother was a midwife. She's the one who delivered the baby and cut the cord. But she was old and in failing health . . . often disoriented," Miss Widdich murmured.

"Three days after the baby was born, I wrapped her puny little body in towels, and I put her in a cardboard box. Then I folded the flaps over it. It was November, in northern Saskatchewan. You can imagine. I put on my grandmother's coat and hat, and I wrapped a scarf around my face, and then I set the box upright in my grandmother's shopping cart. I wanted people to think I was a homeless person as I wheeled the cart to a nearby convent. It wasn't far to go, and that was a good thing, because I was very weak. I was fifteen."

Ken blinked. Running through the math, he calculated that in that case, Miss Widdich would have to be in her early fifties at best. She looked in her seventies.

"You're surprised," she remarked, narrowing her eyes over a thin, acerbic smile. And then she continued.

"I laid the box on the step by the back door. I was afraid to ring the bell, so I waited across the alley behind a car. I thought maybe someone would just . . . divine that she was there. They were nuns, weren't they? If they were any *good*," she said with a sniff, "they would have known. But no one came."

She went on with her account, speaking in a low voice that was calm and devoid of emotion. "It was quiet in the alley. The baby was quiet. I wondered if maybe she had died. But then she began to cry, softly at first, more of a whimper. Still no one came. It began to snow, heavily. I could see the snow getting inside the hole between the overlapping flaps. She cried more loudly then, and for a long time. Finally someone opened the door. It was a very young nun, hardly more than my own age; she had a bag of garbage that she was taking out.

"She heard the baby crying, and in her shock, she dropped the bag of garbage on the step. I remember seeing coffee grounds spill out onto the white snow and wondering how it was that nuns got to drink coffee; I thought their diet was bread and water. The nun didn't even open the flaps to look; she just lifted the box and went inside with it."

Miss Widdich paused, not so much to control her emotions, Ken thought, as for dramatic effect. "And that is the last I saw of my daughter until she tracked me down in Chepaquit."

"How could you be certain that Sylvia was your daughter?"

"She had my eyes," Miss Widdich said dryly.

He had another thought. "Obviously you were never contacted by any adoption agency. How did Sylvia find you?"

"There had been an investigation—*obviously*," she added with contempt. "Eventually it led to my grandmother, who was well-known in the area. By that time, she had no idea where I was, since by then I'd run off again. Sylvia had newspaper clippings with her; it was quite the story at the time. Armed with those few facts, she managed to find me. She was quite a clever girl," Miss Widdich said in a quiet and altogether unexpected boast.

"Do you know where her father is?"

"I have no idea. Prison, most likely."

"Was she ever legally adopted?"

"Naturally. After the newspaper articles, a line formed to take her. People are such idiots," she added, rubbing her temples as if her head hurt. "Sen . . . timen . . . tal idiots."

She seemed to sway in place, and her speech was slowing down. Either exhaustion or alcohol was taking its toll. Ken had to repeat: "Do you know who ended up adopting her?"

"Oh, some couple," she said. "But he died shortly afterward . . . and his wife went to pieces . . . and Sylvia ended up in a series of foster homes. In the last one, the man sexually abused her."

"She told you all that?"

"Oh, yes. She was here to hurt me back."

"So the ten thousand dollars—"

"That was nothing," Miss Widdich said, dismissing the notion with a wave of her hand. "I told you, she didn't come after me for money. She came to put me in a cardboard box of her own. To have complete control over me, over my destiny. That's why she came. To ruin me. She wanted revenge."

Gone was the sadness; in its place was the kind of bitter resentment that only a controlling person being manipulated can know.

"That had to be hard for you," Ken ventured, treading carefully now. "To have her threatening the life you'd made for yourself."

"She was enjoying herself," Miss Widdich admitted. "Bit by bit, she planned to make Chepaquit turn on me with contempt. She told me that; she wasn't secretive about her intentions. Ultimately, she wanted everyone to loathe me."

Ken was thinking, *What the hell difference would that make? We were all scared to death of you.*

Naturally she read his mind. She said simply, "I don't mind being feared—but I would never abide being scorned."

If he was waiting for her to say that she murdered her daughter and then buried her to prevent that from happening, then Ken was disappointed. Miss Widdich had nothing more to relate. She sat in stubborn silence until Ken said, "What will you do now?"

"You mean, after you tell everyone what I've just said?" she asked with a wry look. "I'm not worried. What I did when I was fifteen is just a colorful footnote to a much bigger story now. No one will care about what I did then."

It offended him, that nonchalance. There was something heartless about evaluating your murdered daughter in terms of a media event. He thought of his own mother, who would have moved—would still move—hell and high water for him. It boggled his mind to imagine Camille Barclay dumping him off in a cardboard box somewhere. Rich, poor, or in between, the thought would never have crossed her mind.

He was angry, and it must have shown in his face, because Miss Widdich stood up so abruptly that she teetered. "You can go now," she ordered.

"And if you *do* end up a suspect?" he said, somewhat malevolently.

"Why would I be? I gave Sylvia the money she wanted."

Not exactly what Ken would call an outraged denial; but on the other hand, he didn't know of a single piece of evidence linking Miss Widdich to the murder. Laura's insistence that the woman had had the strength to drag and then bury a body was hardly incontrovertible proof.

He had one last question for the inscrutable woman who, against all reason, could legimitately be called a mother. "What did you think of your daughter when she finally did find you?"

"Sylvia? Arrogant—and yet she didn't love herself. Well, how could she? Look at her life."

The girl's life was over. What Ken was looking at now was her death.

Chapter 28

The door to the house opened, and light from inside spilled onto the porch and out to the car where Laura sat jumpy with curiosity.

She pounced on Ken as soon as he got in the car. "Well? Is she?"

"Her mother? You bet."

"How did you get her to tell you that? I'm jealous!"

"I lied," he said, turning the key to the ignition. He slung his arm behind her seat and turned to peer over his shoulder down the unlit drive as he backed out. "I told her that they'd found the money, and that on a hunch, I went over the bank's records of withdrawals for around that time and came up with her name—but then I made up something about the bank being required to keep serial numbers on cash withdrawals of ten thousand dollars and over."

The car dropped into an extra-big pothole and Ken interrupted himself with a healthy oath, then said, "But, to tell the truth, I think she's been waiting for someone to step forward and accuse her of being Sylvia's mother. She seems pretty confident that no one will be able to make any more of a connection than that."

"But we have to, Ken. We have to be able to make more of a connection! Was she grieving, do you think? If she were innocent, she would have been devastated when I told her earlier that it was Sylvia."

"She'd definitely been crying. Maybe if I were a woman, I would have been able to read her emotions more accurately, but—damn, I couldn't tell why she'd been crying. There were some really creepy vibrations going on in there. That is one strange woman. If she *is* innocent and she *is* sorry, she's buried it deep. I have to tell you, the whole experience threw me."

She was so touched by his honesty. How many men would have admitted to that? She said, "Snack has the same reaction to her that you do. It's only Corinne who thinks she's a sweet old lady."

"She's in her early fifties, tops."

"Are you serious? She looks decades older than that!"

"Drugs? Grief? Illness? Maybe a combination of them," Ken speculated.

They were at the end of the drive. Before he pulled out onto the dark country road, he said, "Where to? I assume O'Doule's, to get your car?"

"Your place," Laura said softly.

Instantly, the air inside the car became charged in a whole new way. Ken let out a surprised half-sigh. He turned and stroked her cheek with the back of his fingers and then tucked her hair behind her ear. The gesture was as beguiling as it was electric.

"Are you sure?" he said.

"I've been sure for a while now. You?"

He shrugged. "Twenty years, give or take."

The smile in his voice enfolded her like warm honey. "You should have come after me, then," she teased.

"I was a fool. I worked out instead."

"And dated."

"Well, sure. I was a fool, not a monk."

He was irresistible. Funny and blunt and smart and . . .

irresistible. She grinned and said, "Drive on, Jeeves. Before I change my mind."

"Too late for that," he promised in a voice that sent an entirely new kind of chill rippling down her back.

He backed onto the pitch-black road and began heading east the short distance to Triple Oaks. Laura listened quietly, her heart ticking off seconds with a palpable thump, as Ken recounted the conversation between Miss Widdich and him.

The tension she was feeling between desire and dread was so keen that it hurt: a hard knot behind her breastbone told her that something, somewhere, somehow, had to be resolved. And soon. Or she would explode into a million bits and pieces of nothing at all.

Ken said, "If those news clippings were still in the satchel with the money—and assuming they haven't turned into dust—the police will easily figure out that Sylvia was in Chepaquit to blackmail someone; they just won't know who the mother was. Even without my two cents, it wouldn't take them long to figure it out. For starters, you have two dozen customers with herbs named Sylvia sitting on kitchen windowsills as we speak."

"And don't forget, I personally saw Miss Widdich's stricken reaction when Billy told us what he thought he'd seen that night."

"Maybe so, but the police will take anything *you* say with a grain of salt," Ken warned. "In any case, none of it proves anything except that she's Sylvia's birth mother."

"I know," Laura said, sighing. "And nothing we know so far gets my brother off the hook, which is all that I'm praying for."

Ken pulled into the drive of his stately house, looming large in the amber glow of twin brass porchlights. Laura got out of the car, then stood and stretched in place after her tense vigil back at Miss Widdich's house.

It was a beautiful night, with a warm west wind, the

kind of night that was made for magical journeys over the ocean and up through the stars. The fancy took hold of her, and as Ken approached her, she offered him a wistful proposal.

"Maybe . . . on the beach?"

He laughed softly and shook his head.

"Bad idea?" she asked, because she knew that Max would have thought so. All that sand.

"Such a good idea, you have no idea," Ken said. He slid his fingers through her hair and pulled her close, his mouth searching and finding hers in a kiss so deep, so yearning, that when he released her, she felt exalted. Some kisses were explorations, and some were promises. This one was akin to a vow. She felt it in her heart, she knew it in her soul.

He reached inside the car to pull a blanket from the back seat, and he tossed it over his shoulder. The simple act, a New England ritual, filled her with such joy. They were going to the beach.

Ken wrapped his arm around her shoulders, and she slid hers across the trim expanse of his lower back. Through the finely spun cotton of his polo shirt, she felt corded muscle, still a surprise to her. She had seen men strut who had so much less to strut; how delicious that she was being offered this man, in this exciting body. The realization of where they were headed—a blanket spread out under the stars—began flooding her with anticipation. And heat. Her awareness of him was so intense that it was making her light-headed, a unique experience for her.

"I don't know *anything*!"

"No problem; we'll work it out," he said, sounding amused.

"Oh, Lord. Did I say that out loud?"

"Or I'm telepathic."

"I meant, not that I didn't know *anything*, just that I

didn't know anything . . . about *this*," she said, struggling to explain herself.

Ken's voice was soft and low and sexy in his effort to help. "You mean, about making love under the stars?"

"Well, that too," she said in ongoing frustration. She had never been as fluent in describing her feelings as some of her women friends back in Portland. When they all got together, she was always the quiet one. It was the curse, she supposed, of being born a Shore; with the exception of Corinne, no one in her family had ever seemed very good at expressing words of love.

She tried again, because it was so important to her. She stopped on the path, in the middle of the stand of high-branched pines that separated the house from the beach and its ocean, and she took his hand in hers.

"I mean about *this*," she said, laying his hand over the beat of her heart. "See how my heart is when I'm with you? Can you feel it? It lifts, I don't know how. But it does. That happens to Corinne, too, when she's with Gabe. I didn't believe her—maybe I was jealous—but now I do. And I'm not jealous of her anymore."

It was a dark night, and in the narrow grove, darker still. Even so, she could sense a melting tenderness in his expression as he dropped the blanket and then cradled her face with his hands. "Laura . . . you have me aching for you . . . you, and no one else. I didn't even know I was hurting for you, not until I saw you come out of the house looking for Corinne that day."

A shaky laugh caught in her throat. "I remember it well. I was a mess."

"I wanted to kiss away every smudge on your face."

"I wish you had. We've wasted so many days . . . years. Oh, God. *Years*," she moaned, overwhelmed by the realization.

"We'll make up for lost time, I promise you," he said, his mouth tracing the delicate outline of her ear. "I love you, Laura," he whispered in the wake of his caress. "I love you, I love you. Can you see yourself living out your life with a skinny geek from Chepaquit Elementary?"

A surge of surprised bliss coursed through her, leaving her schoolgirl-giddy at his apparent proposal. She arched her neck, offering it for him to explore; there was teasing laughter in her voice as she said, "Is this one of those male, before-we-have-sex assurances?"

"Marry me and find out."

Oh—no ambiguity there. She let out a joyous, emotional gasp and bit her lip against a surprising, stinging rush of tears. In the back of her heart was the realization that this is how it should feel when a man wants a woman forever. So happy, so right.

But she wanted to be fair—because she knew about men before sex—and so she said, "Ask me again—after."

"Too long to wait." He pinned her in a new, fierce kiss that thrilled right through her and left her gasping with need.

"Yes. I will," she said. "Yes. Yes."

"I'll take that as a yes," he said, smiling against her cheek. He picked up the blanket and threw it over his shoulder again, and they half-walked, half-stumbled the rest of the way to the beach, grabbing at buttons and stopping for passionate kisses along the way. By the time he snapped the blanket open and let it float down, her bra was undone, her breasts loose and feeling sexy under her tee. His own shirt was half in, half out of his waist; the belt that circled it was completely unbuckled.

They were a laughing, disheveled mess, an embarrassment to the neighborhood. Laura was gleeful at the prospect of making love under the stars on a Chepaquit beach. She had fantasized about it since puberty—such a doable fantasy, and still not done.

Ken took her in his arms and they kissed, then kicked off their shoes and fell to their knees, exploring, reaching, snagging fabric and pulling it up and away. His shirt went sailing, and her top, and when he slid her bra from her shoulders and tossed it aside, she felt the cool night air across her naked breasts and her desire went ratcheting higher. It was all so fresh, so new, so glorious.

"Take me, I am *yours,*" she cried, laughing and falling on her back. She threw out her arms and spread her legs. "*X* marks the spot," she said wantonly, happy and reckless in this respite of passion.

"I'll make a note of it," Ken said, grinning. He bent his head over her and kissed the zipper of her jeans and said, "Yeah, I think I can find my way back here."

He stripped away his slacks and underwear and she thought, *Almost there*. His nakedness was shadowy and alluring; even in the jet-black night, she could see how aroused he was.

Impulsively, she reached out for his thick, engorged penis and slid her hand over the velvety skin in a single, slow, up-and-down stroke. "Mine? Truly?"

"Ho," he said in a shaky voice. "Always."

He undid the brass button of her jeans, and then the zipper, and she lifted her buttocks to help the disrobing. Peeling away her jeans and underpants to just below her knees, he paused to slide his hands up the sides of her thighs, circling inward, heading for the spot marked X.

She held her breath as he lowered his head again over her, this time softly kissing the tight curls of hair there. "I shall return," he promised, and he finished undressing her.

He came back to lie alongside her after that, and the novelty of her bare skin against his was made more so by the exquisite beauty of their surroundings.

"I've dreamed of you . . . this, with you," he said simply. He kissed her, slowly at first and then again and again, warm, wet minglings of her mouth and his, tentative explorations that became easy forays into the depth of her hunger for him. She murmured his name, murmured her love, and he answered in kind, the low, sweet cry of one lonely creature for its soulmate in the scary vastness of God's universe.

Down he trailed, heating her with kisses everywhere: her throat, the curve of her neck, one aching breast and then the other, then a hungry detour back to her mouth before resuming course again. But always, always, she knew that he was bound for the X.

He arrived. Writhing under the hot caresses of his tongue, she gripped the blanket's edge, found sand, rolled it through her fingers. Breathing deep, she sucked in the tang of the ocean. She opened her eyes: the scattering of stars had become a thick spill of glitter across a bolt of velvet. So much beauty, so much pleasure, all for her.

She was on that beach at last. Her heartbeat became a drumbeat and her long moans crumbled into mere whimpers as he took her to the next level, and the next after that. Hot, hot, she was burning all over, her eyes glazing over as she arched herself into his kisses. Her mouth opened in a gaping effort to draw in breath. The glittery swath in the sky above her pulsed blue and then red and then burst like a fireball, showering her with licks of flame, consuming her completely.

She lay in a state of inertia, too spent to move.

Ken came back up alongside her and kissed the tip of her nose. "So. What do you think of making love on the beach?"

She sighed and said, "Oh . . . you know what they say: location, location, location."

He laughed at that and smoothed her hair and seemed in no great urgency at all. But she knew he was—she could *see* he was—and so she said, "You do realize that you yourself are zero for two now?"

"Not by my reckoning; I look at it as two for two," he said gallantly.

To die for. Any man who put a woman first was one

you didn't let go. She said softly, "Hey, how about letting me drive now?"

"Uh-h . . . let me get the keys."

She could tell he was startled, and that gave her yet more new pleasure. Everything about him was new and pleasurable. She nudged him gently on his back, and he didn't seem to have any problem with it. At all. She leaned over him and with her tongue brought his erection to a rock-solid state, reveling in the aroused pace of his breathing.

"You'd . . . better . . . slow . . . down," he said, his voice breaking on the breaths outward.

"Yessir." Immediately she straddled him, fitting herself over him, filling herself with him. Her nerve endings flamed back up, after all; she was aware that with this man, the fire would probably simmer deep for the rest of her life.

He cupped her buttocks in his infinitely capable hands and said, "You are so beautiful."

She laughed, because he couldn't possibly see more than a shadow of her on the dark beach, but she knew what he meant: she was just as aware of his own beauty.

"Don't look at me," she said anyway. "Look at the stars. Aren't they wonderful?" She began a slow, tentative rhythm over him with every intention of making him weep with joy.

He groaned softly as she picked up the pace, and he said, "You *are* the stars." She moved faster, sliding nearly to the tip of him, teasing and taunting before plunging down hard. Again and again, leaning over him so that she herself could savor the strokes, stealing pleasure when she had meant only to offer it to him.

"The stars, the moon, the sun . . . oh, *lady,*" he moaned in her fierce, pumping race to the finish. "I love you, Laura . . . I love you . . . I . . ."

Suddenly he pinned her to him, plunging deep, deep inside, taking her; and Laura felt herself slide, as well, into satisfaction, more gently this time.

After a long, quiet, perfect moment, she rolled off him and lay on her back, nestling on his arm to gaze at the stars with him. There seemed, now, no need for words . . . just a sigh or two, a touch, a kiss.

The night was truly spectacular, the beauty of the star-studded sky crushing in its magnitude. She and Ken were as insignificant, in the grand scheme of things, as any two grains of sand on the beach. But in the smaller world that they had just made their own, how vastly important they were, each to the other.

Chapter 29

Because she wasn't used to walking around strange houses naked, Laura donned one of Ken's white T-shirts. The sleeves came down to her elbows, and the hem came down to the top of her thighs, but it did the job. More or less. She was staring into the refrigerator, looking for something unhealthy to eat, when Ken caught her from behind and slid his hands under the shirt. He pulled her to him as he nibbled the lobe of her ear, something Laura hadn't a clue that she loved until the night before.

"Mmm," she said, still thrilling to his touch. "Morning. I'm starved, and there's no chocolate cake in here. Orange juice, eggs, whole wheat bread—that's it? What gives?"

"Who knew?" he said, rocking her lightly in his arms. "I haven't had anyone stay here overnight since—well, how about that? I've never had anyone stay here overnight."

She looked up over her shoulder at him and said, "You lie."

"Honest. I bought the house from my mother only a couple of years ago, and. . . ." He shrugged off the rest of an explanation.

Which Laura was only too happy to supply. "And when you dated, you were the one who was invited inside for—shall we say—coffee, am I right?"

"Are you jealous? Cool," he said, burying his face in her hair. He nipped at the back of her neck, confident and possessing. "I'm seriously flattered."

"Can I be jealous retroactively?" she asked, sighing happily. "If so, then put me down for some of it."

He turned her in his arms and said, "That's one emotion you will never have to know. And that, lady, is the God's honest truth."

She had no doubt; she could see it in his eyes. "I love you," she said, lost in that emotion for him. "Here's an awful cliché: I did not know it could be like this."

Her gaze was drawn to the gold band with its high-pronged setting of a single, small diamond that she was wearing on her ring finger. Ken had got up in the middle of the night and had come back with it to bed; he'd had to wake Laura up to give it to her.

Bemused and enchanted and droopy with sleep, she had murmured, "Where did *this* come from?"

"I caught the last shooting star before we came in from the beach," he'd told her, and at the time it seemed like a lovely, plausible explanation.

But in the hour before dawn, when they awoke and made love again, he explained that the ring had belonged to his grandmother, and then to his mother, and that his mother had given it to him after his father had died.

"Because you never know when you might need it," she'd told him at the time. "You have to be ready to strike when the iron is hot. That's how it was with your father and me."

A simple, motherly remark. It gave Laura hope that someday, despite the obvious differences between them, she and Camille Barclay would be friends.

Over a breakfast of juice, toast, and eggs and no chocolate cake, the talk turned, as it had on and off all night, back to the ongoing investigation. Despite her euphoria—maybe because of it—Laura was more deeply concerned than ever about Snack.

"It's the knife that I'm worried about most," Laura said.

Ken had told her everything he knew about the investigation so far, and part of what he knew was the knife.

"Yeah," he conceded. "I was hoping it was your father's."

Laura shook her head morosely.

She said, "I'll have to tell them—won't I?—that I personally saved up to have it engraved for Snack's graduation present. He must have given it to Sylvia as a gift."

"Or lent it to her for the day. You don't know. You all use knives."

"Yes, but when I think back . . . Snack really did have a fierce thing about her. There's no point in denying it. And the knife was a proud possession. You know? Kind of a little like—?" She held up her hand with the ring on it.

"I understand," Ken said, nodding.

"I *hate* this," Laura moaned. "I feel as if I possess all the testimony they need to string my brother up. I know who the knife belonged to. I know about the horrible fight Snack had with my father late that awful night—the same night that, earlier, Billy says my brother fought with Sylvia. I know that Snack ran away from home right after the beating my father gave him. And I remember, now, that I wondered if maybe he'd eloped with Sylvia. Which is *your* fault, by the way," she added glumly.

"Come again?"

"After last night . . . after the beach . . . all kinds of dams seemed to break," she said. "Things came flooding back that I haven't let myself think about in years and years. And one of them was the quaint idea that Snack had eloped with Sylvia after she said that she was thinking of quitting her job at Shore Gardens. Snack was only fifteen, then; but never mind. The point is, why would I even have had the thought if he hadn't been wild about her?"

Ken smiled and said, "Maybe because you like happy-ever-afters?"

She laughed. "Oh, yeah. Snack and Sylvia. There's a wedding-cake couple. Actually, do you know what kind of woman Snack really needs? Someone who'd be half girl-friend, half mother to him. That would work. But a bad boy and a bad girl . . ." She snorted and said, "That's not generally a recipe for success."

"Have it all figured out, do you, Miss Lonelyhearts?" He reached over and gave the ring on her finger a tug. "As soon as we get ourselves properly wed, we'll find someone for your brother. It can be done. He's a good kid."

"With a rap sheet. Which is another thing."

Laura sighed and broke off a piece of toast, but each piece had been going down harder, and she was merely playing with her food now. She folded the bread onto itself over and over until it was a tight little ball of gluten, ready to string on a hook for fish bait.

"Add to that, Billy's account," she said, going down the list of damning circumstances. "Oh, and let's not forget Uncle Norbert's homicidal genes. A jury sure won't."

Ken said quickly, "Now, that's the kind of fact that would never be allowed into evidence."

"But it's a fact that everyone knows!"

"*Some* people know it. In Chepaquit. You're much too puffed up over your notoriety, lady," he said, polishing a broken yolk with the last of his bread. "Few people know, and fewer care."

She smiled forlornly and said, "You're just saying we're nobodies to make me feel good."

"Ha. If I wanted to make you feel good," he said with a Groucho Marx jiggle of eyebrows, "I'd go a different route altogether." He pushed his chair back and went around to her side of the table to clear her plate, and then suddenly he stopped.

"It doesn't make sense," he said, frowning. "Miss Widdich claimed—and I believe it—that Sylvia wanted to get back at her. That Sylvia wanted to put *her* in a cardboard box. That money wasn't what Sylvia was after."

"So—?"

"So why would Sylvia say thank you very much, and then be content to pack her bag and start to walk away?"

"Interesting point," Laura said. Unexpectedly, she began to take heart again. "After all, Sylvia was planning to have a really fun time hanging around Chepaquit and sticking pins in Miss Widdich. So to speak. At the very least, she could have got more money out of her."

"Lots of it."

"But . . . would Miss Widdich kill her own *daughter*?" asked Laura. The woman in her refused to believe it.

"She left her in a cardboard box. In the snow."

"But she hung around until Sylvia was found."

"True," Ken conceded. "And then there's the matter of how Miss Widdich would have killed her. You said yourself that Sylvia was tall and in her prime. Miss Widdich could not have been a match for her, physically. No matter how big a hole she can dig."

"But she does know everything about herbs," Laura admitted. "She easily could have poisoned Sylvia. She—no, no, what am I saying? We *all* know a lot about poisons," Laura blurted, distressed that that was true, because it was just one more thing to worry about. "I want to believe that Miss Widdich did it—but I can't. I can't believe that any woman would murder her own flesh and blood."

"Ever hear of a lady named Medea?" Ken said grimly. "You don't have to go back to the Greeks, either; just pick up a paper nowadays."

Laura nodded. "Still, in the myth, Medea was spurned by Jason. People kill from a jealous rage, I'll grant you that. But not from a fear of embarrassment."

"Point taken," said Ken. He took her mug and his over to the coffee machine for refills. "All right. Who, at the time, might have gone into a jealous rage over Sylvia?"

"Besides Snack, you mean," she said, forcing herself to think like Chief Mellon.

She said hesitantly, as if she were picking rubies out of a box of broken glass, "Billy claims that he heard Snack arguing with Sylvia. And that may be. But I heard my father blistering Snack late that night. It was my father, not Snack, who was the enraged one. Who was the violent one when he took Snack out to the shed. Who could easily have been acting out of jealousy. My father, not Snack."

Ken was deeply interested in what she had to say. "Snack didn't put up a fight?" he asked, setting her newly filled mug in front of her.

Laura shook her head. "I think he was so used to submitting to my father's fury that it never occurred to him. Snack would always just cover his head and hunker down. He was a boy. Whatever he felt for Sylvia, he was still a boy."

"And he never said what the beating he got was about?"

"Never," she said. "He's always refused to talk about it."

Ken kissed the top of her hair and pulled her gently up from her chair. "It's time you asked him, then. Because the road to proving Snack's innocence may well lead back and not forward."

Even bankers worked once in a while, Laura learned: Ken actually had a meeting to go to that morning. He dropped Laura off at O'Doule's to get the pickup, and he continued on to work.

Laura headed straight back to the nursery to try to force her brother to confide in her. She was surprised to see that

Corinne was in the shop and that Snack was back at work on the Deere, moving trees to the site of the old compost pile.

"Great news!" Corinne informed her. She was madly running around, watering everything in sight with a wand-end hose. "They're done, at least for now, and we have the garden center back."

Laura glanced at the parking lot outside and said, "Now all we need are our customers back."

"We have built it; they will come," said Corinne with serene optimism.

Her mood rubbed off on Laura like fairy dust. "Does this mean that they're done with us, too?"

Was it possible?

It was not. Corinne looked sheepish as she said, "They want to talk to Snack again. He's going down to the station in an hour or so. No pressure, though. Really, it's just routine. Chief Mellon said whenever it was convenient. I think that's a *very* good sign, don't you?"

"It certainly sounds that way," said Laura, fudging confidence.

"That's exactly what I told—Laura! What is *that*?" Corinne said, grabbing her sister's hand for closer examination. "Ohmigod. It's a diamond ring. Ohmigod. Laura—you didn't. You aren't." She let out a squeal of joy. "You're engaged? To a guy from *Chepaquit*? This means you're staying? You're staying here? Oh, my *God*!"

"Well, Ken and I did talk about that," Laura said, laughing between life-threatening squeezes. "And we decided it was easier for me to move my computer than for Ken to move his bank."

"Oh, this is . . . you don't know . . . this is the best—" Tears began rolling freely. "I'm so *happy* for us."

Excited to be sharing her news, Laura said, "You know how I tend to mull over things until I'm exhausted. This time—no mulling! If Ken hadn't asked me last night, I'm pretty sure I would have asked him."

"It's so romantic, so *New York Times*!"

Laura had been clipping the "Vows" column from the Sunday *Times* for years and sending it to her sister. Corinne had always loved the whirlwind marriages best, so her reaction was no surprise. But Laura herself was still trying to come to terms with her blind leap into another commitment.

"This doesn't feel at all like with Max," she said, amazed at the difference. "Before he dumped me, I considered Max . . . suitable. I don't have a clue if Ken is suitable. All I know is—oh, boy—all I know is that this feeling is big. This is huge."

"You're coming home! I can't believe it!" Corinne said, hugging her joyously again. "When you called to say that you wouldn't be home last night? I had a feeling. Call me psychic, but I just had a really good feeling."

"I definitely will *not* call you psychic," Laura said with a little shiver. She had no desire to ruin her sister's happy mood with a morbid account of Miss Widdich's confession, so she said, "I have to talk to Snack before he goes to town."

"Good. Maybe you can calm him down a little. He's on the jittery side."

"Gee, I wonder why. Don't tell me he's taking all this hounding personally," Laura said on her way out.

She flagged down her brother before he went off for another load of shrubs and trees, and they walked over to a rough-hewn picnic table that Snack had hammered together just so that customers could pause in their labors and enjoy the view.

The view itself was one of the best at Shore Gardens: Cape Cod in its natural state. The ground here was covered in long grass, shimmering and rippling in the early breeze as it sloped gently to the waterfront property below. Tucked on the land once owned by Laura's family sat a beautifully discreet house, built by someone with lots of money and no interest in flaunting it. It scarcely intruded on the expansive vista of blue ocean, already fluttering with distant sails. Somewhere out there crouched Nantucket in a bank of offshore fog, but immediately to their south, the low, flat profile of uninhabited Monomoy Island stretched like an eel in the shallows surrounding it.

It was a perfect place, a gift from the gods, and Laura had no intention of letting it slip through their fingers.

She turned to Snack, who was slugging water thirstily from a bottle he'd brought along. She hadn't really noticed how tan and fit and sinewy her brother had become in the last several weeks. Unlike Ken, Snack had never had to endure a painfully skinny, geeky phase as a kid, and now he was in his prime. Young, healthy, with a breadth of skills—what a catch he'd make, give or take a few issues.

"The life agrees with you," she said.

"Yeah," he muttered, wiping his beaded brow with the back of a bare arm. "If only they'd let me live it."

"I guess you're going to see Chief Mellon after you shower?"

She was sitting on the table, with her feet on the seat; Snack was sitting below her. He looked back over his shoulder at her with a wry smile. "Shower?"

Just like her brother to insist on putting his worst foot forward.

"Snack, this is serious," she said in soft reproach. "Remember that knife I gave you for eighth-grade graduation? The one with your initials in it?"

"Yeah?"

"They found it among the bones."

He said nothing, then let out a long breath. "Shit."

"Did she steal it from you, by any chance?"

"Well, actually—!" He paused, sighed, and shook his

head. "No. I lent it to her. She couldn't find her own, so I lent it to her to use."

Staring at the sea, he let a few seconds pass. "No, that's not true either," he admitted. "I gave it to her as a present. No strings attached."

"Why? Because you liked her so well?"

"Liked?" he said with a melancholy smile. "It was a little more than liked."

"But you were a boy. What did you know about women?"

"Just about nothing. I was a virgin."

"Oh," she said vaguely. And then: "*Oh.*"

He looked directly at her, and she was reminded that his eyes were the same shade of green as the shallow waters around Monomoy. When they were kids and if they got the chance, they used to go clamming together at low tide there. How long ago it seemed.

"Will you tell me why you ran away?"

Turning from her, he shrugged, but he kept his gaze fixed on the sea. Laura didn't know if that was meant to be a yes or a no. She stayed where she was, afraid to move down to the seat next to him and frighten him away. He might just as well have been a dragonfly sunning on a post.

"She had this way of getting you to talk," he said at last. "The opposite of you. You're good at the head-on approach. But with Sylvia—I think it was because she didn't really care what you said. You couldn't shock her. She was kind of like a priest in a confessional that way. So one day I told her how much I hated Dad, and that I planned to split. She said, 'Do it. Take your chances out there.' She told me that she stayed, and that she was sorry. After that, she used to stick up for me against Dad."

"I remember that she liked to take him on," Laura said. "I guess I didn't realize for whom."

"Yeah, well, I was whom. Some of the time, anyway." He paused to finish his bottle of water.

"Then, the day I left, Dad had to have that root canal, remember? So naturally, that meant time off for me. I was hanging out in the greenhouse, watching Sylvia work. We talked. She was curious about me. She said she'd never had a virgin. I didn't even have to tell her I'd never fucked anyone. She just knew, I guess," he said.

He glanced over his shoulder at Laura, and with that half-smile she knew so well, he asked, "Did I really look that green?"

"You're asking *me*? I was just as green."

"Anyway, she took me to the toolshed, and that's where she—let's say—made a man of me."

"The toolshed! The same place that Dad—"

"Beat the shit out of me later that night. Yeah. That toolshed. And if you don't think I get weird vibrations when I'm around that building, then you've got another think coming. I about lost my lunch when those guys found the satchel there."

"Did you know it was Sylvia's?"

"Of course. Didn't you?"

Laura shook her head. She was becoming almost light-headed—but whether from the sun beating down on them, or from her brother's rambling confession, she had no idea.

"But if Dad was at the dentist, how did he know?" Because that was obviously why Snack had been whipped late that night; Laura didn't even have to ask, now. "Did you leave a condom around or something?"

Snack's laugh was loud and incredulous; even she had to smile, once she saw it from his side. She said, "Well? How, then?"

"Someone told Dad. I never quite got around to asking who," he said dryly. "I was too busy howling in pain."

"It wasn't Mom; she'd never tell on you, even if she knew anything. Maybe the help?"

"Syl *was* the help."

"Not Corinne. It must have been a customer, then.

Someone saw you two and told someone who told Dad in town at a bar, the drugstore, anywhere. Probably they did it to bait him; anything to get under his skin."

"It doesn't exactly matter, does it?" Snack said, reaching for the pocket of his T-shirt. She knew the gesture; he needed a smoke. He had cut back considerably—but there were times.

"I gave Syl the knife after the toolshed. It was the least I could do," he said with that macho tone Laura always hated to see.

"Then when did you have the fight with her that Billy remembers so vividly?"

"Ah, *that* fight," he said, lighting up a Marlboro. He inhaled, held, let go. "Right after the toolshed, I hung around her like a puppy. I wanted to play some more, but, alas, Sylvia was done with me. 'I did it just to be able to say.' Those were her exact words. I was cut to the quick," he said, collapsing his chin comically on his chest.

"What did you do?"

"There was nothing I *could* do. I ranted and railed at her, which Billy saw, and then I went off for the rest of the day—and night—and licked my wounds and plotted vengeful things against her, like blowing up her car."

"Oh, don't even joke. Especially not with Chief Mellon when you tell him all this."

Again he laughed. "Get real. I'm not telling him anything. You think I've got some kind of death wish?"

"But . . . you're telling *me,*" she said, confused.

The sardonic tone disappeared. "Because I trust you, sis. For no other reason than that."

She wanted to say, *I'm not a priest. This picnic table is not a confessional.* Didn't he understand that she was bound to say what she knew if asked under oath? She began backing away from the subject altogether. What if she were wrong about his innocence? Suddenly she didn't want to know.

"I didn't do it, dodo!" Snack said.

"Oh, God, I'm sorry." She was mortified that he'd been able to read her thoughts. "I don't know what I was—too much stuff has been going on."

"So I see," he said, nodding at her hand.

So he'd noticed the ring. That surprised her. She smiled ruefully and said, "Let's hope I'm not doing a Snack."

"You're a big girl now," he said. "I think you got yourself a good one. Which is more than I can say for that clunker in Portland."

"What nerve," she said, laughing. "You never even met the guy."

"I've met guys like him." He was already putting out his cigarette in the sandy soil, sinking it deep.

Laura climbed down from her perch and said, "After you shower, wear the yellow polo shirt we got you. You look more innocent in yellow."

Her brother looked up from his task and smiled. "You always did have a way with advice."

He stood up to go. Still smiling herself, Laura said, "Hey, little brother." She put her arms around him and hugged him close. "Just be nice—and tell the truth—and you'll do just fine."

He sucked in his breath and let it out in a rush. "Yeah." For a split second, he was her little brother again, mad at an unfair world but scared of it, too.

"Fog's starting to roll in," he said gruffly, breaking with her. "You'll have to paint inside, not out. Incidentally, I owe you sixty bucks."

It would have been pointless to pretend she didn't know what he was talking about; Snack knew that she kept track of her money. So she nodded and said, "Okay," and said a little prayer of thanks that he had come clean about taking it the day of their arrival.

They walked back to the house discussing the work list,

which hadn't got any shorter during the lockdown.

And that was the last that Laura heard of her brother until two and a half hours later, when she learned that he'd punched out Andrew Mellon, Chepaquit's chief of police.

Chapter 30

"James Mandaren! Gabe uses him. Call him! I can't wait for you, I'm going now. Call him!" Corinne grabbed her purse and was out the door before her sister could tackle her.

Laura was covered in paint spatters from head to toe and cursing herself for not taking the time to put on a zip-up plastic coverall. But it would have meant a run into town to buy one, and it was too clammy to have worn one in any case. And now she was paying the price.

Damn it!

After calling the attorney and leaving a message, she decided to contact Ken at the office. She got his assistant, whose voice and manner changed entirely after Laura identified herself.

"Oh, *yes,* Miss Shore. This is Nancy," the assistant said in a breathless voice. "Mr. Barclay is with someone now, but I'll put your call through."

"No, no . . . if you could just say that I called. Actually, don't even do that. It can wait."

"Are you sure?" Nancy said, hesitating.

"Really. It's not important," Laura insisted, and she hurried off the phone.

The last thing she wanted was for Ken to associate her

with a new scandal every time they talked. He would wonder what the hell he'd got himself into. Eventually, so would his mother.

Angry—for different reasons—with herself, with Snack, and with Corinne, Laura treaded carefully across the half-torn-up floor of the bathroom, stepped over the deep claw-foot tub, and turned on the wobbly shower. Twenty minutes would not make a difference in addressing Snack's latest run-in with the law.

What was he thinking, assaulting a cop? He *did* have a death wish. It hardly mattered that Snack's "assault" consisted of poking the chief in the chest while he vented his outrage at being so clearly under suspicion. What mattered was that Chief Mellon was within his rights to charge Snack and lock him up until a bail hearing. Very handy, if they were putting together a case against him and were afraid that he might run.

She soaped up a loofah and scrubbed her arms and legs viciously. The spatters came off; the blobs did not. She had neither the time nor the patience to clean up thoroughly, so she dried herself off, wrapped the towel around herself, and headed to her room for clothes and a comb.

At the upstairs landing, she jumped back and let out a cry: a male figure was coming up the steps at her.

"Gabe! God, you *scared* me!"

"Yikes—sorry, Laura," he said, looking sheepishly away from her towel-wrapped body.

"Couldn't you *knock*?" She tucked the towel in more firmly and hurried across the hall to her room.

"I did knock," he said to her retreating back. "Where is everyone? The nursery's deserted. I just assumed that Corinne was up here, showering. She told me to meet her at the house after I got off work; we're supposed to go out. Sorry," he repeated, and then added, amused, "I didn't see anything; does that help?"

"Oh, yeah, a lot. My heart attack is nearly gone."

She heard him clumping down the stairs.

"I'll be down in a minute," she called out from her room. "There's been a slight hitch. Snack's just been arrested."

"*Arrested!* For what?" Gabe yelled up. He sounded as shocked as they had been, which was gratifying. At least he hadn't jumped to the conclusion that the arrest was for the murder of Sylvia.

Keeping it deliberately light, Laura said, "Oh, you know Snack. He couldn't help getting testy during the latest interview with Chief Mellon, and he poked him a couple of times on a shirt button."

"For crying out loud. What's the *matter* with him? You know, when this is over, that kid's gotta get professional counseling. This goes beyond just having an attitude."

Dragging a comb through her dripping hair, Laura yelled down, "It's not as if he flattened the man or anything, but still. Corinne is completely traumatized," she added. "It's incredibly discouraging. I don't know what it is about our family: we keep trying to snatch defeat from the jaws of victory."

"I've noticed that!"

"A few minutes ago, my sister was running around thrilled that we could finally reopen."

"That's why I'm here," he called up. "We were going to go out and have a meal to celebrate before she dives back into work. God. I can't believe it. All these years, and Snack hasn't changed at all."

"Yeah. He needs a Big Brother, a mentor," Laura said, pulling a challis sundress over her head. "Someone like you. Look at the tragedies you overcame: losing both parents, giving up law school . . ."

She didn't point out that running a fence company wasn't quite the same as running for United States Senator, which was what Gabe had announced in his senior yearbook that he had every intention of doing. After all, sooner or later, he might very well do it.

"I'm happy enough," he said quickly. But there was a hint of defensiveness in his tone.

Laura was afraid that she might have offended him, so she said warmly, "Well, sure, why wouldn't you be happy? Town councilman . . . mayor next. Who knows what's after that? You're living a dream life," she said, slipping into a pair of sandals.

And she would be, too, once they finished muddling through the current mess. It was amazing, how everything seemed more doable now that she had Ken by her side.

She took the stairs too quickly, stumbling and grabbing the banister in time to save herself from tumbling head-first down the stairwell.

"I'm going to kill myself," she said, annoyed with her choice of shoes.

Gabe was waiting at the landing. "Don't worry; I would have caught you," he said gallantly.

"Oh, for—I don't have a car!" Laura said, amazed that she'd overlooked the detail. "I wonder how Corinne thought I was supposed to follow her—on the tractor?"

"No problem; I'll give you a lift. I want to see Corinne anyway. Have you retained an attorney?"

"Yours—if he ever returns my call. Oh, but how can he? I won't be here!"

"Why don't *I* try?" He reached in his pocket and pulled out a cell phone, then hit an autodial button.

They had made it to the porch. Laura waited impatiently while the attorney's secretary put him on hold. She was antsy, ready to go. If she had a bike, she would have hopped on it. Gabe smiled reassuringly, and she smiled back, and that's when she saw it.

A Timex watch on his wrist. An exact copy of the one she'd found in the greenhouse on the first day of her return.

"I've seen that watch," she said, surprised.

Gabe shrugged and said, "Probably. I've used these for years. It's self-winding: no fuss, no muss. Whenever my

Rolex is out having its annual tune-up, I slap one of these Timexes on my wrist. Not fancy, but they do the—"

"Job. Yes," Laura said, smiling faintly. "Excuse me. I just remembered something."

She turned back into the house just as Gabe got connected to Attorney Mandaren. "Jim, yeah, this is Gabe. How're you doin'? Listen, I've got a—No, I don't think they'll appeal. Why would they?"

He was instantly deep in conversation on some other matter than Snack. Laura hurried up the stairs and went directly to the top drawer of her dresser.

It was the same watch, all right. The pattern on the flexible band might have been slightly different, but other than that . . .

Was it Gabe's? And if it was, did it matter? She hadn't thought about the rusted timepiece since the night she'd ignored Snack's command to throw it out and instead had dumped it in a drawer. Now, suddenly, it seemed to have moved to stage center in her thoughts. She switched on the bureau's lamp and studied the Timex more closely. A watch. An ordinary watch missing a pin from its band. She held it up to the light. For the first time, she noticed a strand of long hair caught in the links of the band.

Long, straight, jet-black hair.

"Ah, you found it," came his voice from behind her.

She whirled around so fast that the room spun.

Billy sat fidgeting in the same leather armchair that Laura had chosen when she and Corinne came to Chepaquit Savings to see about a loan. Ken had been thrilled to be able to free the two sisters from the clutches of a predatory lender—but he wasn't nearly so sure what he could do for Billy.

"You want to know about . . . getting a shot?" he asked, baffled by Billy's rambling request.

"Like in the movies," Billy said, trying his best to explain. "I seen it where the guy got a shot, and right away he started telling all this stuff that he wouldn't even tell them when they were beating him up. It was because of the shot. The shot made him tell."

"You mean, truth serum? But why would you want to get a shot of truth serum? You've already *told* the truth."

"Well, I don't *want* to get a shot," Billy admitted. "I'm kind of afraid of shots. But if that's the only way . . . unless . . . could they give it to someone in cough syrup, do you know? Because that wouldn't be so bad. I could take it in cough syrup," he decided, nodding his big, teddy-bear head. "Especially if it was cherry."

Aware that with the exception of Laura, Billy was the only witness who had come forward with information about that infamous night, Ken decided to probe a little further into his memory.

He came around to the front of his desk and leaned ever so casually back on it. "Billy? You're not keeping anything from me, are you? You've told me everything that you can remember?"

"I don't *know*!" Billy said in a pathetic wail. "That's why I want to have the—what do you call it?"

"Truth serum?"

"Yeah, that. Because maybe I know something else that I just forgot, and if I can just remember it, Snack will be okay. I got Snack *into* trouble," he said, pounding a massive fist into the palm of his hand for emphasis. "I have to try to get Snack *out* of trouble."

With a pleading look at Ken, he said, "Why did he have to fight with Sylvia, anyway? Why couldn't he be like Gabe?"

The muscles in Ken's thighs tightened with the effort not to jump up and grab Billy by the shirt. "Like . . . Gabe?" he said, aware that his heart had just made a crashing attempt to break through his chest. "How do you mean?"

"Well, Gabe was much nicer to Sylvia. He talked real soft to her. He laughed. He hugged her. He even kissed her. That's how much *he* liked her."

God Almighty. "Yeah, a lot of people liked Sylvia. I guess Gabe was one of them. So . . . Sylvia was in a better mood with Gabe than she was with Snack?" he asked carefully.

Billy snorted, as if he were blowing milk through his nose, and said, "There's no comparison."

"Yeah. And Gabe came over on the same day, did you say?" He hadn't said, but never mind.

"In the morning. My mom says I'm a morning person," Billy volunteered. "Maybe Sylvia is, too. Used to be, I mean. And Gabe, he's always going off somewhere early. So he must be a morning person, too. But Snack! He overslept all the time. His dad was always getting on him about that."

"Mm. I'll bet." From what Ken had learned about Sylvia, he wasn't surprised that she had Gabe under her thumb as well. Maybe the attraction for her was Gabe's naughty little secret. Obviously the councilman wouldn't be in a hurry to volunteer information that might make him look just as callow as Snack.

If Billy was telling the truth and not simply fantasizing. After all, the golden boy of Chepaquit with the prettiest girl in Chepaquit: Billy's romantic heart might want to pair up Gabe and Sylvia, regardless.

But if Billy *were* telling the truth . . .

"Billy, do you remember that foggy night you told me about, the one where you fell asleep in the delivery van listening to a song you liked? When you woke up, you saw someone dragging something heavy into the compost pile, right?"

Billy nodded, but he was clearly nervous about being questioned.

Ken said, "I want you to think very hard. Even without truth serum, I'll bet you can remember: was there any other vehicle in the parking lot when you woke up after your nap in the van?"

"I don't even have to think, because there wasn't!" Billy said triumphantly. He'd aced the test, and he was very pleased. "That's why I thought it could be Snack—because he lived right there!" he explained with Watson-like enthusiasm.

Unfortunately, it wasn't quite so elementary as that.

Why did the chicken cross the road?

To get to the other side.

The riddle came and went like a flash of lightning, leaving Ken both dazed and jolted in its wake.

Gabe walks across the road, tries to pick up where he left off earlier that day, gets rebuffed or, if she's a tease, even worse. A kid with hormones amuck—Ken could testify about hormones amuck at that age—*he loses it, kills her, panics, hides her.*

Could the chicken cross the road and then go back without being caught?

On a foggy night? All too easily.

"Thanks, Billy. You've been a big help. You've been more than a big help."

"Really?" No one was more surprised than Billy. "You mean I won't have to get a shot?"

"Not at all." Ken slapped Billy on the back and shook his hand and got him moving up and out of the leather chair. He saw him to the door, then went back to his desk and, still standing, called Laura. He had plenty to say and he wanted to see her, his afternoon's schedule be damned. When there was no answer, he became uneasy. Unnecessarily so, because she and her brother and sister could have been working anywhere on the grounds, but . . . he was uneasy.

In the small anteroom to his office, his assistant sat in front of a computer monitor. "I'll be gone for an hour," he told her. "Call me on the cell phone if it can't wait. If Laura Shore calls—"

"She did call," Nancy said, surprising him. "She asked me not to leave a message, it wasn't important, but—she did call."

"Oh. Okay. Well . . . hmm. In that case . . ." He shrugged and went back into his office.

And in less than a minute, came back out again.

"I'll be at Shore Gardens," he told Nancy on his way out the door.

He was in the bank's parking lot when Andy Mellon hailed him over to the police station's parking lot.

"I've got a bone to pick with you, pal," the chief yelled over.

Ken had a strong hunch that the chief wasn't flagging him down to invite him to go fishing aboard his beloved boat.

Chapter 31

His knife was at her throat.

Laura felt the bite of its flat blade against her skin; in a state of shock, she thought, *He doesn't want to kill me, only to frighten me. Please, God. Only frighten me.*

Nausea swept over her; she was going to be sick.

"Write exactly what I tell you to," Gabe commanded. His voice was taut.

She had to slide the paper farther away from her on the kitchen table just to see what she was writing. She held her head perfectly straight, perfectly stiff. The pen he'd found next to the phone was poised in her hand.

"Say: 'Snack didn't kill Sylvia. I did.' "

Laura did as she was told, but her hand was shaking so much, and the angle was so acute, that the crabbed handwriting barely resembled her own.

Gabe was watching her progress. "Okay," he said, "now write, 'Sylvia was coming on to my father. We fought, and she hit her head on the greenhouse sink.' "

"D-did she?" Laura asked without moving her head a millimeter.

"No. I strangled her. Write."

She shaped the words in what seemed like slow motion.

He said, "Now say, 'I panicked and buried her in the compost pile.' "

"Did y—?"

"Yes. *Write*, goddammit."

Laura was giddy with fear, adrift in an adrenaline rush so strong that every pore of her skin felt needled with pain. She did as Gabe said, clinging desperately to the time she was buying.

Still staring straight ahead, she pleaded, "Me? Gabe—*me*?"

"Why not? Half the town hates you, anyway. And the other half will understand your dilemma: you want to save your brother, but you know you'll lose your lover. You decide to do something right just *once* in your sorry life—so you throw yourself on your sword."

The simple poetry of his plan was enough to make her angry. Without moving a muscle, she said, "They'll never believe . . . this bullshit."

"You wish," Gabe sneered.

"You're the one . . . who hates us," she said, staring immobilized at Corinne's cheerful new valence.

"Not anymore," he said. "Back then—oh, yes. I didn't think much of having to take a number for Sylvia after your brother—and your old man."

"Not my father," she said, rejecting his twisted view.

"Wrong. After I killed her—which I hadn't intended to do, incidentally—I told your old man that she'd boinked Snack in the toolshed. I knew there'd be war after that. I figured either Snack or Ollie would end up taking the blame for Sylvia, but I never dreamed it would take this long to find her." He let out a bitter snort, and she felt the knife again. "Only the Shores."

He said, "Too bad I lost my watch. Or none of this would be necessary. I looked everywhere. Where did you find it?"

He actually seemed curious enough to expect Laura to answer, so she gasped, "The greenhouse."

"I *looked* there," he said, surprised and almost petulant that he'd missed it.

She thought he might be replaying the fatal struggle in his mind, because there was a pause before he abruptly said, "Let's wrap this up. Write: 'Whatever I've done, I'm sorry.' That should leave a good taste in everyone's mouth."

It was an incredible effort to keep on going. Four sentences; she could have been writing four chapters.

And then her scrawl stopped altogether.

Almost in a faint, she said, "I'm out of ink."

"I can see that!" he snapped.

He began to look around, his motions sending shivers of horror through her. One bad nick, that's all it would take. She was close to passing out from a runaway heartbeat.

Apparently he spotted a pen, because he grunted and turned to take the step or two to the counter to grab it.

It was the chance Laura needed to break free and run. She bolted like a rabbit out of a hole, knocking over the chair in her panicky flight. She heard Gabe trip and curse behind her as she ran out the kitchen door and down the steps onto the grounds. The fog was soupy enough to hide her, if she could just get far enough away.

Her panic gave her speed, but her sandals slowed her down. The sandy, gravelly road that led from the house back down to the shop and the road beyond it made for hard going. Where were the cars? Where were the damn customers? She caught a stone the wrong way and slid, falling with a twisting wrench of her knee to the fog-damp ground. Did it hurt? She didn't know. She scrambled back to her feet and took off again, afraid to look behind her in her flight.

Which is why she had no idea that he'd got close enough to grab her arm and yank her violently to a halt. She opened her mouth and started to scream but nothing came out, because a tidal wave of blackness suddenly washed over her, carrying her off in an easy rush to oblivion.

• • •

Town scion or not, Kendall Barclay III had very nearly ended up in the cell next to Snack's. The chief was hot, hotter than Ken had ever seen him.

Snack knew about the knife. While it was true that Snack had not divulged his source, it didn't take a rocket scientist (said the chief) to figure out that in a colossal betrayal of trust, Ken had rifled through the file on his desk. If it hadn't been for the fact that Andy Mellon himself had earlier leaked information to Ken, the situation might have been even dicier than it was.

Ken apologized profusely. As compensation, he offered the chief what he had just learned from Billy.

"Gabe too, now? Come on. Billy is seeing boyfriends behind every bush, don't you think?"

The chief, in short, was not impressed, which wasn't surprising. It was easier to suspect the devil you knew than the councilman you didn't. Fair enough. You had to go with the odds.

But as Ken drove out to Shore Gardens, he found himself conjuring up a compelling profile of a small-town golden boy, deprived of both his parents and his burning ambition in one fell swoop, who might be nursing a serious grudge against life. Who might not take kindly to being toyed with by a transient nothing, no matter how blindingly beautiful she was. Who might lose it altogether in an act of violence, and who was strong enough and lucky enough and hardworking enough to hide the deed for a good half of his life.

Psychological profile be damned. Gabe had the motive, and Gabe had the opportunity: as part-time help, he wouldn't have looked any more out of place on the grounds than a family member.

But when he came right down to it, Ken was zeroing in on Gabe for the simple reason that he was being overrun by an eerie, creepy feeling. At that moment, he felt a little the way he had at Miss Widdich's place, as if there were forces at work that he didn't know and didn't understand but did have to face down. When he had Laura in his arms again, that's when he'd feel reassured.

He speeded up as he approached the nursery. He couldn't help himself; the pull of Laura was too great. Corinne had left her sister behind in her rush to get to the station, and since the only taxi he saw had a group of passengers inside when Ken passed it, it was clear Laura hadn't gone that route. Hitching a ride from a local was her only other option, and Ken had been watching the few cars he passed on the way; she wasn't in any of them.

He was tense, no doubt about it. Billy had set him on edge, and the thick, chill fog was keeping him that way. Houses and hedges alike were shrouded in a ghostly gray vagueness that perfectly echoed the mystery that had pervaded all of their lives.

Uncertainty. Bankers, of all people, didn't like the feeling.

He was about to turn into the nursery when he saw Gabe's new, monster SUV come roaring out of his drive, sending sand and gravel flying before heading down the road.

It was Gabe. Without Laura. Going too fast. In a split-second, instinctual decision, Ken turned the wheel hard, crossing the center line, and aimed his little Boxster squarely at the nose of the giant SUV in a head-on crash. He hadn't felt so outsized since the day he took on the eighth-grade bullies attacking Laura in the woods. His airbag activated instantly, stunning him with its speed and force; he sat pinned behind it, trying to recover his wits.

He squeezed out of the crushed Porsche in time to see Gabe Wellerton running toward his house nearby. Ken started on foot after him, and then—heeding the same instincts that had guided him this far—turned on a dime and headed for the nursery. He had no doubt that Gabe had left Laura there; the only question was, had he left her for dead?

His heart was galloping now as he barged through the main shop, screaming her name. The house, the greenhouses, the outbuildings, the well—she could be anywhere or nowhere at all.

Gabe ran. She's somewhere.

He ran up the incline to the house, breathing hard, shouting her name. The sense of panic he felt was profound. He burst through the front door, racing through the rooms, calling her name, up and then down the stairs again. He was about to exit through the kitchen when he pulled up short: there was a note on the table in her handwriting, throbbing for his attention.

He scanned it incredulously. His heart seemed to stop altogether. Taking out his cell phone, he punched in 911 as he dashed outside, trying to re-enact a crime he couldn't be positive—didn't want to be positive—had taken place.

Where?

The operator answered, and he fought with her. No doubt he was incoherent, but he vowed he would pay any costs, and the upshot was that they were sending an ambulance.

He called Laura's name, over and over, cranking up the volume each time as he ran through the greenhouses and across the grounds; it seemed to him that the fog was hushing his rudeness, as if he were acting like a yahoo in a sacred place.

He stopped and listened.

Yes. A diesel engine; he knew the sound of it from his father's old Mercedes. Only it wasn't a classic sedan, but a classic John Deere tractor. Just as old, just as venerable; just as lethal. He ran to the shed where he knew they kept the Deere, hardly able to hear the engine anymore over the thundering thumps of his heart.

The swing-out doors were barred from inside. He threw

his shoulder into them repeatedly, but they withstood the fury of his assault.

If Gabe got out, Ken could get in. He raced around the side of the building and found a single-paned window that swung horizontally on center pivots. The closed window was tucked under the eave, ten feet off the ground; easier to climb out of than to climb into. He looked around and found an old wooden ladder with missing rungs at one end. Propping it against the wall with the broken end at the bottom, and keeping his feet on the outside edges of the remaining rungs, he began his climb.

A rung broke anyway, sending him crashing down to the next one. But that one held, and his only harm was a jolt to the knees. He scrambled through the window with a contortion of legs and dropped onto an old scarred workbench beneath it, noting the upended stool that Gabe had kicked out in his escape.

There was no one in the tractor's seat. Ken circled the machine and found Laura lying under the exhaust pipe, semiconscious and in acute distress.

How long has she been here? was his single thought. He scooped up her limp form and carried her to the wide swing doors, never imagining that not only would they be bolted, but padlocked.

Padlocked. The concentration of carbon monoxide was enough to have his head already aching; they had to get out. He laid Laura to one side on the cement floor of the shed and climbed the tractor, aware of dizziness as he did so. It was dark in the shed, and the knob of the gearshift was worn smooth; but reverse was reverse. He found the right gear and floored the aging beast, heading with abandon for the locked doors, gambling that Laura would stay where she was. The old tractor crashed through the doors with ease, clearing the air, freeing them both.

He jumped down from the Deere and carried Laura outside to fresher air still, then laid her on the ground. Conscious? CPR? Those were the questions that consumed him as he hovered over her, trying to assess the extent of poisoning.

She moaned. And then she threw up. He rolled her to one side, clearing her mouth, trying to keep her from further harm. *Don't let this be too far,* he prayed, well aware of the long-term damage of carbon-monoxide poisoning. *For her sake, my sake, our children's sake . . . please. Don't let this be too far.*

So absorbed was Ken that he never heard the siren, never saw the strobe cutting the fog until the ambulance was almost upon them. When he finally looked up, he was himself disoriented: it seemed to him that he was with Laura on his boat in a life-and-death storm, and the flashing light was from a lighthouse, a beacon of reassurance in a world of threat. He felt a relief as profound as his previous fear had been deep.

Laura was safe.

"You saved my life," she kept repeating, but Ken seemed ridiculously nonchalant about his part in the affair.

She stared at him in continuing wonder. "Don't act as if you were just passing by and had nothing better to do than ram a tractor through a set of garage doors. Stop being so damned modest. You saved my life!"

"Shh," Ken said as the ER surgeon approached. "I'm in enough trouble with my insurance company as it is."

She laughed, giddy with joy despite her piercing headache. She was safe, Snack was innocent, inevitably Gabe would be run to ground. If it weren't for Corinne's hurt and disillusionment, Laura could honestly say that the Shores—the Shores!—were on a roll.

More good news. The physician said, "Your tests are fine. You're free to go. I'll write out something for that headache—"

"Oh, no, thanks, Dr. Brown. I doubt I'll need—"

"We'll take the prescription," Ken said, interrupting. "She may change her mind."

"So conservative; so like a banker," she teased.

Unperturbed, Ken said, "You'll thank me later."

They left the hospital and squeezed into the front seat of the nursery's rusty pickup alongside Corinne, who said with a tentative smile, "Where to?"

She was so sad. So thrilled for her siblings, but . . . so desperately sad.

Ken said, "How do you feel about jail? We'll go spring Snack."

"*Can* we?" Corinne asked, her spirits picking up.

"Yep. I just got off the phone with the chief. He's decided not to press charges."

Corinne burst into tears. It was all too much.

"Why don't I drive?" said Ken softly. "C'mon, kiddo; out."

Nodding helplessly, Corinne climbed down from the driver's side and went around to the passenger side. Hunched over with lingering sorrow, she said to her sister, "Too bad Gabe took the watch from you; now he can claim the prints were from today."

"Corinne! That watch is just frosting on the cake. Gabe *admitted* to me that he killed Sylvia. His prints are not only all over the toolshed—but on that very high window. Not to mention, on the pen for my suicide note and the knife that gave me the cut on my neck. Plus, new fingerprints or old, there aren't any of Snack's on the watch, only yours and mine and Gabe's. The watch will be one more piece of evidence. Not the whole picture, but a piece of it."

"But you said he yanked out the strand of hair from it."

"A tiny bit is bound to be still in the band," Laura said confidently. "You know how those expandable types are."

Corinne sighed. "Will they find him, you think?"

"Yes. I'm sure of it. He's not the type to swing an escape to Venezuela."

"If they do catch him, how long do you think he'll be in jail?"

Laura said grimly, "Let's put it this way: Gabe won't be running for mayor anytime soon."

"No." Corinne sighed again and said, "He had such plans, such ambitions. When we sat on the porch . . ."

She bowed her head. "We were making plans, the two of us."

"I know, honey. I know."

"Why did he sleep with me?" she asked, anguished.

Because you were willing. For no other reason, damn him, than that.

All Gabe had wanted was an excuse for being able to poke around for the watch and to keep an eye on the compost pile. Courting Corinne gave him his excuse. Taking her to bed was a bonus.

Laura began to rub her sister's back again, aware that it would be a long time, if ever, before Corinne's happiness would match her own. She tried to pull her own joy down a notch, because it seemed somehow mean to feel so much of it when her sister was feeling so bereft.

She exchanged a look with Ken and saw a depth of sympathy for Corinne that matched her own.

And she thought, *Here's a man just made for family.* Her heart lifted at the thought that someday soon, Corinne was bound to come to the same conclusion and welcome her new relation to hearth and table.

"You know what I think?" Laura said softly to her grieving sister. "I think that Gabe recognized that you had something he didn't, something he lacked. I think that's why he slept with you, Rinnie. Because you're you."

"I'm *nobody*," Corinne moaned. "Not without him."

"Oh, honey, don't ever say that, because it will never be true. Gabe, even Gabe, would never have slept with you if you were a nobody. He saw your goodness; he knew that you would have forgiven him for Sylvia, and he was drawn to that."

"Then why did he do what he did today?" she said in a choked voice. "How could he do that?"

"He lost it, honey, that's all," Laura said in motherly tones. "He just lost it. He's always been wounded; we all knew that. It was just too big a wound to heal. Sometimes wounds heal, and . . . sometimes they don't."

"It hurts so much," Corinne said between sobs, turning onto her sister's shoulder for comfort.

With aching tenderness, Laura continued rubbing soothing circles into her sister's back. "I know, honey," she whispered. "I know."

Corinne's pain was utterly wrenching for Laura to see. It would end, as all pain must; but it wouldn't be anytime soon.

"We'll work it out, Rin. All of us, together. You'll see. You'll be so much stronger after this," Laura gently insisted. "You'll see. And I'll be right there, telling you that I told you so."

She smiled and kissed her sister's hair. "You'll see."

Epilogue

"Married. I can't believe it . . . *married*! I kept waiting for him to say, 'Let me go home and think about it.' "

Corinne's whisper was sweet and giddy; she was trying hard not to bawl. She managed to stop the worst of the sniffles by slapping her hands over her mouth and nose, but her eyes were streaming with tears.

Laura hugged her, cheek to wet cheek. "Married, married, married!" she said, because she so loved the sound of the word.

The two sisters stood up and furtively brushed the wrinkles from their linen dresses before stepping from their pew into the aisle to join the procession out of St. John's Church. Ahead of them walked their brother, straight as a soldier and easily as solemn, his arm linked through the arm of a tiny slip of a woman with dark eyes, a quick smile, and just the right mix of deference and sass to have the guy constantly spinning in circles.

Lucy in the sky with diamonds! Laura blessed the day that Lucy Souza dropped by and offered to set their nursery straight once and for all. Within weeks Lucy was telling them all what to do, and that's because she knew more than all of them combined about how to grow anything and everything.

Although it was Laura who'd hired Lucy, it was Snack who had worked with her day in and day out at the nursery for nearly three years. Snack may have thought he was teaching Lucy the ropes; but it was Lucy who'd actually held the reins the entire time, taming him into a calmer, infinitely more appealing version of his former self.

The church was full. Didn't that say something about the new and improved version of him?

Of course, a great many of the guests were from Lucy's extended Portuguese family in Fall River, including the sobbing woman walking directly in front of them: Lucy's widowed mother. There was a time when Laura would have assumed the worst about those sobs; but today, she had no doubt that Mrs. Souza was simply expressing her joy.

"Beautiful flowers, *beautiful*, dear," said one of the seated women guests, reaching out to clasp Laura's hand as she stepped over the petal-strewn carpet. The Portuguese knew a thing or two about horticulture; Laura was deeply flattered.

"Thank you, Mrs. Ferreira," she said, squeezing the woman's hand. "Of course, our nursery is now bare."

"I'm sure it's not," the woman said, pooh-poohing the notion.

The chancel, the pulpit, the pews, even the church steps were adorned with an extravagance of white flowers, all of them accented with blossoms of blue. Corinne and Laura had worked like women possessed for two full days creating the charming arrangements; they'd stripped the nursery of lilies, roses, delphiniums, clematis, baby's breath, cranesbill, and whatever else they had in white or blue. Some of the effects were deliberate, some of them purely spontaneous, the inspired creations of two sleep-deprived but romantic horticulturalists who happened to be sisters to boot.

"Love the flowers, Laura," whispered Rosie Nedworth from a pew. "You girls did very well."

"Why, thank you, Mrs. Nedworth."

Food was important, the gown really mattered; but as far as Laura was concerned, it was the flowers that had to come first.

That's how it had been at her own wedding, in the very same charming white-steepled church. It seemed at the time that all of Chepaquit had tried to get inside, and some of Chepaquit hadn't quite fit; but Laura and Ken had remained on the steps to receive everyone's good wishes until her feet throbbed and she had to kick off her heels. It was the last time she'd worn a pair of uncomfortable shoes.

For this wedding—despite the linen dress—she was wearing Birkenstock sandals. She had to: the baby inside her felt as if it were growing by a good five pounds a day. Laura glanced down self-consciously at her feet, but she couldn't see them anyway, so she shrugged and said happily over her shoulder to her husband, "Married! Snack! You believe it?"

"Believe it?" he said in her ear. "I was the first to predict it."

It was true. "Beginner's luck," Laura teased, lifting their awakening three-year-old gently from Ken's cocooning embrace. "Hey, you," she crooned softly. "Who fell asleep?"

"Not . . . me-e-e," said Maggie, rubbing her eye with a fist. With a yawn, she turned her face back into her father's broad shoulder and snuggled deep.

"*Well,*" Laura said, pretending offense. "I see who's the better mattress."

Ken was beaming, as he tended to do whenever Maggie showed an outright preference for him over her mother. "She's too much for you to carry, anyway, right now," he said kindly.

Also true. It was hard lately to find a place to tuck Maggie comfortably, now that all the available real estate had been claimed by the baby-to-be.

Laura licked a thumb and wiped away a smudge from

their daughter's cheek. "A Shore to the core," she sighed. The child had the family affinity for mud and dirt.

The wedding guests were bunching up now, waiting to congratulate the happy couple. From somewhere, one of Snack's ushers took advantage of the cheery confusion to pounce on Corinne. As usual, she smiled politely at him and began sidling away, despite his effusive attempts to converse about a variety of topics, from her dress to the vows to the weather.

Ken leaned over to whisper in Laura's ear, "George is wearing her down. She doesn't run away crying anymore. I think he's got the inside track."

Laura smiled at her husband's fearless prediction, but she herself wasn't so sure. As steady and reliable as George was—Mister Fixer himself—he wasn't nearly as dashing as Gabe. Did that make a difference? Or was Corinne simply not willing to love anyone ever again?

Corinne, of all of them, had been the most deeply traumatized by the events of four years earlier. When the developer Joe Penchance came sniffing around her a year after Gabe went to jail, Corinne had sent him packing in no time flat. She wasn't ready to let anyone come courting, least of all the man who'd just bought the waterfront property below them that once had belonged to Shore Gardens. Talk about ulterior motives.

But George? He was so sweetly transparent. Laura elbowed her husband to take a closer look. George had his hands on his hips. And then he nodded. And then he scratched his balding head. And then, not knowing where exactly to put them, he planted his hands on his broad hips again.

"Good grief, he reminds me of me," said Ken, chuckling.

"Not at all. When *you're* nervous, you jingle your change in your pockets."

Ken started. "Woman! Is there anything about me you don't know?"

"Yes. I don't know how I let you talk me into *this* one," she said, laying her hands on her huge belly, "before *that* one got out of college."

"Uh-oh. Backache again?"

"Mm. Getting there. I think I'm going to have to jump this line."

"Oh, all *right*," they heard Corinne say rather sharply to George. But she ended it with a giggle, which left Laura confused.

"What was that all about?" she asked her sister as soon as George returned to join Billy for what was left of ushering duties.

"Oh, nothing. He just . . . wanted the first dance."

"*Did* he now?"

"And the last."

"Ah. Now *that* is a very wise man."

Corinne gave her sister a withering look. "I know you think so."

"Oh? Have I mentioned?"

Smiling, Corinne lifted one shoulder demurely and turned to take her place in the line.

Laura whipped around to give her husband a bug-eyed look of expectation. Suddenly her back seemed a lot less sore.

"Lucy, you look beautiful!" Corinne said to their brand-new sister-in-law.

Amid hugs and kisses all around, Laura said, "Welcome to the Shore clan, Lucy. I honestly don't know who's luckier, Snack or us."

"I'm the one who's lucked out," said the bride, and Snack all but fell at her feet on the spot. (He had proposed on his knees, they all knew, so it wouldn't be the first time.)

"And Snack, you be good to her," Laura said. "Or you'll answer to your big sister why not."

"You know what, big sister?" said her wicked brother. "In a few more years you're going to stop bragging about that age difference."

"Congratulations, Snack," Ken said simply. "You done good."

"Don't I know it," said Snack, taking his hand.

Ken threw his free arm around his brother-in-law and they hugged, and instantly Laura teared up: it was a moment to savor, a dream come true. Family who got along.

They moved on and exited the little town church. There were bystanders hanging around, of course; everyone loved to see a bride. The sun was shining, the breeze was warm, the flowers were holding up well.

"The rice!" cried Laura.

"Right here in my pocket," Ken said, shifting his daughter so that he could double-check.

"You think of everything," Laura said in wonder.

"I have the time," he answered with a smile. "Banker's hours, remember?"

Indeed she did. And every non-banking minute was spent with his wife and his child. Every once in a while, Laura thought of the life she had almost ended up living back in Portland, and the thought sent her virtually into a panic. She took Maggie from Ken just so that she could hold her child close and convince herself all over again that she wasn't dreaming.

"Hey, look who's finally here," Ken said in mild reproach.

His mother was rushing toward them. Laura was amazed to see that Camille Barclay looked . . . hot. Sweaty. Close to disheveled. It was a first.

"I've missed it!" Camille wailed. "What a disappointment. A truck rolled over, spilling diesel all over the highway. Four and a half *hours*, I sat in traffic. Even for Boston, it was a nightmare."

Ken said, "And yet you coulda come down last night . . ."

"Oh, stop being so smug," his mother chastised, and somehow she made him thirteen again. "Laura, you went with the lavender dress for her, after all. I'm so glad. It's adorable!"

"You have a much better fashion sense than I," said Laura, without much hope that her belly was hiding her Birkenstocks from her mother-in-law's keen glance.

"Maggie, Maggie, don't you look pretty!"

Maggie went over to the next welcoming embrace, something she was used to doing. Camille held and hugged and cooed and did all of the wonderful things that grandmothers did when they held their youngest progeny in their arms.

It was Maggie who was the glue that held Laura and her mother-in-law together. Finally: something they had in common. The initial awkwardness in their relationship had begun disappearing immediately after Laura had announced that she was pregnant with Maggie. The women had grown steadily closer ever since, so much so that Laura felt comfortable just then in tucking an escaped strand of graying hair back into the artfully arranged bun on the back of her mother-in-law's head. And when Camille gave Laura a quick, grateful glance, Laura returned it with a warm one of her own.

The women had never discussed either Laura's purloined letter or Camille's forged response to it. And that was a tiny bit of an issue, still, with Laura. But she had hopes—she had no doubt, really—that someday, when they were sitting on a beach together watching Maggie and her sibling at play, they would talk about the letters, and laugh, and say how long ago it all seemed.

She watched as her husband dug deep in his pocket and came up with a scoop of rice for Maggie. Pouring the grains into their daughter's outstretched hand, he said, "Okay, now practice by throwing some at Mommy. Let's see how you do it."

Maggie giggled and heave-hoed the rice across the front of Laura's dress. She enjoyed the experience so much that she demanded another handful, this time to aim at Corinne.